FIRST FELL THE GARDEN

E.D. Sanders

PROLOGUE -In the Woodlands of the South, Alee, the princess nymph of Avalon awoke. Created with the powers of the magical isle, she was born. —

VERSE I

Noon was the busiest in the Woodlands of the South, between the edges of the savanna and rain forest. In the cleared meadows, the tall, majestic trees sang songs to the golden grassy blades while both swayed in the wind. The trickling gullies and creeks from the Great River rumbled a low percussion in accompaniment.

Nature's uninterrupted melodies drowned out a township too sparse and spread out to warrant ever being named. Shaded beneath the green arms of trees so old and strong, homes grew to embrace and fully entangle one another. Made of wood and stone, they had a humble life below the songs of the trees.

One house was home to a family, whose warmth of their devoted love radiated like the fire from its hearth. Inside, a young girl listened like the grass reeds of the savanna. Underneath the canopy called mother, the girl sat while her hair was brushed and groomed to the tune of a song.

What do they say when the rain falls?
Do they know the Sun shines again?
Finding your place in the moonlight,

Let the stars guide the way to the end.

The song was mostly hummed, with the words more so spoken than sang. Karwynn told her daughter a lesson she felt the need to impart through the song.

"Beloved Alee," said Karwynn, still brushing as she tilted her head, "do you like tonight's song?"

The young Alee, both beautiful and smart, normally took every opportunity to absorb the loving wisdom from one, whom she considered to be not only mother, but also friend and teacher. However, Alee was not entirely focused on its meaning as much as she was on its melody. As of late, the young girl focused on tomorrow. Her birthday was only a day away and Alee lacked the clarity to decipher anything but the love from the lyrics, so she replied,

"Mother, sing it again, please."

And so Karywnn did. She sang from her heart. Her message stated that no matter what darkness loomed in the future, hope remained to guide her homeward.

Alee uncurled her legs from beneath her. The hardwood floors and the duration of her position caused her discomfort. She sat looking over the home that was as familiar to her as her mother's face. The fire lit the room of a home, which was larger than most in the Woodlands. The stove and kitchen were opposite the fireplace. It worked well to heat the home entirely when the light winters came. Karwynn sat in one of four chairs meant for the dinner table. Dense and smooth, the table was patterned with the likeness of Woodland landmarks.

Everything from the Creek Sea Fishery, the Lamke Market, and the Trajan Buck Farm was carved into that table. If slightly more ordered, it could have been a map. But just as the table's edge met with air and nothingness, Alee, like many other people of the Woodlands, knew nothing outside of its tall green-treed gates.

Alee looked to the stairs. They were the rarity that made their home of a greater class compared to others. Up the stairs were the rooms of Alee and Karwynn. They were little more than lofts with beds, though Alee was fortunate enough to have a window. The view of the forest was a beautiful sight. Leaves from trees and petals from flowers were the colors of a tapestry. But now, with a birthday soon to come, her tapestry was simply a wall. She did not see the color in it anymore. Now the Southland was an obstacle against her ever-growing curiosity for more.

Karwynn brushed then twisted the last strands of hair. Alee hopped away towards the doors to meet the dawn. Karwynn saw her urge to escape from those four walls. Even as a child, Alee seemed to be a force not easily contained. She always learned and explored with pure joy.

Indeed, Karwynn saw her. And truly, she had thoughts that Alee might leave one day too soon. Since Alee was a small child, Karwynn had spoken of a prize to be issued on her seventeenth birthday. If not for that promise Alee would surely be gone. True enough, curiosity kept her longer than Karwynn would care to admit but the days before Alee's birthday dwindled to an end.

Coming at last, though seemingly halted by anticipation, was the day. Calm and bright, as it should always be on a birthday, the young girl Alee, looked forward to the celebration of her seventeenth. She stumbled down the stairs with dainty jubilation. With the anticipation of a magnificent bestowing since the age of nine, Alee sought the attention of her mother.

"Well. What? What is it?" asked Karwynn.

"You don't know such suspense," Alee exclaimed anxiously, "I'm young but I have the wrinkles of an elder." she blurted.

"Hush, child. Your beauty is ageless." Karwynn uttered, "Now go on to meet your studies with your teacher and your friends. Enjoy the day."

Alee's desire to know consumed her. But somehow she set out to relish the day as instructed. She delighted in her short journey to the home of her teacher, who lived in the green of the Southland's rainforest. It was a change. Something to get her mind away from her desires. As she walked, Alee took in all the beauty of the land. Her senses never grew tired of it. The smell of the air and flowers, the look of the sky and trees so tall, even the feel of the dirt between her toes was a soothing familiarity. She maneuvered through the forest and trekked over bend and under branch. It was no maze for Alee, though had it been a maze, she would have bested it.

Alee came to the door of the modest home. She did not knock or announce her coming in any manner. Though slightly late that day, she was expected. With no lock or hinge, she simply opened the door. She pushed its brass handle inward and tiptoed inside. Her steps were naturally light for the petite teenager. Inside, the tiny house was larger than it appeared from outside but its size did not matter, for rarely did it entertain more than a few.

Alee immediately drew her eyes to the artistry above the mantle. There above the fireplace hung three woven embroidered drapes. The hierarchy of their position told the tale of a father, a mother, and a child. Most children near the Southland realm were not permitted to studies. They could not be spared from the labors that their mothers and fathers required. Alee, however, could be spared for a few hours in the midday before the sun peaked. As Alee settled in the house of studies, she saw her cohorts preparing in the adjacent room. Alee took her eyes away from the drapes to be cordial to her beloved friends already engaged in scholarship.

"Many greets and blesses to all. Lyla, you rarely arrive before I," said Alee.

"True. And if at all possible, I bet you wish you could arrive here before Awana," said Lyla.

"It is also true that a birthday is a rarity in a set of seasons," Awana proclaimed as she smiled at her friend.

"Thank you, friends. I appreciate the thoughts, but let us begin our studies together and then celebrate later, if time permits and your favor allows."

The ladies re-entered the study hall of the simple house. They walked in file. It was clear by their order that Alee held the middlemost age among the three. Lyla preceded as the youngest, since her need of knowledge was greatest and her experience the weakest. She was also the shortest in stature, but awkwardly thin. Beautiful still, she had long falling copper-brown hair and a plucky nose. Many men were waiting until she was old enough to be courted and wed. Lyla's eyes were a cooling green that eased and weakened men's hearts. Her look, exotic and fair, was so powerful. Oddly, Lyla knew it not and was dim to the roots of her popularity.

Behind Alee walked Awana, the oldest. She was beyond the age for a young woman to receive studies over chores. Awana stood tall and womanly. Her eyes were bright. Her form more curvaceous than Alee's or Lyla's. Awana spurned many men who wanted her to love them. Her father remained foremost in her care and attention. At times, Awana mocked the men who would court her, knowing that they feigned needing love when truly they desired labor. Not bitter towards love or romance, Awana believed that if love was revealed truly then it would be accepted. In the meantime, Awana had no love to spare as her father still secretly mourned the death of her mother who fell to illness nearly two years ago.

Her father was Aswan, the teacher. He gave Awana leave to do as she desired, but her only desire was to study and know all that he knew. The home's tapestry showed him on high beside wife and daughter. Aswan was content as the lesson began. The old man amassed joy and peace in teaching. He spoke merrily.

"Blessings, young minds. How fare you? Good, I hope." he said rhetorically.

"I hope you all have something," he added.

"I have mine, teacher.," said Awana.

She held respect for her father's title and opened her hands for all to witness.

"Good. Look, ladies. The Sleeping Leaves are found outside the reach of the Great River. Remember the look of them," said Aswan.

"And you Lyla? What do you have?" the teacher asked.

"I have mine. The Masking Leaves! They hide the pain of injury or sickness, but do naught to cure them. They are found below the moss of the open groves."

"Impressive. And well stated." Aswan said before turning to Alee.

"Uhmm…" Alee grumbled as she looked into the eyes of all upon her.

"Surely, you have done your task?"

"You assume knowledge well, Alee. You listen and you recall the work and lectures of myself and your sisters of study. But you must seek out the world, not await it. It is rare to have true knowledge surrendered. Seize it!"

Alee heard the criticisms of Aswan, but smiled at the compliments, which lied within them.

The lesson came and went. Everyone was enthralled and engaged. Aswan taught life then dismissed the girls, but

Alee still had a task to complete. Alee understood the comments of Aswan and made no excuses. For the past few days, she had thought mostly of Karwynn's gift. After Aswan's session, she rededicated herself to finding the Healing Leaves, albeit, in merriment. She made a game of it with Lyla. Awana was not able to join for long. She frolicked only to the ridge and headed back to tend to her father. Lyla and Alee jumped and somersaulted in the forest most of the afternoon. They laughed and played until they had little energy left. The two finally settled on a patch of soft leaves. Lyla looked back in the direction of Aswan's house as though she were able to see it from so far away.

"What did teacher mean about seeking out the world?" Lyla wondered.

Alee smiled and giggled at the young one, but did not answer.

"Come on. Are you going to help me with my task or not?" She asked.

Lyla nodded in affirmation as they moved onward.

Near the outskirts of Karwynn's home, Alee found the vines that wrapped a stone and knew what they were.

"These are they. The Healing Leaves. They swathe the leaves of the Blacker Stones. Beauty, they are in bloom! Karwynn would love the look of them."

Alee motioned towards the Black Stones. She ran her

fingers along the vines, which gave root to the buds. The flowers themselves seemed nearly black as well, but they were a blue so dark that the black spots only appeared to give the petals texture. The crimson sepal outlined the bloom and its glowingly white center. Alee gently reached for it. She did not tear at the vines. She lowered herself and worked to free the stone by the root. Alee pulled the blooms away and smiled. Lyla marveled at the control of Alee's touch. She knew she lacked such tender precision.

"They are beautiful are they not?" Alee asked.

"Yes, but still, I prefer the subtle pink of the Masking Leaves." Lyla replied.

Alee gave her final departure to Lyla. They embraced and laughed. Alee ran to her home with the flowers secured in her hands. She flung open the door and called for Karwynn.

“I am home. Karwynn! Karwynn?” Alee said.

She saw Karwynn seated before her.

“I have these blossoms for you, beautiful mother. I thought you might like them so I picked several. What have you for me?” She asked gleefully.

“These blossoms are a beauty indeed. They have grown so well with little tending."

Karwynn's face softened.

"My dear Alee, I have watched you grow over time. I have done little in the matters of your upbringing."

"Ah, Mom," Alee moaned modestly.

Karwynn paused. Her face went flat.

"That is just it my dear. I am not your mother. Today is the day you know your past, that you know yourself. This is the gift I finally give to you. Fate brought you to my doorsteps and that very night, my only task for you came to me in a dream. I was to raise you carefree and happy. You were not to spend one moment with need or concern until today," said Karywnn.

"I have heard the minstrels tell these stories frequently. You have also told a few of them before bedtime." Alee interrupted jokingly.

"This is no jest, my love. The ones who come for you will be here within moments. Now is the time we say our goodbyes."

For all of Alee's plans and desires, deep down she never thought this day would come. She never truly imagined a day without Karwynn. Her eyes widened. Her home, which seemed so small for so long, was seen through child's eyes once more. It grew immeasurably vast to her. Space filled the room again. Unfortunately, space seemed to push between Alee and Karwynn. She wept. Through her tears she called out the question,

"Why?"

She ran to Karwynn and gave her a tight embrace. She held her with the intent to never let her go. Karwynn had no answer, but conveyed that it was not for any lack of love or wrong doing on Alee's part.

"There will never be a bridge between us," said Karwynn.

Her statement resounded with gloom and detachment in her ears. Karwynn continued.

"Through it all, we are and will always be connected. What bridge is needed when our hearts are bound as one by love? And for longer than breath allows, I will be with you."

Needed belongings already packed and made ready by Karwynn, Alee waited alone. She could hear the muffled sounds of Karwynn sobbing from upstairs. Her cries let her know this had to be. Trusting Karwynn was easy, but time played games as the moment came faster than expected.

Goodbye - Karywynn's last word became an echo, which grew fainter as the line between Alee, and her former caretaker became immeasurable. Alee's thoughts were clouded with the reality of the situation. Her life tugged upon, tugged towards the point of being totally flipped upside down. Just as she was told, two figures came in dark green hooded robes with their visible bulge of sword and scabbard.

The two figures led the way beyond the Woodlands. Their robes dragged the soil below and seemed to be the only part of them connected to the Earth. They walked with an elegant stride and appeared to float on tirelessly while a saddened Alee had grown weary of a journey newly embarked upon. They came in silence, traveled in silence, but Alee would not continue the journey in silence. With no semblance of the place in which they were, and no trail of the way to where they had been, Alee's confusion and fear changed. Curiosity and frustration became her signature emotions. A signature that she was forced to sign then and now. Unexpectedly, Alee reached out and grabbed the hood of one.

"Who are you?"

Her actions revealed great beauty. A blinding illumination caused Alee to shield her eyes. The light's intensity dimmed and the first figure, a gracefully strong and beautiful woman dressed in the finest of silk spoke.

> "We've tread many miles, little one, and now you finally do that which was a desire from the beginning."

The other figure decloaked to also reveal a woman. This one wore the sturdy garments of war. Decked in leather, iron, and robes of armor, she spoke with ease to the child.

"All the tricks of light I could do as well, but I wish not to follow her. Hear me now though, child. You have many questions. You can ask only three."

"Only three?" Alee inquired, "Where do I begin...Wha... How?"

The woman smiled. She teased at Alee's expense.

"I jest, child. Begin your total inquisition."

The second figure succeeded in her comedic mission to ease Alee.

"Who are you?" asked Alee.

"In satin and silk, I am none other than Gaia and in rainments of battle, she is known as Bellia."

Questions - Questions came as a barrage and traveled with them on their journey. Gaia and Bellia promised answers, but continued to press the ground and move onward. It never crossed Alee's mind that the two women would not honor their word. She hoped they would soon stop to pitch camp. The sun gleamed over the distance and removed its touch from the sky above. They came to a stop. Gaia gathered a steady fire and unrolled three blankets. While Bellia, stuck with the dining duties, prepared her specialty of an abundance of dried meat and stoutly beans.

Alee moved towards the food as Gaia began.

"I guess the best place to start is the beginning. God

created all. His spirit moved over many days. The purity of the universe was complete yet closed. The plants and animals lived on the plane without mind to grow and had only the simple impulse of survival. But more was to come. He created man to walk the earth."

Alee blurted in interruption.

"I know this stuff. Karwynn told me that."

"And did you interrupt your Karwynn?" Bellia asked.

"No."

"Alright then, child. Be quiet and don't interrupt. You have asked the questions and we will answer as best we can if you're patient."

Gaia continued.

"Bellia! Behave yourself. She is only a child. Ah, yes...as you know, God ended his work and rested and blessed what He had made. But God did create again."

Gaia paused to gather herself as her story turned.

"Mankind does not know of what I am about to speak because no person should know the origin or nature of his master and judge. God created Avalon and three beings to rule the land of Earth and judge it as a divine triumvirate.

Avalon is the land behind the mist, which is blind to the human eye. Those three beings were to keep the land of Earth pure and righteous without directly interfering in man's affairs. They possessed great powers of will and wisdom, which is their main distinguishable characteristic from those of man.

Changel the changeling, Nympthia the nymph, and Pixsus the pixie took watch over Eden from Avalon. God watched all from Heaven. Unbeknownst to anyone, God prepared a *test* for all. The test stirred evil. All the while, Changel wished to gain favor with God and used his signature power to change the form of evil into a snake. Nympthia and Pixsus wandered the Great Garden in the form of woman unseen and unable to be seen. They never thought to suspect one of God's own creatures in deeds so treacherous.

In the end, everyone failed but everyone was not punished. The humans were exiled from the Great Garden for their part. Pixsus and Nympthia were banished from the mystical island of Avalon. Their ability to tap into their great power was blocked. As for Changel, he was warned not to fail, for his new task was to watch and judge them all from Avalon.

I see it in your eyes, child. You wonder how this story leads to you doorstep. Be patient. I will continue.

Over time, man became fruitful and multiplied. As for Nympthia and Pixsus, they discovered the treachery of Changel. A watchbird owl that witnessed the evil snake's manifestation told them but they could do nothing. Eventually, they married men, children of Exiled Eden, and were also fruitful and bore many children. Time came and went and brought great knowledge and endeavor to the two children of the mystic isle. Their knowledge and their strength of spirit brought about their Awakening. The line that blocked their mind from their own powers broke down. When this happened, Pixsus rushed to arms. Pixsus sought out and battled Changel. But, he had been gathering strength, power, and cunning for far too long. The battle was quick and Pixsus was slain with ease. Changel then came to Nympthia. He said to her, *"Do you wish my death as well? Let us end this now."* Nympthia, in her wisdom, knew she burned to destroy Changel and set right the scales of truth. However, she was nowhere near his level of strength. She said to him, "God does not want death. Yours nor mine. I want what He wants, peace and pure souls to dwell in the Earthly kingdom as well as the Heavenly one. I love you and wish you well, brother."

Understand this Alee, Changel is still about in our world. Throughout the centuries, he has placed himself on a godly mantle. Many places would worship him in their own contrivances as Zeus, Ra, Odin, Bakuldu, Brahma, or Kami. Now he plans not only to be worshipped, but also to rule every land on Earth. He has spread and planted his seeds. And with them, he has created an army to conquer all. His many sons and daughters who have thought to be long dead have only trained and prepared on Avalon since the point of their supposed demise. Villains, heroes, and titans alike all wait on Avalon.

It comes now to you. You are the firstborn daughter of Nympthia. Your name is Aleeia. We are the descendants of Nympthia and Pixsus."

"How can that be?" Alee replied with disbelief.

"We don't really know. We do know it involves some form of time displacement. We do know that you are who we think you are," Gaia replied.

"How so?" Alee added doubtfully.

"We have a translation of your mother's tablets. It is a letter to you."

The Letter of Nympthia - The tablets she wrote are nearly as old as time itself. Nympthia wrote them in a language of her own creation that pre-dates most others. Soon after the fall of Pixsus, the discovery of her own Awakening, and the meeting with Changel, she began. Everyday, day after day, Nympthia carved and chiseled. She worked and labored to create what everyone thought to be a great monument to the sun gods. Gods that nourished all with merciful warmth. Some suspected otherwise of Nympthia.

Indeed, Changel himself maintained a watchful eye over Nympthia. Ever since the opposition of Pixsus, he made her doings his personal business. In disguise, he would sometimes spy himself. With his own eyes, he saw nothing. He bared witness to a Nympthia defeated, subservient, and non-threatening. In his eyes, she spent the remainder of her years doing nothing. She worked and carved. And for twenty-five years, she toiled until it was complete. Until it read.

"Daughter of mine. Daughter Aleeia. I see you now as you are. With my Awoken-Will, I see you through the rivers of time. The children of Changel are capable in the mystic arts so my cheap parlor tricks shall go unnoticed for now.

Aleeia, Alee...I have not given much to you, though I have paved a way. Karwynn gave you blissful youth as I commanded her in dreams to do. But now you have a purpose, a great crusade awaits you. You, and you alone, have the power to defeat Changel. Your power is the purest, not tainted by seas and seas of human lineage. First daughter to me among four brothers younger. This truth, the righting of my wrong is your birthright. It lies upon you to make God's name once again glorified above all others, by removing Changel the False. He should not be credited with the many loving faces of a true Lord.

This message, indeed, maps your journey. But it is only a guide, for the decisions you shall make are yours. Trust in Gaia and Bellia. They are there to help and protect you as your training begins.

"What training?" Aleeia stopped to ask Gaia.

Gaia pointed to the letter-scrolls and Aleeia continued to read.

Awoken-Will, the mystic gift from God, is a tool like any other. You have it coursing through you but you need to know how to use it. Your Awakened

Will is the understanding of everything's inner chemistries. For example, in order to see all, you would first have to know what it means to see. How do we see?

The Great Library will teach you such things. You must go to Egypt. There you will begin your tutorial. And there you will find another letter, an actual piece of the great tablet I carved. Once your learning is complete, you shall be able to read it yourself.

I know this burden would throw anyone into fear, but you must be strong. Cast aside your fear for now and journey onward. Or use it to make you sharp and focused. You would first have to know what fear is before you could do otherwise. May God bless you and be with you, as I cannot. I am but a ghost dwelling in the past. I love you my daughter.

P.S. Tell Gaia no more light shows. She can be so vain at times. And always stay as discreet as possible.

Aleeia finished the letter. She did not cry. Any sadness, shock or sorrow did not show. She held it well. She was amazed and proud. But most of all she was obedient. Fear and intimidation had no signs upon her face. She took in the burden and made it her own.

She folded the letter-scrolls and spoke.

"Let us sleep now. At first sun's wave, we go to Egypt."

The Education in Egypt -Three women were directed to the land of the Pharaohs. Gaia, Bellia, and Aleeia traveled steadily, without incident or danger. For Aleeia, her journey marked the first time she would gaze upon foreign places, intermingle with different people, taste exotic foods, and hear novel melodies. For a few moments at a time, she imagined she was once again a child. For in her childhood, she delighted in exploration. The experience of the voyage unwittingly became part of Aleeia's education. She learned, among other things, to be patient in understanding and to have reverence in judging.

Their journey continued. Some days they tread on by foot, other days they borrowed passage on carriages of hay. On the final leg of their voyage, they approached the land of the black sand on a barge that championed the Great Nile. They touched soil on the Nile's western bank and made their way to the city of Abydos.

The city was a metropolis with an infrastructure that supported all the needs of its citizens. With streets of sand, the center of the city was built on an oasis that sustained Abydos for centuries. The fortress Obelisk, a simple, tall and rectangular structure with a pyramid at its apex, stood adjacent to the Temple of Amon-Ra. Home to soldiers and visiting diplomats, it gave off an odd silver hue at dusk, and turned golden when the sun jumped at dawn. Obelisk was the heartbeat of Abydos. The tall building was covered with the stories of the pharaohs, but the building's story was told in its lower base. There, a siphoning pump connected to an underground river that drew water perpetually. From there, the water rose high to the top of Obelisk where it flowed out to four aqueducts. The aqueducts stood nearly eighty feet off the ground with key stones connecting each part. Two traveled to the Pharaoh and his servants at the Temple of Amon-Ra, one brought refreshment to the aristocracy to serve their waste systems and bathhouses, and the last one went to the Hall of Ancient Scrolls and Manuscripts. The laborers of Abydos kept the system at work. Below the Obelisk, they turned the gears and pulleys of an upward spiraling wheel with an effort that made the pump swirl at remarkable speeds.

Aleeia and her chaperones entered Abydos. They saw the bustling civilization in its everyday practices and conventions.

"Let us find shelter now. The journey has been long. We will begin our studies in the morning," Gaia stated.

"Indeed, our long tour has tired me. I require food

and rest. With a greater concern to my hunger," Bellia added.

"I have no idea how you manage your figure, Bellia. It must be *magic*, an image spell," Gaia noted.

"No, it's my metabolism." Bellia grunted.

"Yeah right. Metabolism." Gaia scoffed.

"Metabolism?" Aleeia inquired. She did not know the word.

"Tomorrow, child. But first let us lead our Bellia to a trough fitting for her appetite."

They crossed into the heart of the city. Gaia sought domain in the local inn for merchants, wanderers, and caravans. They unloaded their supplies, washed their garments, bathed their exhausted bodies and ate to replenish themselves. Finally, they slept deeply and serenely.

Never before had Gaia or Bellia been to the Egyptian City, yet somehow when they rose from slumber, they knew the way to the Hall of Ancient Scrolls and Manuscripts. It was grand, with its comers and goers. It seemed to be pulse of the city, the way a temple or a palace should be. All things led to it. Revered as an antiquity, inside the Hall of Ancient Scrolls and Manuscripts the atmosphere was unbothered and still. For it was a monument to the past while the city grew around it.

They ventured to the Hall. Aleeia saw the same city,

which bustled the day before. She saw the merchants, the caravans, and the consumers. Off in the distance, she saw great tombs and monuments being built by skilled builders. The closer she came to her place of study, the more closely she saw the builders and their extraordinary works of architecture. Her eyes went skyward to take in the massive structure. The Hall looked so complete and immaculate to Aleeia, it was as though it were carved from a small mountain. At that moment, her eyes drew away from the top of the Hall. She looked mistakenly into a cloud that moved to reveal the sun through an opening. She drew her eyes back downward sharply. Her vision was blurred at first but then her eyes connected with those of a young boy. The boy moved and swayed in the straw filled mud in almost mesmerizing motions. Aleeia wondered why some builders, ornamented in gold and jade, only stood and watched while other builders worked. Before she could give a second thought, she reached her intended destination.

Ahead of them loomed stairs, wide and tall. They seemed to number in the hundreds. The women made their way upward. Alee became winded. At the summit, the opening threshold of the Hall was surrounded with Egyptian pillars. Detailed marble floors and high lantern-lit ceilings ornamented the hall. Two of the three figures crossed the portal into The Great Hall. Bellia observed the Hall and saw its single entrance made protection and security most favorable. She remained outside to continue her assessment.

Gaia visually panned the layout of the interior before she began a lesson plan. Her memory served her, as she went from shelf to shelf to remove needed scroll titles from their resting places. The scrolls were so numerous the cubbies of the shelves made the shelves look like humongous wasp nest. Row after row of shelves and tables packed the Hall. Gaia continued to prepare. She walked intensely. Alee tried to keep up.

While in Egypt, Gaia was empowered to lead Aleeia's tutorial and training. She gave her dozens of scrolls so she could begin her reading. Gaia also placed a huge piece of dry papyrus at the head of the chamber for the explanation and elaboration of matters from the reading. Passages of history and philosophy marked the first session of her day. Alee took it all in as she consumed the literature. Learning how some civilizations came to be satisfied her greatly. No longer did she have to stare out her window and wonder. Aswan only taught things that applied to the Woodlands of the South. But, Alee always knew the world was much larger. She read the scrolls of philosophy after history. She found the concepts harder to relate to. At times, they brought an ominous air to her. The scholars' theories on life and death, or life after death, were despairing depending on the argument she read. She had never given thought before to the idea that there may be nothing beyond the lives mortals led.

Alee paused frequently when she read. Sometimes, she did not know where myth ended and existential reason began. Gaia returned when Alee was done. She expected questions that reflected the confused look upon her face.

"Questions, Alee?"

"How can infinity be all and nothing at once? If chaos is a natural state, then how is the universe balanced? Where…" Alee began.

The questions were a rather pleasant barrage to Gaia. She took the time to answer them as best she could. More importantly, her answers prompted more questions from Alee to the point where they discussed her own views and opinions.

Gaia asked, "In your short time here, what is your perception of the true nature of man?"

Alee did not hesitate for the topic was fresh and still at the forefront of her mind. She understood the question completely.

"I guess I believe man is good." Alee said.

Gaia waited for more but soon realized that Alee only understood the question to the point of an answer without explanation. She smiled and replied.

"Not bad for the first day, Alee. Not bad."

After her tutorials, Gaia and Aleeia descended into the lower Chasms of the Hall. It was a vault for the lost passages and texts that time worked to destroy. The thinner air lessened the wear of time on the scrolls left there. In addition to the decaying scrolls were artifacts of time and spoils of war. The items stayed there instead of the trappings of The Temple or some other grand place. However, the Chasm had its own grandeur that was not overlooked by Gaia. The stones on the wall were smooth and appeared like silver. The stones arched to the center of the ceiling with no crease or layer. If not for the dust, the entire room would have surely shone. There, in the Chasm, they would be protected by the astrologically aligned structure of the hollowed spaced. Gaia would be free to teach and demonstrate her mystical abilities to Aleeia.

They noticed a tablet piece hid under a mountain of dust near other heirlooms of the Chasm. Gaia circled it once. She wiped the dirt away with her left hand.

"Is that it? The tablet Nympthia carved?" asked Alee.

"The very same," replied Gaia.

Alee said nothing more and waited for her session to begin. Gaia found it hard to pull away from the tablet. She saw a luster of purpose and history about the tablet and revered it.

She turned to Alee and quickly saw the same luster.

Gaia started Alee with breathing exercises, which calmed the mind. It was the first step towards stirring her Awakening, for the Will does not work well for an unsettled mind. The thin air made the exercise rather difficult for both Aleeia and Gaia. Everyday they followed their routine, studies from morning to noon and spiritual training from noon to night. Bellia, the sentinel, remained outside. That was the beginning as Aleeia made her way towards understanding the humongous piece of tablet.

Everyday she took the same route to the Hall. Often, she saw the same boy she laid eyes upon the day she entered the city. The boy, a bit younger than Aleeia, was also drawn to her. Late into the night when the others rested, he snuck into the Hall and passed a sleeping Bellia. Inside, he saw what drew him there. He descended into the Chasm. He saw Aleeia engaged in a slow mesmerizing dance of her own. Gaia led the dance beside her. She directed the slow fluid wave of their arms, the pivot of their hips and torso, and the steadiness and intensity of their breathing. He entered quietly and subtly. He fell in line behind the two women. He stood beside Aleeia and mimicked Gaia along with Aleeia. Several minutes passed before Gaia even noticed the little one.

"How…?" Gaia exclaimed.

"Who are you? Where did you come from?"

Gaia's questions fell on ears deaf to her language. In the safety of the Hall's Chasm, she enchanted the whirling air among them.

"Speak to the air in your tongue. It shall translate. Hear any language and the air shall translate."

"My name is Hat-kaptah. That was fun. What were we doing?" he said to Aleeia.

"I'm Alee. I mean…Aleeia but you can call me Alee. I have seen you building," Aleeia said.

"So young and yet you build all day?" she asked.

"Yes, Alee. I build but do not wish to. We are slaves to the master of this city, who is the servant to Amon-Ra. We must build for them."

"Slaves? I have learned much. But even without education I know a thing unjust. It is a despairing thought for me to hear you speak it," she replied.

"Indeed, I felt this. When I saw you come, I knew you would liberate us. That you would set us free," Hat-kaptah said passionately.

"I'm sorry. And as we are aware of your sorrow, we can do nothing for you now," Gaia said.

"But Gaia? This is not right." Aleeia declared.

"No." said Gaia.

For the first time since they met all those months ago, Gaia harshly raised her voice at Aleeia with strict implications. At that moment, she undid her will that allowed their communication. She also removed any knowledge of her mystical exploits from his memory. They all proceeded to the upper chamber and made their way towards the exit. Hat-kaptah stumbled along in an unconscious daze. Gaia guided Hat-kaptah by the arm as they passed Bellia, still asleep. Alee trailed from the rear.

"Better let her sleep. If she wakes, she'll be hungry," Gaia said.

They exited the gate and descended the stairs. A guard who circled the area near the tombs nightly looking for robbers, raiders, and vandals spotted them. The guard also caught sight of the young slave who he assumed was trying to escape. Moving like a rabid dog, the guardsman made his way to kill him and arrest those who helped him.

"This can not be good," Gaia said.

"What do we do?" Alee asked in a panic.

"Take the boy. Go back inside to the Chasm," Gaia stated, "Now!"

Gaia, skilled in the ways of the sword, though admittedly not her specialty, drew her blade. The guard was upon her. She dodged the knife and lance of the guardsmen, but in the late of night grew fatigued quickly. She parried and thrust, punched, countered and kicked, each time with the intention only to disable her opponent. They fought on different levels with different objectives. When Gaia realized that the combat could end with her death, she began her retreat. Gaia ducked and shifted the guardsmen's blade as if it were the sole task of some obstacle course. She called out.

"Bellia! Bellia, I need you," she shouted.

Still in a deep dormant sleep, Bellia was summoned by her counterpart, but paid no heed. Bellia, although capable of magic herself, was also an expert markswoman, archer, swordswoman, and war tactician. At that moment, Gaia was backed against the stairs of the Hall. She could not yell any louder. She did not want to alert other soldiers and guardsmen. His lance rose to distract Gaia from his blade, which moved to swipe and pierce Gaia just below the shoulder. The cut drew blood. It was deep and painful enough for her to act instinctively. Gaia lost control. Her Will was poured on the guardsman. With a hard cringe of her brow and a clenching twiddle of her fingertips, her mind exploded and heaved the guardsmen far across the sand. He slammed against the sun-baked bricks of a temple wall with a hollow boom. He felt as though he had been pushed by an angry hurricane. The force of it caused the dust and sand to stir around him. He stayed imbedded into the temple before falling face first to the ground. He lay there unconscious. For Gaia, everything happened in an instant and she was slow to realize what she had done until, finally, her head cleared. She staggered to her feet and held her open wound. She climbed the stairs to retrieve Bellia. She kicked her boot and shouted,

"Bellia, we have a situation here."

The two moved the live, but motionless body into the Chasm where they tended him and cleared his memory of the night's events. They ended the night's drama by stashing the guardsman beside a nearby tavern.

Meanwhile, somewhere on the great Isle of Avalon, heroes and villains, all sons of Changel, feasted with their father, who said,

"What was that? I felt...something."

Mind of the Otherside - In a citadel, a strong impenetrable fortress on The Great Isle of Avalon with walls higher than most mountains, a feast was being held. The citadel was a culmination of home and battle station where men, women, and other unimaginable beings ate, drank and were extremely merry. A hallowed hall and a dining chamber with a long table existed in the heart of the structure. The table's length could not have been adequately described in neither feet, cubits, nor yards. Its seating capacity could not be comprehended as anything other than infinite. The delights to eat seemed unending as well. One fried deer or dozen of baked peaches disappeared by way of gluttony, only to be instantaneously replaced by another portion. The food on the table, the table in the hall, and the hall in the citadel housed an army. And not just an army, a family of several hundred generations. There, fathers dined with founding fathers, great great grandsons shared with grandsons, even mothers-by-marriage talked with sons-by-marriage. Changel's children replenished themselves after a day of tremendous training, which would soon be followed by a night of demanding drills. No one liked training, conditioning, drills, or exercise. Everyone despised them as some sort of cruel foreplay, which was the discussion at this particular sitting. They debated everything. Historical what-ifs were very popular since several people present had a hand in an historical outcome. Tonight, the topic was training.

"How can you drill to kill someone? It's just something that comes naturally." one man said.

"Yeah, either you have it or you don't," a woman replied.

"You tormented souls. Remember not all of us here are evils without remorse. A great deal many have only taken up arms for a cause out of loyalty," a soldier said.

"Regardless of why, I fail to see how doing a few

drills will change anything. No mere human can defeat me. It has never happened and never shall. They are just sheep, no less than a minor inconvenience on the battlefield. They infest the world and soon there will be only us, only our father," responded one brawny figure in passionate soliloquy.

"Ha, Ha, Ha." clamored Changel himself, "My children, enlightened yet limited. You all carry some truth, some wisdom in your fractured words and meanings. Do not be misled. What we do we do for the "*mere humans.*" We hold "*loyalty*" to them, but indeed they are sheep. And all sheep need a shepherd to protect them, and also to destroy the beast that would prey on them. We are at war with them, the beasts, not the mere humans who are righteous, not the sheep."

"But, Father! How can we distinguish those that are wolves from those who are sheep?" one asked.

Changel paused and pointed towards his own eyes with his middle and index fingers. He then pointed his fingers in the opposite direction in a sweeping motion, which scanned across everyone. Counterclockwise his arm motioned until it stood still, straight out next to him, parallel to the ground. Then out of nowhere a watchbird owl sat atop his forearm, just below his elbow. The bird clutched Changel with his blade-like talons. Changel bled, but his blood did not drip. The blood of Changel sprouted and entangled the legs of the watchbird owl like the determined vine of a rose bush. Changel laughed. He quickly mended as the blood retreated. He cleared his throat and spoke once again.

> "The wisdom of this owl, a friend to me since the very beginning, will guide you. You will see with his eyes and gain the ability to look into the souls and minds of men. You will read their impurities and sins aloud. The day is not near, it does not even begin to peak round the road's upward bend. So for now, eat, feast, and enjoy one another. For late night drills begin within the hour."

Changel and the watchbird owl proceeded to retire to his personal quarters for a one-on-one discussion. As they reached the threshold of the chamber, the gigantic twin doors that sealed it from the rest of the fortress slowly creaked open. It was as if the door expected them and knew its job was to open. But indeed, it was the Will of Changel. They entered and Changel raised his arm. The watchbird owl flew to the top of an oak tree, which grew in his chamber across from the fire mantle. Changel slipped off his shimmering armor and reddish-purple cape, which he wore at all meetings, dinners, speeches and battles. He situated himself in his chair beneath the tree. The huge doors slammed simultaneously and he looked at the owl perched at the height of the oak tree.

"Watchbird owl," he said.

"I have known thee for as long as I have known the rule of Avalon. I have known thee for as long as I have championed the praise of mortal's myth. It is the way of the mortal, but in all this time I have neglected to ask your name."

"Yes, it is a mortal desire to name and classify beyond necessity," the owl replied.

"It is not enough for me to be a bird, not even enough to be an owl. I have been named by renamers more times than memory recalls. I say nothing to them but what I say to you is this, name me what you will, but not of the land or of the sea or of the sky or anything upon them. If I like the name, I shall claim it," said the owl.

"You know nothing of Heaven. Nothing of the celestial. I shall name thee Caim, an angel's name in the order Seraphim. I beg you not to reject this gift! Claim this name."

"Very well. But be not surprised if I do not answer to it," the owl proclaimed.

"But what is the true matter in summoning my

council? You have always danced around true motives," said the owl.

"While I dined I felt some force. Tell me, is it another magician who dabbles in the arts, who commits crimes against the order of nature? Surely humans have not grown so powerful in the magical arts? If only they knew it would be their undoing, dim to the price, they would not commit such crimes. Tell me, watchbird owl! Speak to me, Caim! Does trouble stir in Egypt?"

The Tiles of Uriel - For the past three weeks, Alee had not been allowed to sleep in. She was forced to awaken well before the sun. Because of their conflict weeks earlier, Gaia thought it best that their comings and goings be under the cover of darkness. Thus, Gaia shook Alee to rise so that they could travel the empty streets of Abydos, from the inn to the Hall.

"Rise and shine, sleepyhead!" called Gaia annoyingly.

"You know, where I am from that phrase is ignored if the sun is not out yet. If the sun gets more time then so should I," argued Alee.

Gaia ripped away the sheets from atop Alee. Despite the

desert climate, the nights were fairly cool. The air hit her in a rush. An uncomfortable Alee let out a groan then curled herself upon the bed.

"Are you sure you are supposed to treat me this way? I am sure those scrolls and tablets have a passage about letting me do whatever I want in there somewhere." Alee ranted.

Gaia smiled.

"Nice try, but no. Speaking of scrolls and tablets, let's move, young lady."

Alee made no more arguments. She washed up and tidied her hair. She put on a blouse and a pair of trousers, both made of light flax. She wore a heavier poncho made of leather over them, tied her hair back in a single ponytail and was ready to depart.

"What about Bellia?".

"Let her sleep. Unless there is a battle, she is useless before sunrise," replied Gaia.

Alee's face fell when she heard Gaia. Her steps became unusually loud and heavy as they walked by Bellia's room, which emitted roaring snorts and groans. The women reached the Great Hall well before sunrise. When Alee reached the apex of the grand staircase at the main entrance, she turned back and seemed to look down on the sun. She wandered for a moment, lost in thought. She pondered about the places, people and the things that lied beyond the horizon. She had already learned so much but much more learning awaited. *The world is so big,* thought Alee.

"Come," said Gaia.

Gaia's command quickly snapped her trance. She turned to follow Gaia through the library to the entry of the Chasm. Gaia opened the hatch where a short ladder led to a room the size of a closet. The door held the secrets of the Chasm on the other side. Once inside the safety of the Chasm, Gaia raised her two middle fingers upward. The lanterns, candles, and flares that were scattered around the room ignited. Although Alee had seen it before, she never grew tired of Gaia and her displays of power.

"Take your seat, young one," insisted Gaia.

Alee took her seat. Gaia went to the section of cubbyholes and pulled at least a dozen scrolls. Gaia placed the scrolls on the table in front of Alee. She then turned to another corner of the room in search of something else. A curious Alee unfurled a scroll.

"It's blank," she said disappointedly.

She rifled through a few more to the same end. An eager student, Alee saw nothing to consume. In the weeks prior, Alee had been presented with books and texts that explained the language of patterns. The study of logic, trends, space and time as well as how all things interrelate in a quantitative manner were the precursor, lessons necessary for the translation of the tablets. Gaia returned with a box, no bigger than the size of a book, in her hand. She placed it on the table in front of Alee. Alee looked over the box made of thin copper with embossed layered designs. Alee looked at Gaia for permission to touch. Gaia nodded. Alee ran her fingertips across the box.

"Listen carefully, Aleeia." said Gaia.

Alee quickly focused on Gaia whose tone, coupled with the formality of her name made it clear her words were about to be more pertinent than usual. Gaia continued.

> "Inside this box is the first task you must complete by yourself. I will not help you. I cannot help, so please do not ask anything of me."

Gaia paused for a moment to read Alee. She saw an eager smile on the young girl's face, a smile Gaia was glad to see.

> "These are my final words. Inside this box are the Tiles of Uriel. These tiles are stones with the symbols of your mother engraved upon them. They push and pull one another. When one has ebbed, others flow. Play this puzzle. Master it, and when you do, you will be a step closer to mastering *that*."

Gaia pointed at the tablet. She spoke the last words Alee would hear from her for the greater part of the day.

Alee opened the latch and emptied the contents of the box on the table. Twenty pieces of a red stone, too dull to be rubies, scattered across the table. Each one about the width, length, and depth of Alee's two middle fingers side by side. Each had a symbol on them. Alee looked back to the tablet. She saw symbols of the same style and artistry. However, none matched completely. The symbols had a few things in common, but no characteristics ran across them all. Most had a stem, but some were nothing more than a curved line. Some tiles looked to be duplicated or at least transposed in some way. Alee looked to the blank scrolls that Gaia laid down.

"Ah, notes…" Alee realized.

She quickly grabbed the stiff quill and dabbed it in some ink. She wrote down her observations as quickly as they had entered her head. She looked to Gaia who sat in the corner reading a legendary romance chronicled on a set of ancient parchment.

The redstone tiles were scattered across the table face-up. Alee reached for the farthest tile to corral them all closer. When her fingertips touched a tile that looked like a plain, straight line, all the tiles realigned and the tile with the straight line stood on end. The nineteen other tiles stayed flat on the table, but all were positioned somewhere in rows of four and columns of five. The straight line tile stayed balanced on its end.

"They moved by themselves!" exclaimed Alee. She looked to Gaia who had been completely enthralled in her story. To Gaia's dismay, Alee's outburst took her out of her story. She let out a low sigh.

"Pipe down," said Gaia, "Lahmi just gave up the priesthood to be with Kehren."

Alee rolled her eyes. She had thought maybe the movement of the tiles was something done by Gaia but quickly rejected the notion and returned back to the task at hand.

"What am I supposed to be doing here?" she asked of herself.

Alee gently thumped the ridged tile. The moment she touched it, it flipped face down and four other tiles rose on end.

"Whoa," said Alee.

"Shhhh." Gaia scolded, "Concentration is best when silent." she added.

Alee quickly jotted what happened. The symbol of the tile, now facedown, was easy enough to remember. Alee then proceeded to document the symbols of the four new tiles. Two symbols looked to be simple, curved lines, but were the mirror image of one another. The other two symbols had a small circle at their base, though one had a curved spine and the other a straight spine.

"Why did only these four tiles protrude, when the other subsided? Push and pull," murmured Alee. "Twenty tiles...one relates to four."

All of a sudden, Alee heard the faint murmurs of Gaia followed by a moan and wail. Alee looked back at Gaia. Her frenzied eyes moved across the words on the scroll as she dried her tears.

"Concentration is best when silent." scoffed an upset Alee.

"Sorry," replied Gaia, "...but Kehren followed Lahmi, who went away to find himself. He said he *needed to, to be a better man* for her."

Alee ignored the tail end of Gaia's apology. She remained focused on the puzzle and the Tiles of Uriel. Alee tried to raise another tile. She touched the tile in the first row of the first column. Nothing happened. Alee grabbed it, sunk her nails beneath it and pulled. It would not budge.

"Odd," stated Alee.

She tried to move another flat tile but it also would not move. Alee considered the four tiles *in play.* Two of the four tiles were in the same row and the other two in the same column. However, the two symbols from the same row were more similar in style to the two symbols positioned in the same column. Alee took a chance. She chose the tile of the first row, in the fourth column with a circular base. She touched it and as it laid face down, so did the tile in the third row, last column that also had a circular base.

> "If I had to guess, I would say that the object of the puzzle is to make all the tiles lay flat in as few moves as possible. I have made two moves, picking two tiles and there are only two left standing. Their symbols look similar so maybe moving one will move the other as before."

Alee chose again. The tile with the symbol of a line curved down and inward was in the fourth row and the fourth column. Alee hoped that it would also affect the tile with the symbol of a line curved down and out. She touched the tile. However, nothing happened as she had hypothesized. Two tiles arose at the farthest corners of the tile alignment. The tile of row four, column one and the tile of row one, column five were now *in play*.

Alee quickly became frustrated with the game. She spent the next few hours reviewing her three moves. In a timely manner, Gaia completed the twelfth scroll out of the eighteen scrolls that chronicled the tale she found so compelling. It was now time for a break. Gaia approached Alee to offer her a moment to rest and retreat.

"Time for lunch. Let's go topside," said Gaia.

Relieved, Alee popped up out of her seat. She saw the practicality in the exercise but doubted her ability to find a pattern. She needed a break. Every intuitive observation thus far resulted so conversely when acted upon. Alee led the way back to the main Hall of the library. Gaia was close behind to dim the fires that lit the room. It seemed as though a breeze or draft strong enough to extinguish the flames followed Gaia.

Gaia and Alee met Bellia out front at the top of the grand staircase. Bellia's privilege of sleeping in meant she was responsible for bringing the midday meal. This particular day, she brought dried meat seasoned with a rosemary pepper, bread, and raw beets. Alee had water while Gaia and Bellia drank wine. Although Alee cringed at the beets, she enjoyed the meal thoroughly.

"So what is happening in the scrolls?" asked Bellia.

"You know, you would not have to ask if you read it yourself," replied Gaia.

"Maybe, but I would rather ask you than be bored out of my mind," said Bellia.

As Gaia indulged Bellia in regards to *The Legend of Kehren and Lahmi*, Alee grabbed a few scraps of food and her cup of water. She returned to the Chasm alone to continue her pursuits to master the puzzle. Without Gaia, Alee had lit only the three candles on her desk with spark stones. She continued where she left off and randomly chose again.

"How about this one?" she decided.

Alee randomly chose the tile in the lower left corner. When she selected it every tile already on its end then faced down, but every title that was not already faced down stood up. The remaining twelve tiles had risen, but it mattered not. Alee saw the symbols for what they were. Each symbol represented a numerical value. And any choice she made had a bearing on the multiples of that value. Her last choice was the number ***one***. Alee reviewed what she had learned. She finished in eleven moves. And when all the tiles were flat and faced down, they then flipped up to start a new game.

Alee was engaged in the puzzle for the entire day and far into the night. What she learned seemed small but would become the cornerstone for her translations to come. The Tiles of Uriel were a puzzle game made by Nympthia as a means to understand her cryptic language. Gaia returned to the Chasm along with Bellia.

"So, child, are you ready to retire for the day?" Gaia asked.

"I think I am," replied Alee.

"Good, because I have no more of my story to read. Poor Kehren." stated Gaia.

"Yeah, all she had to do was love him with all her heart." Bellia fawned.

Gaia and Alee looked at one another. They were thrown by

Bellia's soft, melodramatic character critique. They laughed while Bellia shrugged them off. The three walked back towards the inn under the cover of night.

Trial And Translation - Almost a year had passed since she, Alee, had been called. Two months of travel and nearly ten months of studies had consumed her life thus far. At times, when weary, she thought the studies pointless and of no substance. She felt as though the lessons stood on their own and failed to remember her studies were the grounds to a greater purpose. But when she forgot, she touched the translated scrolls from her mother or the Tiles of Uriel. Her drive would return and she would make her way to the Chasm of the Hall to the tablet. More times than Alee would admit, the tablet bested her. The patterns were complex, more so than the tiles, but she continued to try alone. It seemed logical for anyone as a student who struggled to get help from their teacher in order to succeed, but out of respect for her mother's wishes Alee never asked Gaia. However, out of pity and the urge to see her pupil succeed Gaia would descend into the Hall's chasm with her knowledge and notes. But as she approached the tablet to read, the markings would fade away. Though it did not stop her from trying at other times, when she felt Alee could not proceed by herself. At those times, the words would sometimes fade or the patterns would rearrange themselves. Once, in a plain, readable language, the tablet read:

Alee alone to read and translate.
Bellia to watch-protect the gate.
Gaia must guide and trust in Fate.

"Where is Alee?" Gaia asked.

"Where else but the Chasm." replied Bellia.

"I should go see to her."

"Look...you have done all you can. Trust in that. Besides, sometimes you have to lay back and let things work themselves out," Bellia said.

"Oh really! Is that what you did all those months ago when I was nearly killed by that guardsmen? Did you just let that work itself out?"

"Are you still on that? Gosh! You're fine. And you logged in some much needed field time. So quit your whining," said Bellia.

"You could have compromised our whole mission," Gaia retorted.

"But I didn't. Besides, if you can't handle a few weak guards then what good are you for the battle ahead? I'm not your babysitter, Gaia," sneered

Bellia.

"Yeah, well! A babysitter is what your stomach is. That pouch you have is why you are rarely ever courted." said Gaia.

"See... Why did you have to take it there? Anytime I make a point you go and..."

Bellia continued on and on while Gaia laughed and reveled in her psychological victory over her friend. As they argued and laughed at the same time, they once again did not notice young Hat-kaptah. He swayed in as calmly and naturally as a person could. He waved a greeting towards the two women and quickly made his way to the Chasm where he knew Alee would be. Over the months of their stay, since the day Gaia described as Bellia's Blunder, Hat-kaptah studied with Alee, not in the mystical arts but purely in scholarship. It soon came to Gaia's attention the best way to help in the slave's plight was to educate him. Knowing knowledge is great power, Gaia made Hat-kaptah more self-aware. But that was not the bargaining chip, which motivated Hat-kaptah to stay. To be near Alee was more than enough for him. He entered the Chasm's Den where Alee studied and greeted her.

"Alee, greetings." he said.

"Oh, hi, Hat-kaptah. Wait one minute. I'm almost there, almost done and this time I know its right."

Alee exclaimed.

"The tablet?" Hat-kaptah asked in uncertainty.

"Yes, the tablet."

Egyptian Rain -The day came upon Alee, dank and gloomy, saturated. She arose from her slumber. Since their entry into the city, the inn in which Alee, Gaia, and Bellia resided had rarely been the place where Alee would rest. The Hall, full of all its knowledge and wisdom, was her sanctuary. Every waking moment, she toiled and studied before the tablet. In the presence of the tablet, in the cold, dark, dankness of the Chasm, Alee had slept many times before. She awoke and some how knew it was the Day of Egyptian Rain.

There in Egypt, rain was a seasonal rarity, but she felt the overcast skies. Beneath the ground in the Chasm, the Nile shook and grew. Yet somehow, she saw the purple-black sky outside in her mind's eye. The waters of the Nile reached out for more. Alee felt everything with instinct rather than mysticism and her instincts found the day to be greatly symbolic. Aleeia had been there for many sunny days in sequence, but the day the purpose for her stay found its end was the Day of Egyptian Rain.

Alee loved these rains. She rushed outside to meet it. She saw the beauty and power in the black clouds that floated majestically above all. It was the same beauty she had seen in the people and places over her journey thus far.

> "Sunny days are not always bright. The day they came was so sunny," she vividly remembered.

Then she smiled even more. She wrapped her arms around one another and tipped her head back a little. As a way of showing her gratitude, she let the respected rain softly hit her face. The purple-black clouds hid the sun's nourishing glow but also did their part to bring the rains that nourished the land.

> "Life from the Darkness. Death from the Light. Death from the Darkness. Life from the Light," rolled off her tongue.

Her words contained wisdom far beyond her years, but they came from her experience. The sorrow she felt the day she had to leave Karwynn compared to the sorrow of her accomplished goal that would soon cause her departure. The joy of truth and purpose that Gaia and Bellia brought from her mother mirrored her pride and anxiety in finishing that chunk of the tablet.

The day before, close to the time of Hat-kaptah's arrival, she finished it around noon. It was not the first time she deciphered the tablet. On that particular day, it was her seventh pass over its translation. But that minute, that hour of that day marked the first time Alee felt completely confident in her translation. All she could do was wait for Gaia and Bellia to arrive. She was excited but did not want to cross paths unknowingly while trying to spread her enthusiasm and news. She came out from under the pouring sky and pulled a chair to the portal of the Hall where the height of the stairs allowed her to see all on-comers. In the meantime, she thought aloud and sometimes not. She tried counting raindrops to pass the time. Her counting started causally enough for she only counted the ones she could see and track clearly. Somewhere around drop number two hundred thirty-six, her scholastic mind took over. She estimated, extrapolated and created mental graphs and schematics in her head.

"My studies have taken over," she mumbled humorously.

"Such a simple counting game made so rigid and serious. Now I know it's time to go.," she thought.

Goodbye Again - As the carriage bearing her life, or at least the last several months, grew nearer and expanded over the orange horizon, Alee felt a great relief. She let her heart breathe and sigh for she did not need to continue her preparation. Purely out of routine, rather than impending commencement and exodus, she dreadfully anticipated the coming of Hat-kaptah. To say anything to him who had been her friend, ally, and confidant at the time of her departure would be too great a burden. Her journey began with a goodbye. A goodbye that echoed. Aleeia knew full well to say again the things she said to another for whom she cared so deeply, would not echo, it would burn. So with that in mind, heart, body and soul, she lingered back into The Great Hall and remembered bittersweetly. And bittersweetly she sang.

His loyalty,
Was certainly,
A friend to me,
La La La La

So desperately,
I wish for thee
To Stay with me,
La La La La

How Bitterly,
That times should be,
Unfair to me,
La La La La

I wish that he,
Could somehow see
My need for thee
La, La, La La --Love

She sang her song downwards and sideways to pass the time, until Gaia and Bellia returned. She gathered the last few cartons that were filled with her belongings: scrolls, books, and trinkets. They stacked and surpassed her line of vision till she could see nothing in front of her. Her other senses, more than acute, aided her awareness. And her awareness came to be a sudden misfortune for Alee.

"May I help you with those?"

She knew the voice all too well. It startled her immensely. The Hall reverberated with the crash of the scrolls and books she carried. The trinkets hit the ground with a boom that caused a fair amount of dust to stir. Alee took her eyes away from the entropy in order to look through the sullen air. At that moment, she knew she had to bear it.

"Hat-kaptah, you are here."

"Yes, I came across Gaia and Bellia and came with them."

Cautiously, she inquired. "So then you know what is going on?"

"Of course, ***we*** are making preparations to continue our journey," he calmly stated.

"Uhm…Could you excuse my clumsiness and gather these items for me, please? I must speak with the ladies," said a flustered Alee.

Alee marched down the stairs and met the women at the wagon. They secured material and took inventory for their long journey ahead. Alee came to them, her feelings of compassion and regret on edge.

"What is the meaning of this?" she shouted.

"Alee, calm down. The meaning of what?" Gaia gestured for softness by lowering her hands.

"He thinks he is coming. Coming with us." She stated as her voice became raspy.

"I implore you to ease yourself. Obviously, when we told him we were on our way to pick you up before ***we*** set out, he felt as though that were an invitation," Gaia said.

“It’s understandable, you know. The little guy has grown attached, Alee,” Bellia added.

“Are you implying this is *my* fault? That the pain I feel and that he is going to feel is because of me?”

“Hold on, I was not implying anything. But in all honesty, this is your mess to clean up. So I suggest you do it.” Bellia said with a fierce tone.

In that instance, Aleeia let her emotions get the better of her. All of them culminated: her love, her anger, her regret and her fear. They were brought to the surface in a manner that Gaia soon recognized.

“No,” Gaia said as she reached for Alee.

But it was too late. They felt the earth move and turned to The Great Hall. They could plainly see The Great Hall flew taller than both of them. It sat there and seemed to rest on air. Hat-kaptah dropped the crates he carried the instant the ground beneath his feet moved. Fearing for Alee, Hat-kaptah raced outside in order to see to her safety.

“Alee, what is happening?” Hat-kaptah asked.

He jumped down towards her from the lowest steps of The Hall. Alee's mind was on her emotion and all she could do was answer to them.

“You can not go with us. I am sorry, so sorrr…”stated Alee as she murmured into unconsciousness.

Alee passed out and fell into slumber with those last words. Her unexpected exploit weakened her. With her mind now at peace, the base of The Hall met the ground with the greatest roar ever heard before. But Alee's few short words were enough. Catching Alee in his arms, Hat-kaptah understood. Gaia turned to him and said,

> "We are going now, with a greater urgency than before. But now your staying has a purpose bigger than your trials alone. If anyone comes looking for the mover of The Hall…
>
> *Retreat into the chasm when the way is clear.*
> *Speak these words so I may hear -*
> *Verba mentium traciecto caelo it*
>
> Make sure you do so while standing over the buried tablet. Good luck, young one. I feel as though Fate will bring you back to us someday."

Hat-Kaptah repeated the words to himself until he could write them down. Bellia scooped up the weary, slumbersome Aleeia and placed her gently in the coach. Gaia took to the reigns and set their journey in motion. For a new arrival in the City of Abydos was only a matter of time.

Mission of Alonard - On the Great Isle of Avalon, Changel, Lord of the land, took to his day-to-day duties. The land behind the mist always had an engaged and busy air about it. With hundreds of thousands of servants and warriors under his charge, Changel delegated the Isle's every pulse. From the highest tower of his fortress, he saw the entire lay of the land, yet his attentions focused on matters in some distant place. Changel, who already had the counsel of his most trusted, awaited the company of his truest emissary.

Alonard of the Western Bank was the strongest heir of Avalon. As the son of Changel, he garnered great respect. Alonard enforced the will of his father upon the Isle from the West to meet his father's direct rule, which came from the East. Born with the same abilities of change, Alonard's natural state was one of great beauty and fairness. His fairness as a man made Alonard the perfect choice for the task at hand.

"Greetings, First among many. Come," commanded Changel.

Upon the order, Alonard came before Changel. He entered the throne room of the Isle's citadel. Alonard marveled at the artistry and simplicity of the room's décor. Strangely enough, no one before had been within the walls that contained the throne, not even the First among many. The room, though vast enough to hold the entire regiments under Changel, was his sanctuary. It contained several beautifully made iconographies, paintings and statutes. Each one was older and even more ancient than the one before it. Though each shared a subtle continuity, the images depicted were drastically different. The beauty of each mural captivated Alonard, until he almost forgot himself. Quickly, Alonard came to himself bent upon one knee and bowed his head. He realized he had yet to give courtesy to his master.

"My lord, what is thy bid?" Alonard asked humbly.

"You paused before you gave me glory. Were you taken by the power of your surroundings? Taken to honor them over me?" asked Changel.

Alonard knew his father's imposing tone, but despite the hysteria he felt and his urgency to show respect, Alonard calmly responded, "No master, I…"

"Worry not, son." Changel interrupted.

"I am these iconographies. You know full well I have been many saviors to many a people. And they have done their best to immortalize me. I have kept them as a reminder of where and who I have been. And also as a reminder of what lies before me. So fear not. For you to stand in reverence of me is your courtesy to me."

Alonard, while still bent in the presence of Changel, raised his eyes to make one final sweep of time's beauty.

"Alonard, I have need of you. You must go to Egypt at once."

"And upon my arrival?" inquired Alonard.

"The powers I have felt are indeed great, but raw. I have no doubt one of my children has experienced an Awakening. You must find this one and bring them to me. A power such as that must be nurtured quickly before we move," said Changel.

"And Father, if the power proves to be hostile, then how should I proceed?" asked Alonard.

"Well, I have an army and this force is nearly invincible. I am more than enough to tip any scale of war. If this power, indeed, holds us in ill favor or will not join with us, then you must rid the Earth of him. Death to him and his allies."

Changel smiled. The thought of anyone standing to deny him was extremely amusing. Changel approached Alonard and ordered him to stand. He then placed his hands upon him with a father's consolation and favor. Alonard smiled. They both laughed aloud. When the laughter subsided in them, Changel spoke.

"The greatest sadness of a life, my son, First among many, is to die before ever having discovered your own reason for being and living in this life.

Originally, the task of watching was given to me. I was created to do so. However, I knew my destiny would lay not simply in looking, but shaping man in the image the Creator intended. I have not spoken to Him since long ago. And I have not received His guidance; therefore I know the path I tread is true, because He allows me to continue. The greatest sadness will not be my fate. I have been allowed in my ways thus far, so I know I shall make my efforts come to fruition."

Alonard pondered the words of his father. He looked upon his father with an even greater sense of admiration. At that moment, what he knew was reinforced. For Alonard, his purpose was to make the Will of God come to light through an undying loyalty to his father, his master.

"I will set out at once with my trusted few. I will not fail you," stated Alonard.

"I know, Alonard," Changel replied.

"You know the penalties of failure, but all failures will be forgiven. Such mercy is the mark of grace and divinity. Go now. Keep your flock to a minimum, to those as inconspicuous as yourself. Do not use your abilities openly if at all possible. But of course, I trust your judgment in the use of adequate discretion. The mist of the Isle will hurry your voyage, its winds and sea will carry you to the Eastern bank of Soxor," he added.

Alonard gave one last courtesy, kissing his master's hand before he retreated out of the throne room. He left the chambers and ordered his aides. To his rightenant, Mage-Sciona, she was to accompany him along with Xamare-Jacobb. And to his leftenant, Vale-Kain, he ordered him to prepare the ship and then to remain behind to assume the Westland in his stead. Alonard's followers received their duties, but a few objections followed.

"My Lord, I would be by your side."

Alonard turned slowly and smiled.

"Kain, it is because you would stay by my side that you must stay here. Protect my people and, most importantly, protect our master. I would have no one else do that which I ask," said Alonard.

"But, Sir…" Kain insisted, before being comforted more by Alonard.

"Please, do as I ask. And have faith. Not only in me, but also in your colleagues. Jacobb is my finest solider beyond the two of us. And Sciona is my foremost tracker and strategist. If not for those abilities, I would surely have her stay in place of you, my friend."

"Of course." Reassured, Kain sprang up to carry out

his master's will.

"Ready the ship! Pack the rations! Saddle the Horses! Prepare to sail! Prepare to sail!"

Moments of Rest and Rowdiness – Three days passed since Alee last saw the light of sun or moon. Since then, her caretakers kept a constant eye on her while she slept peacefully. Alee's actions, all those days ago, drained her. Her body's sudden lost of pure, flowing energy could only be replenished by her slumber. While unconscious, Gaia and Bellia discussed the journey ahead and thus far. They laid out their plans of travel. Like most of their other discussions, this one also embedded an argument. They barged ahead and continued to squabble. Their stern debate fierce, yet quiet enough as to not awaken their young companion.

"Gaia, it was your responsibility to train Aleeia in the proper use and restraint of her Will. And now, someone is bound to pursue us from behind the mist," said Bellia.

"I know I'm to blame. During her studies, we discussed control through her understanding of the world and herself. We considered emotion through pain, death, grief and other emotions foreseeable in the battle ahead. But I did not consider or see that she would care for him so much. All within my view, but beyond my perception."

Gaia riddled with guilt looked at her student. She had the feeling her failure hastened the plunge toward their inevitable battle. Bellia knew the face Gaia wore and motioned towards her with a softer than usual stare.

"Did you see that though? Wow!" Bellia said.

"I mean I'm still shaking from the crash of that monument. You sure taught her how to procure her Will. Impressive."

Gaia smiled and raised her head with a little bit of pride. Although she still felt remorse, Gaia took solace, not only in the gestures of Bellia, but also in the notion that their situation was not yet dire. She knew they were safe for the moment. They had a few days distance and, most importantly, there had been no word of warning from Hat-kaptah.

"The scary part is what she did in Egypt was just a fraction of Alee's potential," Gaia stated with the truest sincerity.

"Speaking of scary, look who is finally waking up," Bellia remarked.

In that instant, Alee's eyes creaked open to witness two

figures in a blurry haze. It took her only a few moments to gather her bearings. Clarity returned slowly, though Alee knew that she was in the safe company of Gaia and Bellia, she did not know where she was.

As the camp cleared along with her vision, Alee saw a blazing fire that lit the faces of her beautiful matrons. The moonlight placed their wagon and two horses, Requi and Reques, near a small pool. She saw the strong animals drinking and knew she, too, was thirsty. Both Gaia and Bellia observed her without comment. They examined her like they would a horse before a journey, though only from a distance. They did not prod, but as Alee quenched her mouth's dryness, Gaia approached her.

"How are you feeling, young one?" Gaia asked.

"You have been out for a few days," Bellia added. Alee stopped for a moment. She quivered lightly. She quickly grabbed her robe near the resting place from which she had arisen. Gaia, who had used the robe to wrap Alee tightly as she slept, helped her put on her garments in hopes that its warmth would quell her shaking and allow her to speak.

"There you go," Gaia said with hearty comfort. Alee turned to both women and took a single step towards them. She thought about her actions thus far and began.

"I could hear you both while I slept. I am sorry for

my lack of control. I did not intend to place us in any immediate danger. He was a friend to me, someone I could talk to without weight. And I knew I would miss him and that he would miss us."

Gaia put her arms on the shoulders of Alee. She looked deeply into her eyes in order to assess whether the tears of past emotions would surface again. Bellia also came near the two women and uncharacteristically opened her arms to both women. Alee and Gaia, who were both surprised and amused by the gesture, looked at each other and laughed. As they all prepared to pack camp for an early morning's departure, Bellia had an idea.

"Hey! There is a wanderer's inn beyond the pass. I am sure we all could use the distraction of music, a few drinks, and a dance or two," an excited Bellia suggested.

"I don't know," Gaia said in a doubtful tone, "It seems like asking for more trouble."

Gaia glanced at Alee and noticed her demeanor regarding the idea. Gaia saw her curiosity and knew the distraction would do her well. More importantly, Gaia doubted Alee would have reason to lose herself as she did in Egypt.

"Okay," Gaia said to the delight of Alee and Bellia. "But you two go and I will stay just beyond the pass with the supplies and horses. Besides, someone has to mange the journey in the morning. Bellia, I am sure you will try to make a night of it."

Bellia grinned and looked at Alee. Alee wondered what such a stare meant, but did not ponder it for too long.

"Oh and Bellia, leave your armor and weapons with me. We would not want you to draw anymore attention than absolutely necessary," said Gaia.

"Of course," replied Bellia with a simple smile.

"I wouldn't have it any other way." She added.

They all walked the pass of the road, which would take them to the inn. As they continued to press and guide the horses, Gaia met her stopping point just before the land dipped into the inn. The structure was sizable, but completely isolated. There were no other signs of civilization besides the hut itself. Gaia wished the two ladies well and took a small moment to advise them both before she took her leave for the night.

Now free of Gaia's instinctive mothering, Bellia had the opportunity to do her own advising to Alee. Bellia took Alee's full flowing, just above shoulder length hair that was normally free of any constraints and twisted and braided it into a short style that made Alee seem a different person altogether. Bellia pulled out a small piece of glass painted black on one side. It was a mirror, which had just enough of the moon's light, to reflect the women before it. Alee smiled and stared. All the while, she turned cheek to cheek and caressed her previously concealed neck. She stroked her neckline from shoulder to ear. Alee thought briefly about how ridiculous she must seem. She giggled and stared as if she had never seen herself before, but in some ways she indeed had not.

"There you go. If you plan to dance at least half as much as I do, you will need your hair up." Bellia stated with practical humor.

As they drew closer, they heard the wondrous sounds of music full of life and energy. Pulsing drums and waving wind instruments told the story of the inn, called Menin, no doubt named for its keeper. The music was another exotic that seemed to intimidate Alee. She doubted whether she could keep up with its aggressive tempo. She also hoped the inn's patrons were not so aggressive as to match the music. Bellia stopped Alee just before the threshold.

"Oh, and for the rest of the night my name is Shael and yours is Shai. Understood? If anyone asks you, your name is…" Bellia paused as she waited for the proper response.

"Shai," Alee replied with quick wit.

"Good, and if you need me don't hesitate to ask okay."

"No problem, Shael," Alee said with a smile.

The two women went inside where a crowd beyond their expectations danced and intermingled in festivity. They made their way to the far table at the edge of the room. They walked around the dance floor and sat near the bar. Bellia removed her robe, but Alee did not. Bellia quickly caught sight of several handsome men. They also met eyes with her. Still seated in her chair, Bellia moved and danced a bit. Alee then took off her own robe.

"So what do you think?" shouted Bellia.

Throbbing band music played from the upper balcony. Bellia immediately took to the dance floor. She swiveled alone for only a moment, but quickly attracted the attention of several men. Bellia enjoyed the dance and made sure to mind each partner equally as best she could. Dancing gingerly, Bellia still maintained a watchful eye over Alee. She beckoned Alee with smiles and waves that were seamlessly integrated into her dance. Alee, still not forthright, continued to watch while she drank the delectably sweet beverage Bellia ordered on her behalf. Bellia felt no fatigue just yet, but decided to rest for the sake of Alee. She politely excused herself from the company of at least a half-dozen men and glided back through the crowd towards Alee.

"Come on." Bellia insisted.

"The festivities here are grand. Feel the beat. Besides, why come if you only mean to grow roots?"

While she twiddled her thumbs and patted her feet, Alee lowered her head.

"Come, dance with me." Bellia said.

She grabbed Alee by the wrist and led her to the center of the floor, before she could utter any objections. They danced and did so quite well. Alee let the rhythm and melody move her with ease. She smiled and became carefree. Before long, Bellia's rabble returned and so did another half-dozen due to the presence of and their interest in Alee.

Alee danced in a pure, yet sultry fashion. She tried her best to mind each man as she had seen Bellia do before. Bellia now felt the fatigue that eluded her before. She cut through the men towards Alee and leaned nearer to speak to her.

"Shai, I am going to sit now for a moment and order myself something that quenches me. I'm overheated." Bellia shouted clearly so Alee could hear her. However, others heard along with her.

"Okay, Shael," Alee called with a grin.

Bellia made her way to the table once again. She sat and continued to watch Alee happily. Alee seemed to show a great sense of joy. She continued in the dance without realizing or caring that she entertained a full dozen men. One-Man, incredibly handsome, arched lower to her ear and asked of her name. He had shining bronze skin, polished by his sweat and carved by his build. Alee seemingly favored him more. She ignored the other men and turned towards One-Man while she danced. She tilted her head back and leaned on her tiptoes to speak. With a dynamic strong enough for his ear, she said only one word.

"Shai."

"Beautiful, indeed" he replied.

Alee felt the tight pull of her wrist and knew the coarse grab was not Bellia. Her hand felt as though it was being dragged across sand. Alee locked eyes with one of the many men whom she had forgotten. The man had a menacing grin upon his face.

"My dance is not over." He said with rough grit.

One-Man stepped in front of Alee to confront the man. Someone struck him across the head from the back. He crashed into two other men, who crashed into another and fell quickly to the ground with a thud. Alee swooped down to see to her pseudo-protector. As soon as she lowered herself below the plane of the men's sight, one of the jostled men turned, only to see the hostile and ragged face of Alee's assailant. As swiftly as a fist could be thrown, the center of the dance floor quaked like an erupting volcano.

Biting and kicking ensued. Alee dragged the dazed One-Man towards safety. She pulled him underneath a nearby table on the other side where the crowds cut her off from Bellia. Bellia was drawn from drink to attention by the igniting mêlée. She was no longer able to see the whereabouts of Alee. Bellia became concerned as to Alee's state and whether Alee, or the absence of her charge, was the cause of the clash. Bellia ran to the floor and shouted excitedly,

"Shai! Shai!" She called out hoping that Alee would answer to that name.

When she did not, Bellia wondered for what reason. Was she no longer conscious or did the frenzy cause her to forget her guise? But neither explanation was the reason. The clamor of the brawl resonated and drowned Bellia's call.

Meanwhile, at the top of the valley near the edge of the pass, Gaia awaited and saw a scurry of people exiting the tavern. She shook her head with a closing eye, and impatiently sighed. She then brushed the brow and mane of her mighty beasts.

"Requi…Reques…I know. I knew it." Gaia said and sighed again.

"…*'I wouldn't have it any other way'* she says. I knew it! Darn! But at least that makes us even," Gaia said to the horses with surprising humor.

Back inside Menin, under a table lay two: One-Man and one woman. Alee saw that he was not terribly injured, but took to his care as best she could. Alee also would not have him leave her and return to throw blows, but neither would he.

"Are you okay?" Alee asked as she plowed into the dark beauty of his eyes.

"Fine, Shai…Fine," he said.

Bellia, now deep within the conflict, detracted brawlers left and right. She showed amazing speed and strength, as no man could challenge her alone or even in droves. Bellia had a keen awareness of the fight. She ducked an unseen blow that came from behind, then leapt atop a table in front of her. She turned quickly and deterred three foes with one swift kick. While on the table, above the confusion, Bellia saw Alee across the way holding One-Man in her arms. She plunked back down onto the floor and waded through the sea of men with several forceful blows guiding her. Some men ignored her and some ran. While others, who danced with her merrily less than minutes ago, confronted her only to be put down quickly.

Bellia was now upon Alee and her accomplice. She witnessed them exchange a soft kiss. The kiss fueled by circumstance, the rush and passion, continued uninterrupted until Bellia was finally noticed by Alee.

"Shael. Um…."

"I do not want to hear it," Bellia said in interruption. Bellia once again grabbed her by the wrist and herded her towards the exit of the inn. As Alee was being pulled away, she looked back at the man. He rose quickly and reached out to her, only to bump his head again against the bottom of the hovering table. Alee smiled. So did he. He rubbed his head and soon vanished from her sight behind a crowd still in an uproar over forgotten ends.

> "You know, it is not that you were out of my view. Not that you started a brawl. I don't even care that you were kissing a strange man." Bellia scolded.
>
> "But how could you leave me to fight, while you were hiding under a table?" She wondered.
>
> "Never mind, when we reach our next destination and your studies become my responsibility, I will never again have a need to ask such a question."

Bellia continued to rant in her usual manner as Alee reflected. As they headed back to the wagon, Alee knew she enjoyed every minute of their little *distraction* as it was called. She thought about One-Man and his kiss. She wondered if she would ever see him again, although she did not need to. Alee thought about the fact that she never got to hear his name, though she did not really want to. What Alee received from the night was something exciting and unexpected that stood on its own. As restful Gaia and a weary Bellia set out to journey by carriage once again, Alee could not sleep. She sat awake and thought long about One-Man's kiss.

VERSE II

The Kingdom of Kush - The beauty of the land had been the object of Alee's attention for her days of travel. The land had shown great, indescribable majesty as they traveled further west. No longer arid and dry, the air had cooled when they entered into the upper savannas. The grasslands of such calm and beauty marked the boarders of Lower Kush.

"Surely, blackness can shine and not be called shadow." Alee thought to herself.

She witnessed the people of the land. They were somewhat like those she saw in Abydos. The people were of equal stature and appearance of face. But they were darker and reminded Alee of One-Man's bronze luster although darker still they were. She looked and smiled at the people of this land as they worked the rivers and crops. All the while, Alee avoided her companions and their barrage of doubt.

> "Alee, just allow me to look over the translation. At this time, we cannot afford to be led astray," Gaia stated.

She clasped her hands to her sensible plea.

> "So, do you not trust my skill to translate or do you doubt your ability to teach?" Alee replied, then paused before continuing to speak.
>
> "I have no doubts. And I am not to reveal my

findings until some later time."

"And how do you know this, Alee?" Bellia added. She was partially involved in the discussion but never took any sides.

"I just know. All will be revealed in time. I am sorry to remain so cryptic, but maybe all the better for it. I know where I stand in the eyes of your confidence, Gaia," said Alee, releasing a small but audible sigh. "Dear child, I hold you in the utmost confidence and truly you are a better pupil than I was. Understand, I am charged with your care and the fulfillment of what Nympthia feels to be your destiny. But you are right, the simple fact you have not relented shows you have no doubts, so neither should I," said Gaia.

Alee left Gaia's statements as the last of their debate and continued to be in awe of the land. She turned away from Gaia towards Bellia for she would be the master of her instructions for the next unknown span of time. As they drew further inward beyond the boarders of Kush, they neared their destination. From a far off distance, they could see the walls of a great city. The wall, tall and strong, stretched out beyond the eye's view. It would take more than many generations to bury such a wall beneath the sands of Kush. Made strong of baked straw-stones and mahogany, it stood as a force all its own. As they came upon the wall, they could see a portal guarded, though not by man.

Two lions bound by thick iron and leather around their necks slept. The beasts stirred. The rightmost lion let out a rumble that shook the eardrums of all who heard the roar. Though it was only a yawn compared to the next that came violently from the other lion. The two sentinels gathered their legs beneath them as the wagon carrying the three women grew in closer proximity. Before the lions could pull their restraints to a tension, Bellia withdrew from the wagon and leapt down towards them. Bellia walked through the portal without pause. She never acknowledged the beasts beside her. Gaia then leapt down and again the lions came forward as they did before. Gaia, a bit anxious, continued as Bellia did while Alee watched intently. In that instant, the rightmost lion who seemed the leader to the other jumped at Gaia swiftly and fiercely. Gaia then threw away her cloak from her neck at the lion to her left. She did so before the lion was able to pounce to follow the right. She then retreated over towards the lion, which she blinded. She used its body and bonds to shield her from the other. All actions occurred faster than the clap of two hands, certainly before Bellia could turn and know of Gaia's obstacle. Bellia now saw Gaia at a safe distance. She kept to her travel through the short corridor and soon came to the other side.

“Who goes there?” asked one of the guardsmen.

“I…Bellia. I have come,” she said.

The guards quickly hurried to her and surrounded her. She lowered her head and grinned. Before the guards could gather themselves, she sprang about among all of them. She delivered one blow to each of them before they could even react or retreat to the attack against the first guard. With all of the men lowered and bent before Bellia, a figure descended from the upper stairs connected to the top of the wall.

“I see I have much more training in store for my troops.” The figure said to Bellia.

“That you do, Matron of the Guard. That you do,” Agreed Bellia.

Bellia looked over her former protégé. She had beauty fairer than Gaia’s. She strode towards Bellia with her long dark hair held up and bound. It was proper for women of war to wear their hair as such, if they so decided not to cut it in a shorter fashion. Her armor was of similar style to that of Bellia’s, but made to suit her beauty. She wore a snug sleeveless leather tunic with brass gauntlets that stretched from her wrists to the middle of her forearm. Strangely though, she had a silk dress that flowed from belt to ankle. Bellia recognized this as purely ornamental and of her own personalization. She assumed her armor continued to adorn her underneath. Bellia noticed that her skin was smooth, but bore more blemishes and scars than a Guard Matriarch should have. That led Bellia to think that the days were harsher than days gone by.

"Greetings, Meroe! Have you taught these soldiers that the first attack should always be yours when outnumbered?"

"Indeed, I have…but they knew not that *they* were outnumbered." Meroe said as they both laughed.

"Please, allow my friends entry.," said Bellia.

"Sure…ahmmh. On your feet. Back to your post," Meroe commanded as she and Bellia went back out to the threshold of the portal."

"Kashta! Shabaka!" She yelled. The beasts retreated and yielded away from Gaia and the gate.

"You would think that after all my visits with Bellia these two would like me by now. That I should have gained some favor." Gaia said as she motioned toward Meroe and Bellia.

"Don't take it personally. A thousand visits with the King himself and you would still be a foreigner to them. It is a good thing you know people here in high places," said Meroe.

"Indeed, my friend." Gaia said as she greeted Meroe with a hug.

"Welcome to the Wall of Nubia and the Kingdom of Kush." Meroe said.

"Indeed. It is great to be back home," said Bellia.

"Will you be visiting your home in Nuri?"

"No. We head straight for the third city, the daughter city - Dorginarti and the house of King Alara's daughter."

"Is there anytime for you and I to catch up?" Meroe inquired.

"As much time as it takes for the horses to be watered and fed, I am afraid. I hope to begin my new pupil's training by tomorrow afternoon," said Bellia.

"Well then, let's eat and drink as well. But lightly so we may still speak, for I have missed your company." Meroe lamented.

The horses were led away by a careful crew of guardsmen. Bellia, Meroe and the rest of her friends retreated to the wall's dormitory for those who would protect the lands' boarders. There inside, old friends spoke of times past and the hopes in their hearts until the moment of their departure.

In a manner of a few hours, the women set out yet again towards Dorginarti. They passed deeper within the Walls of Nubia. The thought that anyone who followed would have to negotiate the Wall's fortitude brought ease to

Gaia. Bellia, however, thought of Meroe and the woman she had become. Bellia had been regaled with stories of Meroe's successes in battle and in combat while they dined. She felt even more ready to impart her knowledge and training upon the young Alee. Alee's mind was surprisingly void of thought, worry, or concern. She did not see anything behind or ahead. She read the pages of a book she had read once before. Bellia spoke and unknowingly she ended Alee's peace of mind.

"Meroe was one of seven pupils I trained in competition for the purpose of succeeding me as Matron of Guard."

Alee did not mind being brought out of her trance since she was curious about Meroe at the time of their meeting. She asked the questions she had then.

"Only women hold your former position?"

"No, five of the last seven great warriors were male. I was the first Matron. My uncle taught me fighting philosophy. He'd learned it from his mother who was a child of Pixsus. Most men are either unable or unwilling to understand and execute the technique of that style in accordance with its ultimate philosophy."

"But didn't you say your uncle taught you?" asked Alee.

"Yes, Alee. My grandmother raised him alone, so her way was the only way he would ever know. He is a fine man, true and strong," replied Bellia.

"What do you mean by philosophy? How does philosophy apply to fighting?"

Alee asked as she waved the book she read. Gaia smiled, but did not say anything. She looked at Bellia and waited for her reply.

"So what do you think fighting is? Strength versus strength? It is much more than that. Philosophia is the love of wisdom. Not just wisdom of books, wisdom of the past, or wisdom of places…No! It is the love of all things to be learned, understood, and or mastered. For every skill you master and fact you acquire, there will always be another genre of which to begin your studies. The arts of war and battle are the wisdoms I have chosen to master. Not to become some master of death, but to become an enforcer of peace and justice," stated Bellia.

"So what is your philosophy of fighting…exactly?" Alee asked.

"Oh, you'll see soon enough. We are here. And we will start as soon as I have greeted the princess properly."

Alee was caught somewhere between excitement and dread.

She had never before truly endured a hard day physically, outside of play and simple chores. But Alee took what Bellia said to heart. She now felt her mind was open and her first lessons had indeed already begun.

The Palace of Dorginarti - They were upon it finally. The Palace of Dorginarti, the home to the princess of Nubia. A palace it was. However, to unknowing eyes, it seemed less. The single realm of the palace looked to be the village of many. One modest structure at the center stood tallest among the rest. It was surrounded. A ring of buildings made the first, but the people who lived there called it *The Last Shield.* The guarded armies and amenities to the princess sat at her doorsteps in that ring. There were beautiful gardens with sod and blooms from far off lands and fountains fed by the tears of the Great River. There were libraries for the counsel and counselors to the princess and tombs great with the bodies of the sleeping and fallen. And there were arenas spacious with a style and architecture not Nubian in appearance compared to that of other great halls. As followed, there were nine more rings and the people of The First Shield were the common of Dorginarti. They slept at the foot of both the fruited land and the sheen of the inner palace city. Other rings held the markets, theaters, and smithies as their central theme of use. More than one theme repeated themselves among the rings, but each had their own guardsmen, granaries, and chieftains. These men or women chieftains would take the concerns and needs of their ring to the Counselors of the Last Shield. There the counselors, so wise and just, dismissed fruitless claims or those wishes already met with planned foresight and then the surviving pleas would go to the princess. Her ear favored the needs of The First Shield on more occasions than others. She knew if the day came, they would be the first to answer her call, the first to prove their loyalty to the ruler that heard their cry.

And so it was told to Alee as she and her governesses passed the playwrights, dancers, minstrels and artists of the seventh circle. They entered The Last Shield and yielded Reques and Requi to the stables of the armory. Bellia moved with familiarity and made haste towards the Den of Counsels. She entered with Alee to her right and Gaia to her left. Both walked a pace behind her.

> "Bellia, former Matron of Guard and Nuri ambassador. I request lodging in this Shield and word with the princess."

When Bellia spoke, it seemed as though the room shook. The people there, mostly aged counselors, moved at her will.

"It does me great pleasure to see you, Bellia." An old man said, and then nodded greetings to Gaia and their unfamiliar companion.

"Uncle? You give counsel to the princess now?" Bellia asked, taken aback.

"No. Since I am no longer of use to Highness, I have retired to the First Shield. I am Chieftain there and here on behalf of business." He stated with the pride of duty and service.

"Did Highness say *you were not of use*?" Bellia asked with a mask of shock upon her face.

"No, of course not. By her grace, I would still be serving her to train and lead these young warriors. No, my dear, it was I who stepped aside. Upon instruction one day, I endeavored to correct a young captain's technique. Correct in my philosophy I was, but I could not move as my philosophy would wish. The young captain flung me down. There his strength proved to justify his manner," said Buhen.

The old man spoke with a little sorrow in him, though he continued to speak his heart.

"But worry not for Buhen, former Patron and teacher to Matron who taught the Guarding Matron."

Bellia asked briefly his business as chieftain and he stated, in full, the wishes of his charge. They were in need of leave and passage past the wall. Buhen's request was reasonable, a troop of escorts into the Southland for trade. Buhen returned the intrigue and inquiry.

"So what brings you back? Have you learned and seen all you have wished?"

"I have learned more than I wished. I am here with this one," Bellia said as she grabbed Alee by the arm and thrust her before Buhen like a goat inspected at the market before its purchase.

"She is to be trained." Bellia added.

"Oh really! She is thick at the hips for one so young, though her legs are sturdy and dense. She would seem to make a better wife. A dancer at the least."

Alee's mouth dropped. She marveled at the blunt critique Buhen spoke to Bellia as if she were not even there. Alee also felt a slight spurn. She considered her hips normal, even small, for her people near the forest in the Southlands. Before she could complete her thoughts and voice her displeasures of his words, Buhen spoke again.

"A woman's stature in that of a child. Maybe not a warrior yet, but reminiscent to me of Bellia and Meroe younger."

Her exasperation stirred no longer. Alee held Bellia and the beauty recently seen as Meroe in as high regard as their skills in arms. She retreated behind Bellia to smile and blush. Gaia stood back all the while. She frequented the land and held some regard among its people. Though now, Gaia felt slight shame. Buhen trained her in partnership with Bellia. And though she tried greatly to gain a mastery of warfare, she was not adept. And, more so, distracted by scholarship and her Awakening abilities. Frequently, Gaia used her abilities exclusively instead of in the union of skills that enhanced the instincts, strength, and speed of a warrior. Gaia kept her opponents at a distance with wind, vine, and loose objects and even an unseen shield or wall. Thus, she did that day in Egypt.

"Greetings, Gaia. Come, ladies, I will escort you to the feet of Highness."

They turned away from the Den of Counsels and set their motion towards the heart of Dorginarti, the princess's palace. Alee looked about as they walked in single file. They passed the garden. She saw beauty new and beauty familiar. She halted and looked upon them. Gaia stepped beside her.

"Come, Alee."

Alee did not move. She stared at the bloom before her.

"The Healing Leaves." Alee said softly.

"They grow plenty in my land. When last I looked upon them they were adorning Karwynn. Now, I think of her."

Alee stepped back and turned to follow Buhen who continued to lead the way. Through the gardens, they passed the stables and then came to the doors of the palace. Strangely, two guards stood alone at the portal. Bare-chested men with long bow-staffs in hand stood at attention. Word of Bellia came before them from a counselor's messenger. The guardsmen allowed Buhen entry without pause. Inside, a modest staircase made of engraved wood with rails of ivory and gold led to the upper level of the palace. They walked along the wide room towards the stairs that marked a regal dwelling. They came to the foot of the staircase and never before felt the shadow of such greatness upon them even those who had ventured there before felt a reverence reborn within them.

Alee had no thoughts or words to describe her anxiety. Moreover, she did not know why she felt so. They gathered themselves and ascended. Bellia now led the way. She came to the top of the spiraling stairs, and looked upon Highness and waited. They all waited for the princess to speak.

Through a translucent veil that surrounded a small bed raised on a platform, Alee saw Highness. Her anxiety grew for she could not see her clearly. From Alee's perspective, she saw the back of royalty and thought she slept angelically before them. However, the princess did not slumber. She knew, despite their complete silence, that people stood in her presence. Highness rose. Alee looked to the others for their model in convention. She followed as they all lowered themselves.

"Blessings to Highness, Blessings to Princess Aalarae." they all said.

"Please, friends. We are past such ceremonies. Get up. Up. Up!"

Alee would have never thought to see another more beautiful than Gaia and indeed when she set her eyes upon Meroe she thought her beauty formidable. But in Aalarae, Alee saw a tall, regal beauty that seemed to pierce the soul. She credited that for her anxiety at the foot of the stairs and gazed yet again. Aalarae's brown eyes held a faint glow of red in them. Alee saw the fullness in her lips, the stoutness of her nose, and the intricate beauty in her bushy braided hair. Aalarae's figure melted through a long crimson gown that flowed so freely. The fabric of it was finer than any silk, and though the weather was dry and hot, she wore the gown elegantly and comfortably. Her wrists bore ivory bracelets that matched the headdress upon her brow.

"I was to dine with the counselors shortly and was weighing needs in the meantime. But entertaining you, my guests, will pardon me from the dinner.

Wait here while I dress in something more to my liking."

Aalarae then retreated to her bedroom by way of another staircase adjacent to the far wall, climbing instead of spiraling to the final floor. Alee moved as if to follow her. Buhen spoke and halted the young girl.

"Yes, indeed, our Highness is beautiful. Do not be misled. She has the heart of a warrior. As our land's protector, she has shown this on many occasions. When Bellia was Matron, our Highness insisted she be taught so she need not be altogether helpless and at the mercy of her guards' defense. Her training went well enough, but she did not complete it. Bellia left so suddenly, and Aalarae would not continue with her successor Meroe or Faras, the captain of the center palace that threw me down."

Before Buhen could speak to further describe Aalarae's love for Bellia's tutelage, she returned. She'd removed the ivory bracelets, tiara, and gown she wore before and now wore bronze gauntlets, leather pants, boots, and a sturdy thick-hide corset that left her shoulders bare. Aalarae was comfortable enough to speak plainly and embraced all her guests.

"Greetings, what brings you all, dear friends?"

Bellia stepped back in gesture to the needs of Buhen on

behalf of his Shield. Buhen, aware of Bellia's gesture on his part, noticed the courtesy and spoke first.

"Princess Aalarae, I have come with matters from the Ninth Ring. In doing so, I met these ladies while in passing and offered an escort," said Buhen.

"Of course, Buhen. I am always eager to answer the call of the First Shield. More so now that you head their governing matters. Speak please." replied Aalarae.

She sat among a bunch of oddly scattered chairs that held no apparent design. Aalarae then motioned with the flapping of her hands for everyone to sit where they might feel the most comfort. Alee sat beside the princess in a chair that faced Bellia, but her eyes stayed steady upon the princess.

"As you know, Highness. My ring has the task of bringing in the spoils of trade and the riches from the wilderness. We have heard of worthwhile trade near the outskirts of the Wall. We would hope to have guarded escorts accompany us past the Wall, in order to bring back these goods and trade."

Buhen paused as he awaited the princess's answer.

"Regretfully, Buhen." Aalarae said in a somber and lower tone, "I cannot grant this. As you know, The Kingdoms of Egypt would not have peace and share the graces of The Great River. For ages at peace and oddly now, Egypt wishes to conquer our lands. To add to that, foreigners across the waters have come. A people with a pale and lifeless appearance, who speak in a rhythm-less tongue, have come to our shores. Although they have yet to show hostility and claim no ill will, we must still stay ever vigilant. Also, the horse raiders across the sea bring death and seek to have my people bow to their god. So as you can see, I cannot allow you escort. However, I will send those troops to help fortify and protect the First Shield in the North and in the Southeast. You may trade Southwest in the grasslands and with Nuri within the Walls."

Buhen understood and was pleased to receive a decision with such a clear explanation from someone so high. Other rulers most certainly would have sufficed to say a simple *NO* and then move on. Buhen bowed again and gave his thanks to Aalarae.

"I will conscribe the guardsmen to your ring after we have eaten," Aalarae said.

She smiled and then turned to Alee beside her.

"And what brings you here, friend?"

Aalarae spoke to Alee. Alee lost all breath and ability to respond. Alee yet again shrank in the presence of that which she revered so greatly. Alee looked to Bellia distressfully. She realized the princess solely asked of her, and Bellia either would not or could not bail her out. So Alee spoke.

"I am Aleeia, a child of the Southlands. I have come here with my caretakers Gaia and Bellia to be trained by them in the arts and philosophies of combat."

Bellia looked at Alee and thought she could not have said it better, if she herself had answered.

"Oh, you are a student to Bellia? How I envy you," said Aalarae.

Her statement brought a smile and a small giggle sprung from her mouth. *Her envy me?* Alee thought.

"Bellia, if it would not be so burdensome, I would like to join in as a pupil for a session or two."

"Of course, Highness. But only if we can use The Arena of Adindan as our place of study."

Bellia and Gaia paused and held their breath. They knew the extent of Alee's maturation in her techniques depended upon that location. Like the Chasm beneath The Hall of Ancient Scrolls and Manuscripts in Abydos, the arena kept those who had awakened from revealing themselves. Before Gaia and Bellia could fully entertain their worry, the princess responded.

"Certainly. I will have it cleared out before sunrise.

Twas made into a museum of sorts. My father's spear and shield, as well as a few other heirlooms, reside there. But my brother always wanted them to reside with him in the second city. I kept them here, childishly, just to spite him a bit."

Aalarae turned again to Alee. Alee was relieved that her training would not begin tonight. Oddly enough, she knew Aalarae regretted it.

"Let us eat. Buhen, come dine and sleep before your journey back to the Ninth Ring.

Gaia, allow me to feed you, please. Or do the men in your land find your lankiness attractive?" asked the Princess.

Gaia made no comments. She regarded the personal jab spoken so plainly as a compliment to their growing respect and friendship that lived absent of Bellia. She also knew she would take out Aalarae's witty retort on Bellia at a later time.

"And you, Aleeia. I have tales to tell of what you are in for," said Aalarae.

"My friends call me Alee."

Aalarae replied, "Alee? Indeed!"

Art and Philosophy - The dawn came and Alee woke in the

comfort of her quarters near the center palace. The room in which she slept was generally reserved for ambassadors and foreign dignitaries. Bellia was against such comfortable manners of living, but of course, Aalarae insisted. In a beautifully spacious suite, Alee dressed when Bellia entered the lordly confines.

"Did you sleep well?" Bellia asked.

Alee looked at Bellia bewilderedly. She saw that Bellia wore a long white gown and had bracelets and flowers upon her. Bellia stood with what seemed to be her weighty armor, anklets, and gauntlets in her arms. Alee continued to dress and turned to speak.

"What is with the dress? Hardly, seems appropriate for battle training." Alee said.

Bellia grinned preceding her reply.

"More appropriate than you think. Put these on."

Bellia dropped the shiny new garments on the floor before Alee. Alee stood confused and awaited further explanation from Bellia.

"Once you are dressed, meet me at the stables. Be quick."

Bellia left the room without another word. Alee stripped to her undergarments and reached for the armor Bellia had left.

"This is Nubian-Kushite armor, not unlike Bellia's and Meroe's. I hope I wear it well."

Alee grabbed the ironclad leather vest that she placed upon her shoulders. She finally saw the weightiness of it. She could barely lift the vest above her and once it was there she could not ease it down. It quickly lowered upon her shoulders and forced her to the floor. Alee set her wobbling legs below her and tried to rise to her feet. She pressed against the ground so forcefully that the weight of the vest caused her an awkward imbalance. Alee nearly fell back.

"Wow! Doesn't seem practical. I mean... It's heavy."

She grunted.

Alee moved back to the floor in order to lift both gauntlets. She did so methodically and knew she did not wish to make more trips than necessary to the ground and back. She placed the gauntlets upon her wrists and felt those as well. They pulled at her shoulders and stretched on her arms. She tried to bend her arm against the weight and slowly did so before dropping her arms again.

"And now the anklets." She sighed.

Alee put on the anklets and slowly made her way to the stables. She struggled as she walked. However, every step seemed to bring greater comfort she had yet to notice, since nearly all the muscles in her body burned. She trotted slowly and eventually reached the stables. She saw all who were there.

"So you made it... Finally." Bellia said.

"Took her long enough." Gaia added.

Alee saw that Gaia, Bellia, and Aalarae wore the same style of dress and noticed Buhen atop a horse fully loaded for his travels to the Outer Ring. Princess Aalarae came towards Alee and placed her hand upon her right shoulder. With her vest on, her hand had the weight of a stone to Alee. She grimaced at the touch.

"Enjoy!"

It was all that the princess said to Alee. Alee saw that the princess knew of her strain and also the effects of her own touch. In that moment, Alee stood taller.

"I will do my best, Highness."

Buhen's horse grew restless. Bellia moved towards the horse and rubbed its brow. As she began to give Alee instructions, Alee moved closer to them both.

"Alee, how does the armor feel?" asked Bellia.

Bellia paused for a response, but got no verbal confirmation to match what her eyes could see.

"It is beautiful. I am honored to wear it." Alee said.

"As you should be, Aleeia. That armor was Aalarae's for a brief time. She was younger than you though, when she first wore it. I remember when I first had to bear armor, it was indeed heavy," Bellia said.

Alee's eyes dropped as silent affirmation.

"Listen, Alee. Your training begins today, but you

are not able to study battle or combat skills just yet. Your body is not strong enough, and though my philosophy would have you use your opponents' strength against them you still must be able to muster your own. Once more, I am sure you would tire if a battle drew out. So we have to get you into shape."

Alee understood. Gaia and Bellia already possessed a toned stature that showed their strength. Alee knew her own strength had to rival that. Bellia grabbed a bottle of water and strapped it over Alee's shoulders.

"Buhen will trot back upon his horse and you will escort him on foot. Pace yourself but do your best to keep up. His conscripts will follow once they have all been assembled, but by that time you should be returning. I will look for you at dusk. I hope you do not miss dinner. Gaia and I will accompany Highness today. She has requested our counsel regarding the threat of the Egyptians. Farewell, Alee."

Buhen nodded to Bellia and motioned the stirrups ordering the horse's direction. Alee turned to jog with Buhen. Her burning body continued to feel the effects of the weight. Alee was now off and away. Not too long afterwards she wondered,

"Did...Bellia..." Alee panted a few words before Buhen interceded.

"Do not talk for you will need every breath. Did Bellia accomplish this task? Did she have to do it? Yes and no," Buhen said.

He slowed the horse to a graceful stride. He knew they were out of Bellia's sight.

"Back when I trained her there were only seven Rings not nine and she started from the third not the center. But believe me child, I was modest when I spoke of your comparison to her yesterday. She was in worse shape and had not the travels you have had thus far, but she was indeed younger."

Buhen quickened his pace back to a light gallop again. Once more, Alee jogged. She pondered Bellia and Gaia's task while she struggled so readily.

While Alee ran and wondered, Gaia and Bellia stood beside Princess Aalarae in the Den of Counsel amongst all nine ambassadors and her royal advisors. They had just finished giving praise to Highness and prayer for the good graces of the land. They then went well into discussion on the main agenda for the day.

“But Highness, the will of the First City's people,

your father's vote would insist you unite to mount an offensive against Egypt," said the voice of a foreign advisor. The Princess rose and said,

"Yes, but my brother and his people of the Second City have voted we stay safe behind the Walls. I would not cast the vote of this city at a whim and send an entire nation to war. Remember counselors, you are not here to convince me of a single decision. You are here to advise me of the after-effects of either decision ***I*** should choose."

Bellia listened and took note of every detail that allowed her to calculate an effective defense or attack strategy that would help the Princess no matter what her decision may be.

"And what prompted my father's choice? Ambassadors, what is your report from that meeting?"

As the princess finished her question, two men stood. One represented Dorginarti at the King's Counsel and the other represented the King at Aalarae's Counsel. The King's Ambassador spoke with a persuasive lowness in his tone.

"No other city is built to defend like Dorginarti, Highness. The King would not risk his city or breach of the Wall," said the king's ambassador.

"Yes, Highness. The King does fear the breach of

the Wall, but he is hesitant to attack head on beyond the Wall's protection," said the Princess's ambassador.

"And the Prince? What are my brother's thoughts?" asked Highness.

Two more men arose and spoke as the previous group of ambassadors sat and listened.

"The Prince, as you know, still tries to negotiate peace and a union of nations by wedding the Pharaoh's daughter. He loves the Egyptian princess, but the Pharaoh sees any such union, whether of nations or blood, as an insult to his mantle as *The Living God*, thus his daughter has been exiled. And for the love of his new wife, your brother would not attack her homeland, not even to save his own from future attack."

As the Prince's ambassador finished, the other expounded on behalf of his report.

"It has not been affirmed, but the Prince still orchestrates stealth tactics just beyond the Wall to deter the Egyptian forces."

Aalarae cupped her chin with the smooth touch of her hand. She leaned her elbow on the armrest of her chair that stood center between Bellia and Gaia who sat slightly lower. The three women carried themselves from on high with a powerful mode of sovereignty. They stared out at what seemed to be an ocean of advisors, all men. It was amazing so many were able to give counsel and debate in an orderly manner.

Somewhere in Dorginarti, near the Seventh Ring almost two-thirds of the distance from the center palace to the First Shield, Alee drank to quench her thirst. Bent and nearly broken by her fatigue, Alee lowered upon one knee, lifted her leather container above her head and drank more. Before the water flowed past its brim into her mouth, Alee heard Buhen speak.

> "Ahtt, Ahtt...Not too much! You wouldn't want to get a cramp. That would indeed make your journey much more laborsome."

Buhen held his laugher and reduced it to a mere stare. Alee saw his face and read it well.

> "Hohh...How's...muhh pace?" Alee asked as coherently as she could.
>
> "You are doing well. Actually, you have endured so well I have been pushing my horse a bit more than I did for Bellia on her run."

Alee smiled and gathered her feet below her. She then placed the bottle across her shoulder again and jogged ahead of Buhen on their current bearing. *She's pretty tough. And will probably make it back in no time by her own will, without the empty threat of missing supper.* Buhen's thoughts brought yet another smile to his face. He felt as though her spirit possessed a potency he had no choice but to admire. They treaded on for the remainder of the down trip. Finally, they reached the outer level of Dorginarti - The First Shield.

Back at the Den of Counsels, the heads of state continued to plead and advise on behalf of their land's better interest. Princess Aalarae had not yet voted on a plan of action to send or keep her beloved kingdom from going to arms. The hearing was in a brief recess. Gaia and Bellia had heard all the intelligence offered to the Princess by the advisors. The two women both formed a body of advice for Princess Aalarae. Aalarae allowed Gaia to speak her thoughts.

> "Gaia, speak to me. You are wise. I have for a long time valued the counsel of one who is impartial to the land," said Aalarae.
>
> "Well, Highness. I have heard the motives of the Prince and King. But purely out of scholarship, I suggest you side with your Father. The Nubian forces outnumber the Egyptians by a manner of four-to-three. A slight advantage, I know. But with

the River and the Wall as fallback defenses, it is highly unlikely Egypt could defeat us."

Bellia's brow rose as she heard the word *us* erupt from her counsel. Bellia motioned toward the Princess ready to impart her war-just logic upon her.

"Princess, although Gaia speaks true of numbers and draws well from historical battles long past, I say it is not wise to support the King. Your vote should lay with your brother. I do agree the Wall is a strong defense, not only in the absence of an offensive assault, but because it is a solid structure, fortified by Nubia’s best. Let us stay behind the Wall. The Pharaoh's son has not revealed his mind regarding our land. We may need only stand strong against the Pharaoh until his sun has set."

The Princess did not speak. She stood still and heard the advice of two whom she held so dearly. Aalarae placed her hand on Gaia's shoulder showing favor to her counsel thus far.

"Highness, please!" Bellia cried before Aalarae interrupted her.

"Fear not, Bellia. I only wish for Gaia to elaborate her counsel with a formal battle strategy."

"Battle Strategy! Highness, with all due respect, Gaia is not qualified to give such a report." Bellia retorted.

Gaia's eyes swelled and her cheeks tightened. Her teeth clenched a bit. Bellia took notice of Gaia's face, but did nothing to trace her words.

"Bellia, I wish a new defense strategy from you too," said the Princess.

"I will decide at the end of the hearing tonight before dinner. Go now, the both of you, and prepare."

As the two women exited the Den and the company of Princess Aalarae, their eyes met. They had stern words for one another.

"Not qualified. How dare you, Bellia? You think me incompetent?" asked Gaia.

Gaia's voice was harsh and ridged but stirred with underlying pain closely resembling betrayal.

"Not incompetent, certainly. You are learned, but you do not have the knowledge that real war inspires. Plus..."

Bellia trailed off and held her present thoughts from passing beyond her lips.

"Plus, what?" shouted Gaia.

Gaia insisted Bellia complete her thought, not so much with a verbal command as with her piercing glare.

"Gaia, these are not your people. As the Princess said you are *impartial*. I doubt you see the casualties that will inevitably stem for your counsel," said Bellia.

"You have succeeded in calling me a heartless monster. I have come to think of Kush as my own home," replied Gaia.

With Gaia's words, they parted ways and retreated to their confines to prepare their counsels. The rift between them was indeed thicker than the wall that stood between their rooms. They worked in anger but also in love, for both of them thought of the well-being of The Kingdom of Kush.

The sun was now well past its peak and Alee had replenished herself as well as her water supply. She rested briefly. While she said goodbye to Buhen in the commons of his chieftain home, Alee removed her armor at Buhen’s request. Buhen brought in his ring's healer to tend to Alee.

"It is okay, young one. The Healer will tend to your blisters and massage your soreness away."

Alee looked surprised. Her feet were horribly sore and peeled. Every place on her ached but she said nothing of it on her journey.

"Come now, Alee. Of course I recognize your distress, my feet hurt with the memory of it," Buhen said.

"Healer, bandage her feet and make sure she is

stretched and loose," he added.

In that instance, Alee laid upon a small bed and was then tended. An assistant to Buhen came and took Alee's musty armor, which was saturated with the sweat of her journey thus far. She saw the man taking her armor away and for the moment was content to see it gone as the Healer's hands gently oiled away her soreness.

Nearly an hour passed. Alee let out a low moan. The Healer finished her massage. At the same time, Buhen returned with Aleeia's armor in hand. He saw that she had a smile on her face.

"It is time to go, Alee. Keep the pace that brought you here and you will surely be home before the sun sets. But, be careful. Alone there may be hooligans within the inner rings who might look to take you."

Alee took note. Alee gave Buhen a hug and said her goodbyes. She had the armor placed on her shoulders by Buhen's aide. She made her way to the portal of Buhen's hut and stopped. Alee slowly turned back to Buhen.

"Thank You,"

Buhen smiled and simply nodded his farewell.

The recess had ended and once again the Den of Counsels was bursting at the seams. The statesmen were presided over by Gaia, Lady of the Nile; Bellia, Matron of the Guard Returned; and Aalarae, Kushite Princess. The King's ambassador came forward on behalf of the King and his illustrious first city and awaited a ruling from Alara's daughter. He stood and waited as Highness rose to make her voice heard.

> "Distinguished sons of Nubia, I have pondered the information brought forth by you all. Additionally, my special advisors Gaia and Bellia have both made their cases, each one on the opposite side of the debate. I have instructed them to prepare a plan of action for their supported policy. I will now call the advocate of my decision forward to submit her report and explain her plan."

After Aalarae spoke, the men grew silent. They awaited the name of she who would stand before them. Bellia felt a confidence in her counsel to the princess that made her sit taller in her chair. She peered at Gaia over the words they exchanged earlier and saw a grin upon her. For Gaia's part, she masked her anger incredibly well and thought to herself about the last time Bellia and she had such a rift between them. Before the memory swarmed back to the forefront of Gaia's thought, Aalarae's pause ended along with her final deliberation. The princess stepped forth with a name.

> "Now, speaking on behalf of the mind and body of Dorginarti. Captains, Advisors, Ambassadors,

Listen. Come forth, Gaia."

Gaia came forward to address the counsel as Bellia's face fell. She turned to Aalarae as she came back to sit upon her high throne. Aalarae read Bellia's distress and only held her right hand in comfort. Suddenly, Bellia left the Den of Counsels. Aalarae did not hinder Bellia as she calmly marched away. Princess Aalarae desired to follow Bellia and only stayed out of respect for Gaia. As Bellia walked out, Gaia began.

> "Counselors, I wish, for the sake of Kush, we take the offensive. We have the Wall and the River as points that will not yield. Fear not the numbers and chariots of Egyptian forces, our warriors are formidable. Thus, here are the details of our first campaign…"

Gaia continued on. The ears of the counselors heard and cheered. Gaia's confidence made the people there believe themselves a nation invincible. Aalarae applauded Gaia's strategy and believed it to be pure genius, but the princess could not help but think of where and how Bellia faired.

Somewhere near the Seventh Ring, Alee plodded toward the Last Shield. Weary, she felt only the pains brought upon her by her journey. Her mind lost all sharpness. She was not aware of anything she saw, heard, or felt except for her own soreness. She did not notice the man who followed her since she traveled past the conscripts that marched to Buhen's aid. The man kept to the shadows made by the approaching dusk. Alee was distracted by the familiarity of the stables that housed Reques and Requi as a sign of her proximity to the center palace. Being closer to the Last Shield brought clarity to Alee's mind, thus she further focused her energies on completing her journey.

At the foot of the Gardens that Alee knew for their Healing Leaves, the lurking man assaulted Alee without warning. The man said nothing and pinned her against the sandy streets. Alee wailed but the streets seemed vacant. Alee's head throbbed. She was too weak to overthrow the man, but she still struggled fiercely considering her current state of fatigue. Alee was left with little recourse and, for once, she intentionally tried with desperation to call upon her gifts and abilities as she stared at the face of the man. However, as Alee's eyes took in the man's scarred, bloodshot eyes, his grim, expressionless face and his foul, sour breath, she could not will anything from her severely drained temple. Her hands waved. The ruffian bound her at the wrists. Alee mustered her last stock of strength and gave out another yell. She slid her knee from underneath the man's restraining thigh and lifted it towards the sky. The scarred man immediately relinquished his hold on Alee and bellowed like a lame ox. Alee let out a small sigh to catch her breath, but could not move in the armor. The man lay cradling himself. He rolled about in a curled position like a baby. Alee locked her eyes upon the man. He stumbled to his feet still holding himself with one of his hands. His emotionless face showed pain but soon shaped itself into an expression of anger. The man came upon Alee yet again. A figure from the shadow of an alley called out.

"Yield, solider. Stand down." The voice said.

Suddenly, the man fell on his bottom. His face scowled again with pain.

Alee heard the voice and was relieved, but surprised to hear it. Out of the shadows came Bellia, who stood over the motionless Alee.

> "Interesting battle, Alee. Good to see the will in a body less willing."
>
> "Uhmm…Yeah...Well." Alee spoke solemnly feeling the need to apologize to Bellia.

Though her body's final cry prevailed, she did indeed attempt to strike the man down with her Awakening gifts.

> "I saw everything, Aleeia. I know what you tried to do and thus I hoped you would try. Listen, Alee..."

Bellia kneeled lower speaking to the stock-still Alee.

> "Our abilities, even yours, reign best with a clear mind and body. Until now, you have seen the

undisciplined slips occurring from emotion and subthoughts in a rested body. Emotion can trigger your will, but only when your body retains a considerable level of strength. Gaia still had strength in Egypt at The Great Hall, but her pierced flesh evoked her will. Gaia's skills in battle endangered us as she surrendered herself to her emotions. Therefore, I did not fear. You struggled until you could not struggle anymore. You tried to use you Awakening-will but did not have the strength or wit to do so, and with what little strength you had you struck the solider in his manliness. I applaud your discipline. Comparatively, it rivals Gaia's exceedingly. Lie here a while longer as I tend to the solider. Okay?"

Bellia stood. A still motionless Alee saw her move towards the lurking man whom Bellia revealed to be a solider under her charge. Alee was not angry, though surprised at the lengths of her instruction. Alee overheard Bellia speaking to the solider who was just beginning to feel his throbbing pain subside.

"Good job, solider. Can you stand?" Bellia asked.

"Yes, Madam. Just give me a minute," he groaned.

"Take your time, Sufra.," said Bellia.

Bellia extended her hand to help the disguised lancer to his feet. Alee shouted to the man. He reached his feet and leaned against the wall of a market hut.

"Sorry, Master Sufra. I did not know."

As Alee called out to ease his pain, both Bellia and Sufra laughed.

"Do not concern yourself, Young Matron," said Sufra.

"It was a good and timely blow."

"Indeed, Sufra. Get back to your wife in the Sixth Ring. I assure you, you have earned some leave of duty. At least a week's worth, in my opinion." Bellia smiled

"I will put in a word for you. Thank you for your help." said Bellia.

Bellia left Sufra to journey back to his family. She turned back to Alee and removed her armor. First, the anklets and shin guards came off followed by Alee's gauntlets. Bellia then pulled Alee to a sitting position. Together, they flung away her vest and chest guard. Alee felt like she was floating after the burden of the armor was removed. Though still weak, Alee rose to her feet with Bellia's aid. Her arm draped around her teacher's shoulders. Alee limped and turned her eyes to Bellia.

"So did I make it in time for dinner?" Alee asked.

"Surely. And then some." replied Bellia.

"And then some."

The Captain's Return - Day came again. Alee fell into a deep slumber after gorging at the diner table and awoke ready. She suited up for Bellia's morning session. Although Alee still felt a lingering soreness, sleep rejuvenated her. She carried her armor about with slightly greater ease and experience. Alee raised her armored vest above her shoulders and slipped it on, followed by her anklets and then her gauntlets. Alee dashed to the Arena of Adindan as soon as she strapped her armor securely. In Adindan, Bellia waited in full battle gear. For the first time since they arrived in Dorginarti, Alee saw Bellia alone. Absent were the likes of Meroe, Aalarae, Buhen and especially Gaia. Alee moved urgently to Bellia. When closer, Alee noticed a scowl set upon Bellia's face. She thought her tardiness caused Bellia's expression. Alee stood attentively before Bellia awaiting instruction, but Bellia stood lowly and mellow. Alee saw the darkness about her and felt her heart connecting with Bellia's in that moment.

"So where is Gaia?" Alee asked.

Bellia said nothing but turned her eyes to Aalarae's study. Alee dared not ask again and simply waited for her instructions to begin with her first session.

"Aleeia, run along the borders of this Ring. It will

warm your blood and loosen you to better handle your lesson. Run quickly and finish before I complete my song. Go."

Bellia pointed northward. Alee ran counterclockwise along the outskirts of the Ring between the Eighth and Ninth Shield. Bellia began her song, though she did not sing it aloud. The song flooded Bellia's mind with memories of her and Gaia as they traveled the Southlands along the Great River seeking Alee. Bellia sang with her eyes shut so that she could visualize her Gaia whom she loved with no contempt. Suddenly, Bellia's eyes burst open. A man upon a mighty steed stood before her.

"I know you, do I not?" The man asked Bellia.

"I do not recall you, Sir?"

Bellia replied with respect to his authority. Although she could not recognize his face, Bellia recognized his arms and garments as a Captain of Kush.

"Are you sure? It vexes me that I cannot place you."

In that instant, Alee returned behind Bellia and the man opposite the way she departed. Alee moved closer to Bellia. She saw the captain's face and recalled it. Before she could retreat away, Bellia called out to her.

"Good time. Quick pace. Come."

As Bellia spoke, the Captain turned his eyes to Alee.

"Shai." he said.

The Captain's eyes froze. He instantly placed Shael and Shai from the depths of recent memory. He knew them and admitted his slowness in wit as a matter of his drinking on that night.

"Shai! You are her, are you not?" The Captain asked.

Alee looked to Bellia for counsel, but Bellia in her heart of hearts grew tiresome of people giving and accepting counsel so readily. The Captain dismounted and stepped towards Alee. He gently placed his hand upon her cheek. As he moved towards her lips, Alee turned away from One-Man.

"Yes, I know and I remember our kiss. But I do not wish it relived. I have no desire to kiss a stranger."

Alee whispered and kept her eyes away from the Captain. But the Captain could not take his eyes away. They remained set, fixated on the beauty of whom he thought was Shai.

"Shai, I am no stranger. And even still, that did not stop you before," The Captain said.

"Good Sir, I do not know your name and you do not know mine. For it is not Shai," said Alee.

"Faras Morvs, Captain of the Center Shield and Heart of Dorginarti." he proclaimed.

Alee knew him as soon as he spoke his name. She instantly

thought of Buhen and Aalarae, for Faras was dominate over one and rejected by the other.

"Good Sir, please. You hinder my training. Bellia and I--" Alee pleaded but was interrupted.

Faras turned away from Alee and ignored her petition. Instead, he stood face to face with Bellia. With a tenor and groan akin to gravel in his throat, he said.

"So, Shael! Bellia! Your lessons are golden are they not? I mean Highness would have none other, save you, to teach her. So, how about a lesson?" Faras asked.

Bellia saw Faras was resolute in his challenge. He removed his sword and scabbard. Bellia, feeling foul from yesterday's matters, also felt sympathy to Faras. Her counsel was placed aside for Gaia's. However, Bellia believed her skills over Faras's compared equally in superiority to her counsel over Gaia's. Fueled by reason and the desire to confront the man who had dishonored Buhen, Bellia spoke,

"So, without sword or spear then?"

"If you wish it, Matron of Guard. If you wish it.," said Faras.

Bellia knew she could defeat Captain Faras easily enough but to what extent depended upon his willingness to yield.

"Fetch the wooden sabres from the cases there. This demonstration will serve your training well, no matter who is victorious," said Bellia.

"I agree," added Faras.

Alee handed Bellia and Faras their weapons and found a comfortable place to observe. She sat upon the large crates filled with the trinkets that formerly made the arena a museum. There atop the crates, Alee had a splendid vantage to witness the exhibition. Bellia, ceremoniously, gave honor to her opponent by saying a few inaudible words in his favor. Faras showed no such respect towards Bellia and stood at the ready. Bellia's fighting stance showed little concern for Faras. Her hands and swords stayed low by her side. Standing tall, Bellia read the breathing of Faras and also saw his weight was primarily on his back foot. And so Bellia waited, knowing Faras held a strong defensive position.

"What are you waiting for, Matron? Is the lesson mine or yours to give?"

Bellia heard his words and although they riled her a bit, she did not satisfy his bait. Bellia did not attack and waited silently.

"Shai, I will teach you," Faras yelled.

"Let me know you and I promise I will make you into the greatest warrior to ever walk the sands if you so desire. Bellia does not attack me because she knows I will triumph. Her style is flawed and her so-called philosophy is Buhen's joke."

Bellia felt nothing. The disciplined fighter within her heard the banter and held it to no esteem. She only felt the air. She noticed impatience growing in his stance. Soon, as she predicted, Faras replanted his back foot. And when he did, Bellia attacked. She swung her wooden sabre low at his forefront knee. Faras quickly moved his front leg back from the slash causing him to stand legs closed with his torso bent forward to balance the sudden jerk. As he moved his face and chest forward, Bellia saw to it that they met her sword free fist. The blow did not topple Faras though it did cause him to fall back by two steps. Bellia abandoned her attack in those two moves and allowed the Captain to regroup.

"See, child, how important balance is? Remove it and the opponent will be at your mercy trying to regain it." Bellia shouted calmly so Alee could hear her instruction.

Faras heard Bellia speak to Shai and felt his pride sink. As his face grew flushed, Faras felt the moisture of a small scar on his bottom lip. Faras had never been made to bleed in any demonstration. He grew agitated. Bellia saw the scowl on his face. She also saw the position of his feet and hands and knew his offensive was to come. Faras leapt blade first towards Bellia. She parried the sword with her own then sidestepped behind him. Faras turned to swipe head high at

Bellia. In a smooth yet fierce motion, she ducked, falling back on her shoulders. She then immediately kicked both feet skyward at the chin of Faras as she vaulted back to her feet.

> "Never lead blade point first. It leaves the attacking warrior open most times. A blade-point attack usually is a death blow that ends a combination."

Faras hesitated. He flung his head back down. His eyes glared at Bellia. Faras, now bested on two consecutive engagements, did his best to calm himself. He was indeed a savvy warrior and had never been provoked in such a way. He felt that Bellia's instruction also mockingly addressed him. Faras saw the calm about Bellia and noticed the opposite embodiment of their demeanors. Faras scoffed at the role reversal. Faras, usually calm, normally dominated the other combatant.

> "You have riled me, Bellia. I give you more credit now than when we began. But you will not best me. You will come to fear me as does our illustrious Matron of Guard, Meroe." Faras declared.
>
> "Meroe! Fear you?" Bellia exclaimed, "Maybe she does. Or maybe she honors your ego by not accepting any challenge from you. Maybe she respects your skill and strength enough to grant you a high rank at the center palace. Or, maybe she fears

you. You tell me."

Bellia's words once again set Faras's mind into motion. He lost all the recently reacquired calm. He charged Bellia. Their wooden swords clanked and clamored like flashes of thunder. Faras was momentously aggressive and Bellia could find no opening to halt him as the captain backed Bellia towards the outlying Pillars of Adindan. With her back against the column, the wooden sword grazed Bellia. She dove beneath his back fist. Bellia came to her feet near the center of the arena and changed sword hands.

"Shai! In the spirit of this exhibition, the Good Captain has skillfully rendered my favored sword-hand limp. I cannot use it. But let us continue."

Bellia intentionally used the false name as another subtle jab at Faras as the moment Faras had attempted to reclaim with Alee when she was *Shai* slipped further away. Bellia then placed her right hand behind her back and wound it in the loose straps of her armored corset. *That...She continues to mock me.* Faras thought. Faras let out a yell and charged Bellia. Bellia leapt high into the air over Faras and landed behind him in a crouch. Faras quickly turned to meet the blade-point of Bellia's sword at his throat. Upon one knee with her right arm bound and left arm stretched upwards towards his neck, both Bellia and Faras froze in their positions like newly chiseled statutes.

"Yield?" Bellia inquired.

"Reset." Faras stated.

"If our simulation were real you would not have the luxury to *reset*. Please, good Captain. You have wounded me and shown your skill. I must now tend to *my* student," said Bellia.

Faras released the tension in his neck and recoiled. He took a step back away from Bellia's wooden sword. Bellia came out of her crouch all the while reading again the signs in Faras's expression. If Faras meant to attack still, it did not show to her.

"My leave of duty has left me with too much drink in me." Faras said as he looked atop the crates.

"I have no wife and there is no other way for a young captain such as myself to pass the time of a dull holiday. I will leave you two to your playtime."

Faras gathered his sword and scabbard and refastened them to his belt while Bellia threw her wooden sword down near his feet. Faras turned and walked towards Shai.

"I will return, Shai...or whomever you are!" Faras stated.

"I leave you with a gift. And though I wish it were another kiss, I'll simply leave you with the ability to respect and admire your master." Faras stated.

And with that, Captain Faras Morvs mounted his horse and

trotted across the way to the palace stables and the Den of Counsels. Alee jumped down from atop the boxes and moved to Bellia.

"So did you learn anything?" Bellia asked and then they both laughed.

"If I had known he was such a jerk, I would never have kissed him." Alee stated while she chuckled.

"Oh, never mind that, child. You didn't know. Besides, the cocky captain is very handsome and somewhat skilled, but cocky still."

The ladies reverted back to their studies and dissected the fight. Bellia taught breathing, reading, and proper stances to Alee and she indeed took it all in. The Faras-Bellia demonstration echoed in her mind. She tried to recall the moments in the fight when Bellia herself might have used these same techniques. It brought a smile to Alee's face, as well as Bellia's, for Alee learned the arts quickly.

Across the way at the Den of Counsels, Captain Faras entered the halls to the sight of war at strategy and deliberation. He set his eyes first upon the fair Princess Aalarae and then the maiden beside her. He began his courtesies.

"Blessings to Highness, Blessing to Princess Aalarae!"

Faras paused and turned while still kneeling courteously.

"Blessing to you as well, Lady…?"

"Gaia," she answered.

Gaia, seeing the handsome Captain, blushed before him as he arose. But as the Princess spoke, Gaia turned back to the map table and set her thoughts back on the plans of battle.

"Captain Faras, Welcome." said the Princess.

"I have returned early from leave at your request Highness. How am I to serve you?" asked Faras.

"We are in the early stages of planning a great offensive against Egypt.," replied Aalarae.

"So you have voted with your father then?" Faras inquired.

"Yes, Captain, and I need you at the Wall in place of Meroe."

Faras contained his content as she gave the order. He felt the appointment was long past due and relished his new post. But his happiness in Aalarae's words was short lived.

"I need Meroe here for she will lead the Legions of Dorginarti as General. I trust your skill and you will substitute her well as acting Patron of Guard. Protect the city while we are off to war."

Faras clenched his teeth, but said nothing. He stood still. Suddenly, his clever mind set itself in motion.

"You are to join the battle, Highness?" Faras

inquired.

"I must. My father is not well and my brother will send his armies, but wants no part for the love of his bride," she replied.

"Then who will govern Dorginarti? Who will keep it safe?" asked Faras.

"All military forces will be at and beyond the gates. The high counselors will preside over the chieftains and ambassadors. In the city, they will rule together and embody the will of their people through debate and consensus."

Faras smiled within himself. With no warriors left behind, a couple of well placed assassins could make Faras Morvs the new Master of Kush. But Faras left that villainous thought behind. He realized the thought manifested from the spurns of his recent defeats. By his humiliation at the hands of Bellia, Faras felt feeble. Now, with the orders of Aalarae, he felt another great dishonor as Meroe was again chosen before him.

"But I would fight with Meroe by your side, Princess, to prove my worth." Faras stated.

"Good Captain," Aalarae said as she placed her hand upon his cheek.

"Your worth *is* nor has ever been in question. You are skilled and fierce in battle and I trust you now with the task to safeguard all of Kush as the last line, not just Dorginarti."

"But Princess, you call upon Meroe to fight and die as a General. She is good enough to do that for you. And Bellia good enough to train you, when I am not."

Aalarae's eyes lightened. She stared solemnly at the captain.

"Faras, I see now that I have hurt you in my choices. Understand, though lady warriors are more common here, it is still unorthodox for a lady of royalty to seek instruction. No one could spare the time for the task except for the retired Matron Bellia. As for Meroe, it was Bellia's right to choose her successor and, if I recall, you had yet to arrive here from the Second City. Meroe did not know who to choose as her successor. All she knew of you was your legend, but nothing of your heart. She deferred the choice to me and I chose you as protector of the people, Good Captain. Rank means nothing for that title is paramount."

Faras's heart grew heavy. He realized his folly and dishonor towards Bellia. More so, he realized his boorish nature, which he regretfully displayed before the young maiden, still known to him as Shai.

"I shall never receive another such kiss," Faras

mumbled to himself.

"What was that, Patron Faras?" asked Gaia.

The voice of Gaia eased Faras. He sat beside her amongst her plans. His presence gave her goose bumps. He showed even greater charm in the eyes of Gaia after the Princess humbled him.

"Captain, I wish for you to work with Gaia. She is the leading counselor as Dorginarti leads the way to war. She will benefit from your wisdom as well as Meroe's when she arrives. I will leave the two of you."

The Princess smiled and left the corridors of the Den. Aalarae read the heart of Gaia and found beauty in her favor of Faras, especially on the many eves before an oncoming war. The two of them pined away together at the maps and models of fronts and geographies concerning the war. Gaia received all the input Faras offered concerning every possible scenario and contingency that may befall during the battle. As their work wore on for a few hours, Gaia grew closer to Faras and he grew more comfortable with her. They spoke without reservation as the day faded.

"So, Gaia…If I may...I was wondering…?"

"Yes." Gaia said anxiously.

"You arrived with Bellia and the young girl. Did you not?"

Gaia's face fell. She did not want nor expect to hear words regarding Bellia. Gaia withdrew from the table and moved to the door of the Den. She stood peering out across the way at the Arena of Adindan. Gaia looked back at Faras to reply.

"Yes, I am in the company of Bellia and Aleeia."

"Aleeia, eh," sighed Faras.

"Excuse me, Lady Gaia. I have given my counsel to its greatest value and it has grown thin. When Meroe arrives, I am sure she will completely accommodate your survey with her full and fresh body of wisdom. I take my leave, Lady Gaia," stated Faras.

Faras kissed Gaia's hand and then made his way to Adindan. Gaia felt enraptured by the Captain's departing courtesy, but as he became more distant she regarded his interest in Alee bitterly.

Deep in thought, the newly appointed Patron of Guard moved towards Adindan. He was silent. He walked past the Pillars that marked the entrance of the arena. Unseen, Faras looked upon Aleeia from behind the crates she sat on during his skirmish with Bellia. Aleeia stepped to the beat of Bellia's choreography. Secretly impressed, Faras looked on. He saw Aleeia's intensity in training and admitted having doubts earlier regarding her true commitment. As he watched Aleeia now and noted the expression of determination on her face, Faras became swayed. He revealed himself from behind the crates and strode towards teacher and pupil.

"Greetings, ladies." Faras said with a full smile. Aleeia showed intense discipline and continued her stances. She completely ignored the handsome Captain. Bellia stepped between Faras's path to Aleeia.

> "I wondered when you would reveal yourself from the cover of those crates." Bellia stated.
>
> "Indeed, Bellia, you are a treasure to the Majesty of Kush. One of her finest warriors and most compassioned ambassadors."

Faras kneeled before Bellia catching her slightly off guard.

"To what do I owe this courtesy?" Bellia asked. Aleeia continued to train while at the same time listening to their exchange.

> "I did not properly honor you and your pupil earlier. By the grace and wisdom of Highness, I realized jealousy drove my actions. Please, accept my apology."

Bellia, despite her concern for Alee, accepted the Captain's contrition. She knew the days ahead had enough malice and spite within them.

"That is enough for now, child. Rest," said Bellia. Alee walked away towards the beautiful fountains in the

Arena of Adindan to replenish herself. As Alee moved away, Bellia turned back to Faras.

"Good Captain, would you mind assisting me in the next part of today's session?"

"I would be honored."

With the soothing beauty of Aalarae's words in his head, Faras did not challenge Bellia. His pride still bore wounds from their previous encounter. The Captain accepted Bellia's invitation only to be closer to the object of his heart's infatuation. Faras felt raw and naked when close to Aleeia. He also felt somehow Aleeia could see into him and the sight was not a horror to her. To look at her from afar, knowing what her lips tasted like, added to the Captain's anguish. He approached her. Faras was mindful of his offensive actions from earlier and knew they repulsed Aleeia.

"Shai…that…name is false," Faras thought aloud confirming Aleeia's disdain.

Before Faras could speak a word in an attempt to endear himself to Aleeia, Bellia immediately enlisted the Captain's services for the sake of their training session. With her right hand, Bellia motioned Faras to take a stance to the right and with her other hand Aleeia took the left. They walked by one another to take their places. Aleeia looked into his eyes. He smiled and slightly brushed her forearm with the tip of his index finger as he passed Aleeia.

"Captain Faras, attack and subdue her," instructed Bellia.

"Do not let the Captain pin you. And remember what we have done today," Bellia added.

Faras looked at Aleeia and saw the solid expression that stared back at him. He wanted Aleeia to see him as she did that night when they danced and held one another. Faras stood ready to attack and took comfort that he would hold her again, even if it was an aggressive grappling exhibition. But first Faras spoke to lighten the tension in her.

"Have I told you that I like the style of your hair? Up suits you, Aleeia." Faras said.

Aleeia's brow rose. She held back a small grin. She clenched her fist. Any trace of a smile completely vanished. Aleeia did not say a word, but Bellia did.

"Faras, today, please."

Faras lunged at the beautiful young warrior. She quickly retreated outwards of the Captain's reach. Aleeia then stared intently at the form Faras held. Like Bellia earlier, Aleeia meant to judge the weight and balance of Captain Faras in order to predict his next move, but he showed no favor Aleeia could see. The good captain swung both arms low towards her feet. Aleeia jumped into the air, which allowed herself to be vulnerable to the Captain's exceptional speed.

Before Aleeia could hit the floors of Adindan, the Captain held Aleeia securely. In his grasp, her feet flopped just above the ground. Oddly to the Captain, Aleeia did not struggle. His arms wrapped around her waist, clasping Aleeia's arms tightly at her side. Aleeia looked at Faras and glared into his face. Faras felt her eyes piercing him. He could not place her emotionless face. Faras set her down. *Aleeia, what are you thinking? What do you think of me? Do you hate me?* He wondered. Faras awaited her response intensely as if his entire existence depended upon the things that would pass beyond her mouth. Aleeia was still. Her demeanor was very cold. She revealed nothing to the Captain. She cut her eyes to Bellia. Bellia gestured a subtle nod.

> "The man I kissed is not the man before me. He was pure and mysterious. Noble. Even a little weak. I remember feeling those things as I held you. I remember thanking you for coming to my aid. For being my hero that day," said Alee.

Aleeia looked at Faras. For a moment, his expression showed a frailty that reminded her of him all those days ago. Aleeia held back those thoughts as she spoke again.

> "Captain Faras, who stands here now, is arrogant and vengeful. He is to be respected for his abilities and stature, but offers no respect to anyone else's

stature and abilities. I have seen your good courtesy to Bellia as well, but it comes after you failed to gain my favor by besting her. Which ***You*** do I accept? Whom do I trust?"

Faras paused. He knew the words of Aleeia were honest. He lowered his head in shame, but more so to mourn the feeling that lied at the bottom of his belly. Faras wanted to know Aleeia. He wanted to love her and for her to return that love fully, but doubted she ever would. Faras grew weaker and lost all interest in physically confronting Aleeia in her studies.

"Bellia, the day is nearly done. I must regretfully retire. If you need my service for anything, you need simply call for it."

He nodded to Bellia. She confirmed the captain's statements by returning the act. Faras turned to Aleeia and once again lowered himself before her.

"Farewell, Lady Aleeia." Faras said.

Captain Faras, the newly appointed Patron of Guard, turned to depart. He expected no reply from her. He knew he did not deserve one. The expression of a tender man was stapled upon Faras's face again and Aleeia saw that it was. Thus uncontrollably, Aleeia uttered back unto him.

"Alee. Those who know me call me Alee."

Pressures of Ceremony - A looming sun rose high, three days after the coming of Captain Faras. Under the swelter created by the golden orb, the City of Dorginarti made plans for war, while the Center Palace made their preparations for a grand ceremony. Titles and Guards would be passed later that night. Meroe would be appointed General of Dorginarti and Faras would succeed Meroe as Patron of Guard and Master of the Wall. Decorations for the night's dance were made around the streets of the centermost Shield. Two women, however, could be found in the same place, partaking in tasks that had not been altered from routine by the oncoming ceremony. Alee was there training and improving immensely under the watchful eye and expert tutelage of Bellia. In the Arena of Adindan, Alee learned to fuse her newly acquired battle skills and her special gifts into an amalgam of power and confidence Gaia and Bellia deemed to be her birthright. Alee's mind sharpened and showed improvement by the day, but for some reason Bellia had not seen her as zealous on that day. Bellia continuously caught notice of Alee gazing at the Den of Counsels where Captain Faras dwelled in study with Gaia. Alee again wandered during Bellia's demonstration. Bellia walked calmly behind Alee and struck her gently on the back of her head.

"What was that for?" Alee groaned while rubbing the back of her head.

"You have the nerve to ask me that?" Bellia paused then let out a deep sigh, "Alee...Aleeia, you have come far. It has only been a matter of weeks, but already you know and do more than I under Buhen after an entire season. With your skill improving so and a battle possibly at our heels, I feel more so now it is best we leave here and move on to the next phase of your journey. There are other places like Adindan and other methods of keeping your gifts hidden."

Alee interrupted with a stare. Bellia grew silent.

"It is not yet time to depart." Alee stated.

"Alee, I trust you completely but don't you think you have kept your translation from us long enough?"

"No." Alee said lowly, "We wait. A sign is coming."

Bellia did not press. She listened to the words brought forth assuredly by her student. Bellia looked at Alee and noted that something else lingered amongst her thoughts. For the past few days, the Arena of Adindan held visitors who bore witness to Bellia as she endeavored to train Aleeia. But more importantly to Alee, she had been in the presence of Captain Faras at times. Alee left a door open by uttering her name to him. Faras endeared himself to Alee and spent every minute he could spare at her side. He spoke to Alee and told her all the things he had seen on his many travels. He even shared stories of his time in Kush as a youth. But today, the good captain left Alee with something else that scurried restlessly through her mind.

"What is it, child? I know all the looks now. Ask the question. Let me be an advisor to you," urged Bellia.

An odd visible blush hued over her sultry auburn complexion, Alee held back for a moment before she spoke.

"Faras asked me to escort him to tonight's dance and ceremony. The invitation left me speechless. I have yet to answer," said Alee.

"Why so?" inquired Bellia.

"True, he rose to the challenge of being the hero I met at Menin. But how much of his interest lies in the chase? If I let him know how I now feel, will he still be there?" Alee wondered.

Bellia covered her lips and held back a laugh.

"Alee, he asked you to a dance, not to be wed or to lie in your lap. Have fun." Bellia said before her expression suddenly changed.

Alee heard the words beneath Bellia's counsel and, having done so, quickly put all back in perspective. She remembered wholly the pressures that lay on her shoulders. As Egypt had taught her, Alee knew she could not afford to fall for anyone for the sake of destiny parting them. Bellia placed her hand on her shoulder after seeing a face the likes of the one she held on departing day in Abydos.

"Wait here, Alee." Bellia said suddenly.

"Of course, but what would you have me do while I wait?" A confused Alee asked.

She figured Bellia to be pulling another trick.

"Take a break." Bellia blurted before she sprang towards the Den.

Bellia entered the Den of Counsels for the third time in as many days. Bellia visited only to update Gaia on the progress of Alee. At times, Gaia felt she came to the Den to spy and pass judgment on her plans regarding the upcoming battle. The two women were more distant than they had ever been in recent memory. Bellia came to the Den to satisfy two aims. Her first objective was carried out rather quickly. She approached the soon-to-be Patron of Guard, Faras Morvs.

"Greetings, Good Captain," Bellia said, smiling from ear to ear.

"Hello, Bellia. How fare you and the fair Alee?" Faras asked.

"She is well, but if you could spare your expertise, she could use your help with something," said

Bellia.

Faras arose slowly from his seat and bowed to the graces of Gaia. He asked to be excused and made his way to the Arena. Gaia smiled but knew her endearing gaze went unnoticed. She knew full well Faras favored Alee completely. Bellia came upon Gaia as Faras left the Den.

"Gaia, you and I have known one another for quite some time. And it has been a hard thing for the both of us over the years. We have been in competition ever since I can remember, but it has never driven us apart, only together," said Bellia.

Bellia paused. Gaia came away from her plans and letters and gave Bellia her full attention. Gaia's mind went back to when she received the call. She lay motionless. The Heavens opened before her as she gained clarity, purpose and experienced her Awakening. From that moment on, Gaia knew what life meant and what road she was destined to travel.

"Do you remember that feeling, Bellia? How our bodies and minds felt after all of a sudden knowing."

Gaia smiled and so did Bellia.

"Shortly after we met, we even argued about you Awakening before me." Bellia added.

"Listen, Gaia. We both have our roles to play. We knew them back then, but somewhere along the way we let those roles keep us from growing. Our pride kept us from nurturing one another. I think we both could have grown to be more well-rounded. But we were held back for a reason," said Bellia.

Gaia's eyes watered.

"You are right, you know. Look at you playing the philosopher," said Gaia.

Gaia stopped to wipe the tears.

"If I were the battlemaster you were and you were the wisemaster as I, then Aleeia would be the worse for it. We would proclaim ourselves true heirs of Pixsus and Nympthia and thus the world would go into ruin."

"I could not have said it better myself.," stated Bellia.

"I know," added Gaia as the two ladies embraced.

Moments earlier, Faras approached Alee in the Arena of Adindan at the request of Bellia. Though, by his truest wishes, Bellia gave him a viable excuse to see the young warrior. He came upon her while she continued to practice, even though Bellia left her to rest. Alee moved gracefully. She exuded a powerful and unexplainable aura, but Faras was one of few who could peer through. He lovingly saw all her fear and uncertainty mixed with her confidence and purity. The two made eye contact as Faras reached out to her. Alee, feeling the weight of her mission, pulled back to the dismay of the Captain.

"Alee?" said the Captain with bewilderment.

Alee heard his voice and moved to reply.

> "Good Captain, I would be delighted to accompany you to tonight's ceremony for a single night of lighthearted joy so that you and I both can take a breath before our respective plunge," said Alee.

Faras was relieved and overjoyed to hear Alee offer him such a favorable response, though he stood confused about the totality of her comments. He took Alee by the hand, somewhat quickly as not to give her cause to retreat. Faras kneeled before a melancholy woman and began working to ease her mind so he might see her smile again.

> "I am taken by you. I would have love take me wherever you would go. And if my body must forebear the journey, know my heart and spirit will never falter," said Faras.

Alee grew weak by the words uttered by Faras. She turned and tendered a smile to him, all the while holding back the urge to cry. Alee thought of others as loyal who were now gone. The thought of those who loved her the same nearly caused her to break down. But now knowing Faras was with her gave her security and she doubted him no more.

"I await tonight anxiously. I shall see you then.," said Alee.

Faras took her words as his leave to depart. However, before he did, Alee tiptoed to him. And just as she did that night in Menin, Alee gave him the smallest kiss on the cheek.

Faras turned to depart and two figures came upon Adindan. Gaia and Bellia returned to Alee together for the first time in days. Faras left and passed Gaia. She hastened her stride to Alee. Gaia's face fell at the thought of Faras denying her in favor of a child. Knowing she felt jealousy, she tried to calm herself to inform Alee of the potential danger her involvement could cause them all.

"Alee, a word please?" asked Gaia.

"Yes, Gaia." Alee responded.

"He has made it plain, Captain Faras, that he favors you. I implore you not to continue on this road. It does not suit our interest," said Gaia.

"Our interest?" Alee questioned boldly, "You, Gaia, have made it plain you favor the Captain."

Gaia began speaking slowly. Her eyes turned down low.

"I will admit to my liking and also to my jealousy, but understand I speak aside those things. You have come far. Further than Egypt, but you still play with emotions that can bleed through your discipline.

And I, for one, cannot let you rock the Palaces of Dorginarti as you moved the Hall. Please, Alee. Do not fight with me. Bellia and I have just recently mended our bond. I need your understanding."

Gaia extended her hands to Alee and Alee cupped them in her own.

"Forgive me, Gaia, but I have come to terms with it."

Gaia paused as to provoke Alee to elaborate.

"I know lonely is the road ahead. Just as the path already tread has left me without mother and friend." Alee stated before smiling grimly.

"Not to worry, Gaia. Tonight is tonight."

Alee turned to the Palace to leave in preparation for the ceremony. Gaia looked at Bellia and knew Alee's wisdom derived from her.

Alee shuffled off her haughty doubts and sorrow. She returned to her ambassador's suite, adjacent to the palace. Alee moved beyond the threshold into the dominion that became her newest resting place. Her eyes drew vision upon a beautiful gown stretched out across her bed. Alee sprang towards the bed to give the dress a look over. Her face brightened as she marveled at its exquisite beauty and style.

"It is beautiful. It is not?" A familiar voice peered from the portal.

Alee turned speechless as she lost the words that stood waiting on her tongue. She paused and took a moment to form new words for Princess Aalarae.

"Truly, it is." Alee said.

The princess came from the portal to the open area of Alee's suite. She stood across from the foot of the bed. Alee gently placed the gown back on the bed and moved closer to the feet of Aalarae.

"Highness, the dress is amazing. It reminds me of the ones seen in the Southland," she added.

"That is because it is." replied the princess.

"It is a dress befitting an Honorary Ambassador of Kush from the Southlands."

Alee paused as she heard Aalarae in her sovereign glory make the appointment. Once again, Alee had no words. Aalarae saw Alee struggle and smiled. Alee smiled to thank her once.

"And thank you." Alee said to thank her twice.

Aalarae departed to prepare for the ceremony. But before she reached the door, Alee called out to her.

"Highness…"

Alee's thoughts turned to serious matters once again. Alee knew the private ear of the Ruler of the Third City came very rarely. The concerns of Alee gave way and provoked Alee to seize the opportunity and acquire some answers.

"I know the campaign march begins in seventeen days. If it pleases you to answer, Highness, would you have Gaia and Bellia join the efforts if they were not in care of me?" asked Alee.

"Most certainly, Gaia's plan is primary until Meroe comes to amend it and Bellia has shown her skills time and time again." said the Princess while still giving thought to the question.

"I would *not* order them to fight. If that is what you mean to ask." The princess added.

"No, I do not presume you would but…" Alee added.

"But what, Alee?" inquired Aalarae.

Alee's face became hallow and grim as she lowered her eyes before Highness. Aalarae placed her arms around Alee and pulled her closer to her bosom. Aalarae began patting and stroking Alee's hair to comfort away the grimness that troubled her face. Alee felt at ease and imagined the Princess to be her own dear Karwynn. She spoke through small tears.

"I wait for a sign, Karwynn. When it comes, I will be alone…without Bellia, without Gaia…and without you."

Aalarae said nothing and held Alee as she wanted, as her Karwynn. The Princess understood Aleeia's burdens a bit more. Finally, she realized why she trained and traveled with Gaia and Bellia, not as some point of privilege but as a trial of destiny. And in that thought, Aleeia came out of her trance and knew the arms of Aalarae instead of Karwynn. Aleeia realized the consoling comfort caused her to maybe say too much. Aleeia pulled away from Aalarae and looked deep into her.

> "I take great pride that I could tender you. That you would *confide* in me.," said Aalarae.

Aleeia nodded as the princess turned to the door to leave.

The Coming of the Sign - A few hours before the ceremony, drums, brass, and woodwinds rang out at the spectacle. The procession announced near the Third Shield drew a crowd. Meroe entered the City of Dorginarti with a legion of followers conscripted from throughout Nuri, the Second City. The broad road to the heart of Dorginarti was filled with thousands of Nuri-Kushite warriors. Marching proud and strong they followed an awe-inspiring Meroe. She walked commandingly along side Shabaka and Kashta, the Guardian Beasts of the Wall. The lions were reined by Meroe. She reluctantly brought them from the gate to

Dorginarti as a matter of ceremony, for she would pass their care to Faras later that night. Shabaka and Kashta let out a roar that added to the thunderous drums. Alee heard the rumbling clamor and stared intensely at the dress she was to wear. She knew the ceremony began soon.

In the lower level of the Center Palace, a crew of handmaidens tended to Highness. Princess Aalarae stood elegantly with her arms extended like a bird in mid-flight. Her hair was being braided and her gown was being wrapped around her body. They placed a headdress upon Aalarae. She stood there in purple silk that flowed from shoulder to hip and waist to ankle as a belt made of twisted brass and pearls held the single seamless piece of fabric to her body. Princess Aalarae also held herself together despite the weight of leadership and the impending war. The sorrow that would consume the average person in her place was bred never to manifest within her. She beat down the thoughts of sending hundreds of soldiers to a possible doom and carried on regally and statuesque as the handmaidens finished their tasks.

"Highness, the ambassadors and guests await you,"

said a messenger standing at the palace portal.

The princess nodded and signaled the leave of the handmaidens and messenger. She then met her two ambassadors outside who escorted her in procession to the

Den of Counsels where the ceremony and dance were to be held. Her liaisons to The First and Second City walked quietly beside her. They both wore long brown robes with a purple silk sash that represented the royalty who could not attend. The streets were lined with people as Aalarae entered the Den. Inside, five chairs sat atop the platform. Princess Aalarae took her place on the center chair. Her ambassadors sat at the furthest ends and left two empty chairs on either side of the Princess. The drums played as the roars of Kashta and Shabaka could be heard as near as Adindan. Every dignitary turned to the doors of the Den as Meroe was but mere moments away from her entrance.

Meanwhile, just outside the foreign ambassador's suite adjacent to the Palace, Captain Faras pleaded to the door of a suite. He waited for the beautiful Alee to escort him into the Den behind Meroe who neared her entrance.

> "Alee, I assure you your beauty is not to be matched," Faras stated.
>
> "Go, please. I do not wish to make you late nor do I wish to rob you of all deserving eyes," replied Alee.
>
> "My dear, I wish to walk with you...to be with you.," said Faras.

Faras heard no immediate reply as he placed his hands and ears to the door. The Captain heard nothing and took a step back as to knock open the door. Alee spoke before he could do so.

"Go ahead. I will see you towards the end of the ceremony before the dance begins," said Alee.

Time took all objections from Captain Faras. He rushed away from the door as if pulled by a strong swirling wind. And thus, Faras made his way to the Den. He fell in line directly behind Meroe and the Guardian Beasts. He looked back in hopes of catching a glimpse of Alee. He turned back disappointed. Meroe and Faras took their places at the foot of the platform and stood directly in front of the empty chairs beside Highness.

"Here before you, people of Dorginarti, two of your finest warriors will be honored today. One with the important charge of leading you in battle. The other with the equally, if not more important task of protecting you from it. Warriors, step forward."

Meroe and Faras ascended the platform as the people in attendance at the Den of Counsels let out a huge clamoring applause.

"Meroe, our Matron of Guard at the Wall of Nubia, a Dorginarti daughter, champion at *The Siege of the Fourth Cataract*, and my dear friend has come forth. Answering the call, I give you the burden to lead us in the upcoming battles. People of Dorginarti, I give you Meroe, General of Dorginarti."

The crowd gave the announcement all the honor it was due and beyond. The soldiers took to a knee and bowed before their new leader. Captain Faras, as well, lowered himself before her as he turned from the Princess to honor her more readily. The Princess began subsiding their applauses as she motioned for the soldiers in the Den to stand. Captain Faras remained bent while the Princess spoke.

> "Faras Morvs, our Captain of the Shields, a Nuri son, hero of *The Third Invasion,* and my finest warrior has kneeled before you, Meroe," said Highness.

Meroe stepped before Faras. She had a secure grasp of the thick iron-leather reigns that held Kashta and Shabaka.

> "Answering the call, I pass on the honor of defending us and all the cities of Kush, not only from the upcoming battle, but all conflicts to come. People of Dorginarti, I give you Faras Morvs, Patron of Guard!" proclaimed Meroe.

As Faras arose, Meroe handed him the reigns of the Guardian Beasts. They let out a thunderous roar that mixed with the applause. It shook the Den. Searching, Faras turned towards the audience looking them over. He hoped to get a glimpse of Alee. However, nothing nor anyone seen by Faras could even closely resemble the beauty Faras knew as Alee. The newly sworn Patron of Guard let out a sigh. He grew restless waiting for Alee as time continued to drift away. For now, as Patron, Faras had to return to The Wall and leave Dorginarti at dawn. He handed the reigns to the tamer who would take the two lions to the stable and have them fed and watered as the ceremony drew on. The tamer walked back down the aisle through the portal of the Den. The Princess continued on with the conclusion of the ceremony. Aalarae, Princess of Dorginarti, the Third City, had a resolve upon her face that energized the crowd. No weakness or fear could be found upon her face and her words also showed no signs of frailty.

> "My people, I know what makes a war. When people who would not be conquered take arms against those who would conquer them. For countless years, we have stood at the Bank of the Great River with our backs to the Barren Sea sharing the life that it has granted us with those who also depend upon it. But as time has gone by and kingdoms have grown, the life of this kingdom has been too closely tied to a fragile peace. Now, in these times, Egyptian rulers, Pharaohs, who think themselves man-gods, wish to take our lands to eliminate us for the sake of their own peoples' lives and survival. And so I ask you this, my people, Is this land not yours, are your lives of less

importance? Will you not fight?"

The uproar of the crowd rippled out of the Den into the streets of Dorginarti like a tidal wave. Aalarae's speech set in the hearts of her people. She knew her skills in oration paled in comparison to her father's, but Princess Aalarae knew her father, King Alara, would be proud.

Once again, Aalarae muted the Den with the wave of her hands. She then yielded the platform to Meroe. Meroe stepped forth to give her address, which was no more than a brief issuing of orders and her endorsement of Patron Faras. With wisdom, Meroe chose to save all fiery words for the first offensive.

"All attending guardsmen and soldiers, you have been assigned to your post. Taharqa Legion, I will brief you as soon as I have reviewed all courses of advancement," said Meroe.

Meroe continued as Faras, still staring out amongst the onlookers, waited for Alee to arrive. He grew anxious as the burning urge to leave and find her came over him. However, he remained composed. As Meroe finished her address, Faras readied his mind for what he was to say to his soldiers and the Dorginarti people. He stepped forward.

"The gift of a safe and sound sleep has been a treasure the people of this nation has taken for granted. And rightfully so. I have slept in Nuri as well as this Great City knowing that the Wall of Nubia and its guardians keep us safe. It has been so for years and so it shall be, for as long as I draw breath with all the will to protect the people I love."

In that instant as Faras Morvs spoke of protecting love, three magnificent female forms entered the Den. Their presence caused Faras to stammer in his speech as he beheld the elegant beauty of Gaia, Bellia, and Alee. He looked out into the eyes of Alee. His mind fell back and connected to the words she inspired.

"Yes...Love. As a captain, I have seen many battles. And in those battles I have fought to protect this city as a place...as a space...and done so successfully. But now I protect Dorginarti with something stronger, with love for its people. Your love strengthens me and I shall not fail."

The crowd responded cheerless, but in pure applause. The heartfelt words of Faras Morvs, Patron of Guard, reassured the already confident people of Dorginarti. He took his place beside Aalarae while many continued to salute Faras. Princess Aalarae concluded the ceremony as she ordered the bands to strike up the music. People in the streets and in the Den celebrated the night and the peace and freedom brought to them. All the dignitaries who sat atop the platform came into the crowd and met various people therein. Meroe came down from the platform with a new weight and sought the comfort of her former teacher, Bellia, who was dressed immaculately in full ceremony armor. Aalarae met with Gaia to speak about the final transition of ideas and strategy. Aalarae only appeared at the dance to show a strong, unwavered assurance to the public.

And then there was Faras. He dotted out into the crowd searching for Alee. Face after face he encountered as he maneuvered around the dancers in the Hall looking for Alee. Faras stood taller than most of the crowd and stopped in the middle of the Den to get his bearings. In the farthest corner of the Den away from the platform, Faras caught sight of her. Alee, in her emerald-green dress that draped across her left shoulder leaving the other bare, glided towards Faras. She wore a brass headdress and two arm bracelets with two rings connected by a single glowing silk shawl. It gave Faras the illusion that, with wings, she was flying towards him.

Amongst the music, their eyes met as they did in Menin all those weeks ago. Alee, held closely by Faras, smiled and placed her head on his chest. She listened to his heartbeat for a moment before she led him out of the Den towards the quieter Adindan. Just outside the Den, dancers lined the streets. The sound of the bands playing became more faint. The crowd grew lighter and more dispersed the closer they came to the Arena. Faras and Alee entered Adindan and shared a small, yet intense kiss before he held her hand. They exchanged words.

"I feared leaving before ever having the chance to properly say goodbye. To tell you that I love you," Faras said while holding her hand.

"So did I," replied Alee. Her words left Faras a bit bewildered.

"You knew I'm to leave at dawn?" Faras asked.

"You are? No, I did not know.," replied Alee.

Faras paused to reassess what he had heard.

"So were *you* going to leave here soon?" Faras asked.

"Possibly," Alee said as she stepped out of the moonlight near a pillar, "Remember when I told you I spent time in Abydos? I...I..."

Faras saw the struggle within her and came closer to settle her but Alee backed away while she continued to tell her tale.

"A tablet holding one of several keys to my destiny, I translated there in Egypt. It said:

You must go into the desert - The Barren Sea,
To trek no more as group of Three.
Receive a sign through agony,

Through mouths of two so meant for Thee.
Receive a sign of Earthly doom,
You bound to the messenger towards Pixsus' tomb.

...So clearly, I have to leave but I know not when nor with whom. I have already packed, to be able to leave in an instant; however, my nights have been haunted with the thought of going on without Gaia or Bellia."

Once again, Faras tried to take in all he heard for it shook him severely. The thought of Alee going West into the Barren Sea sent chills up his spine, but another thought concerned him equally. Provided he trusted in the tablet as Alee did, Faras wondered, *who bound to Alee would be the messenger? With whom would she go?*

"Do you have any idea who this messenger will be, Alee?" he inquired aloud.

"Not to a certainty, but the tablet was clear. It would not be Gaia or Bellia, but would be someone to whom I held a certain responsibility and they to me. *Bound* as it states in the verse."

"That should narrow it down, shouldn't it? Maybe me, Alee?" Faras suggested.

Alee remained silent. She wrapped herself in her shawl, which did little to soften the cool night's wind. She then looked farther off towards the Den. Suddenly, amidst the band play, Alee faintly made out a screeching wail. She saw four figures rush to the Arena. As they moved closer, Alee saw Meroe and Bellia led by Princess Aalarae. They held Gaia on their shoulders and guided her to Adindan. Gaia could barely stand as she let out another howl.

"Hurry, Hurry! Get her into the Arena!" Bellia cried,

"Let it out, Gaia! Don't hold it. It's okay."

Aleeia ran to Gaia stretched out on the floor of Adindan. Gaia continued to moan. Aleeia asked Bellia the cause of the pain.

> "It's Hat-kaptah! Gaia fell out in the Den. She tried to hold it back so Dorginarti would not be endangered." Bellia then turned to Gaia, "Its okay, Gaia. You made it! We are in Adindan."

Faras and Aalarae looked at the disturbing spectacle. Aleeia's mind went back to the translation, *Receive a sign through agony, through mouths of two so meant for Thee.* Aleeia looked back up at Faras. He stared past Aleeia in astonishment. Suddenly, Gaia stopped all wailing and arose from the ground as if the Heavens and the Hands of God pulled her. Her eyes glowed in a bright blue hue like a star burned within her. Suddenly, she spoke with a deepened voice that sounded not unlike two people speaking at once. Seeing the Chasm of the Great Hall in Abydos through the eyes of Hat-kaptah, Gaia communicated his words:

They came days and days ago, here to Abydos.
They are Three who have taken the ear of Pharaoh.
The Pharaoh has moved on Kush,
Egypt is two days from the Wall.

Gaia saw the Chasm stairs as Egyptian soldiers swarmed in. She saw Hat-kaptah surrounded on the buried tablet. Gaia still connected to Hat-kaptah breathed deeply and uttered a single word as Hat-Kaptah was being overtaken.

...Alee!

Gaia fell to the ground. Aalarae and Bellia stooped beside her. Meroe, knowing the trueness of the Awakening Will of Gaia, rushed to her captains and prepared to set out for The Wall at dawn with Faras. Gaia looked like someone who suffered from a fever as Aalarae and Bellia moved her to the Healers Realm. Bellia turned to Faras and Aleeia for help to carry Gaia, but when Bellia glanced back both Alee and Faras were gone.

"Where is Aleeia?" Bellia asked.

Gaia, still dizzy, began clearing her head and soon after stood under her own will. She looked around and also wondered the whereabouts of the young Aleeia. Seeing that

Gaia faired a bit better, Princess Aalarae moved to clear the Den. She then assembled all the chieftains, advisors, and ambassadors. Aalarae as well felt imposed by the omen of Gaia. Gaia and Bellia followed closely behind Aalarae towards The Den of Counsels and spotted Faras alone in the stables.

"Faras, what are you doing here? Do you know where Aleeia is?" asked Bellia.

"*Alee* is gone," replied a somber Faras with harshness in his throat.

"What do you mean, gone?" Gaia wondered.

"She left for The Wall...to save *him*," he said.

"It's at least a two day journey from here to The Wall. She is not foolish enough to journey that far without supplies." Bellia stated.

"You are right, Bellia. She's probably packing now. We can catch her...stop her!" added Gaia.

Faras let out a laugh as he moved towards the holding pens where Kashta and Shabaka slept. He tossed them slabs of meat from a saltwater container and continued to laugh.

"Why do you laugh, Patron Faras?" Bellia asked.

"You taught her well. She thought of everything, you know. Because of the translation that told her she would have to go on without you two, she packed Reques days ago."

Bellia took a glance around the stable and saw Requi alone, now convinced Aleeia had indeed fled to The Wall.

> "Yes, by the time you pack, she will be half-a-day ahead of all of us. The Wall's guardians will have no reason to halt her, assuming Aleeia gets there before the Pharaoh's forces."

And so Aleeia was gone, leaving behind Gaia, Bellia, Meroe, Faras and their army with a day's distance to soon be between them. She made her way toward The Wall of Nubia to rescue Hat-kaptah from the torment of Alonard.

The Incursion Of Abydos - By way of Soxor on the eastern shore of Egypt, they came days and days ago. Alonard of the Western Bank of Avalon, First Son to Changel, came to the city of Abydos with a mission hard pressed within him. Determined to find *the power* Changel felt on Avalon, he arrived with just two others, leaving his crew at the harbors of Soxor. Mage-Sciona, the menacing huntress, entered the city at the right side of Alonard. Sciona dressed in blood-red leather straps that enwrapped her impressively strong feminine form from head to toe. She trotted on with her ear to the ground and her nose aloft, waiting for the smell of raw power to surface amongst her senses. With two small blades holstered to her thighs, Sciona prepared her skills to pick up the trail in Abydos. Xamare-Jacobb, the bloodthirsty juggernaut, stood at the left of Alonard. And although the massive behemoth stood taller than any Earth bound mortal, standing in the place of Vale-Kain was a test for Jacobb to prove his worth in his stead. Jacobb, despite the arid weather, wore the fur and carcasses of dozens of beasts he had slain.

"Have your senses discovered anything? Have you tasted *the power*?" Alonard inquired of Sciona.

"No, not yet, Master," replied Sciona whose alluring voice vibrated like a mesmerizing serpent.

"You find *power*! I KILL DEAD!"

Jacobb's voice sounded like a wild boar tried to speak. In a low grumble, he ranted with all the clarity that his meager wit could muster.

"Were those men in Soxor not enough for your insatiable bloodlust?" asked Alonard.

He spoke then paused awhile to stare deep into Jacobb's hollow, white eyes.

"I will only say this to you once, Jacobb! If you kill in this city without my order, you will be no more."

Alonard mandated and the huge, intimidating figure shrank away like a frightened dog.

In shimmering silver armor with an oddly dark

luster in its shadows, Alonard traveled through the streets of Abydos. All who witnessed his coming through the metropolis took notice and gave Alonard and his company the regard of foreign dignitaries, except for one.

Hat-kaptah had seen many comers and goers since the time Alee and her governesses departed, but took none of them at face value. He worked directly across from the Great Hall of Scrolls and Manuscripts, near the temple struck by Gaia's attacker. He kept a watchful eye on everyone as he toiled through the day. On that particular day, Hat-kaptah's concern grew considerably. He looked observantly upon the woman in the company. She said nothing but broke away from the two men accompanying her. She staggered randomly with her nose turned up. Her behavior seemed odd to Hat-kaptah, but the two men with her only paused and looked at her as though they expected it. She sniffed profusely with a scowl that crimpled her nose and brow. She moved as though overcome by some magnetic odor and frantically moved to the base of the temple.

"The smell is strongest here. It fades from the street.," said Sciona.

"Can you determine the origin of *the power*?" Alonard asked of Sciona.

"No." she replied.

Suddenly, Jacobb turned and met eyes with the young man at the base of the temple. The giant Xamare-Jacobb groaned and rumbled towards Hat-kaptah. Hat-kaptah was afraid though he held his ground and went back to his duties. The hulking man made his way towards him. Jacobb was upon him with his boulder-like fist raised high above Hat-kaptah's head ready to deliver a definite deathblow. Jacobb let out a horrific yell and began to drop his arms to deal out instant death, but suddenly he was halted.

"Jacobb." shouted Alonard.

The giant paused.

"Have you forgotten my order so quickly?" Alonard asked as he made his way towards the slave.

"You would have ended your life over a slave if I had not stopped you, and next time I will not."

Jacobb backed away. Alonard moved to the slave and looked him over. For a brief moment, Alonard second guessed his decision to bring the brute, realizing the alternative meant leaving his realm on Avalon bare of proper leadership as well as Changel without an able aide in his absence.

"You would do well not to stare or make eye contact with him again. Unless you wish to sign your life away with the act," explained Alonard to the slave.

"Thank you, Master." Hat-kaptah mumbled in his

own tongue with his eyes to the ground.

That slave did not even flinch. He's either too stupid to know his life hung by a strand or too disciplined to care. Alonard thought.

Hat-kaptah brought the words Gaia told him from the depth of his memory to the front of his mind. He prepared to go into the chasm and signal his warning from atop the buried tablet, but as he made plans to enter the Great Hall, he heard Alonard speak to Sciona.

> "Stay here and continue to assess the source and whereabouts of *the power*. Jacobb and I will go seek an audience with Pharaoh." Alonard said with a sinister smirk.
>
> "Yes, Master."

Alonard silently walked the streets and alleys of Abydos in the direction of the Pharaoh's stronghold. The Temple of Amon-Ra stood immaculate and pristine as a spectacle so readily visible that it was able to been seen from half-a-days distance away from the City of Abydos. To many other travelers and passersby, the temple would have inspired considerable awe and praise. Most people would have been so impressed by the landmark's vastness they would say the hands of the gods built the temple, but Alonard feigned the effects of the temple as he approached the sanctuary. Sarcastically, he awed, mocking the Temple and all those who ever laid eyes upon it. Onlookers who came to the Temple to present sacrifices and prayers fled. They feared to be near someone who dared to dishonor the gods.

"To look upon the meager labors of mortals is of great humor to me when compared to the majesty of what lies beyond the Mist." Alonard said as he came to the foot of the Temple's stairs.

Alonard climbed the stairs with Jacobb close behind. He reached the final step at the height of the Temple. Just outside the main corridor, he stopped before two sentinels. The two men were adorned with golden necklaces and head ornaments that resembled the columns that stood across the grounds. Alonard looked at the massive support pillar that was carved with the likeness of both man and bird, with the head of a phoenix and fiery eyes that peered down upon all who entered, Alonard laughed.

"Father, you always did like birds.," said Alonard to himself as he entered the Temple unhindered.

Back at The Great Hall of Scrolls and Manuscripts, Sciona continued her search for answers. Brought to these shores knowing her abilities as a tracker remained her ultimate responsibility, Sciona was left with a trail that had apparently gone cold. She concentrated intensely at the foot of the staircase. Hat-kaptah, still taxed with his mission to warn Gaia, examined the stoic Sciona for an opening into The Hall and down into the Chasm where the tablet lay buried. Sciona, seemingly immersed in some meditative trance, did not move or respond to the outside world, but Hat-kaptah made no move. He showed caution and went back to his labors once again. Even as he worked, Hat-kaptah made his senses as acute as possible. He felt that before he made contact with Gaia more information would be best. He saw Sciona and made note of her pale grey eyes and full, thick lips. They were the only signs of expression behind the dirty leather-straps that incased her entire face. Sciona sat and waited with a menacing smirk.

In the inner corridor of the Temple of Amon-Ra, two figures were surrounded by dozens of Egyptian warriors, protectors to the Pharaoh. From behind the circle came a voice engulfed in shadow that produced the authoritative vibration. The guardsmen halted and lowered their weapons from the two figures, which they deemed as hostile by the word of the mysterious figure.

"We seek the ear of Pharaoh," Alonard demanded.

"You seek death, strangers. No one enters the temple

under their own accord. Those who do have thus forfeited their life."

The voice was the Body of the Pharaoh, who was not the Pharaoh himself. Clad in silks and jewels with the Golden Helm of the Phoenix masking his face, the physical go-about of the Pharaoh questioned the intruders with all the authority of the living god he represented.

"State your business and if it suits the Body it may serve the Soul," said the emissary.

"I have no desire to share my concerns with underlings. However, I will allow you to lead me to the Pharaoh himself, and then divulge all that concerns you."

Without word from the Body, nearly sixty guardsmen lowered their lances and drew their swords the instant the stranger uttered his mocking reply. Similarly, Jacobb became riled and ready to move before an order from Alonard needed to be issued. The hunching behemoth still stood tall to the fright of the many guardsmen who were to challenge him. Jacobb's presence was enough to cause a standstill. He made no advancement however, for he was in no mood to anger Alonard with another disobedient aggression. Alonard waited. He saw the Body considering his advantage and reveling in it before he ordered death upon the strangers.

"Allow us to pass. Or die, all." Alonard blurted.

The order came swiftly from the Body. All the soldiers rushed against the strangers like a crashing wave. They moved in on Alonard, but were held back by some unknown force. And like a wave against a rocky shore, they broke against him as he stood there calmly. Jacobb, however, was the focus of Alonard's attention as he looked on safely. Jacobb bore wounds from several spears, but they were only as insect bites to him. His skin was tight and hard as stone. And with his stone-like hands he clubbed away at the sixty. He crushed skulls with his brutish strength. The guardsmen dwindled in number. Alonard looked on with a smile, for the same force that held his assailants at bay also kept the fearful guardsmen from escaping. When the guardsmen numbered only thirteen Alonard spoke.

> "Enough, my friend! I love the number thirteen! Such a fair and abundant number. Think about it. Thirteen. But I also love the number, one. Would you like to see the number, one, represented here, Sir?" Alonard asked, as he looked deep into the Body.

The Body of the Pharaoh quibbled. Astonished at the sight of an entire battalion of soldiers annihilated, he lost all godly and noble resolve. Slowly, he rose to his feet and led Alonard and Jacobb to the Pharaoh's altar-throne. The corridor opened to reveal the chambers of the Pharaoh. The hall was vast. Inside, the pillars bore the statues of the Egyptian Pantheon with Amon-Ra and Osiris the more prevalent. Upon the throne sat the Pharaoh. He wore a necklace of golden feathers and bracelets with jade jewels, which complimented the headdress fixed upon his shoulders. The headdress bore the animal likenesses of the snake, the phoenix, and the jackal. Alonard took notice of them. The Pharaoh did not move when the Body and strangers entered his hall. With all ease, he raised his hands to dismiss his priests and prepared to speak.

> "Interruption. Who does my Body bring forth? I commune with my Brethren in the Heavens in order to work our will on Earth. Speak."

With a tone that echoed against the ceiling, the Body fled from the presence of the strangers and left them to the wrath of Pharaoh. Alonard stared as the emissary departed and held back an overwhelming urge to explode with laughter. However, he made no mockery of the Pharaoh as he did outside the Temple.

> "Don't you recognize me, brother?" he asked.
>
> "You will surely be put to death. For all know I am not akin to any mortal." replied the Pharaoh with false resolve.

Alonard slowly walked towards the footed base of the altar-throne. Pharaoh called to his Body and guardsmen to halt Alonard's advancement.

> "Guards, kill these infidels.," said the Pharaoh as Alonard lurked ever closer.

But the true man, who by birth was fed the lies and mantle of the Pharaoh, felt a real fear upon him as no guards or servant came to his summons. Face to face with the Pharaoh, Alonard laughed aloud with all the intensity he held back earlier. Jacobb stood silently still below. Alonard suddenly ceased laughing and peered into the face of Pharaoh. The Pharaoh looked back upon his face. Fear increased greatly in the man who was Pharaoh. The face of Alonard boiled and twitched. To the Pharaoh it looked as if something beneath the stranger's face fought to escape. A jackal-like snout peered and protruded in waves. The Pharaoh, though utterly fearful, was wise and clever. He feigned calmness in order to speak.

> "Ah! Yes, Brother, it is a strange form you take these days. What brings you here, Lord of the Dead?" said Pharaoh.

Alonard smiled within himself for he knew the clever tact used by the Pharaoh was fully to his design. Alonard now had the ear of the Pharaoh who knew he himself was no god. But still, Pharaoh believed himself divine enough to carry one in company. Alonard stepped back from the altar-throne where Jacobb stood like a hibernating beast below.

"Brother, I know your eyes are ever watchful upon this Earthly realm. Have your senses and far reaching hands touched anything of a peculiar nature?" Alonard asked of the Pharaoh.

The Pharaoh paused and let his mind review the innumerable issues of news that passed before him. Being careful that the question posed was not a test, the Pharaoh went back to the most obvious and bizarre occurrence of memory.

"Well, Brother, the ground shook for a day when the Great Hall of Scrolls and Manuscripts jumped."

"And do you know who is accountable for that?" Alonard asked.

The Pharaoh still pondered these questions for a riddle, which the Jackal-god knew full well the true answer. And fearing a wrong answer before a god, Pharaoh set his mind to work again. He replied as cleverly as possible.

"There are few witnesses. I, myself, was in a deep slumber of spirit that spanned far before the quake, but I do recall my Body spoke of three, often cloaked, who frequented the Hall from the Southeast Inn."

Jacobb stirred. He could smell the growing stench of fear, which poured from the Pharaoh. Alonard perceived it as well. Thus, having the ear of the Pharaoh and a slight of information, Alonard rested on his questions. He was satisfied with the intimidating control he now wielded over the Pharaoh.

> "Thank you, Brother. I will stay here for a period unknown. Prepare a throne beside you. But for now send a dozen of what is left of your temple guardsmen to the Hall to keep watch," said Alonard.

Alonard and Jacobb departed the Temple of Amon-Ra and the company of the Pharaoh who was still fearful. The Pharaoh exhaled frantically as he marveled at his own genius, for he was still alive. He then commanded the order for Alonard.

Within a few moments, Alonard was back at the Hall among Sciona, Jacobb, and the temple guardsmen he requested. Sciona still examined the street and broken temple wall and made no progress in finding the source of *the power* despite hours of hunting and tracking. Hat-kaptah was still there, even as the sun neared setting. All but a few laborers remained behind with him. Hat-kaptah saw the guards take to their posts and decided he would better accomplish his goal by retreating to his quarters, then returning in the dark of night. Hat-kaptah left the foot of the Great Hall and made his way to the small mudholes beyond the center of the city. As he departed, Alonard took notice of him as the last slave to leave. He thought to himself, he might make a fair witness on the morrow.

Moving towards the mudholes of Abydos and the forgotten borough of the city, Hat-kaptah committed the positioning of the guardsmen to memory. He heard by the order from Alonard, four at the foot of the Hall's stairs, two outside the main corridor, two inside, two at the height of the Chasm, and two within the Chasm's depths. With the men set, Alonard and Sciona went into the Hall as Jacobb waited. The mounts and shelves of books stirred Alonard. He had been an avid pupil of lore under Changel. Sciona, though, was not impressed. Her interests lay only in the experience of primal physical pleasures such as hunting among the lot. She shadowed Alonard. He sat amongst a hive of maps that marked the lands near and far beyond the sea. She touched him and leaned over his shoulder to stroke his chest. Alonard ignored Sciona and her frequent seductive attempts at satisfying her incessant lusts.

> "Master, the lights are dim in this place and any onlookers would be more than welcome for my taste." Sciona whispered, "Will you deny me here, Alonard? Master? It has been too long since you last touched me."

Alonard pushed away the arms of Sciona and rose from

where he sat. He turned and peered at her. Sciona was still. Whether by the pure will of Alonard or the intimidation he impressed upon her, she did not move as he looked about the Hall.

> "Here in this place with all its knowledge of space and secrets in time, you wish to satisfy your animal-like desires, just as Xamare-Jacobb wants to kill and maim as a manner of fulfilling joyful instinct. I fear for the two of you. When Changel has brought peace to this Realm and your thoughtless desires and barbaric skills are no longer an asset, you will not survive in the New World. I strongly suggest you find more in life and show passion for more than what simply lies within you. Otherwise, and I will say this again, you will become a tool that is no longer needed. And like any other useless tools, you will be cast to the wind and fall into the fire."

Alonard made his way to the Chasm. Sciona silently followed after briefly looking over a scroll, which she then tossed back amongst the pile. Alonard sighed for her and what was possibly the destiny of many who gathered beyond the Mist. Alonard passed the guards and stepped slowly downward into the Chasm. Looking about its dank hollows, Alonard saw the arches and pillars as well as the markings on the walls.

"Here of all places, for me who has seen so much, to see something of such beauty like I have never seen before," Alonard remarked, while he touched the symbols, not knowing what they meant.

"Sciona, do you feel the history of this place? The answer must lie in the scrolls above."

Midway down the stairs, Sciona coughed and hacked. The stale uncirculated air inundated her highly acute sense of smell and taste. She covered her mouth with a squinting wrinkle about her nose and brow.

"What is it?" Alonard asked, reading Sciona's displeasure.

"Time is static in the air of this place. The odors of dozens of comers and goers still roam about," she said.

"And can you find the strongest amongst them? The Pharaoh said no one has entered after the quake since the three who studied here."

Sciona removed her hand from her lips and took in a deep breath, which choked her. She held it in order to distinguish the flavors among it. The eyes of Sciona watered before she spat then spoke.

"Strongest I taste are three who bled, but there is another musk that is all too familiar," Sciona replied as she showed her obvious discomfort to Alonard.

He replied and gave her leave to get relief from outside the Hall. Alone in the dimmed dark of the Chasm, Alonard thought about what Sciona said. He grabbed a handful of dirt from the floor and cast it aside.

> "I think the Pharaoh knows more about the three than he let on; trying to outwit me for the sake of saving his life," Alonard said to himself, "I can learn no more from this place as of now. It is time I rested for the sun is low."

Alonard left the Great Hall of Scrolls and Manuscripts as dusk settled. He walked back to the Palace of Obelisk with Jacobb and Sciona. The Pharaoh offered them kingly rooms in which to rest and continue the search to follow the trail that was growing clearer. Sciona was allowed to sleep in the vacant dwellings that formerly belonged to the Pharaoh's Daughter and found the accommodations to her liking. Jacobb was given the room belonging to the Pharaoh's body who was never again seen in Egypt, but was quickly replaced by the next able priest of Amon-Ra. Jacobb did not care for where he slept. Even in the plush trappings of his room, he slept on the floor, the bed too small and frail to satisfy. As for Alonard, although he was offered his pick of seven rooms, which the Pharaoh shuffled in use, he picked none. He did not sleep that night.

Usurpation - Alonard stirred awake all night thinking. The morning brought the return of a captain in a distant land. From Obelisk, the palace adjacent to the Temple of Amon-Ra, Alonard made his way to the throne room at the Temple to speak again with Pharaoh. Alonard pondered whether it was fair to associate the three that the Pharaoh spoke of with the women whom Sciona uncovered in the Chasm.

"What matters do three women have in a chasm of a house of knowledge? Ah, but Sciona caught wind of another," he said aloud.

Alonard returned to the Temple alone. Sciona still slept and Jacobb gorged on his fifth ration of breakfast. As he entered, Alonard's presence was met with reverence from all he passed. The priest and magistrates followed him. He walked to the Pharaoh's altar-throne while every soldier-guardsman shrank away and bowed before he whom they knew to be a god. Beside the Pharaoh was his own mantle, on which Alonard sat. The Pharaoh prepared his wits and continued to secure his claim of equal stature with Alonard. He was certain that Alonard was Anubis, jackal god and shepherd of the dead.

"Did the night please you, Brother?" asked the Pharaoh.

"Yes, and so did your news of the three," replied

Alonard. "Tell me, Pharaoh, do you know to where they departed?"

The Pharaoh once again feared a riddle as a trap and manner for him to forsake his claim as an immortal vessel. However, through arrogance he was less afraid and more confident to play his game. The Pharaoh stood and descended from where he sat. His mind was in full motion.

"They walked towards the Nubian Sands, Kush," said Pharaoh.

"Are you sure of this?" inquired Alonard of Pharaoh.

"As sure as I am of the soldiers who witnessed it. Remember, Brother, I told you, I slept."

Alonard took in what Pharaoh said although the arrogance he perceived annoyed him. Pharaoh reascended his altar-throne and sat beside Alonard again. The new Body of the Pharaoh came forth with all the news to be read before them.

"Soul of the Land, Great Pharaoh, I have seen and heard and touched the people of the mortal realm and they have these things to say: Your daughter plans to wed the Nubian Prince. The Nubians do not retreat from the outer cataracts of the Great River. They do not stay behind their wall. The marauders from across the sea have departed back from the Northern Port. A slave was seen trespassing at The Great Hall of Scrolls and Manuscripts in the dead of night. The guardsmen killed yesterday have been buried and replaced--"

Alonard took in all that the Body had read but more importantly he was concerned with the news of the trespasser. Thus, he interrupted and addressed the Body.

"The trespasser at the Hall? What of that news? Speak." Alonard commanded in interruption.

"A young man seen at the Hall was identified as a slave who labors at the nearby temple," said the Body.

"Was he captured?" asked Alonard.

"No, he claimed to have left some belonging near the temple and thus was not seized nor slain," answered the Body.

Alonard moved as soon as the last word came forth from the Body. He went with all speed back to the Obelisk and sought out Sciona. He came upon her bathing in her quarters. Sciona saw Alonard. Knowing his mind, she stood tall from the waters. Sciona took her two leather straps and began wrapping herself from her ankles up to the top of her head. Now clothed before Alonard, she went with him without a word. In mere moments, they were back at the Hall amongst the guardsmen and the laborers who toiled on the nearby temple. Sciona was moved as she looked at Alonard. Their minds connected as he spoke to her.

"What story do your senses tell, Sciona? Tell me of the three!"

Sciona moved about hundreds of slaves. The fourth musk from the Chasm was faint amongst them.

"Be wary of the slave who had eyes upon us all the day before," added Alonard.

He was nearly certain that he was the one whom they sought. Alonard was the first to lay eyes upon him but the slave did not alter his work. Hat-kaptah spied Alonard and Sciona who approached.

"Him, Sciona. Walk by him and if it is he, continue past them all and meet me 'round the huddle," instructed Alonard.

Sciona lurked and kept herself open. However, like some demonic hound she knew that he was once in the Chasm. Sciona doubled back and showed no awareness of the slave, known as Hat-kaptah. She came back round to Alonard.

"What does this mean, Master?"

"Aside from the obvious, it means we set a trap! He was there with the three who by now are either in or beyond Kush," replied Alonard. "But why does he lurk and creep by the Hall? What is there months after they have left? Yes, I know what we must now do."

When Hat-kaptah saw Alonard and Sciona about the laborers that day, he was afraid. He thought his failure to negotiate the guards the night before placed himself in grave danger, even though they did not move on him. Time grew shorter for him, or so he felt. He made plans to secure the tablet and send his message as soon as possible.

A short while later, back at the Temple of Amon-Ra, Alonard and Sciona along with Jacobb pressed themselves upon the Pharaoh once again. Alonard took his seat beside him again and began to put his plan into motion.

"Pharaoh, what are your plans for the Nubian's? Will you march on them?"

"Although my daughter is dead to me and the water is precious, Egypt has not warred with Kush since the last Dynasty of long ago," Pharaoh replied.

Pharaoh spoke plainly and felt no need to be cryptic in his reply. Alonard heard the complacency in his explanation as it lacked the resolve to carry on his deception. Alonard for the sake of his motives picked apart the Pharaoh.

"What does war matter to a god? It is but a trifle, a means to an end. It is of no consequence to the everlasting." Alonard stated.

"Of course, but I wish it not, my brother," replied Pharaoh nervously.

"Send your forces out on Kush at once. I wish to see the pleasures of a great battle."

"But not I, Brother." said the Pharaoh, seeming stern.

"Brother?" replied Alonard as he lost his patience.

"You are a mortal and are subject to the death that binds you to the sands. Surely enough, you are greater than most mortals for you have wealth and a legacy of lies that tie you to something great. But you are no god, and comparatively, I am. So I will ***ask*** you again to throw all your forces at the Wall of Nubia."

Pharaoh stood speechless as Sciona and Jacobb looked on. Pharaoh heard the ultimatum of Alonard and thus he responded thinking he could stay in the deception.

"Comparatively, Brother? You humor me.," said Pharaoh.

"And you anger me. Jacobb, kill him." ordered Alonard.

Jacobb moved slowly. Alonard threw the Pharaoh from his altar-throne. The Pharaoh's mouth moved but no sound came from it. He grabbed his throat and scurried about like a wounded bird. Jacobb crept ever closer as Alonard destroyed the altar-throne the Pharaoh formerly occupied. Alonard sat alone atop the mantle in his throne and took the form of Pharaoh. Pharaoh looked upon Alonard as himself and pleaded upon his knees. Pharaoh-Alonard removed the sting, which made the Pharaoh mute in order to listen to his final cries. Jacobb's shadow cast itself upon Pharaoh. He raised his left foot high above the Pharaoh and lowered it violently. He crushed the Pharaoh's legs into one bloody gushing pulp. The Pharaoh let out a horrific scream.

> "So Pharaoh, did you ever dream you would see yourself so vividly when you met your end?" uttered Pharaoh-Alonard.

Jacobb lifted the Pharaoh with his bare hands by his head and mutilated legs. And as Pharaoh-Alonard waved his arm, Jacobb tore him asunder. Thus passed the Pharaoh, here unnamed, whose Earthly presence persisted long beyond the span of his lifetime. For he moved Egypt to war against Kush.

Raptus Cruciatusque Hat-katptus - The Cities of Egypt were uneasy as they mustered and dispatched soldiers towards Kush. Abydos was the first among them to do so. Everyone within the nation knew the mind of the Pharaoh and Hat-kaptah was one of them. Pharaoh wanted to fiercely conquer the Nubian Sands. Every night since the order, Hat-kaptah desired to infiltrate the Great Hall, but could not risk another capture as time grew shorter. However, as the days went by and the armies assembled, Hat-kaptah noticed the dwindling numbers of the twelve who guarded the Hall. He decided to wait until they were few enough to where he could make safe passage into the Chasm. Day by day, they left in pairs. Hat-kaptah was both certain and impatient. Tonight, he would make his move.

"What news of the slave?" inquired Alonard still in the guise of Pharaoh.

"Every night he stalks the grounds," replied Sciona.

"And does he suspect anything?" asked Alonard.

"No, Master, he has showed no signs," said Sciona.

"Good. Ready the troops for tonight, for he will surely make a move with our armies moving ever closer to those with whom he conspired. Then, he will reveal them and their secrets that lie in that Chasm to me."

Throughout the day, Abydos stirred as the weight of war moved its people. Night fell on the bare streets that were lit with the lanterns of the stars. A young man roamed. He moved towards the Hall with a cat-like stealth that had allowed him to elude spot and capture. Hat-kaptah entered with comfort and dread knowing that nearly every soldier marched for Kush. Hat-kaptah thought about the safety of

Gaia, Bellia, and especially Alee as weeks went by without his warning. And now so close to the Chasm and the tablet, Hat-kaptah's thoughts turned back to his fondness for Alee. He regarded her as strong and true as well as able to handle any challenge that came forthright. Inside the Hall, Hat-kaptah descended into the dank Chasm. In the center of the room, he moved aside the dirt and rock that covered the buried tablet. Atop the tablet, Hat-kaptah stood fearful. He knew full well the vast power Gaia held as he braced himself.

"I know the power in these words, for I have seen the wonders of Gaia and Alee," Hat-kaptah uttered. He made himself ready, while recalling the words that were pressed into his memory. And with a final long, deep breath, Hat-kaptah spoke:

Verba mentium traciecto caelo it

Suddenly, the dirt unsettled and a muggy wind swirled in the Chasm. The dank room shifted from cold and damp to dry and hot. Hat-kaptah began panting through the swirling humid air that was hard to take in. His muscles burned. His eyes flared and widened as if a fire was lit behind them. The extent of the pain and discomfort he felt was unexpected. As he stood there, somewhere another felt the tugs and scars that Hat-kaptah felt and thus she was assisted to the safety of Adindan. Hat-kaptah quickly regained his resolve. The laborious days greatly exceeded the pain, which only caught him off guard. Hat-kaptah tried to speak despite the air and his fatigue, but no sound came forth. With every attempt to speak, Hat-kaptah felt like something held back his voice. Hat-kaptah grew dizzier and weaker as Gaia, now in Adindan, was equally distraught. At last, as the winds swirled faster and the heat became more intense, Hat-kaptah brought forth all the essential information he could cram into a single breath. He finally let out the warning that had burdened his thoughts for many months.

The warning was sent and received. Soldiers waited and listened at the height of the stairs then moved by their orders. Entering the Chasm, they surrounded Hat-kaptah. Sciona walked slowly down the stairs and gave the command.

"Seize him." She said.

And Hat-kaptah replied with a single word. A name,

"Alee."

The name marked the warning's end. His connection was severed, the winds ceased, and the coldness returned to the Chasm. In a breath, the soldiers had him. Too weak to fight,

Hat-kaptah lunged at the first comer throwing the strongest right fist he could muster, but he was struck at the back of the neck from behind before the blow could meet its destination.

Sciona loomed over the fallen body, which lay still in the hollow Chasm. She examined him to give his scent her final confirmation. Sciona did not know what to make of what she had seen. The light and wind that made the Chasm so filled with heat was amazing to her, even as one who dwelt behind the Mist.

"Take him to Pharaoh!" Sciona commanded.

The guardsmen took Hat-kaptah and bound him at the ankles and wrists. They lifted him across two soldiers and held him by either end of a lance by which he hung. The Chasm was emptied. All made their way towards the Temple, save Sciona. She lingered behind in the Chasm and kneeled beside the uncovered tablet from which she could not read.

"I feel many of the Master's questions have answers that lie with this," she said.

Sciona rose quickly and made her way back to the Temple of Amon-Ra. She cared little for answers or questions. She simply wanted to see what pain and suffering awaited the young slave.

In the Temple of Amon-Ra, a young slave bound in

chains slowly regained consciousness. As his eyes brought all that was blurry into focus, Hat-kaptah looked about the vast hall with amazement. He had never before walked within the vast Temple. Alone, Hat-kaptah struggled to free himself. He stood before a small flight of stairs with an astonishingly regal altar-throne upon them.

"What happened? Where am I?" Hat-kaptah asked of himself.

Hat-kaptah's head still pounded and his ankles were severely bruised. He tried to remember how he came to be there. The last thing he remembered was saying the words to contact Gaia, and feeling intense pain. Everything that followed was hazy and then black.

"I hope Gaia received my warning," he thought.

Suddenly, the humongous doors of the Temple throne room opened and a small company entered. Pharaoh-Alonard, Sciona, and Jacobb walked with the Magistrates of Abydos and took their places. Pharaoh-Alonard atop the throne, Sciona to his right and Jacobb stood at the left as the Magistrates prepared their tools for questioning at the base of the altar-throne stairs. As the Magistrates heated the cinders and sharpened the blades, Hat-kaptah knew what was to come. He remained brave and calm. Quickly, he reverted to the mannerisms of a simple slave, but also prepared to meditate. Before Gaia departed with Alee, Hat-kaptah's last lesson involved the separation of mind and body through intense meditation and strength of spirit. Almost a daze or numbness, Hat-kaptah used the same skill and discipline to work and toil under the pains of hardships. Shortly after acquiring the skill, Hat-kaptah had felt an overwhelming guilt for his enslaved brethren who could not do the same. Hat-kaptah's ability to separate his mind from his body improved with use, but now it was not as acute from being unused. As the Pharaoh spoke, Hat-kaptah knew he would soon need the benefits of meditation.

> "There are roles mortals play in life: soldiers war, artisans create, clergymen pray, scholars study, and slaves toil. Tell me slave, how has your role brought you to The Great Hall of Scrolls and Manuscripts on this cold, dead night?"

Hat-kaptah spoke words of praise and blessings in his own tongue before the questions posed by the Pharaoh. Ignorance was the best ploy for now, Hat-kaptah thought. But the Pharaoh saw through it easily, given the knowledge he received from all who witnessed him in the Chasm. The Pharaoh raised his hand and motioned two more Magistrates to enter. They carried with them a huge tablet of foreign stone. When Hat-kaptah saw the tablet, he understood what transpired. *I did send the message. They followed me.* He thought to himself as the tablet was dropped, crashing before him.

"My patience is a fragile thing. And as it stands now your life is in your hands, but that can change quickly as my patience is stretched along with my mercy," said Pharaoh.

Hat-kaptah, despite his heroic resolve, feared for his own well-being as the Magistrates placed the tip of their blades in the fiery cinders. He closed his eyes and distanced himself from thoughts of people and places that would steady him and return his courage.

"You still sit silent?" asked the Pharaoh.

The Pharaoh-Alonard arose from his altar-throne and descended before the slave tightly bound to the walls and ceiling of the Temple. Pharaoh-Alonard looked deep into the eyes of Hat-kaptah. He tried reading the stories, which lay within them. Hat-kaptah's eyes were glazed over in deep meditation and revealed nothing of his mind as they peered past Pharaoh. But the Pharaoh's stare did not come back empty. He found no clue to any answers from the mind. But Pharaoh-Alonard looked into Hat-kaptah's heart and discovered the source of his courage and resolve.

"Ah, there is that name again…Alee. You spoke it once in the Chasm and now your heart is focused on it."

"Who is this Alee?" the Pharaoh asked.

Hat-kaptah grew angrier and more fearful. His trance faltered and weakened. The simple horror of her gracious name coming from such a wicked mouth gave him a chilling worry. Hat-kaptah's teeth clenched for a moment. He tried to regain control over his emotions and maintain his body's tranquil composure.

"Nothing still? So it seems it is of no consequence to you that the one called Alee in the Lands of Kush will not see the coming of a new season, Alee ***will*** die."

"Don't you touch her," Hat-kaptah shouted in plain tongue.

Hat-kaptah lunged at the Pharaoh from the strains that held him. Fully enraged, Hat-kaptah's fear and anger grew again as it mounted over the safety and well-being of Alee. Hat-kaptah saw the smirk of Sciona and then heard the rumbling grin of Jacobb. He knew Pharaoh was the one who completed the wicked trinity that came to Abydos. All resolve was gone from the once stoic slave and Pharaoh-Alonard took that as the affirmation of what he knew. Alee was one of three whom they sought in Kush.

"Without inflicting any pain, I have all the information I need from you. But as you sit here

> torrid in your own anger, you no longer have the strength to dull the torture that will ensue as tonight's entertainment. But take heart, your new role carries an extremely greater level of importance as both entertainment and bait. And yes, we all have our roles to play," said Pharaoh-Alonard.

Alonard reascended the altar-throne to the sounds of the young slave's horrific screams. The Magistrates instituted a slow and arduous torture. For hours upon hours, the hot blades met the body of Hat-kaptah from the fiery cinders. Hat-kaptah, never having time nor pause to protect his body, grew weaker of mind. The pain grew increasingly intense. Hat-kaptah told more in pain than he thought he knew. Sciona had her turn in the tortures, all the while reveling in them. She took Hat-kaptah to the edge where the abyss of lifelessness loomed. Finally, Hat-kaptah lay bruised and broken, struggling to breathe, in a cell at the base of Obelisk, where he would stay until transported to the camp just outside of Nubia.

Siege of the Wall - Alee was two days ahead of the winds that stirred one of two great waves that would meet at the Wall. The armies of Nubia led by Meroe and Faras to reinforce the Wall of Nubia rumbled in thousands behind her. Upon Reques, Alee rode on to save Hat-kaptah who was the unknown key to be used in the Barren Sea, although he meant much more to her than that. She galloped towards the Wall. Blind to the troubles beyond it, Alee came to Nuri, the Second City, the Realm of the Nubian Prince and Egyptian Princess, where Buhen Chieftain of the Ninth Ring of Dorginarti held trade and bartership.

As though Fate knew Alee needed the favor of time, Alee reached Buhen as soon as she entered the outskirts of Nuri. There, he packed his caravan for the return trip to Dorginarti with all the treasures and goods native to Nuri artisans. Alee and Buhen met again, to the surprise of the elder Chieftain.

> "Gracious child, brave lady. What brings you and I together so soon?" Buhen looked her over and asked, "Where are your Matrons? Where are Gaia and Bellia?"

Buhen did not know her story completely, but knew enough to sense trouble after he saw her alone without the two who cared for and valued her so greatly.

> "There is little time, Master Buhen! The Wall will be struck in less than two days and Meroe and her defenders are at least that far behind. The few garrisons that hold strong at the Wall will only last the initial rush. If the Prince forgoes his subtle

offenses and dispatches Nuri's western infantry to the Wall then we may have a chance."

Alee spoke intently. Buhen listened hesistantly. He knew that to ring a bell of war was one that could not be undone.

"Alee, are you sure? I mean, how is it that you have come to find this and be the only one sent forth? If what you say is true, then why is General Meroe so far behind?" Buhen wondered.

Alee interrupted before Buhen could pose any other questions.

"I ride to rescue he who has warned us, but certain circumstances allowed me to be ready for the journey in advance. Listen," Alee said with a softened passion, "In the short time you have known me, you know I have come to accept the harsh truths of fate. Fate will not allow me to be wrong because I am **not**. And fate will not allow you to distrust me because you **cannot**."

Buhen looked deep into Alee and knew she spoke wisdom and truth. He simply nodded as he unhinged the caravan wagon and lightened the load of his horse. Buhen turned to Alee atop Reques.

"Good luck, young matron." he said.

"Thank you. Thank you for everything." Alee replied as she rode with the sun high towards the

Wall of Nubia.

Buhen rode to the Nuri Tower where the Prince of Nubia kept his beauty and love, the Princess of Egypt. With the small bits of information given to him by Alee, Buhen only hoped the Prince would hearken and heed the warning for the sake of all of Kush. Buhen also hoped his former name and reputation would carry the burden of Alee’s warning, which came like lightning with a clamorous thunder. He arrived at the Tower of Nuri, which stood tall and wide. The Tower of Nuri was home to Kushite princes since the Third Dynasty whereas Dorginarti was made for the first Kushite Princess who ruled ages later.

“Where kings learn to rule a kingdom.” Buhen said as he came to the guarded gates.

“Who goes?” asked a Nuri sentinel.

“Buhen! Chieftain of the Ninth Ring of Dorginarti, Former Patron of Guard, and Ambassador to Princess Aalarae. I have news and counsel for the Prince.”

Buhen showed confidence as he embellished his titles, past and present. The sentinel knew the name and the face, which had been to Nuri before on matters of trade and diplomacy. Buhen was held only for a moment so his coming to the

Prince might be announced.

He entered the base of the Nuri Tower where the Prince sat side by side with his Princess. Buhen marveled at the man before him. He had not seen the reclusive Prince since the days of his youth. Tall with skin like gold and eyes like *nuri,* the prince stood in long robes of grey and white with an unkempt bread that added to him a kingly aura. The Princess looked on and walked towards Buhen. She wore the similar dress of white and grey with a gold-jade bracelet that marked her ties to her lands and people.

> "Hail and blessings to Prince Ashur and his lovely wife to be, Princess Atratah of Egypt," greeted Buhen.

He bowed with all the manners of etiquette time and repetition had afforded him. Buhen arose and made his plea as the whip of haste was upon the entire nation.

> "Prince Ashur, the forces of Egypt are moving towards Kush. The Wall is bare and reinforcements are more than two days behind. Prince, I know you have hesitations for the love of your bride, but please allow the same love to move you to protect her new home. Your forces can be at the Wall by nightfall."

The Prince paused pondering the words that came from the trusted Buhen. He then looked over to his beautiful wife.

Open war with her people would cause great sorrow for Atratah, the Forsaken Daughter of Pharaoh. Prince Ashur knew that and turned to Buhen and began his heartfelt reply.

> "You are right, wise Buhen. And I would do my all to protect my realm, its people, and my bride, but there are two conditions before you that hinder my decision. First and foremost, you must know I would never do anything to hurt my dear Atratah. Though her heart is here, her home lies beyond the Wall. So ask my Princess for her grace and blessings in this matter and the first condition will be met."

Buhen approached Princess Atratah, moving subtly before speaking. He did not know the Pharaoh's daughter. However, her love for the Nubian Prince was well known throughout the Land of Kush. Thus, Buhen spoke of love as it was his only card to play.

> "Princess Atratah, many blessings to you. I know the pains of being away from home, although I cannot imagine being cast out of a family. I would say that your love for our Prince should compel you to answer the call, but I would not dare cheapen your thoughts and feelings with such a ploy. All I can say is that you should show grace to your home."

The Egyptian Princess stood and walked beside Ashur. She held his hand. Atratah looked at Buhen with an expressionless beauty upon her face.

"Home, you say? True, I have been banished but Egypt will forever be tied to me." she said as Buhen felt enveloped by the cloud of failure.

"But my home is here where I am loved not only by my Prince, but by his people. I have been welcomed here and I walk as a Nubian with no shame. So, if Egypt comes to harm this land's good people then so be it if ***we*** wish to protect it. You have my blessings, Buhen."

Buhen was pleased but showed no signs of contentment for he knew not the second condition yet to be presented by Prince Ashur.

Meanwhile, somewhere outside of Nuri, the sands vallied as Alee saw the Wall of Nubia set upon the horizon. Alee, now only a few hours away and the sight of the Wall in a fair state, was pleased. However, she could not determine much from such a distance. *I may have arrived too early*. Alee thought. *If I pass beyond the Wall too soon, then I will surely be captured as I ride alone with no cover on the desert sands, but if I wait too late then the Wall's siege will begin and passage past the gate will be barred.* Alee continued pondering the dilemma as she took a sip of water from her jug. She placed a sizable portion in a bowl for Reques.

"Yes, I know," Alee said to Reques as he drank. "Even as the sun begins to fall, it remains hot."

Back at The Tower of Nuri, a silence was broken as Buhen awaited the second condition. The Princess had retired to her chambers and now Buhen and Prince Ashur were alone on the top floor of the Tower. There, at the top, was the Bell of Tabiry, which called the warriors of Nuri to arms throughout the ages. Buhen stood before the entire city with the Prince.

"It does my heart well to hear my Princess call this place home," he said.

"Indeed," replied Buhen.

"But there is another condition set before you," stated Prince Ashur, "The Nuri captains left to greet the new Kushite General, Meroe, in Dorginarti. The soldiers wait here ready but leaderless."

Buhen thought over the second condition and searched for a solution for the problem presented. Looking out over the city, Buhen turned to the Prince in order to get a better assessment of the situation. He went down the ranks to ask the Prince for a skilled or worthy soldier to command Nuri's army, at least long enough to hold the Wall until Faras and

Meroe arrived.

"I am sorry, Buhen. But it seems, I cannot grant your request. Even for the sake of your warning, I must at least wait until the captains are back and the threat is upon us."

Buhen became frustrated as the door was closing on his audience with the Prince. He needed an urgent solution to settle the second condition. And from the depths of his mind came a solution that would seemingly satisfy the need.

"Prince Ashur," said Buhen as he turned to face him, "Please, allow me to captain the soldiers. Our land depends on someone who can champion the Wall for a full day at least."

The Prince was taken aback by the proposal. He knew Buhen was once a great leader of men, back in a time before he ever breathed the Nubian air. Knowing the name of Buhen still drew awe-inspired whispers among the soldiers even today, Prince Ashur had no question of his worthiness, but his skill remained a question.

"Buhen, if you were to lead would it be from afar, atop the perch of the Wall? Strategy becomes useless if it cannot be adapted within the battle," he said.

"Indeed, Prince. I know the roles of a captain and Patron of Guard and I ask for them now. What hope does Nubia have otherwise? Trust in me, Prince, as your father before you," Buhen pleaded.

Prince Ashur was quiet for but a moment. He saw the passion and fire that stirred within the spirit of Buhen.

"I cannot deny you, sir. Not only because there is so much at stake, but because I see in you the strength to lead."

Prince Ashur stepped aside. He left Buhen steadfast at the base of the Bell of Tabiry. Buhen pondered the times before that the great leaders of Nubia stood in the very same spot. *To call upon a land's people from their homes to fight and die would be cruel, if not their fighting meant the protection of the families in those homes.* His thought ended there as Buhen grasped the mallet that lay beside Tabiry. Beautifully made with an artistry and skill older than the city itself, Buhen raised the mallet's wooden handle and bronze striker and proceeded to swing the metal striker engraved with the names of all the warriors, men and women, who had held it. Inside the Bell of Tabiry, a balanced pendulum hung, weighted at the bottom of the chains with a five-sided bronze ringer. The ringer was such that two beams crossed right and a third beam stretched longer through the center of the two beams. The center bronze beam peeked through two circular holes on opposite sides of the Bell, where

Buhen was to strike.

> "Hit the center beam with your all and I assure you it will be heard as far as the Wall!" The Prince boasted.

Tabiry rang out. Many men afar heard its low bellowing chime. It stretched out its call like an ocean wave. For Alee, her back was warmed. She walked out of the sun towards the Wall. The sound was faint, but sure enough, it was heard as Alee lurked closer to the Wall of Nubia. With Reques left behind, Alee crept from dune to dune as the soldiers at the Wall stirred with uncertainty at the chime of a bell long silent. The soldiers looked back into the sun, low and bright and saw nothing but the dunes' shadows.

At the base of the Nuri Tower, warriors gathered in numbers that far exceeded any Buhen had envisioned. Swelling so intensely that the boundaries of the courtyard could no longer contain them all, their eyes skyward, fixed on the Bell Tower. They awaited the words of the Prince and he who would lead them. In regimen, in file, and as legions, the last trickle of warriors settled beneath the Bell of Tabiry. Prince Ashur raised his hand to calm the crowd, and orated.

> "All who are here are here for the love of home. Nubia is threatened at the East and I charge you to protect it! Time is against us so my words shall be

few. Follow Buhen, whose exploits surpass legend. Follow Buhen, whose warning gives us a chance to live free. Follow Buhen and fight our oppressors head on. Follow Buhen and fight for Nuri."

Buhen rang the bell and went to meet his men. With no words of introduction or orders necessary those in his charge knew him and saw a fierce lion behind his eyes. Buhen's hand raised with the wooden and bronze mallet, which struck Tabiry, clenched tightly in hand. He soon rode with an army behind him.

Dusk brought darkness in the East. The rouse that came from the faint sound of Tabiry had ceased for some time. The Wall was still as the Egyptian forces came silently towards the Portal of Nubia at the Center of the Wall. Sitting on higher ground, the Wall gave the Egyptian forces no chance of a silent siege. Thus, as the sun finally gave way to the night, a sentinel atop the Wall saw a single flare of fire. When the sentinel knew that the torch seen from afar was no myth of his own vigilance, a great many more appeared lighting the east as if the sun was rising again.

"To arms! To arms! An enemy is upon us!"

Alee heard the clamor and shouts of the sentinels. She sat with her back against the Wall in a pocket of stealth. She knew it would not be long now, for the siege was upon them.

Buhen pushed his forces relentlessly. The Nuri-Nubians were still hours away from the Portal. Time was not an ally, but they raced with a speed and thunder never before experienced by rider nor horse. Buhen knew that still they would arrive to a battle already underway. *Will we make it in time to stand and at least face the winds of our enemy?* Thought Buhen. *Or will we arrive in time to see what stands now be blown away?*

Buhen rode on. The battle began. The first lance was thrown and the first man, a Kushite, fell. Alee raised her hood and entered the gate of the stronghold. Unheeded nor held, she roamed within the Wall freely, for all the soldiers were engaged in battle. Alee outwardly remained calm despite the unsettling conditions that surrounded her. She focused and prepared for the tasks to come and searched the kitchen for food and supplies. Bread and water brought her thus far but her body desired something more for sustenance. She found her way to the kitchen filled with fruits from far-off lands as well as milk and meat. She prepared a plate and sat there in relative silence. Despite her calm manner, her mind was slowly falling apart as she heard the screams from the battle outside. The sound of soldiers fighting and dying echoed. Alee also wondered about the present condition of

Hat-kaptah and whether his pain and screams continued in some dark place unheard.

> "I remember you, Hat-kaptah, and the pain of enslavement. But how can that compare to the pain of knowing me? Having met me."

Alee spoke her thoughts in words, which bore her guilt. Guilt gave weight to her and she began to move so that it would not hold her down. She packed a small ration of food including meat, bread and more water. Then she moved to the top of the Wall. There the warriors of Kush threw volley upon volley of lance and spear at the invaders who worked to break the gate.

And so a count was made. Fifty soldiers stood atop the wall while one hundred and fifty more waited inside the gate. The Invaders of Egypt stood ten thousand strong with more encamped beyond the ridge. Alee heard this and put her mind and cunning to work for the sake of Nubia. With her hood masked to just below her eyes, Alee made what was left of her to be Meroe-like.

> "I need fifty more soldiers atop the East Wall, another fifty lancers atop the West Wall, and the rest with sword and shield outside the West Gate." Alee commanded outside of her own voice.

With that of Meroe, Matron of the Guard, Alee's words gave every solider comfort. They moved without hesitation. Alee continued to speak.

> "Continue the volley atop the Eastern Wall! Every soldier attack with lance and spear and bow and rock. Hold off their entry but let them come. For when they do, they will enter the lower empty yard, funneled and clustered by the gate. There we will rain death on them from atop both Walls, East and West. Wait for my order. For when the advantage of high ground and surprise are no longer, we will open the West Gate and fight them until help arrives or death takes us."

The soldiers heard the voice and harkened it. Never putting logic to the desire of their spirits, the soldiers all wanted to believe Meroe was there so they followed orders without thought of their few numbers.

Ten thousand strong became eight thousand before the gate was broken and the invaders entered. Alee drew her sword and gave thought to the evils of men.

> "What force fools men to kill and cleave one another? Men with the same heart and life, the same needs and desires. I know the answer and go to remedy."

Atop the Western Wall, Alee stood and ordered wrath upon the soldiers who took the yard. Alee spoke, calling out the attack, and in that moment was again Aleeia. With her sword given to her by Bellia and the skill of Bellia made full within her, Aleeia met the force with speed and courage. She gave the order and the West Gate opened. The yard filled. Aleeia cut through the hoards like a bird through the clouds. She took on dozens as the chaos escalated in the Portal of Nubia. She made her way to the Eastern Gate of the Wall towards the Pharaoh and Hat-kaptah as the sun set finally and darkness was upon them. The Wall swelled as soldiers entered the yard from the West.

"Tabiry! Nuri! Buhen!" the soldiers cried exuberantly.

Buhen rode in with the Mallet of Tabiry. Aleeia saw the great breaking wave. The Egyptians were driven out of the yard and the fortune of Kush became more favorable. Buhen wielded the mallet with crushing blows that caused some onlookers to think him a captain of twenty in age.

"Take the Gate! Reclaim the Wall!" shouted Buhen. The Nuri Warriors came in and fortified the Portal as lancers threw volleys at the backs of invaders. Alee sheathed her blade and collected the garb of a fallen Egyptian. And thus she came out of the Wall with the retreating hoards of Egypt, moving with them as a shadow in the dark. Alee moved toward the encampment, towards Hat-kaptah.

The Rescue of Hat-kaptah - Numbering nearly three thousand, the defeated soldiers crossed the apex of the sand and returned to the camp of the Egyptian army. Alee amongst them continued to go unnoticed as the soldiers tended to their own wounds and injuries. Alee held back a smile as she heard the whispers of the soldiers.

"Their ranks seemed endless." said one.

"As...if... they knew...of our coming." replied another through great pain.

Alee searched the camp tent by tent for the captive Hat-kaptah. Still in disguise, she knew the search would take time. The camp housed soldiers, thousands more, and just as many tents to shelter them.

Meanwhile, back at the Portal of Nubia, Buhen laid waste to the stragglers of Egypt while he worked to re-strengthen the Wall. The Wall bustled as the soldiers of Kush were now tenfold what they were before the siege began. Buhen dealt out orders to the Nuri reinforcements and the battlement of the Wall fell in line with them. Buhen knew the Egyptians would soon return in numbers far greater and much needed to be done before then.

"Sure up the door! There is lumber in the store as well as iron and tools. Quickly now!" said Buhen.

"Sir," stated a young commander. "Our spotters speak of several phalanxes approaching from the West."

"The West? But How?" Buhen wondered as he scrambled to reform the ranks, "Warriors at the ready."

All became silent and still. In that very instant, the roar of two great beasts echoed off the sands. Every person who heard the rumble felt at ease and lowered their weapons for they knew the familiar song of Kashta and Shabaka. Once again the Great Beasts marked the coming of the Guard, Meroe and all the Warriors of the Black Sand.

"My lady, glad to have you here." said Buhen, "How did you arrive so quickly?"

"We rode nonstop with a cool wind and our blazon hearts to aid us," replied Meroe.

"Better late than never." added Buhen.

Meroe laughed. She knew the reality of the situation and she rejoiced at the stand of the Wall but knew her numbers came in time to only equal those of the invaders.

"Unload the supplies! Sure up the door! Set up tents

outside the Gate!" ordered Meroe.

Naturally, the soldiers followed. To them, her presence was seamless. In their eyes, Meroe led them to victory and they applauded her for that. It pleased Meroe to see the soldiers in high spirits no matter what the true cause. Meroe called for a meeting of officials while the soldiers rested and ate.

Gaia, Buhen, Bellia, Meroe and Faras gathered to discuss the next move. Faras insisted on coming to the Wall despite his charge at Dorginarti and, given the urgency of the deployments, no objection was made. Seated at the head of the table, Meroe began counsel. To her left sat Faras and Buhen and to her right were Gaia and Bellia. Meroe paused and looked into all who surrounded her. She began by giving praise to Buhen for his courage and leadership.

"Buhen, if not for your gift of leadership and valor as Guardian reborn, we would not have lasted the night. We would not be here now," said Meroe.

"The victory belongs to Alee. She warned me and sent me to Prince Ashur. If not for her then Nubia would truly be lost," replied Buhen.

"And for her, we must attack the Egyptians as soon as possible," added Faras. "She ventured into the camp alone and needs the cover of battle to stand a chance."

Meroe stood and paced a bit. She turned back towards the

small counsel with a stern voice.

"The decision of what to do must be made for the sake and safeguard of Nubia. I cannot rashly send more to die for one."

Gaia looked towards Bellia as if to tell her she should say what they both were thinking.

"What we do here for Alee will not only benefit her but ***all***.," stated Bellia.

"How do you even know Alee is in the Egyptian encampment? For what I know, she has journeyed far from home, and this is her first taste of war. She may have gone home.," replied Meroe.

Her words were offensive to everyone in the room who knew Alee. They became angered. Each person made points as to how and why that could not be. Tales about Abydos and Menin came to the ears of Meroe. The name Alee meant loyalty and courage to those who spoke on her behalf.

"So with all due respect, Meroe, Alee is loved by all here, and you know the least of her. As Buhen has said, she has brought us victory today. We would not ask you to throw away your reason to passion, sending warriors to slaughter, only that you help buy Alee the time she has bought us all."

It was Faras who spoke those words as his heart reached out for Alee through his voice. Meroe saw finally what the other four had long perceived. A victory for Alee would be a victory for Nubia. Meroe, however, spoke with the reason and resolve that had made her General of Dorginarti.

"Numbers bring our forces nearly to a balance. I cannot spare anyone and I cannot give up the position of the Wall. I am sorry, friends. If there is any other way to help her, I am listening."

Meroe was respected. Buhen, Faras, Gaia and Bellia knew that the burden of her charge forced her to make a decision so unpopular. Bellia rose from her chair and gathered her few belongings. Gaia read her yet again.

"So the only thing left to do is to go in after her," stated Gaia.

"Was that not the plan all along? The help of the Guard was just wishful thinking. It is just us again, as it has always been. And appropriately so, Alee is our responsibility. She is our sister.," replied Bellia.

"So we leave now?" Faras clenched his hands upon the table.

"No," replied Meroe, "Do not lose yourself. Who are you? Who are you, Faras, Patron of Guard-Defender of the Portal? Reason more for why a soldier's life is tried more. You have duty above self. You made the vow same as I."

Meroe looked into the eyes of Faras. She was nearly the

same age as he. For a woman, that meant Meroe had her share of suitors, love, and romance. Those things for her were not lasting nor ever could be, not as long as duty drove the warrior and filled her heart with pride and compassion for the weak. Meroe believed duty filled the heart the same as love. It was her belief. Duty *was* unselfish love of all. Meroe fought with love for children she will never play with, kings she will rarely greet, men she could never dance with, even thieves with whom she would loath to meet. Such thoughts gave her the strength to say *nay* and not charge in after Alee. Meroe loved all and her duty proved it.

Faras knew himself. He regarded duty highly, but passion had always given him strength. Sometimes thought to be rash and foolish in that rashness, Faras first fought for the love of his father. Ruhtra loved his son and was proud of him, but his love was stagnant and became harder to see as the years changed. For any triumph or failure Faras experienced, Ruhtra did not move. Never scoffed and never praised, Faras looked for more from his father. Ruhtra, so wise and knowing, never imparted anything to Faras. Even when asked, he stayed cold until the day Faras' mother was taken. Ruhtra loved her, above any other. At the age of thirteen, Faras went with his father to save her.

> "I put *duty* before *love* once. My father finally told me what I had to do against the choice I knew to be

true in my heart," said Faras.

His hands trembled as his mind went back in time. Ruhtra and Faras followed seven men back to a hut where their plans for the women were clear. Faras now smiled at the scars and blemishes suffered through battle, anything that made him less fair. He was his mother's son and she was known across the realm as beauty and joy incarnate. She was Fallah.

"Now is not the time for these thoughts, this story." Faras said to himself aloud. "Duty and love have betrayed me before. The choice is not that simple, Meroe."

Meroe sighed while Faras stood unmoved for a moment.

"I will stay at the Wall. Away from love. Closer to duty," said Faras, an unsettled stare emanated from his face.

Somewhere just inside the bounds of the Egyptian camp, Alee searched from tent to tent although she did not scurry or creep. She wore her cloak and the garbs of Egyptian armor and every passerby who addressed Alee received a quick and stern reply in her deepest voice. For the most part, she was unnoticed. Soldiers hurried to and fro. In such a dangerous proximity, Alee kept her Will at bay although at times she desired greatly to use it. Alee had no mind of which tent held Hat-kaptah, so she checked dozens of tents where inside soldiers slept. They alternated with those who kept watch. Instinctively, she moved towards the middle of the camp to find him.

Entering another dwelling in search of Hat-kaptah, Alee's eyes beheld the same atrocity witnessed in Abydos. Bound together, they laid on the cold and rigid sands. Alee saw the slaves of the Pharaoh who undoubtedly built the encampment, every tent, armory, and trench. Alee turned away to go back into the night. Her heart went out to them, but she knew that releasing them would be death. She turned towards the exit and looked into the eyes of a little girl. Alee did not want the questions of why the girl was present in a war-camp to enter her mind. She halted and whispered.

> "To free you all would mean death for many," she said. "Where would you go in the dry shadow of the night?"

Alee paused and looked out over the huddle.

> "Outside this shelter is a long road back to Abydos and your families, but just across the portal is a new life. If you would not put your life in jeopardy, stay here. If there are others, find them and be swift."

Alee removed a small dagger from a holster wrapped tightly around her right thigh. She cut through the thick leather bonds that hindered the children. She started with the girl first, then placed the dagger on the ground. Alee turned to the little girl for direction.

> "Little one, I see a picture in my head of a young man in the center of the room lying with his hands and feet tied together. Can you help me find this place? You need not lead me just point me in the right direction."

The little girl spoke so quietly. She told Alee of the marks the tents had branded at the bottom of the entryway. Pictographs, for both readers and non-readers, distinguished the contents of every tent.

> "There is a place with no mark. Keep going to the center.," said the young girl.

Alee left them to their own judgment and fate as she reentered the labyrinth of the camp. And so the scatter and scurry of those imprisoned brought the camp to an early rise.

Meanwhile, Gaia and Bellia made final preparations before they left the Portal of Nubia. Packing food, water, and herbs, the two women dressed lightly. No longer in full armor, Gaia and Bellia wore thick leather trousers and vests outlined and ornamented with bronze. With little color, their Nubian style attire was stately, which suggested the presence of war-mastered emissaries. As Reques and Requi were reacquainted, the ladies agreed time was short. The day, marked by a battle, quickly gave way to a new one. They mounted the majestic beasts and galloped to Alee.

The nameless girl was gracious. She led Alee to the place with no mark amongst the encampment. Alee was nervous outside the tent. When suddenly the little girl left to run East, she was more unsettled. She took a breath. She knew not the condition of her loyal friend but she would not let her mind settle on it. What was described as witnessed by Gaia at Adindan gave her chills. But she hesitated no longer. She entered. The room was bare along its edges. It was dark and the light from the lamps did little to fill the space. Alee committed to the room. She opened the portal veil letting in the moonlight. In the center, the lunar eye revealed a chair. Alee walked slowly towards the chair, with gold and jewels that reflected in the light. She paused.

"Much is hidden from my eyes. Someone is there," said Alee quietly.

She stepped back and took a lamp from a pike near the room's edge. Alee tipped slowly holding the lamp out front.

"Hat-kaptah?"

She spoke cautiously into the shadow and wondered why the light had not yet revealed the figure. *Now is not the time to be taken by fear. I must move true and not idly,* thought

Alee. She decided then to tiptoe no longer, but thought halted her again.

"Why do you not answer? Move or wail."

Alee called out louder but still withheld as not to alert the frantic and scrambled guards. For a moment, Alee showed the manner of someone who would turn and flee. It disgusted her. She acknowledged her fear. Bellia had taught her that, but more than ever she was paralyzed by her fear. Alee began to feel small because of fear's frequency. So to be sudden and contrary, she quickly leapt at the seated figure. She thrusted her lamp high above and saw the posture of he who sat in the center of the room.

Aleeia kneeled beside the young man, Hat-kaptah. His body was broken and scarred. Flesh pierced and burnt black through torture gave Hat-kaptah the look of a ragged tiger. It was obvious to her now why he neither moved nor spoke. With his jaw broken and unset, Hat-kaptah was bound by silk to the golden throne. The silky strap was tight, though negotiable, but Hat-kaptah was too weak. Indeed, Hat-kaptah heard her song and wished greatly to heed, but malevolent hands had been set upon him for hours at a time.

"What have...I…done to you," gasped Alee as she loosened the silk.

Hat-kaptah hunched over and fell to her arms as soon as the silk ceased as his anchor to the chair. Alee hugged Hat-kaptah, his pain evident. She backed away slowly wiping and picking away at the crusty stale blood about his body.

"Hat-kaptah, can you hear me? We have to go. Hat-kaptah? Please...Hat-kaptah."

Alee set him on the ground along his side. The only sign of life came from his slow and staggered breathing. His eyes then moved and peered towards her. The back of his hand rose slowly to her brow. Alee grasped it and smiled. Her tears formed now from joy. Alee reached into her satchel and pulled out the Healing Leaves known as Bhena, though she called them Karwynn.

"By Grace, Dorginarti brought these to me," she said.

Alee ground away at the moistened leaves and powdered the water with them. Alee pulled up his head and brought his lips closer. The clamors outside matured as the ruckus of the soldiers and slaves ensued. Alee felt hurried by the noises.

"Drink this," she said, "Your injuries are great and thus the arch water will work slowly. Initially, they are no more than the numbing Masking Leaves."

She poured the water for him to drink, but the dry mouth and throat of Hat-kaptah found it hard to keep.

"Just a little at a time, my friend," she said as Hat-kaptah tried to swallow.

He stirred, fueled by his own strong will, the effect of the leaves hastened in him. She draped his arms about her shoulders to help Hat-kaptah to his feet. Alee examined the body of Hat-kaptah who, although weak, had grown stronger and taller over their time apart.

> "I see your scars...you were scarred for me. You were cut to bleed and burned to stop over and over again. These things in study do not compare to the eyes."

Hat-kaptah's head was low. He affirmed the story with his gaze and a faint grunt.

Finally, they moved towards the exit. Alee moved as a crutch to Hat-kaptah. They reached the portal. Alee prepared for the scatter of soldiers and those who would be emancipated. Alee pulled back the canvas and looked out at the giant who stood ten strides before her. Xamare-Jacobb saw Alee but remained still and as though he waited for her to exit. Instinctively, Alee was frightened and saw him as a hostile Egyptian despite never before seeing the juggernaut. Hat-kaptah made no gesture regarding Jacobb. His head was still low. His eyes set to the sands. Alee retreated back inside the tent to set down Hat-kaptah. She waited. The seconds felt like days. Alee stood ready in what felt like the seventh day, and moved slowly towards the portal veil. She drew it back slightly. One eye peeked outward and met the eyes of Jacobb now standing at seven strides. Alee flung herself back into the tent again. *What game is this?* Alee thought. *Does he wish to keep me here or drive me mad before we battle?* She paused. *If either be the case, then wise or ordered is the Stalker. I dare not look again.*

But, she looked out again at the chaos of the streets and the one standing cold amongst it all. He was at five strides when she saw him move towards her. Alee went back into the tent and wrangled Hat-kaptah again. Alee drew her sword with her free hand. She hobbled to the back of the tent and cut an exit through the canvas. With as much haste as the two could muster, they crept out the back and around to an adjacent empty dwelling. Alee looked out to see the tent they had just occupied come down. She did not see the Stalker, as Jacobb was known to her. Alee darted out as best she could with Hat-kaptah, westward to the Wall with her head and eyes constantly at a swiveled onlook.

It was odd to Alee that she trekked to the bounds of the encampment, but amongst all the bodies that lay on the sands, she was never hindered, save for the Stalker who did not rush her. Alee put her thoughts to words.

"The ease of this quest troubles me greatly," she

said. "Come, Hat-kaptah. We near the outer stables."

Alee and Hat-kaptah came to the horses of Nile. They heard

a thunderous cry that reached far to them from within the camp. Alee turned for a moment back to the camp. She then helped set Hat-kaptah atop a black horse. Clasping the reigns and endearing herself to the great beast, Alee spoke.

> "We do not choose our masters. Only pray they are gracious, for maybe they have masters themselves. My masters brought me here. Name my masters, call them *fate* and *legacy*. Are they gracious? It would seem not, but when fate is a master then faith must accompany."

She paused again to look at the scurrying and the dead. She leaned to whisper to the unsettled black horse, Norequus she called him.

> "Come, my friend. You are my master. I pray, take me back West."

Forsaking Faras - Within moments, Alee had returned to the Portal of Nubia. She had successfully delivered Hat-kaptah from the foes of Avalon, laden in Egypt. Alee felt no joy in the mission complete. The guards opened the gate and Alee helped Hat-kaptah dismount and called for aid. His wounded body caused her guilt to swell. In that instant, burrowed through the pain of a broken jaw, Hat-kaptah spoke for the first time in more than a day. It was only a broken word, or rather a proper name,

"Alee," and it lightened her heart.

"Do not speak. These men will take you to the healers of this fort. I will be with you shortly."

Hat-kaptah made no other gestures and may have heard nothing from Alee as he fell into unconsciousness.

And so, Meroe came to her first astonished, then with dread, and finally resolved with a mind of war. Alee greeted Meroe knowing the outcome of Egypt's first siege. Alee knew the mind of Meroe and, although she showed no favor to the statehood of Kush over Egypt, Alee did love Bellia and Highness Aalarae.

"Meroe, to the matters of this nation, I would deem this information pertinent. Their camp is apparently leaderless and is now in chaos as the slaves have rallied and scattered," said Alee.

Alee did not linger to discover her plan of actions. She motioned to the store to gather more supplies.

"Alee, wait!" Meroe exclaimed, "You have to know Gaia and Bellia are in that camp. They went in after you."

Alee kept her direction to the shock of Meroe. She came behind Alee and grabbed her by the arm to spin her around so they stood eye to eye.

"What is with you? Faras and those women made it

a point to tell me how I did not know you. They said there is no other soul worth the sacrifice of life and all you can do now is walk away. If you keep walking away, then I was right and you have made fools of us all," shouted Meroe.

"Let. Me. Go."

Alee said the words slowly as if every single word was a statement all its own. Meroe stepped back.

"Listen--" Meroe spoke. Alee interrupted with a raised voice.

"Where is Faras?"

"The Counsel Room," Meroe replied.

Alee turned away and with the charge of Nubia upon Meroe's back, Meroe let her be. She sighed to show Alee her disappointment and disgust. Alee continued on to find Faras.

Alee came to the Counsel Room and found Faras sitting at an empty table. The look of the room brought memories of Aalarae. It was obviously made for diplomacy and the negotiations of war among nations. It was a small piece of Dorginarti's splendor in the dreary Wall. The glossy stone floors looked like frozen waves. The long grey marbled table complimented the room, although it was an emissary's gift from a far off land. Faras sat in one of the eleven mahogany chairs that circled the table. Each had terms of strength and trust along the backrest as well as the mark of an animal engraved in the arm. Faras sat on the mark of the elephant, where *strength* and *trust* were written in a language unknown to him. Although darkness covered most of Faras's face, the torches held by the lanterns on the wall lit the room well enough. Mirrors and candles hung from the ceiling ready to illuminate the room like a chandelier. The flickering light hid the whole of the room's beauty. The rugs, tapestries, and urns gave no life to the room that stood for peace and compromise. Alee stepped towards Faras. Her every step echoed in the hall. Faras was still. His eyes confirmed the rumor that Alee was back.

"So you are here," said Faras.

"Gaia and Bellia. You let them follow. You did not hinder them. Does God wish guilt to be the death of me? You did not hinder them!" she stated with a raised voice.

"You are a woman strong. If it were always so, then God smiles on you. But if you have learned strength from others such as Gaia and Bellia, then you should not be surprised," he replied.

Faras rose from the chair at the head of his empty committee and approached Alee. Alee subvertly moved to keep the table between them. Faras saw this, but did not let on nor give chase before he spoke.

"How can I comfort you, Alee?"

"Comfort? I can find no comfort. Not while my friends suffer and fate is the burden that it is."

Alee turned away. Faras moved behind her. He placed his hands upon her shoulder.

"Is this your comfort? Do you still attempt?" Alee asked.

"No, I do not pretend to comfort you in such a way. As you said, your friends suffer and fate is weighty. I would comfort you in this way," he said.

Alee turned to look in his eyes. She had always held Faras in great trust but learned to anticipate promises and to look them in the eye.

"Let us recover your friends and your comfort along with it."

"I cannot Faras. I must travel further West," replied Alee.

"*Must* you? Fate should never be a burden nor cause discomfort. Especially since fate is a book you yourself have license to write. Woe the gods that give our stories intro, theme, and length, for that is all they care to author. You owe the rest of your story to you. We all do," he said.

"That may be true for most." replied Alee, "But my

story, if it is written by God is also of interest to my mother."

Faras sighed softly. He stepped closer to the light of the lanterns that fought the shadows in the room.

"I learned long ago we cannot live in the eyes of fathers," stated Faras.

Alee saw something in his face and heard something in his tone. She embraced Faras. They held each other tightly. The embrace relayed their fears of losing one another and the ache of even two days apart. Faras bowed to kiss her. He pulled her closer. The kiss was soft and filling for the both of them.

"Alee, listen. Fate is ours to make. We can retrieve Gaia and Bellia if it be your wish. And you can stay here with me," he said.

"To say such a thing, was that kiss a mistake?" Alee pondered.

Faras was dazed by the question. He knew neither its meaning nor origin in the moment they now shared. He remained silent and still. Then Faras let her withdraw from their close proximity. Alee, walking back towards the wall, examined a tapestry. Beautiful it was, as well as old and kept. The tapestry depicted the Guardian Beast, forefather of Kashta, along side the hero of Kush who was the first defender. Stitched in gold, it shone well for the story it told.

Alee thought about the past while looking at the artistry. Thinking about the past for Alee had made her think about her mother; and doing so essentially led Alee to thoughts of the future.

> "Faras, since Adindan would you say I love you less?" she asked.
>
> "No," Faras gave shortly.
>
> "Asking me to stay again, knowing the pain of it in Adindan, must mean you think my resolve to be trifle. That what was so important then is miraculously no longer. Oh, if it were so." she said.

Alee turned with a look so intense. Faras spoke to ease her.

> "Maybe I love you more with every passing day and for it I am selfish. And you, Alee, have a right to be selfish too. I question not your resolve, will, nor determination. Just the opposite, my love. Ask yourself what will make you happy and be just a little selfish so that you can make it so," he said.
>
> "You cannot possibly understand. My path is written on a tablet, and you will never understand the feeling of seeing your name written in time, across generations. Sometimes I do not believe. I refuse. But every time I do, I have more fate to follow with my name engraven deeper within it."

Alee said no more and Faras let her be. He wanted to stop

Alee as she walked to the door but knew he didn't possess any words to do so. Their conversation had already begun to go in circles. Points of love and fate left Alee unchanged and Faras let her. He said only,

"Come back to me, Alee"

Where Alee replied,

> "Someday I'll owe no more. Thank Karwynn for the peace of playful youth that someday I may know again that restful part."

Leaving the Counsel Room, Alee took one step closer to that peace. She threw her thoughts away from Faras to matters that became what Alee had called her *new life*. Walking through the corridors made of mudbrick and stone, Alee sought Hat-kaptah who was essential to that life. Her steps were not light as Alee came to his bedside. It was almost a soldier's march. For her, Alee knew where and what for to be her destination. Destiny awaited. Hat-kaptah heard her booming from afar. He sat up when she entered the room. However, Alee spoke in regards to his well-being with a healer and gave him little regard.

"Can he travel?" inquired Alee.

The answer from the healer dismayed Alee, not due to the state of her friend's wellness, but because of the delay it would cause. Her concern to duty was greater than ever. It substituted her smiles for grimaces and her laugher for sighs. And in the moment, Hat-kaptah was not a friend to her but rather a tool of her translations needed in the Barren Sea. Her guilt to his condition even subsided as Alee turned to him.

"You moved well enough in the camp. Can you ride? That is all I need to know." Alee insisted.

Hat-kaptah reached out to her, touching her cheek. It softened Alee for she knew the depth of his love. She closed her eyes and took him by the hand.

"This is hard for me. I have seen Gaia and Bellia be so untouched by circumstances, Faras and Meroe be restrained in the face of duty. Buhen as well be the unreadable leader of his legend. But I cannot. "

"Gaia and Bellia?" Hat-kaptah interrupted.

"Yes, my mothers while in Abydos are in the Pharaoh's camp, but I cannot follow. I rejoice in the fact that they are strong and may find their way back home," she said.

Hat-kaptah rose from the bed and brought a smile to Alee. With his movement, Hat-kaptah made his ability to travel known to her. Alee hugged him then left him with instructions to prepare for their impending departure. Alee made ready things of her own. She walked out quickly. She did not notice Faras whose back rested calmly beside the door. As she went off right, down the hall, back to the armory near the court square, Faras entered the room with Hat-kaptah. He signaled the healers to take their leave. And so, the two men were alone.

Faras did not see Hat-kaptah as an equal, only as an unfortunate peasant from a far off land lucky to be graced with knowing Alee. Alee, who was the only commonality between them, was the topic of discussion started by Faras. Hat-kaptah saw him approach and got a sense of him as he drew closer. Faras was above him, taller by at least one head. Looking down, Faras spoke.

> "Alee has risked a lot for you. I know this because I know the translations. Happiness is here. Safety. Love. All abandoned because of a misguided belief, so called fate. Though I would never say this to her, I believe she was brought to me, once in the inn, then again in the Third City. Fate like that cannot be denied. And to have her taken by the folly of her blindness would be a crime against the gods and a crime against love, which even the gods exalt among them."

Faras crept closer towards Hat-kaptah. Hat-kaptah neither swayed nor moved. He knew not the motives of Faras, nor did he understand the reason for his audience to Faras's monologue. Faras began again.

> "What quest would Alee have if the doors had no keys? Would she continue on if prophecy were written in the moment? Would you suffer more because of her? Look at yourself, broken and weak. Life eludes you as your flesh has become burnt and bones made brittle. And you suffer this, I know, for her."

Faras placed his hand on the shoulder of Hat-kaptah. He hunched lower to be at eye level with Hat-kaptah. Hat-kaptah looked into him as well.

"You need not suffer anymore for her..." said Faras. Faras struck as suddenly as a python. His hand, once upon the shoulder of Hat-kaptah, now clasped the young man's neck like the talon of an eagle. Faras squeezed, trying to purge the life from Hat-kaptah. He did so believing it to be the means by which both Alee and Hat-kaptah would be set free to find peace. Hat-kaptah shrank as Faras perceived him fading. He squeezed tighter.

"...anymore." Faras whispered.

With that, Hat-kaptah grabbed Faras's one hand at the wrists. It was a slow clenching resistance against the hands of Faras. Faras tried to squeeze tighter. Oddly, Hat-kaptah never gasped nor did he try to cry out. The two men seemed to be locked in their positions as if they were subjects to an artist for a sculpture or painting. As Faras squeezed and held longer, Hat-kaptah's grip upon the wrist of Faras became increasingly intense. Faras's face fell. He seemed frozen, though not for some realization of the actions he had undertaken. He knew. He was simply matched and astonished. The hands of Faras moved by the strength of Hat-kaptah, which drew his right hand away from his neck. The arm of Faras moved slowly away while Hat-kaptah's face remained as silent as his voice. Faras committed his left to finish the job but he was caught by Hat-kaptah with the same strength and power that relented the right. Finally, Faras ceased and marveled at the young man as he waited. Silence filled the room for a far longer span than Faras felt comfort in.

"Damn you. Speak, you wretched thing."

Hat-kaptah did not speak nor move and the span of silence came again.

> "You would stand there as if I did not just try to kill you? As if I still do not wish you dead? More so now, to preserve my reputation with all, especially Alee."

Hat-kaptah seemed taller to Faras as Hat-kaptah stepped forward. They stood toe to toe and Faras finally heard the mind of the young man. With a voice gritty and deep, through pain in jaw and throat, Hat-kaptah spoke.

> "Do you see she is safe? With me, she is safe. I saw her for the first time and..." Hat-kaptah paused for a quick moment then continued to speak. "Set yourself at ease. For there is no other choice for you."

Hat-kaptah left and joined Alee at the West Gate of the Wall. Faras, ashamed and fearful, did not follow.

With Norequus, one of two horses travel ready, Alee packed the rest of her supplies. Soldiers and guards by order of Meroe came to send her off. They were lined in five rows and called her name out in praise. Meroe stepped before Alee to exchange words. She knew their last discussion was less than amiable and both Meroe and Alee did not desire to part in such a state. Amidst death and loss unto a backdrop of war, they both felt nothing but love in memory of one another.

> "Good journey, Alee. Worry not for Gaia and Bellia, for together they can be an army unto themselves," said Meroe.
>
> "Truly, let's just hope Bellia has one of her intense cravings for either food or handsome men during their journey for then we will surely see her again." said Alee.

The two chuckled knowing who Bellia was to them. They

hugged and parted. The guards shouted and the two horses grew smaller as they melted into the horizon. Faras atop the Western Wall did not call out his goodbye. He let Alee go. Even still, Alee turned her eyes back to the Portal and saw Faras. And when sight connected them, Faras retreated back into the fort.

"What *love* is love that the heart would not kill for? Only greater is the love the heart would die for.," said Faras as he faded back into duty.

And so going back towards Nuri, Napata, and Dorginarti, Alee and Hat-kaptah traveled. Passing the cities with as much distance as the route to the Barren Sea would allow, Alee sunk deeper into her *new life*.

Silent Crossings - The sand had much memory as Requi and Reques brought Gaia and Bellia to the encampments. Soldiers, horses, and war-trailers were marked in the sands for miles. Despite strong, rolling winds, the impressions were deep and told the story of the past few days. The wind picked up slightly as Gaia and Bellia ascended the last dune that valleyed the land. Their position gave the Egyptians the highest defensible point from the Wall.

The wind tumbled forcefully across the sands to erase all the memory it once held. The sky was clear as the two women rode steadily to the camp. Despite the fact both Gaia and Bellia were unsure of their plan, they traveled calmly. Upon their approach to the camp they heard unrest several fields away. The two women stopped and looked at one another.

"They would not attack again so soon?" Gaia stated as half inquiry.

"No, it takes longer than hours to reform from a defeat like that. But maybe knowing this compels them toward a hastened second offensive," replied Bellia.

The two ladies galloped to the sand's apex near the camp's edge. They could plainly see the origins of the uproar once they reached the top of the dune.

"The battle is here," Bellia exclaimed.

Amongst the bodies of soldiers and slaves, the revolt continued to escalate. Before their eyes, Gaia and Bellia saw soldiers mauled and more slaves cut down.

"Well, we do not need to be discrete. A distraction surrounds us. But finding Alee will be even more difficult amidst the chaos," said Bellia.

"Bellia, are you suggesting we split up?" asked Gaia.

"Of course. First one to find Alee wins," replied

Bellia.

Gaia broke a smile. Bellia succeeded in easing her mind. Gaia saw all the bodies and became clouded with the thought that they may be too late; that Alee lay still somewhere. Before her laugh, her face showed signs of despair.

"Okay, you're on. Save whomever you can along the way. It is still our oath to protect the weak be they Egyptian solider or Egyptian captive," Gaia decreed.

Parting ways, Gaia moved along the Northern edge of the camp. She wove intricately between each encampment's huddle. Witnessing the troubles of the camp, Gaia had no intentions to intervene barring her own decree. By eye, captives out numbered soldiers two to one. Gaia witnessed a young boy fleeing the sword of a solider twice his size.

Standing strong and unflustered, the young boy ran behind her as if she were his own shield and protector. All that was left of her impartiality was stripped away, though Gaia did not mind in the least. The soldier burrowed down on her. He never stated a demand or stopped his rush. The soldier only raised his weapon. Gaia remained calm, although the last time she engaged an Egyptian warrior was not lost to her memory. As the soldier drew closer, Gaia remembered her restraint from before that kept her from using her Will in tandem with her combat skills. Alee needed to be safe and secret and the Awakening Will ripples through space and time connecting all who know of it. Here in the moment, Gaia was not restrained. With Alee revealed to Avalon through the mouth of Hat-kaptah and baited by him as well, Gaia no longer had cause to hold back. As the young boy clenched her leg tighter, she spoke words of comfort to him before the scuffle began.

"This horse is called Requi. He's a good horse." Gaia quickly lifted the young boy atop the horse.

"He knows the way."

Gaia slapped the back of the horse and the boy sped away from the camp. She then immediately turned to meet her assailant head on. The soldier raised his sword high. He made a play at Gaia. Bringing the sword straight down as though aiming at the tip of her nose, he attacked. Gaia, quick, moved smoothly past the left shoulder that the soldier favored. Upon her elusive move, Gaia whispered to him. She was so close that what was said would not have been heard if they were the only souls in an empty hollow room.

Estne tua harpe gravidam

It was all one fluid motion for anyone who saw it.

Gaia was now behind him and the soldier turned and raised his sword yet again. With a leveled swing, he swiped at her throat. Had the swipe been as quick as the first, he might have delivered a deadly blow. However, Gaia ducked and hopped back. The soldier became frustrated, not at Gaia and her seemingly tauntish maneuvers, but at himself, for the blade was noticeably of greater weight.

Screaming, he held the blade to the sky and slashed downward towards Gaia's belly. Easily enough, Gaia dodged it again. But the blade would not be moved again. The sword was so hefty to the solider that it seemed stuck in the sands. Though not by the force of his attack but by its sheer weight alone. The solider still tugged at the blade as Gaia drew her own and approached with a reaping stride. Gaia was upon him and came ever closer. Finally, he let go of his blade while Gaia cocked her own weapon ready to strike. Before Gaia thought about letting go to swing her blade, the soldier was in full retreat. Gaia, of course, did not follow. But when the soldier looked back at her, he saw Gaia lift his sword as though it were a grain of sand. Gaia smiled. She knew that her first encounter in Abydos would have ended similarly, if she were free to act as she was capable.

In that moment at the southern part of the camp,

Bellia was fully enthralled by battle. Bellia, being a daughter of Kush, was inclined to fight the soldiers she saw more outright. Her sense of logic led Bellia to believe fighting would bring Alee to her or at least those who held her. She took on all comers with the same lack of restraint that made Gaia's skirmish so effortless. But for Bellia, freedom in battle meant letting loose a darker, more brutal essence of herself. And every Egyptian who came was unfortunate enough to meet that Bellia. Her left hand gripped the throat of a soldiers while the right hand held him by the wrist. She used the soldier's own arm and sword as her own. She let him go and flung him into the two soldiers who attempted to catch her from behind. Two more came at the right while another charged her from her left. Remarkably, Bellia had yet to arm herself though she had been fighting constantly since splitting from Gaia.

Bellia effectively and fiercely handled the three soldiers. She became lost in it as the battle took her towards the center of the camp. At times, Bellia only saw the enemy and struggled to remember Alee. With a soldier in a headlock, she saw past a cluster of soldiers to an odd sight. A monstrous beast of a man who was clearly no Egyptian stood in front of a single tent and stared intensely. Bellia, with the soldier in submission, dropped with him to the ground thrusting her elbow into the back of his neck. She got up quickly to see the tent's canvas ruffle slightly. And when it did the man who stood nearly eight feet tall took a step towards it. Bellia was blindsided by the broad of a lance. She stumbled back, angry at her lack of focus. Before Bellia regained her balance, she was tackled to the ground from the side. Two other Egyptians came to hold her by the waist and arm.

On the ground embedded in the sand, Bellia lay clamped by three men as a lancer made his way towards her. Despite her own immediate peril, Bellia looked to the man who looked at the tent. Bellia saw the tent's portal sway again and looked at the canvas portal creeping apart. Bellia's eyes cause sight of *her* inside the dwelling. The beast moved closer again. Bellia wanted then to call out to *Aleeia* but was struck across the jaw while drawing breath. The lancer stood above her with his blade point just upon her. Bellia smiled and the lancer paused because of it. Suddenly, she raised her legs grasping the lance with her feet. In the same instance, the solider who held her right arm struck her in the nose with his elbow and by doing so inadvertently loosened his grip slightly. Bellia twisted the lance breaking it in two like a twig. With her right hand free, she gouged the eye of the soldier who pinned her down by lying across her waist. The soldier wailed and rose to his feet running amok. The soldier to her left panicked and quickly reached for the blade piece of the broken lance. He coiled it back and lunged to stab her. Bellia rolled into the soldier at her right. He fell behind her, between her and the blade. She placed her feet beneath her quickly and the two soldiers who remained ran.

It happened so fast. When Bellia reassessed the huge man outside the tent, he began moving more intently towards it. Bellia saw him and ran at him with all speed. She rushed with the intent to cut him off and bring him to the ground. The gigantic foe caught sight of her just inside his field of vision. He stopped and stepped back so quickly that Bellia seemed to float right in front of him. And as she hovered, he raised his boot and kicked her into the tent. Bellia flew through the support pillar inside and the tent came down around her. Engulfed by the canvas and astonished by the feat of strength shone by the brute, Bellia was disoriented for a moment.

Bellia felt the ground rumble and it hastened her clarity. The brute loomed over the fallen tent stomping every hump that could possibly resemble an animate object. Bellia laid flat and still while slowly reaching for her sword to cut through the ensnaring, net-like canvas.

"Where are you?"

Bellia heard the words and trembled for they sounded as though thunder had a voice and spoke in words. With her blade now in hand, she reached to the sky and ripped her way back into the clear night. Standing tall, she called out while she examined the behemoth.

"Over here," cried Bellia, outside of any strategy. The titan turned to her with a grimace about his face. His eyes were white and pale. They seemed blank; although they pierced right through her. The look chilled Bellia but her experience settled her. She knew that anxiety only marked the coming of a challenge and worthy foe.

"Who are you?" asked Bellia.

The man simply stared. Bellia looked around amongst the ongoing ruckus and called out for Alee. The riot muffled her cries. They were nearly inaudible to anyone who was not in the area. Bellia focused again on the man.

"I'll ask again. Who are you? Is Avalon your home?"

"Avalon. Yes. Jacobb."

Jacobb murmured his reply. From his delivery, she wasted no more time with questions. Bellia now thought him to be slow of body due to his size and dull of wit due to his reply.

> "He is just the muscle it seems. I'll get no answers here. And if that was Alee indeed she may be gaining distance." Bellia thought to herself.

Bellia turned to examine the scene while Jacobb stood still yet again. Bellia had no mind of him as she searched the grounds for tracks or clues to help find either Alee or Hat-kaptah.

In an instant, Jacobb charged her. She positioned her sword to the ready. She held the blade low to the right beside her hip with the tip pointing away behind her. Jacobb rumbled towards her with speed that surprised Bellia. When Jacobb was upon her, she attacked. Bellia brought the blade across her body, swinging with an aggression that suggested more than an intent to subdue. Still barreling near, Jacobb raised his arm as if his flesh were a shield. The blade struck him violently and stopped at the bone. Blood stained the sands. The blade hewed deep into the heaping forearm to where only the back and hilt of the sword were free. Jacobb did not wail nor did he break stride. The same bludgeoned arm struck Bellia with a devastating back fist. With both hands holding the hilt of the sword, Bellia was naked to the unconventional counterattack. Hit hard in the shoulder, the force of the blow sent Bellia flying yards across the sands. She hit the sand and finally slowed from the impact, sliding to a stop.

Shaken, Bellia took staggered steps to get her feet beneath her. She first rolled to her stomach, then to one knee and then finally pressed her hand against her thighs to rise up completely. It was not lost on Bellia that twice now Jacobb hurled her through the air. But Jacobb, quietly brooding, stood there bleeding with her sword still protruding.

"You are smarter than this Bellia," she thought to herself, “A head-on attack with an enemy like this…"

Jacobb motored his legs for a second charge just as Bellia formulated a plan. As Jacobb charged, instinctively Bellia did too, for her thoughts were incomplete. In the instant before contact, just as Jacobb lowered his torso, Bellia folded her arms across her head and threw her entire body at the knees of Jacobb. The collision caused Jacobb no noticeable pain, though he tumbled over and fell hard face first into the sand. Bellia rolled into her dive and set her feet before leaping high into in the air. The height of her jump was remarkable such that anyone looking to the sky in the camp might have seen her as a bird in the airy dark blue. Above the body of Jacobb, the jump brought great speed as she accelerated down to the Earth. With her boot heels clamped together, Bellia came down on Jacobb like a bullet striking him in the small of his lower back. As spectacular as Bellia's attack was, she felt the pain of it. For diving into the striding charge of Jacobb was as hazardous as attempting to topple a stampeding elephant. Bellia hopped off the massive warrior and walked away victorious.

"A broken spine is not worse than death," said Bellia

in assumption.

But before she could fully retreat or submit her triumph to the task of finding Alee, Jacobb had risen again.

"I sure hope Gaia is fairing better," Bellia sighed. And so the battle continued.

Gaia, still north of the center of the encampment, searched the sand and read the winds trying to find anything that would bring Alee to her. She even spent some time asking the captives and deserters of Alee's whereabouts. However, Gaia had no idea of how well disguised Alee had been. Thus, the answers she received reflected the matter. Had anyone glanced at Alee, she would have been unnoticed. Gaia was brilliant at times, but finally admitted to her lack of broad thinking. She remembered Hat-kaptah was severely tortured she received the message from him. She knew that Alee was here with him. Quickly, she changed her approach.

The camp became more desolate through those who escaped death and those taken by it. Gaia looked about and came across a body wrapped in bandages. Moving oddly, Gaia kneeled beside her.

"Are you okay?" Gaia asked.

"Are you okay?" the women replied in a duplicate

tone.

Gaia knew naught what to make of such a reply. Amidst all the carnage, such a reply could only come from someone traumatized by the cloud of death, thought Gaia. She lifted the woman's head in comfort.

"What is your name?" Gaia asked.

"What is your name?" she replied.

Gaia's heart went out to the women wrapped in leather. She saw scars old and new written across the body and within the skin of the troubled young woman.

"My name is Gaia, I am here to help you," she stated.

"My name is Sciona, I am here to help you," was the woman's reply.

Gaia grew impatient and suspected something sinister. Sciona's tone did not change. But the change in her mirror like reply, which revealed her name was something more than foreboding to Gaia.

"Where are you from?" asked Gaia in harsher dynamic.

And somewhat expectedly, the question was thrown back.

"Where are you from?" Sciona replied.

Gaia's frustration swelled. She could not determine the meaning behind the strange woman's game. Gaia stepped back from Sciona while Sciona rose to her feet. As Sciona stood tall, Gaia saw the small blades strapped to her thighs, one on each leg. Gaia's face lost all of its pleasant expression. Her emotions raged. Gaia felt trapped and hated she was so gullible to be ensnared. *But what is this game?* Gaia thought. She inspected Sciona and all exchanges up until now. The longer Gaia thought on it, the more she understood. *No questions*, she thought to herself.

"I am from beyond the Barren Sea," Gaia stated.

"I am from beyond the mist," Sciona replied.

Gaia was right. No questions as she walked slightly to her left. Sciona mirrored and moved the same to her left. The two women walked in a circle common centered to one another.

"I came to Abydos with Bellia and Aleeia."

"I came to Abydos with Alonard and Jacobb."

All that Sciona said took Gaia aback. And despite giving up the names, Gaia felt confusion so great concerning the motives behind her answers given so freely.

"Why play this game?" Gaia asked instinctively.

The question was a slip, but surely, Sciona retorted as expected. Gaia quickly got back in the game.

"The last time I saw Alee was Dorginarti."

"The last time I saw Alee was here."

Gaia smiled but only for a moment. She did not know whether the words of Sciona were weighted with truth or lies. She pondered Sciona again. She stepped towards her slightly. Sciona stepped in as well.

"When I saw Alee, she was going out East from the Wall."

"When I saw Alee, she was going out West from the camp."

"...she was only with her horse..."

"...she was only with her slave..."

Gaia's eyes widened. She quickly turned away and began running westward back towards the Wall. Sciona sat still for a moment for she loved the hunt as well as the chase. Gaia called out Alee's name, while she rushed back to the edge of the camp. Her eyes steady on the move. She scanned for Hat-kaptah, more so than for Alee. Gaia was sure Alee wore some disguise or put her Will to work in some manner of cloak.

Sciona still waited. She did not pursue until all her senses lost track of her. When the chase was ripe for Sciona, she sped into the night running with the elegant stride of a panther. Unbeknownst to Gaia, Sciona was closing ground. Gaia had not looked to her rear since her initial departure. The huntress was now at her heels. Gaia reached the edge of the camp. She saw the faint frame of Alee and Hat-kaptah atop a black horse meld into the night. She tried to run after them but found her ankle bounded as she fell to the ground.

She saw a wrap of leather at her feet that hindered her. Alee became lost again.

Gaia turned to see the source of her chain. She saw Sciona, half bare, as one strap from her body was the tie that bound Gaia. It relented. The strap loosened and retreated back like a whip. Back up her thigh, around her waist, and across the shoulders, the leather strap was replaced.

"No more games. Make yourself known," Gaia exclaimed.

"What fun is there in that?" replied Sciona.

"Fun? Of course, you are evil for the sake of evil. You probably feel nothing."

"Oh, but you are wrong. I feel and feel and feel. And to explore *that* is my higher purpose. Pain. Pleasure. Touch. Taste. I embrace my senses as the variable palette of life. The curiosity of knowing what makes a pain more painful than a moment before; they are never the same, you know. I have killed many and they were never the same. But now, I wonder how it would *feel* to choke the life from you and kiss your lips just as they went cold. I have not strangled someone for quite sometime. I am eager to know how the feeling has changed."

Sciona words unsettled Gaia. She cringed. Sciona's lips

curled to a smile at the sight of Gaia's displeasure.

"Let me know the feeling of death. If you are able to speak as it happens," requested Sciona before grabbing her daggers. Gaia drew her sword and they began.

Gaia stood tall and balanced. She held her sword in her right hand high above her head and pointed it at Sciona. Her defensive stance showed confidence. Her left palm faced up beside her hip. In an instant, Sciona ran back behind the tents around Gaia. She moved so quickly. Gaia only saw flashes and faded images of her going back and forth amongst the cover of the camp. Suddenly, Gaia saw nothing and lost all trace of her.

It was silent and still in the clearing among the tents. Gaia held her posture for as long as anticipation would allow. She settled her thoughts and debated whether to give chase or retreat completely. Gaia lowered her sword. In that moment of uncertainty as her defenses dropped, Sciona came out of the sky. Like a dying raven, she twisted out of the air with her daggers aimed toward Gaia. Gaia was truly at the mercy of the attack. Her eyes widened then closed. She waited for the next instant when death would strike.

Then came a great thud. Gaia had been forcefully cast to safety as a body hurled her into the sand. Dazed, Gaia set her feet and looked down while Sciona scoffed at the timely luck. Bellia lay on the ground bruised and beaten. Her pounded flesh was swollen and tender. She lay there still. Her ragged tears and itching wounds filled with stale blood and gritty sand. Gaia ran to Bellia and gathered her in her arms.

"What happened? Who did this?" Gaia asked

As the words ventured off her tongue, the booming steps of the giant Jacobb brought him into the clearing. Sciona halted him. While they talked, Gaia tended to Bellia.

"Bellia, say something." pleaded Gaia.

Gaia raised her hands to Bellia and touched her body to swathe her wounds with the healing of her Will.

"No, stop." stated Bellia.

She grabbed her hand. Gaia was puzzled and did not heed, until Bellia revealed more.

> "I am okay. The brute got a few licks in, but I cannot let you waste the greater sum of your spirit, the fuel of your Awakening Will on me. I have spirit left and I will use it to finish this."

Gaia stopped; though the seconds spent being healed helped Bellia's state considerably. She came to her feet and feigned a powerfully fresh resolve. Gaia stood by her as their presence commanded the attention of their foes.

Jacobb laughed with a rumble, which echoed across

the desert floor. With minor cuts and bruises, Jacobb readied again his bull-like charge. Sciona stood back to take in the carnage for a moment. Jacobb barreled down on Bellia, but Gaia stepped in front of her. She waved her arm and shaped her hands and fingers to the symbol of Uriel. The sand became thin and moist beneath the feet of Jacobb. It slowed him but the mammoth still trudged through the swamp of sand. Unaware, Jacobb continued to sink in the sand. He then struggled uncontrollably until finally, the Earth consumed him. The grains of sand quickly became hard and ridged again as Jacobb was buried.

Gaia ran towards Sciona satisfied with her resourcefulness in dealing with Jacobb.

"Gaia, wait!" cried Bellia.

Out of the sand, the huge hand of Jacobb ensnared Gaia by the leg. Within an instant, Gaia disappeared after she was pulled beneath the ground into the abyss. Bellia hobbled to the spot where the sand closed in around Gaia. Upon her knees, digging and digging, she cried out.

"Gaia! Gaia!"

Sciona walked towards Bellia swaying her hips in a prance.

"No, No, No! We are alone, you and I. And oh, the games we could play," said Sciona.

Bellia stood barehanded. Her sword long gone. Sciona ran in on Bellia and the dance ensued. Sciona led with a swipe aimed at Bellia's ear. Bellia leaned into the attack and blocked her advance. She raised her arm and held her by the wrist, stopping the blade away from her body. Bellia countered with a blow. She thrust a knee to her stomach, which knocked the wind out of Sciona. Sciona stumbled back a step before quickly attacking again. Stabbing haphazardly, Sciona caused Bellia to retreat. She dodged with skillful agility. However, fatigue from her previous battle took hold. Her worry of Gaia was a distraction as well. *I'll have to end this soon,* thought Bellia.

Bellia saw the flaws in Sciona's aggressive style but she did not recognize her own decline in strength and speed. As Sciona's attacks became fiercer, Bellia's counters became fewer by degree. Finding the opening to strike a blow was limited by Bellia's inability to react timely enough. Bellia would not admit it, but Sciona was faster than her and became more so with every passing moment.

They struggled on, dancing on the sands leaving it ruffled and disturbed. But the sands now moved unnoticed by them. Swirling slowly at first, then more violently, the sand turned and toppled upon itself. Like a consuming whirlpool, the sea of sand opened up. The fissure had no draw or pull. A strong air emanated from the core. Suddenly, something came and sprang forth. Springing high into the air out of the whirling sand. It was the body of

Gaia. She reached the apex of her flight then fell back to the Earth landing hard on her side.

Gaia moved slowly, she was bloodied and covered by the dry rigid sands. The battle beneath the desert floor left her gasping. She looked around to gather what she could of the situation. She saw Bellia and shook her head to focus herself. She walked towards her to help. But as Gaia stumbled towards Bellia, the ground still gave. The massive arm of Jacobb came forth, out of the captive fissure. His hands dug deep. He pulled himself up from within the Earth.

"They may be beyond us," said Gaia.

Gaia placed her hand flat against the sand. She closed her eyes. She whispered then speared her hand into the sand. Jacobb neared freedom as the sand burned. Hotter was the ground, until it shimmered and hardened. Jacobb now stood half-encased in the golden glass that was the desert sand.

"Tricks." Jacobb grumbled.

The glass exploded without so much as the warning of a crack. The sound was deafening as the shards of hardened sand flew in all directions. Gaia, too weak to avoid the dagger-like shards, took three to her body. At the thigh, the shoulder, and into her abdomen, Gaia felt the pain of them burrowed into her. Gaia looked at her stomach and fell to her knees. She dared not to remove the shards for fear of bleeding to death.

Bellia's eyes strayed to her fallen companion, while holding on in her battle with Sciona. She saw the blood. She saw Gaia lowered and the maddened Jacobb looming towards her. Sciona paused as well. She stopped to taunt Bellia, making light of Gaia who lay wounded on the desert sand.

"Like the Red Fountains of Avalon. What a beauty." said Sciona.

Bellia had no retort or further discourse for Sciona. She felt the pain of her own injuries. Her emotion from the sight of Gaia flared them even more. Bellia grew desperate. Her body had no quantity of power to equal that of her will. And so it came to her, the thought of merging the two. To let the spirit become the body's fuel was Bellia's means to become almost godly. Despite the dangers, Bellia had to save Gaia as well as herself. And so she uttered the words, which stirred the spirit to be not of the soul but of the flesh.

Cupiam meo animo esse meam fortitudinem

Bellia's spirit emptied from her soul. And from that ethereal urn, it became substantial as it flowed through her veins. Bellia knew that the orb of the soul dwelled in an intangible place and was filled with the fluid of the spirit. Rare it was when that urn was drained, and the soul left hollow. However, Bellia heard the warnings and knew when the soul is depleted without the substance of the spirit, then mortals go beyond death, only to fall into oblivion. In such a way, Bellia was once told:

Think of the soul as a glorious ship, truly homeward bound, and the spirit as the winds that give power and direction to the journey ashore.

For Bellia, she needed that power for her and Gaia to make it through. Her limitless spirit poured into the wells of her flesh. They became one. As her flesh was tried and broken, so would her spirit be left to suffer the slings of that corporeal vessel. If the body failed in its endeavor, then the spirit could not return the soul homeward.

Those who practiced and used their Awakening Will knew the dangers of the technique, which Bellia used. The little known history of it recorded slaves who labored beyond the will of their body or heroes who moved the mountains and the Earth to save a loved one. No one dared to use it in battle. Bellia knew she would soon be the first.

Almost immediately, Bellia felt the warmth of her own blood coursing through her body, making her strong and righting the wrongs of her sustained wounds. Her senses heightened. She saw everything clearer. In the instant after Bellia spoke to let her spirit be her strength, Sciona caught her breath and reared back to attack again. Bellia paid her no mind. She sprinted at the giant Jacobb and left Sciona waving at air. She barreled into Jacobb again, though this time with their roles reversed. He pummeled into the sands yards away, the collision akin to an avalanche. Bellia kneeled beside Gaia. She wiped her brow and pulled back Gaia's hair. She raised her chin so she could look reassuringly into to her eyes.

"Hang on, Gaia. I'll get you back to the Wall."

Bellia scooped her up. She cradled Gaia in her arms with the ease and care of a small child. Bellia's perception continued to intensify in acuteness. Before Sciona and the recovered yet dazed Jacobb gave chase, Bellia followed her ears and ran west with the speed of a wild stallion. Bellia felt them closing and quickly ducked into a tent. She set down the now unconscious Gaia. It was a sign to Bellia that her condition worsened. Bellia left Gaia hidden so she could find a horse. It proved difficult in what was left of the ruined and nearly desolate camp. Amongst the aftereffects of chaos, Bellia raced to the stables. When she arrived, Sciona and Jacobb were already there. A single camel, the last and only animal was still tied. Bellia wanted to avoid confrontation, but needed the beast for a speedier journey.

Once again Bellia was left without a choice. She thought of a quick, devastating plan of attack. Time was fleeting. Alee grew further distant as did Gaia in another way entirely. Bellia made her first in a series of planned out moves. However, before she could balance herself, Jacobb jerked suddenly. He snatched the camel by the throat and put it down gruesomely.

Bellia's eyes widened. She ran back into the camp towards Gaia. With her friend and sister in such horrible shape, the need to stay and fight was eliminated. She gained distance as her spirit, still strong, made her speed exceptional. Suddenly, Jacobb landed in the path of Bellia. His leap was followed by the cold and sinister words of Sciona. And in her own words, so playful to Sciona, she bade Bellia to stay and enjoy the pleasures of a slow and painful death.

In a day full of battle and death, it would begin again. Hopeful was Bellia to the thought that this would be the last battle and that relative safety and rest might follow. Bellia wasted no time. She was upon Jacobb as quickly as he could blink. Delivering hard rights, she turned the heaping man's jaw toward the sky. For Bellia, it was as if her body could no longer contain the energy, which she summoned from her spirit. She felt greater and greater power. It was more than she imagined when she spoke the words. Godly, she heard all and saw so brightly.

She stood over the toppled Jacobb and began wailing away. Every punch was harder and louder than the one before. The sound of pounding flesh against flesh was now the echo across the sand. Sciona made her move, though Bellia did not notice. All her senses were now so heightened that all Bellia heard was an agonizing muffle. All she saw was the blinding light of the stars reflected off of blood, sand, and sweat. Sciona snuck behind her then wrapped Bellia by the throat. With the slack of her leather straps, the same that covered her body from head to toe, she strangled Bellia. Bellia had no balance to push away or break free. Bellia struggled and flailed like a fish out of water.

Jacobb with his tender and bruised face walked towards Bellia. He coiled to strike Bellia and then let loose a devastating blow to her face. In her current state, Jacobb's barrage brought an intense physical pain. But more so, with her body and spirit connected, being hit was something indescribable. The intense pain of the blows felt like that of a broken heart or like sincerest regret, like a mournful lost or the emptiest depression. It was emotional pain made physical and unbearable. The last hit was despair upon her body as if she lost all the faith left within her heart. In all, it was every possible emotional pain that made mortals weak.

It was dying on the inside repeatedly.

Bellia was unprepared for such distress. She had never before used her Will in such a way. Within moments, she could take no more and fell. Jacobb grabbed Bellia and followed Sciona. And with her skills, they quickly came upon Gaia, motionless in the tent where Bellia had left her. Jacobb carried them both, Gaia across one shoulder and Bellia across the other. The two fiends of Avalon, though bruised and weary were pleased at their task completed. They took Gaia and Bellia to the East edge of the camp. There waited three horses, one for Sciona and the other two for Jacobb to guide on a carriage. He plopped the two women inside and barred the door. Sciona and Jacobb left for Avalon by way of Soxor with the bodies of Gaia and Bellia.

VERSE III

The Barren Sea - The night gave way to the morning sun. Alee had been traveling now for hours. Although Hat-kaptah was with her, Alee was left alone with her thoughts. She contemplated every cause and effect up until that very moment. It was all she could do to keep her mind off the waving horizon, as the burning sand grew hotter. The sun reached its apex before falling again. Without Gaia and Bellia, Meroe and Buhen, Faras or Karwynn, Alee was victimized by doubt. Doubts that had festered before now had room to grow without the positive words of loved ones to cut them down. She asked all the questions before she turned back to Hat-kaptah. They both guided their horses by foot in order to rest them. *Did I bring him here all this way to die?* She thought.

Alee continued to walk. Despite all the questions she asked of herself, Alee did not pause to answer. The answers were unknown to her. Cause and effect, the questions and what-ifs kept her mind at work while they both pressed the sand heading West. With less than half a day's travel undertaken, the two were well past fatigued.

> "We will rest in the day and travel by the cooler night. Knowledge of the stars will guide us like the sun does by day," stated Alee.

She held her eyes low and never looked directly into the

eyes of Hat-kaptah. His wounds were now a dark purple, almost black. They were everywhere from top to bottom. There were even markings on either side of his neck, which were strangely artistic and mosaic. Alee glanced at them from time to time, when Hat-kaptah was unaware. She lamented that because of her, Hat-kaptah had been carved into a tortured canvas.

Alee's thoughts grew as arid as the land she was in; where life became so scarce and hidden. It became harder and harder for Alee to champion her own cause. All she had done since first spilling blood a mere day ago was point her finger as to *why* and *how*.

A mother who threw me away. She thought. She had no taste for water and had the ill-gotten foresight to pack both water and wine. She was dim to many rules of travel and thus drank away. She giggled while her thoughts continued. *A mother who threw me away only to have me coddled by another mother who would also give me over.* She laughed again for she had no tolerance for the potency of the drink and quickly became inebriated. Hat-kaptah finished raising the canopy. He also made the beds that would shelter them through the day. Afterwards, he came to Alee. He sat beside Alee while she stared into space looking only at thought and memory. He reached for her satchel. He lowered himself and looked into her eyes.

"Not this," he said softly and took the wine away. Alee leaned into him. He wrapped his arms around her. She felt the form of his scars embossed along his body. She also felt his stature and strength that was greater than when they last embraced. It felt safe to her but oddly, it reminded her of Faras.

Many nights in Dorginarti the two, Faras and Alee, held courtship, and never before in her life had Alee felt the comfort of someone who listened truly. Someone who listened, not for an opening to speak or even for the news by which to settle transgressions, but who listened as pure comfort. It took time for Faras to listen in such a way, but Alee's love changed something in him. Love had not always been a comfort to Alee. For Karwynn's unspoken love, though shown to Alee, at times could not compare to that of Faras. The wine took her mind back there to Faras and Dorginarti. Alee talked to him while he listened.

> "At what stage will my life be my own?" she wondered, "Given purpose, yes. But not one of my choosing. I did not want a life of killing. And what kind of mother would carve that out for their daughter?"

Alee paused. The desert grew silent as she fell into Hat-kaptah's lap.

"Do you know what scares me most?" she whispered, "I was...good...at the killing."

"And only now...hours later, do I even see their faces," added Alee.

She stared distantly.

"I may only now mourn because I do not truly mourn," she said solemnly, "...or that I mourn so little."

She said nothing more. The two travelers fell asleep beneath the cooler shade of their canopy. Now dreams of what Alee had done were left to her mind; for her psyche was unprotected by the anchor of reality. She saw the past and present as well as her apprehensions for the future. Loved ones were dead, lying amongst the slaughtered bodies of those she had slain. Ghosts of the past cried around her with their unrelenting presence. Flashes of pain and torture, scars and sorrow were abundant in her mind. With no comforts like redemption, truth, peace, or good, Alee could have easily fallen into despair had her dream been more coherent. But like most dreams, the imagery and memory of it all was broken. They caused her only a waking jolt after the sun finally set.

Into the night sky was Hat-kaptah. He stood alone. He broke away from Alee around midday for he found it hard to sleep during the day, despite their strategy to beat the heat and preserve strength. Alee tied her soft yet ruffled hair back and walked beside him. He made no motion to acknowledge her presence at first. To Alee, either he was lost in thought or overcome by some greatness in the heavens.

"Which star do we follow?" he asked.

"I should be asking you. You are the key," she replied.

"And if I am not?" said Hat-kaptah.

"Not to worry. If destiny is destined then all we must do is travel west across the Barren Sea. When the time comes and there is no more west or clues to be followed, then the both of us will be free of what people claim to be destiny," scoffed Alee.

"And which path do you desire, Alee?" asked Hat-kaptah.

Alee felt the dryness of the air in her throat. She lost the words that plagued her mind for the last few days. Hat-kaptah saw her and relieved her of his question.

"I have missed you since Abydos," said Hat-kaptah.

"And I you, my friend," she replied.

"About the world in other places, I hope there is some peace and safety," Hat-kaptah stated.

Alee turned back to the canopy as if running from Hat-kaptah's tender words. She felt peace and safety in that moment, which was ironically one of reminiscing. She sang a song of him before, which praised his friendship and loyalty. Months after Dorginarti and Adindan, Alee found strength in her friendship and connection with Hat-kaptah.

About the world, in other places, peace and safety seemed prevalent. The Isle of Avalon, along with Eden, created whispers among men. Perfection, abundance, and paradise were translucent dreams to mankind, but the legend of those places gave men hope. However, no man's dream of it compared to what true paradise was; especially in the case of Avalon. There on the Isle, the seasons changed as they needed. Everything green felt the joy of full bloom for as long as the laws of nature allowed. Winter was white and cool, always powdered by snow, never beaten by ice. And summer and spring seemed to meld together as one.

In the Forest of the Eastern Bank, not far from Changel's stronghold, the grass, so perfect, was beaten by the pounding of feet in pursuit. Vale-Kain ran quickly. He hurdled over stones and ducked branch and vine. He ran with such intensity that the land before him blurred due to the sway of his head in stride. It was hard for him to keep up. In more ways than one, his target continued to elude him. He raced on. Finally, he came to a halt. The forest cleared to the base of a cliff. Vale-Kain paused and looked directly into the eyes of the wolf.

The wolf was a strange hue; so much orange it seemed brown. The wolf circled and paced. Kain anticipated the beast. He was in awe, for it was as large as a lion. The wolf's face drew back to reveal fangs as sharp as blades. The wolf seemed to smile when it growled. The sound reverberated against the cliff walls. The birds, in the forest trees, were unsettled. They flurried from the loud sneering rumble.

> "What now, my Lord? Do you loathe my watchful eye and protective arm so exceedingly?" asked Kain.

In the blink of an eye, the wolf form gave way to that of a humming bird. It flew skyward beyond Kain's sight and reach. Kain walked slowly to the base of the cliff and prepared to climb. He grabbed the first stepping stone. Kain sighed from the game played at his expense. He looked at the face of the mountainside and began the long climb that awaited him.

The climb was well paced. Without rope or harness, Kain embedded his fingers in the stone; his dark green tunic flowed freely off his shoulders. His face made no sign of effort or exertion while he pulled and pushed his way to the top. Within the hour, Kain met the apex of the high ridge.

His eyes surpassed the sight of the mountain rock to that of the western setting sun. Changel-Wolf waited for him. The menacing hound came to attention with ears reared back, and then forward again.

In moments, the setting sun fell and gave way to a purple light that blended just above the horizon. Kain conquered the mountain and made his way towards the beast that was Changel. He stirred before the dog, then paused with a sense of caution as well as anticipation. The wolf leapt to its hind legs as fur began to shed. The ridged hair fell to the ground like a stack of needles. He was now bare, with every muscle through the skin clearly defined. Suddenly standing more upright, the wolf's torso and arms grew more bulky. With foul breath emanating, Changel turned to Kain howling ferociously. Kain remained still while the transformation continued. The ears and snout of the beast recoiled as the man-wolf stood taller. Changel's face became more defined, more human. However his features seemed younger compared to the form that was most commonly seen by most Avalonians. And so, Changel, the younger, stood naked before Kain. Kain saw his choice of apparent age odd. However, he knew not to question.

Changel's skin sprouted vines of rosebuds from every pore. Slowly twitching at first, they all bloomed into the clothes he came to wear. It was a single white shawl, which flowed and melted into the ground. The shawl rested upon him from the shoulders. And though it was sleeveless, it showed the strength of his young stature. The white fabric, accented by the silver of rose vines, was fine as silk, yet strong as steel.

The sun's last ray fell upon the night sky, giving way to the silver moon, which shone so brightly. Kain, after all the extraordinary exploits, finally gave his courtesy to Changel. A slight bow of the head was all that Kain gave to the lord of the land. Changel walked over to Kain. The moon was intense, though it seemed to strengthen the shadows in view. From on high, the trees looked like an ocean as the wind moved the darkness like a gentle wave.

"Kain, whom my son claims as his First Among Many, how do you fair today?" asked Changel.

"Am I not your son as well, my Lord?" Kain replied. Changel paused at the bold reply, which sprang forth so freely from the mouth of Kain.

"Alonard has spoken highly of your courage, but it seems in truth to be stupidity," stated Changel.

"No, my Lord. I merely wish to be enlightened. All who think, love, and live are either children of Eden or Avalon. The *greater* are Avalonians either by Pixsus, Nympthia, or Changel. I would choose to believe my heritage is traced to your line."

"You forget all lines lead to One," replied Changel, before continuing, "He who created all. Do not separate the two. Though one is to rule the other, always remember the *weaker* is a testament to God's omnipotence, an imperfect thing made so perfectly."

Kain stood beside Changel as they both looked out towards the Western Bank. Kain remained still, while Changel continued.

"Freewill is a concept that every father fears, yet also embraces. I know Alonard is loyal to me. He shows it. I do not force him to love, serve, or protect me, though I am capable. It means more that he chooses me. If the day should come when I were to lose his service, it would be a betrayal that would rip the heart from me. The thought of that pain is my fear; and knowing now he is true gives me cause to praise freewill."

Kain grew perplexed. He knew not where the load of words came. Kain's look showed his desire for clarification and Changel continued.

"We all were given freewill. Though it would have been easier to make us love and be righteous. But if that were so, we would not be choosing to make our imperfections perfect. We would simply be."

Changel turned to Kain and looked him in his dark blue eyes. Kain found it hard to maintain a stare with Changel. His skin seemed to grow paler, the longer their eyes were connected. Finally, he looked back to the silver moon.

"You have exercised your gift of freewill as well, Kain." said Changel, "You have made choices..."

Suddenly, Changel drove his arm through the body of Kain. The blow was forceful enough to pierce through the breastplate of armor and bone, yet quick enough to leave Kain impaled without moving an inch. Changel's arm ran deep as it dug into Kain all the way to his upper bicep. Out of Kain's back came Changel's fist in a form that was not entirely man. Black fur and feathers covered Changel's forearm, though they glimmered red from the thick of Kain's blood and the light of the moon. A razor sharp talon, like the griffins of legend formed Changel's hand. It opened and held the bleeding.

"You love my son. You are devoted. You are loyal. But there is no place for the choice you made, love so misguided and friendship so greatly perverted," Changel growled as he spoke.

With a voice increasingly intense and gritty, his face could not hide the severity of his wrath. Kain struggled to breathe, gasping, though otherwise adjusted enough to speak.

Changel's arm kept Kain intact. Changel saw Kain struggle to form words.

"And what would you say with your last breaths?" Changel retorted.

Kain started to fade. His eyes glazed and looked past Changel to the distant silver moon. He tried to speak, but could not call out. Kain never spoke a single word, though Changel did wonder. The last thoughts of Kain were written upon his face. Changel was not able to see confusion or regret. He saw sorrow. Changel wrenched his arm away from the lifeless body.

"Was your sorrow due to your treachery discovered? No, your thoughts were still of Alonard."

Changel sighed before he slowly lowered Kain into position. Both knees met the ground and Kain's arms fell to either side. After tilting Kain's head to the left, Changel filled the hole he'd made in Kain's chest with mud.

"Even still, you deserve peace. I grant you that. And safety from your choices," said Changel.

Kain's skin dried and cracked. His hair and clothes ceased blowing in the wind. Slowly Kain, and all that were about him hardened and turned a dark grey. It was as if a plague of granite infected the lifeless body. Within moments, Kain became the stone embodiment of what Changel knew to be mercy.

"Here you stay. Better as stone than the rotting corpse I wish to leave behind."

The pure white fabric Changel wore was now spotted in black, the color of dried blood. He made no effort to be rid of the stains, leaving it upon his garments as well as his face and hands.

Out of the sky came a foul form. Though indeed, it was only an owl. It seemed to find its perch upon the statue as soon as the last bit of flesh became rock. It settled on Kain, atop his shoulder. The watchbird shook its wings; releasing the moist air that seeped in from flying high on such a cold, damp night. Changel chose to ignore the bird. He continued to walk away from the statue that kneeled to look out over the mountain's edge. The owl called and Changel turned to Caim.

"That was extremely entertaining, my friend." exclaimed the owl.

"What do you want, Caim?" Changel asked.

"What do I always want?" Caim replied gingerly.

"But tell me, was all that necessary?" He added.

"I do not have time for this pointless banter. Leave me." Changel stated.

"That is the problem with you mortals, no patience. You should always have time because there will always ***be*** time."

Changel turned to trek down the mountainside leaving Caim speaking at the Statue of Vale-Kain.

"For mortals will live until time is no more."

The Barren Sea held them captive, the two travelers who set out from the Wall in pursuit of a better world. The arid burn of the desert air was enough to overwhelm anyone. Their lips cracked and their eyes turned red and dry, but Hat-kaptah and Alee continued on. Alee, fully covered, wore a black shawl and shroud. A simple piece with only minor silver accents to distinguish rank among the Nubian legions, it protected her as best as could be expected. It hid all but her eyes to the elements. Though unsophisticated in its design, she wore it elegantly. Alee took the shawl from Meroe's trunk when she loaded up at the Wall. Hat-kaptah, however, had no such garbs. Oddly, he seemed unphased by the excruciating heat. His scars had long since crusted over. The scars created a thick shell, encasing the majority of his body.

Alee staggered across the sands. She found it harder and harder to place her feet beneath her. She lurched ahead of Hat-kaptah who led the horses behind her. It had been several hours since Alee and Hat-kaptah exchanged words that were not logistically related to their journey. Alee seemed colder than before to Hat-kaptah. She brooded across the Barren Sea like a demon possessed. Hat-kaptah sought the cause. However, he realized he had a small point of reference to access the changes in her demeanor.

They had both endured so much from the hardships of the desert and the days before. Hat-kaptah kept a close eye. Alee's clothes flowed, tattered in the wind. They walked on the edge of a peaking dune. Alee struggled to maintain her balance, but continued to feign a sure resolve, both mentally and physically.

Suddenly, the wind began to pick up. Alee grew fainter with every step she took. Dizziness overwhelmed her. She stumbled and fell sliding down the side of the dune into a whirlpool of sand. Hat-kaptah leapt after her and slid quickly over the coarse incline. The friction of the sand heated and scarred his body even more. His old scars chipped and peeled away, leaving only the soft pus of flesh beneath his skin. At the bottom of the sand, Alee laid still. Hat-kaptah found her scarred across the arms, hips, and thighs. The greater part of her robe was completely ripped away. He tried to revive her. Dehydration and heat exhaustion pushed her body beyond its limit and she had fallen deep into unconsciousness.

Hat-kaptah placed her across his shoulder and began

the climb back to the apex of the sand crater. The extra weight made his muscles burn. His legs sunk knee high into the sand. He struggled to pull them out with every step. More than half way up the dune, Hat-kaptah slipped and Alee fell from his shoulders. He quickly reached back and grabbed her by the wrist. There he was stretched out. His right hand and leg anchored him to the sand. He screamed then mustered the strength to pull her up.

Within the next hour, Hat-kaptah made it back to the top of the dune. Weak, he recklessly laid out on the plateau of sand and nearly fell over the opposite edge. He rested his eyes for what seemed like a moment to him. However, when they opened, both he and Alee were surrounded. Three men stood before Hat-kaptah, two behind, with the edges of the dune to either side. As quickly as possible, Hat-kaptah stood to attention, still hunched by fatigue. He studied the men. The three before him wore black tunics, with maroon hide vests that ran from neck to knee. Their eyes were hidden through the shadow of the cloth. Hat-kaptah leered. He turned his chin to his shoulder to catch sight of the strangers behind him. They wore the same garbs, though the shortest one to the left behind him wore a silver pendant. To Hat-kaptah, the rectangular medallion had no decipherable markings, yet, he seemed drawn to it. Enthralled by the pendant, his eyes never turned back to his front. He gazed at the object not noticing one of the three had kneeled beside Alee. Hat-kaptah only regained full clarity when he heard the strangers in front of him speaking.

"This is a foolish one. She has been drinking, completely dry within. We must get her back," said the man with the gritty low voice.

The short carrier of the pendant responded slightly with a nod. Two soldiers moved to gather Alee, when Hat-kaptah motioned towards her. Swiftly, two other soldiers drew their snake-curved daggers. The short stranger looked on. Hat-kaptah began his appeal to whom he clearly thought to be the group's leader.

"Let us pass. We mean you no harm," stated Hat-kaptah.

The stranger was quiet. With a mere gesture of the hand, the stranger ordered the others to escort Hat-kaptah, along with Alee, across the Barren Sea. Hat-kaptah relented. He stopped with a sterner dimension about his face.

"Make your intentions known, now."

Hat-kaptah blurted the order with forceful implications. It was nothing more than a bluff on his part. Hat-kaptah lacked the strength to stand upright. His voice was the only manner about him that matched his false bravado.

"Secure the girl. We must take them back to the

Oasis."

Hat-kaptah heard the leader speak yet again. He envisioned a small watering hole in his mind. They put their feet to the sand and walked in line. From the rear, two of the strangers pulled Alee, wrapped tightly in damp cloth, on a wheeled dolly. Two more of the marauders led Hat-kaptah by knifepoint with the leader of the pack in front.

"Where are we going?" Hat-kaptah asked.

The wind continued to swirl. Visibility was low. A full-blown sand storm made the noses on their faces nearly impossible to see, but somehow, the marauders found their way. They walked for hours and made only slight turns and twists to adjust their bearings.

Sure enough, as the winds settled, they all came upon a watered clearing. Hat-kaptah paid no mind to the soldiers. He rushed to the water and buried his head in it. Until then, he and Alee had been given a traveler's ration. Now, Hat-kaptah indulged himself.

The Oasis was the size of a small lake. With the green of grass and trees surrounding it, the sand melted into the dirt at the watery bank. It was a marvel of beauty and reality.

"How could such a place be unconsumed by the Barren Sea?" Hat-kaptah said.

No reply came. The silent strangers took position and

spread out around the waters. Their feet slightly met the edge of the waters. All Hat-kaptah did was look, although he was capable of much, much more. With the last desert marauder in place, they called out in unison:

Denudate Ouache

The sparkling gray waters fell away from their feet. Slowly upon itself, it flowed back. It was a familiar sight for Hat-kaptah who now thought the desert strangers to be Children of Avalon. The lake continued to sink away until its bottom revealed two cylindrical pillars sprouting from the ground. The water fell back into one that acted as a drain. The other, however, was covered and sat a few yards adjacent to the draining pillar.

> "Hurry, we have but a few moments. Gather the girl."

The orders were given by one of the marauders. Hat-kaptah saw the true power behind the words they spoke to dispense the water.

> "A password," he whispered to himself, "Loud enough with five mouths to be heard through the water and the ground."

The strangers moved the heavy cap of the pillar away. Inside, foot holes led into the darkness. Hat-kaptah could not see how deep it was when he stood upon the brink. He only saw the grey edges of the tunnel turn to pitch black nothingness. Suddenly, the draining pillar rumbled with a loud moan. The water inside flush against the lip rippled and waved.

"Hurry people."

Alee was fixed against the back of the brawniest marauder. Three other strangers followed them into the tunnel. Hat-kaptah heard the moans and creaks grow louder and knew them to be the reasons for their sudden haste. He descended, but paused.

> "Are you coming?" Hat-kaptah shouted to the leader.
>
> "Go, I have to seal the pillar with the mud of this Oasis before I can enter."

The leader yelled over the rumbles. Hat-kaptah hopped back out of the tunnel. He gathered the slightly damp, yet firm mud near the outer edge of the lake with the stranger. They packed the mud to seal the rim. Suddenly, the waters shot out of the drain pillar. The eruption made its own tall pillar of water. The water rained down upon the two. They scurried and worked together to complete the seal that was only half way around. Hat-kaptah waded through water in order to get more mud.

"We have to hurry. The water level will reach the

brim of the tunnel in a few moments," the stranger exclaimed through the sound of rushing water.

The two finished packing the seal as the water met the edge. The stranger rushed Hat-kaptah into the tunnels. He held on to one of the footholds to stop from falling into the cramp dark. Hat-kaptah looked skyward, with water rushing upon him. He saw the stranger. The marauder was directly above Hat-kaptah with the heavy, bulky cap held above. It was an eclipse to Hat-kaptah as the stranger got into position. With nothing but darkness above and below, the water weighed him down. The stranger, with the cap held high above, leapt into the tunnel to stop the waters and seal the pillar with the cap.

In silence, the stranger and Hat-kaptah made their way down. Their sounds made them aware of one another in the deep. A hollow echo made by the water passed the time during their descent. Hat-kaptah spent the time putting his mind to the question of whether the desert marauders were his captors or saviors. The question was left with no answer and before long the journey met its end.

Finally, after a downward trudge of nearly an hour, their feet hit solid ground. The light of blue fire lanterns welcomed them. Alee was there with the others, again on the dolly and still unconscious. Hat-kaptah rushed to her side. He said nothing but stood tall. His frustration swelled.

"Why have you brought us here?" he asked.

Finally, the leader among them spoke, un-muffled by noise nor altered by volume.

"All will be revealed in a moment," a voice softer than Hat-kaptah expected replied.

It was enough to ease him. He followed without further dispute.

Through the Oasis Tunnels, they trekked. Carved out hundreds of years ago, they were a sight of old artistry and engineering. The tunnels had an arched support, though the stones pieced along the sides were spiraled. Each spiraling stone support had markings upon them. Characters that meant nothing to Hat-kaptah, yet still, he stood in awe of them. Ever so often, they would pass the wheels of the tap and the chambers that diverted the waters. It flowed downward and south bound, from the ocean to the reservoir then back southeast to the free waters of the sea.

The Oasis was something of an ancient overflow tank. On this day, the overflow was blocked by the words cried by the desert strangers. So strong was the flow of the ocean and sea that the pressure withstood by the intricate system also spoke to the skill of the ancient builders. *Ancient* they were, in reference to when they were built, not in the advanced manner by which they were used. The tunnels and lines were far beyond anything ever before constructed.

The light in the distance grew brighter. It was a white light that ate away at the lanterns' blue, overcoming them. Hat-kaptah hesitated to walk into the white light. He was more apprehensive compared to the darkness he dove into back at the pillar entrance. He followed for the sake of Alee, who was his concern.

A new world was unveiled to him, a township underground. Hat-kaptah saw the tunnels flowing in from all direction into the buried acropolis that brought food, water, and fresh air. The city was beneath a vast dome of earth that stretched far and wide, perfect in circumference. Every structure was arched and domed as well. They were built keeping with the style of the tunnels, which reflected a resistance to cave-ins and falling debris.

Almost every structure was a dull grey color. To the ancients who built the underground civilization, pride came from the beauty of the build, rather than the shell of aesthetics poured upon a finished product. Wood was finished, not painted. Stone was trimmed, not glossed. Despite the look of the city, Hat-kaptah saw the villa that was center to the realm. They moved through the city towards it. The people held their heads low, parted and made way for the envoy from the surface. They looked at

Hat-kaptah. The sight of his body so bare and uncovered outdoors was odd enough. His battered state also added to their turning an eye.

They came upon a huge treated door made of wood without latch or lock upon it. It swung open by the hand of the short stranger, who had shown great strength to Hat-kaptah once before at the entry of the tunnel.

The seven from the surface entered the atrium. Without word, two departed left with Alee. Hat-kaptah motioned to follow but halted by the leader's glance, and continued behind. Straight ahead, they marched until they came into a room called the Prima. There in the middle of the Prima was the governor upon his seat. Along the wall, carved into the earth were three doors or vaults, two to either side and one directly behind the seat. Hat-kaptah's heart pounded erratically. He felt it harder and harder to breathe there, where the sun was so long hidden from him. He looked upon the man in the seat. His skin was a cool brown, lightened by the missing sun. With eyelids closed, his brow showed the wisdom of age. Hat-kaptah approached, led by the stranger. The old man spoke, while the soft-spoken leader stood beside Hat-kaptah.

"Long have I been...in the dark," sighed the old man. He opened the lids of his eyes. He revealed the black pearls he once used to see. Hat-kaptah remained silent.

"My name is Asal-Iman. I have something to ask of you."

Hat-kaptah paused and awaited the question. Asal-Iman rose from his seat and slowly came towards Hat-kaptah until they stood toe to toe.

"Would you take my hand?"

The old man extended his arms to Hat-kaptah. He cupped them, patiently waiting for the touch of Hat-kaptah's hand. Hat-kaptah moved slowly. He extended his hand as if it were a bird slowed by caution to a feed. Finally, Hat-kaptah's finger touched the tip of the old man's hand. Unexpectedly, the old man's hand reached out and grabbed Hat-kaptah's. Fist over fist, they were connected. Hat-kaptah fell to his knees from the sudden pain of Asal-Iman’s tight grip. Hat-kaptah looked at him with a *why* in his expression. He saw the black pearled eyes of Asal-Iman begin to flood a scarlet red. The pain was intense, though it came not entirely from his grip. It was as if something was being funneled out of Hat-kaptah, then pushed back, but swelled so it did not fit quite the same.

"What are you doing to me?" he cried.

"Be silent. Be still," replied the stranger, as Asal-Iman continued.

Just before the grey room seemed darker to Hat-kaptah,

Asal-Iman let him go. He fell, and then crawled back a few steps. The stranger came to him and kneeled beside him. Unwrapping the tunic, Hat-kaptah looked into the eyes of a young woman.

"Back away, Mhasika. Give him room to speak. He wants to say something," Asal-Iman stated behind a grin.

Whatever strength was gone from Hat-kaptah returned quickly. He rose to his feet and began.

"Who are you?"

"A simple question, with an answer I can give to you unfiltered," replied Asal-Iman.

"Well then? " expressed Hat-kaptah.

"Patience. We all are not as fortunate to wear our age as you do," answered Asal-Iman.

The old governor returned to his seat. And though help was not necessary, Mhasika escorted Hat-kaptah closer to Asal-Iman. Hat-kaptah listened and waited. Uneasiness surrounded him.

"Your coming has been foretold. I have seen that you are the key from a realm afar, but where is the other?"

Mhasika stepped forward.

"She is being treated. The Barren Sea nearly claimed

her," she interjected.

Hat-kaptah was worn by his own curiosity and ignorance. Playing the pawn, being used and led made him more impatient and enraged. His face was now hard and rather blank. Devoid of expression, he spoke with an ominous tone.

"It stops now. You will cease your reference of me, without regard to me. Nor will you speak of me as some trinket. What is this key? Alee has little knowledge of it. And if you have any, give it over by the next pause."

Asal-Iman smiled.

"How stern and poetic. Next time, speak more from the throat, it will make believers of all who listen."

Hat-kaptah did not know what to make of the old, blind man. His taunts and grimaces were daggers to his pride.

"Am I to be mocked now?" Hat-kaptah asked.

"You are to be light-hearted." Asal-Iman replied.

"And fully fed. Go with Mhasika. See the city, and then return for supper. With God's blessing, your Alee will be with us."

Hat-kaptah gazed at the center door behind Asal-Iman, while Mhasika pulled him towards the exit. He turned and walked with her back towards the atrium where they originally split from Alee. Hat-kaptah stopped in the middle of the room. Looking down each corridor, he then turned to Mhasika.

"Where is Alee?" asked Hat-kaptah.

"No taste for sight-seeing?" she replied.

Hat-kaptah lowered his head and rolled his eyes.

> "Does anyone here take matters seriously? Of course not, your leader's ways trickle down to his subjects."

Mhasika's expression changed. Hat-kaptah's comments, made from his brief encounters, thus far, did not speak accurately of a people so noble. And, on a more personal level, Mhasika did not care for his words spoken so unfavorably about her father.

> "Life is filled with sorrow and pain. And so, it can seem a never-ending barrage of serious offenses. Live in infinite despair if you must, but I make the moment. I perceive them as I choose. My father taught me these things. You know him as Asal-Iman."

Hat-kaptah's face fell when Mhasika spoke again. Her voice softened yet again.

> "Alee will be fine, I promise. Come into the city with me. Let go of some of those offenses. Release your sorrow and your pain, if only for a few fleeting

moments."

Her words would have touched Hat-kaptah, had he been there. Instead, her words fell on the deaf ears of someone fixed on a mission. With no knowledge of the labyrinth, he chose to follow Mhasika.

Elsewhere, several twists and turns away, a body was at rest while a mind was in turmoil. Alee was haunted by her thoughts since the days of Abydos. She had always been a heavy dreamer, but her dreams grew darker by the day. Once fielded by the flowering visions of Karwynn, Lyla, and Awana, she now saw a medley of darker things. A continuous barrage of disturbing flashes passed before her. Bodies beaten, bludgeoned and cut down by her hand crept back to life. A nightmarish vision grasped at her. The softer images of Karwynn and the like were buried by death itself. They now became the flashes stretched out amongst her corrupted remembrances.

Those that tended to her saw her unsettled state. Her eyes stayed in full motion beneath their lids. The women in the infirmary kept her swathed with a moist cloth. They wiped her brow and massaged away her soreness while she laid still. It was all they could do until she awakened. And like lightning out of a clear sky, her eyes opened.

"Welcome, back. I am Dorah. Try not to move," the

attendant said.

Alee rose slowly from her back and came off the table. Her face was unreadable though Dorah saw her fierce eyes. The other attendants seem to be parted by her stare. They stepped away from her leaving a clear path between Alee and Dorah. Erratically, Alee came closer to Dorah, who happened to block the exit. With less than a thought, Alee pushed Dorah through the portal with her Will. For Dorah, death had come instantly. And she now lived, only in the terrors of a mind troubled by hellish decay.

Without word, Alee turned right and headed down the hall. The remaining attendants gathered around Dorah, who did not move. They sounded the alarm and cried out, which alerted all in the city to know a murder had been committed. Aleeia heard it and continued her unwanting journey.

Mhasika, by her call of duty, heard and came back to the scene with Hat-kaptah. She bore witness to the covered body and the wake of Alee who had already departed. Mhasika followed and came upon her before her father, Asal-Iman. Deep in discourse, Mhasika stayed hidden beside the portal way. And with Hat-kaptah, she listened.

"...troubled soul warring with your better nature,"

Mhasika heard her father say as they listened more,

> "...you must find what was lost in the Barren Sea. There you were broken. Your thoughts turned. You changed. But, lo, I speak not of things that are unknown to you. Even now, in your battered state, with sanity that comes undone, you know that true despair."

Aleeia said nothing. She heard the words but did not listen. She could not. Her mouth was still dry and the desert winds still roared in her ear. With her face neither to fall nor to rise, she crept by the seat of Asal-Iman to the center door. She pushed it with more force than that which took Dorah. The whole of the subset world rumbled at her cause, yet the door did not move. She thought on it more, she spoke the words, all in her effort to have the door removed. It stayed set. The portal, fixed in the cave, was locked to her.

"And where is your key?" asked Asal-Iman.

Aleeia looked back at him. She whipped her head around like a hawk who found new prey. Asal-Iman did not shrink away from her maddening gaze. He unseated himself and turned to the lost child, Aleeia. The fire in her eyes transferred to the world. The room grew warmer. The wood in the chairs cracked, while the air waved before their eyes. Aleeia walked towards Asal-Iman. Mhasika drew her daggers, but was held back by Hat-kaptah.

"My father," she cried to him.

"No wait..." he replied, pointing at the action before them.

Aleeia loomed closer to Asal-Iman. The air was too thick for Asal-Iman to weather. He fell from his seat, then suddenly, he snapped at Aleeia. Reaching out, he pulled her by the wrist closer to him. He cupped her face and saw her just as he did with Hat-kaptah before.

He felt her disconnection. He saw the troubled past of recent memory, the cause of her grief and anger. He looked deep inside her to find her anchor; that thing that all people have, which grounds them to their better selves. Family, love, and hope are common anchors, yet specific to each and every individual. Asal-Iman looked to find for Alee, that which was lost. The connection increased intensity for Asal-Iman. It was as if something was being pulled out of him, then pushed back faster and in greater volume than before. It was a pain too great for Asal-Iman yet he held on. He kept looking. He saw the flash of a fair man's face.

"Faras." he called.

Aleeia was not moved. She heard nothing. Asal-Iman grew a bit dizzy, while enduring the pain

of it. Despite it all, he continued to see. The black pearl eyes, which saw nothing of the corporeal world, began its change to a scarlet hue. He saw the sword and the star with a flash of two faces.

"Gaia. Bellia." he cried.

His face showed great discomfort. He held his grimace due to the pain of being drowned by the essence of her past. His vision of it blurred a bit. The scarlet ocular pearls faded back to the deep black void that was there before. Mhasika struggled to be near her father but Hat-kaptah held her tightly by the waist. For some unexplained reason, Hat-kaptah desired to see it all played out.

Aleeia looked down upon Asal-Iman. Unable to break his grip, but also in no noticeable discomfort, her face was as cold as the winter mountain peaks. Aleeia glanced back at the door, covered with the language of Nympthia. Still drawn, she pulled away from the hands of Asal-Iman who cupped her about her cheeks.

"Please..." he cried faintly.

"Karwynn...Please..." he added.

Aleeia stopped. Not having the strength to hold on, Asal-Iman let go of Alee. He then fell violently to the floor of the hollowed room. Aleeia drifted above him like a cloud full of powerful light that marked its coming with a thunderous roar. Asal-Iman was now totally blind, in every manner conceivable. However, he heard Alee widen her base, then nothing. No sound, not even a drafting breeze.

Suddenly, he heard the cry of Mhasika. Her passion to protect her father finally gave her the strength to race beside him. The young girl, though a fierce warrior, did not engage Aleeia. Mhasika only came to him, shielding Asal-Iman from her raised hand with the whole of her body. The isolation of the Barren Sea had left Aleeia's mind in shambles. Asal-Iman saw nothing left in her that could bring her back. But in that very instant, when Mhasika became more tense, acting as her father's cradle, Mhasika's pendant slipped from beneath her vest. It was in plain view for Aleeia to read, in the language now primary to her. And so she read aloud past her whispering lips,

Faith Lies With You, Daughter-Alee

It was read in such a way, right, but wrong. For Nympthia, *faith* meant *hope* and back again. Aleeia knew that. Nympthia spoke to her again so that Alee would break free of herself. She who was Aleeia tormented.

Hope Lies With You, Daughter-Alee

Oddly, the pendant read, was not her burden being revisited upon her. Her previous resentment of her destiny was the farthest thought from her mind when she read it. She found comfort in the words and knew her mind again. Nympthia was her anchor, her true mother. For the more Alee traveled, the more she made Karwynn and Aalarae the earthly incarnation of Nympthia's love and guidance. In the face of her matriarchs, she knew what she had done. She wept. She cried for Dorah. She cried for them all.

The Ouache Keepers - In the vast hollowed earth, in what was considered the southern part of a secret civilization, Alee stood near the cave walls. She stood there and admitted to herself that things had changed. She had changed and gone too far. A coffin was placed inside the tomb, in a wall amongst others. They were all marked by name in stone. Alee said a silent prayer, not only for Dorah, but for every life extinguished by her hands. As the body was cranked into its final resting place, Mhasika, who had her pendant in hand, stepped beside Alee. She was subtle and sure not to impose on the moment. Mhasika held out the pendant so that Alee, with her head held low, could see it.

"You saw this. This pendant given to me by my

father and you stopped. Why?" Mhasika asked.

"Is your father okay?" Alee inquired.

"He has yet to awaken," answered Mhasika.

"What was he…" Alee led as inquiry.

Mhasika cut off Alee. She knew the questions to come and spoke before them.

"My father is the governor...yes. But more so, he is Nympthia's Keeper. He cannot see you until he has touched you. Until the energies of your auras come in contact. One aura will always overwhelm the other and therein lies the pain. Hat-kaptah felt it and my father felt it when he touched you."

Alee turned to Mhasika with an eyebrow raised.

"And what does he see," Alee asked.

"It depends of course. Just like you and I, we perceive differently; primarily because we have bared witness to different things. What Father sees depends upon the person. For some, he sees their fears, for most he sees their past, and for a few he sees their future. And, upon doing so, he helps guide them to a place of balance," stated Mhasika.

"And what did he see in me?"

"I do not know."

Alee saw the turn. Mhasika acted to what she knew was to come and Alee did as well. She fiddled the pendant that

Mhasika held by her side and told her what she wanted to hear.

> "It says *daughter have faith!* It was a good token to receive...and it seems a timely message for the both of us."

Mhasika put on the pendant again. She was pleased to know of its meaning after wearing it for so long. She smiled and so did Alee. It was her first in quite some time. They left the tomb, for a ceremony was about to begin. The family and friends of Dorah came from the city to her resting place. Instinctively, Alee lowered her head. Mhasika held Alee's upper arm and escorted her through the crowd. Dorah was beloved by the entire town. In the dark, isolation of a civilization buried, Dorah kept the majority of the nation in excellent physical health as their treating physician. Asal-Iman could not hear the sorrow of all his subjects to subdue their troubled minds. Dorah served as their listening ear.

The stares upon Alee were like daggers. Through the veils and head wraps of the conservative culture, Alee still saw anger, contempt, and fear upon their faces. As the two ladies walked, the crowd parted and paused. For some onlookers, who would let their grief become violent, Mhasika's proximity was the only thing that shielded Alee. Even in rage, no one would dare throw stones near the daughter of their beloved leader. What Alee felt was beyond shame, and part of her wished to them whatever satisfaction they imagined for themselves.

"Do not be afraid," said Mhasika.

"There are few things left for me to fear, Mhasika. But, losing myself again is indeed one of them."

Mhasika and Alee neared the villa. Alee paused at the threshold.

"The moment he wakes, he will want to see you." Mhasika said.

"With all the questions I have, it seems your father is the only one in the world who might have some answers,"

"You would be surprised."

Mhasika's words added to her confusion. Her patience was even more limited by her recent actions. Alee entered the villa looking to find Asal-Iman.

"My father saw you. What he will tell you is what you already know, deep within your soul."

Alee returned to the infirmary where less than a day ago, she committed an unjustified atrocity. She did not try to suppress the memory of it. Nor did she try to convince herself she had killed outside of her own capacity to control her actions. She made herself fully accountable.

She entered and saw seven stone beds padded for comfort. In the room, the lanterns burned bright to overcome the gloomy and dark possibility of untimely endings. Alee had not noticed before, but carved in the stone of the bed base were the characters of Nympthia. She determined they were written ignorantly and only for their decorative stylings due to their randomness. Mhasika stood beside her father. She placed her hand on his chest, while it slowly moved up and down. The smile that followed caught Alee by surprise. Mhasika saw her perplexed.

"My father sleeps because you are strong. What he saw in you, what you told him by touch, was much to take in," said Mhasika.

"How long do you think he will lie still?" Alee wondered.

"There is no way to know. I hope soon he wakes, for both our sakes."

Alee gently brushed back Mhasika and placed her hand on Asal-Iman's chest. Using her Will was never primary for Alee. She searched her pouch for what was left of the Healing Leaves, but found none there. Thanks to her time in Abydos, her mind grew to a near, encyclopedic catalogue of knowledge, which fueled her Will. She searched for the proper method to revive Asal-Iman. A method came to mind, but with it was an even greater risk of Asal-Iman's death. Alee knew the body, more so than any person would for several generations. Its inner workings were a complex system that Alee used her knowledge of to bring back Asal-Iman.

Alee leaned over and placed her other hand upon his brow. Her left hand stayed still upon his chest. She closed her eyes and put her Will to the task of his revival. She moved his blood quicker through its course. Asal-Iman's heartbeat increased. She funneled the blood's crop of fruit, which invigorated the mind and body. Asal-Iman opened his eyes revealing the black pearls that were his legend. His breathing progressed and grew more powerful. His adrenaline pumped throughout. He was revived. He sprang up like a man half his age. Alee had to restrain him and slow the speed of the blood she made to race.

"Try to slow your breathing. Your body is on edge." Mhasika never had the opportunity to object to Alee. It was over and done before Mhasika saw more than a gentle touch upon the head by Alee. Alee gave Asal-Iman time to recover, in the silence, she heard the faintest succession of thumps from afar. Alee was careful not to touch Asal-Iman while he was conscious and fully aware.

> "A spirit such as yours would have had me slumber for weeks. I see you could not wait at length," said Asal-Iman.

Alee nodded and Mhasika smiled at the humor of her father. Alee saw them and stepped back for a moment so they could have time alone. Mhasika placed her arms around her father. They embraced, though Asal-Iman spoke to dismiss her,

> "Close words I require with Alee. Leave us, daughter. Please."

Mhasika left without an ill-gotten demeanor. She was use to the privacy requested by Asal-Iman, when he divulged the imagery of his visions. Mhasika left and Asal-Iman began.

> "Alee, you have a destiny and are fated to do more than most would dare to take on. You know this by the guidance brought to you by your mother. I am a keeper and know your mother as one of the three. You have followed a path to be here; where I am Keeper to the three doors. One of which I know is the Tomb of Pixsus. The others I cannot say."

Alee's eyes glazed over at, yet another speech of *destiny*. However, what Asal-Iman knew in regards to the tomb and the doors explained why Alee was drawn to them when her mind was fractured. She listened further.

> "You, the daughter...came with the son. You both are key to a single door, but only together can you unlock the center door."

Before Alee could fully consume Asal-Iman's words, she again heard the faint thumping in the distance from some chamber across the villa. She remembered that despite the strength gained from her lack of restraint, the center door would not be moved. She then pondered.

"*...the son? Hat-kaptah? Does he descend from Pixsus?*"

Asal-Iman paused to reexamine the memory of Alee's vision. When he touched her earlier, he saw her face a pale color. He saw what Alee truly needed.

"I know there is little comfort in the keys and trinkets laid out by your mother. There are two concerns that burn you from within. The people you love, will you ever see them again? And in the wake of that question you continuously ask yourself, why go on?"

Alee turned away. Being read so well shocked her. Alee had always felt she showed a strong resolve and commitment to her mission. At the very least she thought that her charge and drive was evident to the world. Now, she felt a bit of shame because her inner-self was, at last, naked to someone. When Asal-Iman spoke aloud, her needs did not compare when weighed against her duties. They seemed petty to her. Her shame became guilt. Being engulfed by self-loathing did not stop Alee from wishing for that simpler time. She dreamed of it again, then quickly remembered when she lost herself.

"I was me, until I saw nothing but the Barren Sea in front of me," Alee said to herself, "I wanted to be anywhere but there, doing anything but that."

Alee paused.

"I never even thought of home or Karwynn. I forgot everything. My most selfish moment met with the devilish culmination of a murder. Murder done by me."

Asal-Iman touched her on the shoulder. Seconds had passed before Alee realized his comfort.

"You have finally shown me what lies within," stated Asal-Iman.

"I am blind again. I have seen all there is to see in you. You are more than a mortal, a daughter of Avalon. But in you is the best and worst that is the nature of mankind. Choice is tantamount for all who live and breathe. Find that same freedom in your righteousness. Hope that heaven can truly be and then your destiny will find you."

All that had to be said was spoken by the two. Asal-Iman put on his thick grey tunic and black cottoned robe. They left the infirmary, where Mhasika waited patiently outside, just out of earshot. They walked together through the villa, back to the vault of the Prima were Asal-Iman's chair stood before the three doors. The faint thumps from before became subtle booms as they moved closer to the hollowed room. The sounds were spaced in generous intervals.

Finally, near the threshold of the vault, Alee heard the fullness of a resounding quake, unmuffled. She raced ahead of the others, sprinting to the doors. There inside the Prima, she saw Hat-kaptah who faced the center door. Alee did not allow herself to show any expression of surprise. His presence was indeed odd. Alee's heavy steps stopped him in whatever act he committed. Alee found the scene difficult to ascertain. There was a small dent in the center door that was not there before. Hat-kaptah approached Alee with concern.

"Alee, are you well? Are you, *you* again?"

"I was always *me*," Alee replied.

Mhasika and Asal-Iman followed behind. Fresh from the infirmary, Mhasika assisted her father, despite his assurance that he was completely able. Alee looked past her shoulder, to Asal-Iman behind her. She paused before she inquired of Hat-kaptah.

"Did you hear anything, Hat-kaptah?"

"I was on the overlook when I heard an auspicious yet thunderous bang. One after the next, I followed the sound until it led me here," he replied.

His words did little to ease her. More questions followed.

"How long ago did you arrive in the room," she

asked.

"Just moments before you, Alee," he replied.

Asal-Iman came forth with a look that said it all, which perplexed Alee even further. She had no cause to doubt Hat-kaptah. He was loyal and true beyond anyone she knew in her second life, the life after Karwynn and the Southland. Asal-Iman pointed to the first door, right of the center. Alee saw the words upon it.

"Can you read those words as well?" asked Mhasika.

"Yes," said Alee.

"What does it say?" she added.

Alee looked over the tall stone door. The laws, which governed its opening, were upon it, engraved. Alee answered Mhasika to their own dismay.

Where is God's Sacrifice, Daughter-Alee,
The thanks for the life that is given to thee.
No doubts, nor displeasures for all that should be,
Give tithe and rejoice 'ere death you to see.

Alee knew what she had to do. The words seemed to be nothing more than a riddle in verse to Hat-kaptah and Mhasika. Asal-Iman, however, knew the next step as well. He removed his thick cotton robe and made a place for Alee before the great stone door. She lowered herself to her knees. Mhasika and Asal-Iman stepped back, giving her space. Hat-kaptah followed suit. Alee bowed her head and closed her eyes. She placed her hands together and spoke her prayer.

> *Pater noster quî es in caelîs, sânctificêtur nômen tuum; adventiat rêgnum tuum; fîat voluntâs tua sîcut in caelô et in terrâ. Pânem nostrum supersubstantiâlem dâ nôbis hodiê, et dîmitte nôbîs dêbita nostra, sîcut et nôs dîmittimus dêbitôribus nostrîs; et nê inducâs nôs in temptâtiônem: sed lîberâ nôs â malô. Âmên.*

Alee waited. To her dismay, the door stayed closed and unmoved. Again, she read the words upon the stone. Alee did not understand. She turned back to Asal-Iman. He felt her eyes upon him.

"Where is God's sacrifice?" repeated Asal-Iman, "You have spoken your praise with beauty and formality; but are you truly content? Does your heart accept the slings and arrows of this life, with complete and utter faith that the Divine Hand shapes it with love for us all?"

Alee turned back to the door. In that moment, she gave herself to the Father. She smiled for all she was given, all she had endured, and the test that lay beyond her horizons. She was the sacrifice. Alee now drowned in the light of grace, where faith was more than just a word. As her teardrops fell upon the floor, the mountainous stone that was the seal to the Tomb of Pixsus opened.

Retold Awakenings - All were still as the door wrenched itself ajar. The fresher air funneled from the surface became sullied by the stiff, motionless air. The bare stench, accompanied by the dust unsettled after centuries of dormancy, crept out from within the tomb. Hat-kaptah held back a smile. Alee stepped forward. She turned to Asal-Iman, who had been a worthy guide thus far. She looked at him as if to find cause to not enter. His nod, however, symbolized the alternative.

Aleeia walked slowly to the seal. Her three companions took light steps to accompany her. Aleeia then stretched out her hand to hold them back as if to say *no further*. She waved across her face and the air became clearer, more dispersed. The door closed. Alee was alone and separated from the others. She raised her hands and the lanterns surged ablaze. Aleeia saw the majesty of a final resting place. Nympthia marked the walls, and there the story was told.

The tomb was spherical, arched like the tunnels. Two rectangular pillars stood in the center of the room. At the far end apex of the egg shaped tomb was the monument where in laid the remains of Pixsus. The room had no color, only the red from the flame and the grey from the stone. Aleeia walked closer to the monument with a bit of fear. Fear of the unknown settled. There were no markings or words to indicate what was to be done next.

> "Where is the clear road now? I am left with my own choice."

Alee reached for the latch of the sarcophagus. A sudden flicker of the light drew her back to the pillars. They too had markings of Nympthia upon them. Her eyes were drawn to the monument and the markings that Aleeia did not notice before. She read. It was the beginning to an end:

> Several centuries passed since the Fall and the Exile. Here in the Midlands of the Earth, we worked and toiled. But here as well, amongst the Aaminites, we, Pixsus and I, found a home. The animals grazed, the crops grew, and all was good. The past was unsettling, but as history grew, our memories did

fade. We wanted to forget the glory of the Isle and all that was lost. Pixsus was mother to three, long after my firstborn was thought lost in childbirth a lifetime ago. The chieftain, Adonai was wed to Pixsus; and his brother, Bivai to me. Matrimony brought us peace and the ability to lull the ambition of the leaders. Overall, we experienced peace and lived peaceably.

We were nomads in the Midlands where the air stayed warm. The land was expended before we moved on. One bustling summer day, word returned to Adonai. Scouters told of land beyond the Canyons of Mec. Land so plentiful, we need not pack another tent again.

Pixsus and I preferred the life of the wanderer. For although we called the Midlands home, who could settle for no less than the Isle. We continued on. Eighteen days, we beat the ground, until we found ourselves at the heart of Mec. Forsaking the pergolas, the men of Aamine built homes through trial and error. Finally, we were settled. And peace remained without adversity for many days.

Alee was done reading the face of the doorward pillar. She

wanted to know more than the story told. *How did they meet the Aaminites? Who were the sons of Pixsus?* Her mind showed no regard for those who were outside who wanted to know more. Hat-kaptah pushed the door. Intent to get in, he sat and prayed, but entry was not meant for him. He looked to the other doors, though mainly the center door. Back inside, Alee stepped right to the face of the second pillar. More writing appeared. She continued.

> Twelve seasons of prosperity followed. I thought surely that this land in Mec was another paradise on Earth. The day came when a stranger entered the village. Before Pixsus and I had words with Adonai, the people of Aamine killed intruders without hesitation. Pixsus, personally, prepared the meal, while I gathered the supplies. After a day of refreshment, the wayward traveler was again on his way.
>
> Two days later, the stranger returned with his lord and warriors. They were followers of the god, Tarim, another manifestation of Changel about the Earth. Their leader was Nadad. He was the kind of leader who would do anything to ensure the survival of his own people. And so he came to

conquer, kill, enslave and sacrifice.

Although we had numbers in our favor, we did not benefit from the long-standing peace and prosperity. Of our numbers, the majority were either children, elders, or young men, who had never seen a battle. As the Tarim worshipers were seen from a distance, swords in hand, the able women joined the able men. They formed a line and Pixsus rushed to join. 'You cannot go. What of our oath to God, the covenant we made to be righteous and vigilant.' Said I. 'Know yourself, Nympthia. We are them now. Our promise to God was broken when we lost the means to be bystanders. When we were cast out.' Pixsus replied. 'Do you think this, not to be a test? Do we kill because we face death or do we continue to believe God watches for the right in our actions.' Pixsus turned to the exit. 'All I know is I feel bound to this life. I cannot risk its end for the uncertainty of an unseen shore,' Pixsus stated with dynamic inflection. 'So your question now is faith.'

I saw Pixsus grow more frustrated with me. She was always of strong conviction. She ran to the frontline with a wood-axe in hand. The battle began. In my home, I went to pray. Unbeknownst to the both of us, the eye of Changel was upon the field giving the people of Nadad strength through rage and a fiery bloodlust. It was my thought, from the depth of my mind, that Pixsus wished vengeance against Changel through his misguided order on that day.

My mind was on Pixsus. Her image was here. I prayed for her safety. I had not experienced a time, since my days on the Isle, where I was more still or more connected to everything. I felt her again. I opened my eyes to blackness, and then suddenly my sight was filled with the light of the field where Pixsus and the Aaminites were to do battle. Her face was sour. Such an intense hate resided within her. Had I not seen it, I still would have felt the emotion, so great as it was.

Alee moved to the wall where the story continued. She walked through the cold airy tomb with a heavy heart. Pixsus was family to her. A long lost aunt she would never know. She understood the tale from all that was written on the pillars and the walls. Alee made comparisons, relating the actions of Nympthia and Pixsus to her own choices on the journey thus far. She saw that grief and regret loomed in both lives. Her steps knocked and echoed within the hollowed room.

Alee did not begin reading right away. She stopped

to listen and closed her eyes. She saw nothing, no face or flash from the past, present, or future. She felt no guilt or remorse. Alee was engulfed in the tale of Pixsus. She yearned to know more. It would be a comfort to know if Pixsus felt the same anxiety in battle. The story, which brought such a curiosity, also brought her a moment's peace. She sat on the rocky floor and continued the long read.

> Nadad came. They rushed the outskirts of the village defended by the able. I saw it all as Pixsus and I were connected. She stood by Adonai, pretending to feel no fear. She gripped her axe with the thoughts of her children and me as motivation to be courageous. And with her courage manifested through a need to protect, her skill manifested through her raging vengeance. Life was no longer sacred to Pixsus. All she saw in each marauder was Changel, their god Tarim.
>
> The first assailant slashed high, so close to her neck that I screamed in fear. She moved in time to strike him down across the back. I felt the blood splatter across her face. I felt the satisfaction within her as well. Adonai had her back. With a watchful eye, he protected her. He cut down several soldiers that proved too advanced for her, despite being engaged

himself. As my connection to her and the world heightened, I felt her physical strength multiply. She dodged left then right, blocked high with her axe and delivered a right fist blow to the gut of one seen as Changel. The blow was so abrasive that it seemed to push his stomach into his chest.

Soon, Pixsus was covered in dead flesh and black rouge. She entertained one Tarim follower after the next, and at times, many at once. Hate spilled from her. A wroth that came from her wake of battle. 'You follow the False,' she cried. 'Life is not deserved to those who disturb peace and tranquility.' I was displaced by how she could suddenly, and so easily, make decrees of to whom life is owed. I tried to speak to her. I tried to reach out. 'Pixsus,' I said. She heard me but ignored. She fought on beside her husband. With every Aaminite who fell by Nadadine, Pixsus lost more of herself. 'Pixsus!' I yelled. It rang in her ear, as I heard it resonate in my own. So loud it was, instinctively, she dropped her axe and covered both ears with her hands. The very same wandering stranger saw her distracted and charged her with his short blade outward.

Barreling down on her, Adonai called to her running faster than ever he had ran before. I saw the stranger as Pixsus turned. I felt her eyes widen and the pain in the depths of her stomach. She stepped back from the shock of it. Adonai came between her and the blade, which showed itself protruding from his back, just below the neck.

In an instant, the world changed. It seemed like time stopped. Pixsus saw the price of kindness. She realized each person is as different as the moment they were born. From then on, nothing would be assumed, or given without trust truly earned. Pixsus's grief ignited her rage. It tore asunder the block between her and her Will. Adonai was lifeless on the grass. She looked at the wanderer, the betrayer. Her Will was unleashed, not through skill or control but through pure blind passion. A great flame stretched out from within her. A fiery inferno, so intense, it incinerated all who still fought on the field that day, including the Aaminites, the wanderer, and Adonai.

Rivaling a small star, the pulsing wave of heat left nothing. Only Pixsus stood in the center of barren rock that spanned as far as the eye could see. Pixsus did not question how the destruction was done. She only knew that it came to be from the desires, which now surfaced from the darkest ambit of her soul.

The fires spread out and moved slowly towards us. Eventually, they consumed everything in the Midlands of Mec, leaving nothing but desert and barren sea. Yet, Pixsus was not done. Her rampage fueled by her truest desire, something she longed to have for generations, would now come to fruition through the majesty of her Will. Changel, her greatest adversary, appeared before her. Pixsus made it so. Her pain brought him to her. She summoned him to the field in a form, which personified the demon Changel was to her. The horned beast, the red Minotaur, stood before her. He had auburn skin covered by stiff dark brown hair. The eyes of the bull were a hollow white. His face scarred with his own ruffled expression. His brow and nose crimpled with a snarl. Standing ten feet tall, it motioned towards Pixsus. She was not afraid. I felt that she was not.

I was unable to flee with the others as the fires burned, paralyzed as I was by my connection to Pixsus, or rather from fear of losing it without the ability to regain it once more. Pixsus looked to the ground and saw her axe searing beside her. She picked it up. I felt my own hand burn from the touch of it. We were more as one. I thought the words, which Pixsus spoke. 'The time for a reckoning is upon us,' she said.

Changel reverted, becoming the stately elder that was once a part of a mighty Triumvirate. He was again in his robe, which covered his dark grey, viper patterned armor. 'Put your weapon away, sister. You have no chance to satisfy your sinful desires. It would truly be in the image of the Creator to offer forgiveness and mercy.'

Changel's words took Pixsus towards uncharted points of anger. 'You dare call me, sister. You dare judge me sinful. And you dare invoke the Creator, with forgiveness and mercy on your behalf.' Pixsus clenched her hands upon the axe, twisting and ringing the hilt. 'Darling sister, God loves me. But obviously, He favors you not I. Your meek existence should be a joy to live out, without the burden or worry of the world's fate. Yours is a simple destiny. You will die as nothing and meet God soon. It is envy I have for you.'

The room became warmer; though I felt, more the cold sweat upon Pixsus's brow. Pixsus ruled her Will by emotion alone. It only manifested from the extremes of her purest primal urges. It was unpredictable. The only constants to aid Pixsus were her heightened senses and increased physical strength. The opportunity for what Pixsus called justice was in front of her. Desperately, Pixsus moved to banish Changel with the same fiery disdain in which she had summoned him.

And so, she charged. Pixsus was fearless. She carried all of us with her as she came down upon Changel. In her eyes, she saw Adonai, her sons, her daughters, and me. Battle cries rang out from Pixsus. She brought her axe from on high and slashed at Changel's head. He sidestepped effortlessly as his nails grew to a talon's length. From the rocky soil, Pixsus quickly brought the axe towards Changel's stomach. Changel lunged back out of the way again. Seemingly, he made light of the engagement and sport of Pixsus. She turned to swipe the axe blade across his body. Changel caught the axe by the hilt and delivered a staggering blow to Pixsus's jaw. While Pixsus stumbled back, my mouth began to bleed. Her anger unsettled the dust. The ground shook, yet Changel only laughed at the pageantry of it. Like a mad bull, or a wild dog, Pixsus came at him again. His grin removed, Changel waited for

Pixsus to close. Rearing way back with her axe, Pixsus was open. Changel grabbed her by the throat. He clamped into her flesh at the back of her neck with his razor sharp nails. It was difficult to breathe. Pixsus gasped while she swung her axe. Changel halted her desperate counter attack. He grabbed her by the forearm with his other hand.

Changel squeezed into her neck and forearm. He looked for her pain, though she showed none. I cried and wailed enough for the both of us. Through Pixsus, I saw the smirk on Changel's face. He paused as if to say something, but what followed was only more pain. He held Pixsus and raised his foot. Changel stepped through her knee, shattered her kneecap and ripped her ligaments apart. Pixsus fell to the ground. Shamefully, through her pain I desired to sever our connection. It was more than I could bear.

I was proud of my sister. I wished I had the strength and courage she possessed. Pixsus did not wallow or retreat, despite the battle being over. She grabbed the axe and threw it at Changel. He knocked it away with his bare stone fist. Changel loomed closer. As he crept nearer, Pixsus flung dirt. She kicked, but could do nothing to keep him at bay.

Changel kneeled beside her. 'What does one perceive at the end? I imagine there is a euphoric clarity. A peace, my sister,' he said. He put his arms around her. She flailed. He looked into her eyes and pulled her nearer for a final embrace. It would be their first since the days of Avalon. She bit and clawed. Changel brought her to his robe. He hugged her tightly. Her resistance lessened. Her motions slowed. My breath drew shorter as did hers. My muscles grew limp as did hers. And as all went black, I no longer felt my sister. Pixsus faded while her final image of Changel burned into my mind.

Waking from the nightmare of Pixsus' death, the fires so real, engulfed and surrounded me. I staggered to my feet despite the pain of my knee. I called to Bivai, but my cries were faint. Though they mattered not, for he died on the field with Adonai. I grabbed and soaked my cloak in the water from a vase, so hot it already steamed and boiled. I covered myself and leapt through the flames. It would be days later before the fires were full. All was consumed and the green of Mec completely gave way to the Barren Sea.

When I patted the flames away, I found

myself alone. Every Aamanite not dead, had long fled the village. Nothing remained there for me. I traveled to where Pixsus lay. Her eyes were wide open. Her face held a deathly pallor. Her stale black blood ceased flowing from her hollowed out wounds. 'Oh Father, forgive of her trespasses, her prides, and her sins. I pray you judge in your infinite wisdom, the sum of her life. The fall and the wrath, lay those sins upon me, so she be pardoned and given a place by your side.'

I looked up and saw, just a yard away, her axe. I then wrapped her up and the axe with her. We made the perilous journey to the Canyons of the Barren Sea together. As I journeyed, I felt the Earth. It spoke to me. While I was starved and parched, my Will forced itself upon me. I heard the sound of water in the arid realm. The fluid music came from the Canyon, which the waters built.

In the Canyons, I entombed Pixsus. Digging graves and tunnels with the might of my Will, I moved the Earth. I built the doors and sealed them shut, and at that time it was for a purpose unknown even to me. Destiny was written. It began to shape itself. My firstborn daughter was taken and now I knew why. Changel was beyond my strength to

> redeem or vanquish. So I left the tomb and the tunnels. I covered the great canyon with Earth and wandered aimlessly for months. Until finally, I came unto the remnants of the Nadadine, the same who attacked us. They still wandered as I did. They captured me and took me as a slave. I gave them the tunnels, its location and its passages, in exchange for freedom. And so, they wandered no more as Nadad, for then they became Ouache. And through the children of Ouache, I told my story. I traveled to Egypt and back many times, placing the pieces, laying the foundation for destiny to be realized; so the death of my sister be not for naught. So the kingdom of heaven would be brought to fruition through Truth, not the false.

The words on the wall ended at the tomb. Alee pondered what to do next. She thought of the other two doors and turned towards the exit. Before taking two full steps, she looked back. Aleeia took a slow stride to the tomb. She pushed at the cover and slid it away. The dust rose from the disturbed casket. Aleeia coughed a bit and closed her eyes. When they opened yet again, she peered inside and saw the remains of Pixsus, her dried flesh and bones. Beside her was the axe.

The axe was a dull grey. The blade single-sided with a blunt sledge-mace opposite. The handle was iron, though so well forged it became hard as steel. The base knob was box shaped with a hole through it. The leather straps that ran through were twisted to the top of the axe, crisscrossing along the face where the blade side of the axe met the hammer side. Oddly, the axe's blade was curved inward, crescent like the moon.

Alee grabbed the axe. The leather on the hilt peeled and crumbled away. She shut the cover by the might of her Will and said her thanks to Pixsus. Alee took the heirloom and exited the room. The door shut as soon as she stepped free. Awakened by the rumble of the door, Mhasika and Hat-kaptah rose to their feet.

"Where is Asal-Iman?" asked Alee.

"He returned to his duties. He could wait no longer," said Mhasika.

"Wait?" Alee replied with confusion.

"Yes, Alee. You have been in there for three days," she added.

Alee's surprise quickly faded. To her, it felt like she had been inside only a few hours. She looked at the other two doors, but did not read their markings.

"Then show me to the kitchen. I have not eaten in

three days."

Mhasika laughed and Alee smiled. Mhasika led the way to the dining quarters. Mhasika, though curious, left Alee to what she found behind the door. Hat-kaptah followed slowly. He halted and looked to the dull grey floor, then back to the center door. He was drawn to it. He stared as if he saw through it. From the echoes in the corridors, Alee's voice broke him of the pull. Hat-kaptah looked back towards the sound of Alee. She called for him to catch up and join them, so he did.

The Separation of Shadow - Yards away from the Prima and the two unexplored vaults, Mhasika and Alee dined while Hat-kaptah sat alone on the overlook. The two women talked and shared the tales that made their lives. Mhasika now knew the wonders of Dorginarti, Aalarae, and Buhen's compassionate wisdom. Alee also spoke of Faras and Mhasika envied it. She never knew that type of love. The Ouache men were forbidden to court her simply because she was the daughter of Asal-Iman. Tradition held Asal-Iman would choose for Mhasika one who could succeed him and lead.

They ate the light meal of soup, bread, and water. Alee kept the secrets of the tomb to herself. Even the axe she held was unnoticed, despite its mysterious new presence beside her. Mhasika laughed at the night in Menin and wept for Alee's severance from Gaia and Bellia. She felt somewhat diminished in her company. The grand stories of bravery and battle cast an overwhelming shadow on her own exploits. Mhasika, however, still shared memories of her days as a marauder. Alee immersed herself greatly in the drama of all Mhasika's rescue and retrieval missions. They were trials that brought her face to face with the death in the Barren Sea.

"If time permits, would you care to take in a sparring session with me?" asked Alee.

"I would truly be honored." Mhasika replied.

Mhasika escorted Alee to the sleeping quarters of the villa. Hat-kaptah remained on the balcony. He saw them exit out the corner of his eye. As soon they were nowhere to be seen, he turned to revisit the Prima and the door. However, out of the shadows of the overlook came Asal-Iman. He melted into the surroundings of the balcony in the black robe and head wrap he wore. He came toward Hat-kaptah. Hat-kaptah retreated, making sure to avoid his touch.

"There is nothing to fear. Unless you have consciously chosen a different path since our last encounter, you need not fear my touch."

"All the same, I will keep my distance."

"So where were you off to in such a hurry, Lord Hat-kaptah?"

Hat-kaptah was thrown by Asal-Iman's choice of title. Never before had he heard *Hat-kaptah* spoken with such venerable designation preceding it. He grew curious and uneasy.

"What do you think you know, old man?"

"Old man? I am not a day over eighty-three," he groaned before a chuckle.

Hat-kaptah turned back to the double doors that led into the dining hall. He had not eaten but passed the food with no interest. He jogged down the steps and went back through the atrium. Finally, Hat-kaptah returned to the threshold of the Prima.

"So, you took the long way."

The voice came from beside him as he entered the Prima. Asal-Iman enjoyed the look of frustration upon Hat-kaptah's face. He dared not ask such an obvious question to the master of the villa. Instead, he posed another question.

"Why are you following me?"

"I do not follow. I am your guide in this… My daughter is strong, showing who Pixsus was through her physical prowess. A gift like that is not given to be squandered. Destiny is an intricate system, a puzzle which relies on every single piece put in its proper place."

"So you know my future?"

Asal-Iman grinned and left Hat-kaptah to explore the vaults without interruption. He simply sat on his seat and listened. His eyes were on the center door. Hat-kaptah placed his hand on the embossed script of the Urien translation. Angered that he could not read the marks upon the door, he scoffed. Hat-kaptah reared back. With both hands wrapped together, he struck the door directly at the mysterious dent. The booms resonated in the Prima. They became rhythmic as Asal-Iman swayed his head to the beat. The drumming of the center door continued for several minutes, until Asal-Iman finally interjected.

"The center door is not yours alone. It belongs to both of you. To your left, that door," he said.

"What are you talking about?"

"Remember, I am here to guide you. Inside that door, your path will become clearer."

Hat-kaptah came around to look into the black eyes of Asal-Iman. He paused and thought of Alee and his duty to her.

"How do I open the first door then?" Hat-kaptah asked.

"First, tell me why you desire to open the center door so intently."

Hat-kaptah paused. He turned to the center door and gazed

at it as if under some spell. His mind went back to his youth and the days lived in a carefree paradise, in comparison to the present. Hat-kaptah felt a pull to the center door. A familiar and warm feeling called him towards it. Asal-Iman laughed overtly at Hat-kaptah's gestures. Hat-kaptah grew annoyed and angry with his ridicule.

"Assist me or leave me, *guide.*," stated Hat-kaptah.

"Are you dissatisfied, my lord?" inquired Asal-Iman.

Hat-kaptah's scowl hardened. Disgust grew in him. He had no patience for banter full of puzzles and conundrums. The dynamic in his voice echoed with harsh grit.

"You speak in riddles, answering questions with questions."

"You are right. But I am a guide not an instructor and definitely not a dictator. Reveal your true self and the door will open."

"But I can not read the markings on the vault."

"No one said you had to. Alee did not open the door until she showed her true heart, when she hid no more and was truly sincere. If you stop holding back and cast the cloud away with your doubt, then the door will be opened…my lord."

Hat-kaptah returned to the face of the massive vault. His mind took in the words of Asal-Iman that finally seemed to carry some weight. He stood there silently, pondering his options. His needs, his mission, his logic and lusts were measured; and he who was Hat-kaptah took one step towards his path.

In a soft colored room, full of blues and greens, Alee slept. Exempt of stony grey, the room decorated to remind a guest dwelling in the villa of the surface's beauties. Harmonious greens adorned the vases and the trim of the mirrors. Near the ceiling, baby blue paint like the sky embellished the walls. And near the bottom, there was a bolder blue like the rolling seas. They melted together like the purple horizon at sunset.

The stately room was extremely therapeutic for orphaned vagabonds saved from the desert surface. For those who went from the one extreme to the next, the room helped to relieve some anxiety. For Alee, the last time she saw the light and luster of the sun, it beat her towards madness and darkness followed. Although she was safe below the earth, the pale-faced Ouache's bland and gray civilization left her wanting life and color. Thus, the room soothed her to sleep. Until she met unrest again in her dreams.

Darkness filled the images she dreamt. Voices called out to her from the shadows of a cage. It seemed filled with the forms of tormented people; phantasms cried to be free from the cage and life within. The nightmare continued as the hands of the captive spirits reached toward Alee. In her bed, they pulled her towards the dark place. Louder were the voices and their muffled wails. Alee had no ability to move, which added to the terror of a dream as real to her as a cold black night. Ghosts engulfed her. They pulled her out of the light. Her body and flesh seemed to melt away as it past the threshold of pure darkness.

Hands like cold grey air that had no real substance still pulled at her all over. Pulling at her shoulders, tugging her, and yanking her by her hair, she saw her thighs and hips vanish into the black hole. Every single part of her body that met the nothingness, felt extreme cold, and then went numb again.

Only her eyes moved. Alee had no means to fight. The dream was so real to Alee. She wished she would soon awaken. She witnessed her torso dissipate. Her neck and hair slung towards oblivion, Alee heard a familiar voice call her name. Desperately, she looked around. Her eyes rolled around in her head. Alee stretched and flexed her eyelids, though she could not see where the voice originated.

Suddenly, an arm came across her face and reached into the shadowy veil. She looked down to see her body becoming free. Each part of her regained its form. The voices bellowed louder. With a final jerk, Alee plopped down on a green field. No longer split between the bedroom and the void, Alee looked around in confusion. She turned to survey the land. Alee only saw the tall blades of grass that melted into the horizon on all sides of her. When she stopped her scan, Alee felt the slightest touch on her shoulder. She immediately turned to see a face she *knew*.

"Pixsus?" Alee said.

Alee took notice of the black gown. She wore it hung by her shoulders. Pixsus saw Alee look her over and smiled. Alee looked down upon herself. She saw that miraculously, she wore the same garment. They both stood barefoot in the field. Alee's hair flowed freely with her gown in the breeze. Pixsus's hair was of a short crop, though the ribbons she wore swayed as well.

Alee studied her face. An air of regret diluted her ultimate beauty. Yet still, her eyes were full and wide. Her eyebrows were slight and her nose was stout. Her mouth was full, behind the slight frown of her curling lips. Alee stood a bit taller than the woman before her that was Pixsus. Alee saw upon Pixsus, the bruises from her final battle. Alee reached out to touch her on the cheek, to feel what felt to be real.

"What is this place? What is this?" Alee inquired.

"Thank, Nympthia."

Her voice was softer than before. It reminded her of Aalarae. It harmonized with the wind in a manner that comforted Alee.

> "She brought you here. Her Will, so strong, made the tunnels and the tomb. You were in the tomb for three days so you would have the strength to be here," replied Pixsus.

Alee felt the strings of her mother. Pixsus spoke as if everything Nympthia laid out was coming to light. Less than a week ago, Alee would have fought to be free of someone else's design for her. Face to face with Pixsus, however, Alee was at ease and relaxed. She sat and talked with the aunt she would never know. The story she had read on the walls was given life and clarity. Alee heard all the emotion in her voice. The words she spoke manifested her love for Nympthia, her acceptance of a peaceful life in Mec, and finally, a fiery hatred of one who betrayed beyond all fathomable deceits. Pixsus finished her narrative of the past and spoke to Alee of her legacy.

"The time is…"

Pixsus's words were covered with a loud boom that echoed from a distance. Alee filled in the blanks, however, and knew Pixsus said *now is the time.*

"Alee, if anything were ever a birthright, Avalon is yours. Go and claim…"

Again a quaking bang seemed to supersede her voice. Alee did not hear the last part. Her head turned in search of the cause of distortion.

"The doors are sealed, but..."

The final boom jarred Alee from the grassy paradise back to the dimly lit confines of her bedroom. Alee immediately arose in her beige nightgown and made her way to the Prima. With her urgency came the rumbles that brought Mhasika back from her own slumber. Mhasika looked out her open door and saw Alee running by in full dress with her axe in hand. She slipped on the shawls that she wore the day they met in the Barren Sea and followed suit. They both came to the verge of the Prima and saw Asal-Iman seated motionless on his seat. Mhasika ran to him to determine his state. Alee, however, looked past the seat and saw a cloud of dust, which seemed to emanate from the first door.

Alee ran to the first door. She almost tripped on the crumbled remains of the broken vault. As Alee heard the cry of Mhasika, she saw the silhouette of a well built man that seemed to move and change with the settling air. Alee stepped into the vault and felt a weight upon her.

"Who is it? Who's there?" she shouted.

Alee stepped back from the threshold. Out of the shadows came Hat-kaptah. He stepped closer to Alee. As he reached the doorsill, his flesh seemed to sear and blister. To Alee, he appeared to walk through a waterfall of invisible fire. Free of heat, the unseen flame burned so intense. Hat-kaptah's clothes peeled away with his skin. Alee looked back at Mhasika, less concerned about her cries than the disgusting sight before her that caused her to shutter. She directed her eyes back towards the vault where Hat-kaptah stood. She looked up to a new face. Standing there naked, a fair and pale face stared back at her with eyes like the deep ocean. Alee was dumbfounded for a moment. As Mhasika's cries became louder, Alee knew who stood before her.

"*Changel?*" she whispered.

A great fear washed over Alee. She was paralyzed. She dropped her axe and fell to her rear. With her eyes still fixed on the bare body, she tried crawling away to no avail. Within seconds, the shining silver armor seemed to sprout out of nowhere. It fully encased his six foot, five inch frame and wrapped around him like the wings of a perching phoenix.

Alee could not have known Alonard, Prince of the Isle of Avalon, protector of the Western bank, stood before her, for she did not comprehend the revelation of Asal-Isman when he said to her, *you, the daughter came with the son.*

Despite that, Alonard and Changel were one and the same in some ways. For Alee, no distinction mattered in the moment. Alonard's silver breastplate, with its brass shaped ornaments symbolizing the Western bank and gold ones marking the East, reflected all the light in the room. His brunette hair slightly caught the color of his red cape. He strode towards Alee with his heavy steps. They echoed in the Prima.

With every step, Alee's heart beat faster and faster. She lost all the resolve that won the Wall days and days ago. Alee only remembered her closeness to the enemy who had been in his guise for the past several weeks. Every hug, every word, and every tear meant for Hat-kaptah, she had freely given to an adversary. Her thoughts then turned. The fear she had of the stranger who was Alonard compounded with her concern of Hat-kaptah's true fate.

Alee's body grew as weak as her spirit. She saw the ghost of Pixsus before waking and feared new ghosts to come. Alee wallowed in the thought that Gaia, Bellia, and Hat-kaptah were worse for knowing her. They were her final thoughts before Alee felt the draining flood of hope leaving. Despair filled the void. The whole of the Ouache

Tunnels quaked. Every lantern and candle was extinguished including the Ouache Star, which hug from the center of the massive cave.

Hysteria ensued. In five hundred years, the Ouache Star never went out. It burned by the fuels of the Earth that dripped into its clear circular tank. It was a ring of light, radiating in all directions that few could look upon. As rock came down and the walls caved in, many fled through the tunnels. Death by the Barren Sea outweighed being buried alive.

Back in the Prima, Alee tried to stop. But with every teardrop, the room rumbled even more. Alonard looked on.

"Yes, this is the one." He smirked.

He reached out to grab her by the arm. Alee curled up. The center door cracked. The sound of it all was deafening as boulders fell and iron wrenched itself apart. Before Alonard's hand met with Alee, out of nowhere, Mhasika clasped Alonard by the wrist. Alonard looked up. His face joined a hard right blow from Mhasika, which turned his head away. Alonard then remembered the remarkable strength she showed when sealing the pillar.

"Maybe you should come as well," Alonard thought aloud.

Mhasika fixed her eyes, her face stern. Through her anger, she held back the tears for her father who lay motionless on his seat. With his bruised throat, marked so familiar to Mhasika, having seen the exact pattern on Hat-Kaptah, she reached her conclusion at once. She stood between Alonard and Alee. Holding her stance and ready for battle, the shaking caves set the perfect stage for Mhasika. Her father was her world; and without him, it seemed fitting that the world be torn apart.

Alonard recognized her resolve. He had seen it many times before, from many who would attempt to do battle. He smiled. Despite her exceptional power and her leadership on the sands, he knew she had no chance to defeat him.

"Stand aside, girl. She is mine."

Mhasika turned to the still detached Alee. Her brow crumpled. She slapped Alee to the ground with the back of her hand. Alee did not move. Her mind shifted from the deceit of Alonard to her own betrayal. Without words, Alee accepted the blame Mhasika laid upon her. Her self-control dissipated.

The center door peeled away. Alonard turned towards it as it crumbled and fell to the ground. Mhasika saw her chance. She looked around to find something sharp or blunt. Her eyes came across the axe. Quietly, she picked it up and drew closer to him. Alonard was fixed on the light that peeked from the tunnel. Trying to see past the immaculate glow, he shielded his eyes and took a step closer. Still upon the ground, Alee turned away from the light. She thought of Gaia and felt greatly ashamed. Wailing she cried,

"Do not see me."

They were words for those whom she loved; those whom she knew would shutter at her cowardice and weakness. The more she tried to calm herself, the deeper she fell into despair. And with her wails, Alonard turned. He met Mhasika's attack head on, and grabbed the axe by the handle. Alonard twisted the axe from her grasp. He stood hip to hip, beside Mhasika and threw an elbow to her face. She stammered back. Mhasika found it harder to maintain her balance. Not because of the blow she took, but because of the violent quake of the Ouache realm. Suddenly, the hollowed ceiling gave way and the exit to the Prima was caved shut.

Mhasika turned to her father. She shed a tear and ran towards the light from the center door. She stopped at the illuminated threshold, which cast a great shadow on the room. Mhasika took one last look at the back of her father's seat, where his arms and legs slumped into view and gave her eulogy,

"Here in this place, the Prima, is a grave…A

burial…worthy of you, my father."

She turned into the tunnel and disappeared into the unknown.

Bemoaned, Alonard was disappointed at the brevity of the conflict with Mhasika. He longed to stretch his legs; to not hold back as Asal-Iman advised. Alonard refocused on Alee. He came upon her and grabbed her by the ankle. She feigned a kick. It was all the resistance she could muster. He dragged her into the light radiant from the crumbled center door. What was once Ouache was buried.

The sun met the tunnel at the perfect angle. Its luminous warmth filled it completely. Alonard, with Alee now laid across his shoulder, ran through the inclined passage without ever seeing the ground before him. Alee was still absent. The tunnels came down behind them. Due to Alee's lack of control, Alonard ran with all speed. In the past, Alee's explosions exhausted her and a deep replenishing slumber followed. Stronger than before, the pure energy she unleashed flowed readily like the Great River.

The Prima was lost and would soon become a distant memory for Alonard. It seemed as though he ran for miles up the tunnel. The light subsided. He came to the end of the way. Alonard looked out upon the sun and the waters. The tunnel ended at the high cliffs of a mountainous wall where a single port seemed hidden in time. Alonard stepped onto a wooden deck, which led him to the dock. A vessel, large enough for a small crew, swayed in the waters. Alonard smiled; for all waters of the sea could reach the shores of Avalon given time. And so they boarded. With the cliff so high and bay so deep, Alonard searched the ship for Mhasika, but found no trace of her. Wherever she was, he let her be. Alonard carried Alee below deck and locked her in the captain's quarters. Shaking still, Alee made the waters of the harbor rougher. She curled up on the bed and squeezed the pillows tightly. She had no one. Finally, the loneliness she feared came to be. Her memories were again her ghost in the dark. Bigger than clouds, the arrow-shaped sails unfurled from the mast. The waters settled. Alonard knew that Alee now slept. He stood at the helm and sailed towards the setting sun. As he ventured toward paradise, they left behind the flawed world of mankind.

INTERLUDE - Near the River Nile and the Great Wall, the tides of war subsided until the rise of another full moon. The nations of Egypt and Nubia-Kush rested after the chaos that followed the siege. Leaderless, the Egyptian camp pulled back out of the valley to the next apex. Meroe, leader of the armies of Kush, maintained her resolve despite mixed counsel. She never gave up the advantage of the wall. For weeks, Meroe looked out upon the unpredictable flurry of movement from the disbanded camp. Careful was Meroe. Without a known cause, she thought it odd a force so strong and disciplined would fall apart so readily at the seams. Thus, she concluded it to be a trap.

The sun packed the desert sand. During all the days of stillness, it hardened more and more. The players realigned. The solider, Sufra, returned to Dorginarti to relate news of their victory to King Alara, Prince Ashur, and the king's daughter, Aalarae. All, except for Ashur, met the news with joy and elation. He felt the distress that amassed itself within his beloved Atratah. On the clear morning Sufra was due to return, he was ordered to wait while two kindred hearts spoke to the fate of both nations.

"If Pharaoh, my father, is no more, then rightfully I am now the Egyptian Sun," stated Atratah.

"You do still care. Caring so greatly for the land

across the river," replied the Prince.

Ashur held his head low. He turned his eyes away from his darling wife-to-be and let out a low sigh. Atratah saw the words to come written upon his face. However, she still paused in hopes that his doubts would not manifest themselves aloud.

"And here, I thought, with all the happiness love can bring, that I could make you forget your loss," said Ashur.

"Yes, your love has brought happiness, great and true. And being lost in that love, that happiness, I lose myself. Egypt is me, a part of who I am. It was so when you came instead of your father. You spoke to my father as if you were already a king, an equal. I hope in fairness I can say I loved you then, Kushite Prince, as you loved me, your Egyptian Princess, yours with forbidden glances."

Ashur came to Atratah and wrapped her up in his arms. For a moment, they embraced. They whispered to one another.

"So where are we left, you and I?" asked Prince Ashur.

"I will return to the Wall and then Egypt thereafter. My counsel will be free to Meroe. However, if peace can be reached without bloodshed, then my heart will be truly filled with utter content for both the realms I deem as home," she said.

Ashur wasted no more words. He kissed his much adored love and watched her turn. She walked out of the hall of the throne room. The crimson and gold tapestries fluttered while the chamber doors opened. She walked towards the exit, her steps echoed against the marbled floors in the Nuri Tower. Atratah did not look back. She continued forward as she held back her tears.

Across the sands, the Body of the Pharaoh stayed visible. The people were accustomed to never seeing the Pharaoh and only the Body. Thus power shifted without notice. The Body made his name known. In a moment, a dynasty began and Pharaoh Isohhim ruled the land of the black sands. And where dynasties thrive through the vision of leadership, Isohhim put his ambition to work.

With Atratah returning to the Wall, Isohhim rounded up the deserters and the slaves. The threat of torture and death quelled the anarchy amongst them. His subjects did not take torture idly. An example was made. Isohhim executed all the Priests. He destroyed any vie for the title of the Body, as well as killed all who knew how his power came to be.

Isohhim, no longer a high priest, indulged in the pleasures his power allowed. He lost himself in the delights of the flesh. He bedded a different woman every night and killed at will. He was ruthless. Isohhim realized the only challenge to his ultimate power was the lost daughter, Atratah. Blood outweighed banishment; and thus, Isohhim reassembled the legions of the Egyptian Nation. He made ready plans to march on Nubia. Battle's daybreak was soon to come.

Heavy Sea - With wind's merciless assault on the waters, a fierce tempest shook the ocean surface. A crushing downpour fell upon the vessel that set out from Soxor three days ago. A bombardment of waves nearly toppled the ship. Coming from all directions, the ship's occupants began to think that both heaven and earth were made of water. Yet, the ship withstood the onslaught. During the storm, the huge sails remained bundled upon the three masts. Out port and starboard of the ship were dozens of oars, which powered the vessel while the winds were uneasy.

The clouds blanketed the sun, mixing day into night. Those who had no duty, or fear of the storm, slept in the dark of night. The slaves manned the oars of a ship without its captain; where leadership fell to another. Mage-Sciona slept in the captain's quarters, in the bed where Alonard had laid. Thunder shook the hull in the chamber, where thoughts of him filled her completely. With waves that rose to pound the deck, she soon would be rocked to sleep. Xamare-Jacobb sat still below deck. Before the slaves, his stare was enough to drive them past exhaustion. His eyes alone pushed the ship to speeds that challenged the ocean's will. His eyes, however, were not without its target.

A door lay at the far end of the hollowed room. Beyond the door was a small hold at the stern of the ship. Inside was a room without light, save the flickers from a lantern that crept through the door.

The slow motion of an opening eye came to one who had laid dormant for weeks. A blur from the shadow of waking met with the darkness of the room. A sore body moved. A disoriented soul looked into memory for the pieces to the puzzle. A try of words came from a pasty mouth. A low moan sprang forth instead.

"Be still. I will bring you water." Spoke a figure in the dark.

A brown bowl was offered to the light. The dull water was less than pure. Yet still, it twinkled in the light. The dazed captive snatched the bowl and guzzled the water after a quick swoosh of the mouth. Inquiries rushed soon afterwards.

"Where is Gaia? Where am I?"

"She is safe, here beside me," the voice replied.

Bellia heard the answer come forth from the shadow. She saw nothing, only the light between them. She thought for a moment and knew the feel of the sea. In the next moment, she thought of Alee.

"Show yourself."

And by the spark of two stones, a candle was lit with a flame that fought back the dark. Bellia stepped forward and saw a face she knew.

"Hat-kaptah!"

Despite setting the candle next to Gaia, Bellia looked over Hat-kaptah. He seemed to have aged more than the time that had gone by. He was thinner than before. With less food and the labors of slavery no more, his body looked barely fit to be about. The scars were still upon him, yet his will was a strength to be envied.

"Gaia sleeps as you did. Despite my care, your own strength is cause for your revival," he said.

"Your care?" asked Bellia.

"Yes," he replied humbly, "You both have slept beside me for more than three weeks. I reset the bones; and the honey and thyme which I placed beneath your tongues kept you both from starving."

Bellia attempted to rise up, but her strength had yet to return. Her stitches began to tear.

"Be still or move slowly," Hat-kaptah stated.

"I must help Gaia," she blurted.

"You are too weak. Besides, she is better and breathes with consistency again."

Bellia heard the word *again* and felt cold. She shuttered and looked upon her. Bellia crawled beside her. She brushed back the hair from across her closed eye and thought about the last time she heard Gaia speak.

"Were your words a warning? Did I go too far?" she thought aloud.

Hat-kaptah knew not of what she spoke. His memories possessed its own regret. He was strong, but in the end, not strong enough. And of Alee and her fate from his weakness, he also knew nothing. Bellia paused then slowly moved to her feet. She rested against the wall and prepared herself for what she knew she had to do.

"I have to try."

Bellia stood above Gaia with her arms stretched out. She took a breath and began.

Meus Magnus Deus,
She is my sister
With all my heart, I pray thee-
And thou knowst of what I pray...

No matter in what tongue, the words Bellia spoke held a great power within them. She tried, as Gaia did before, to give her strength to one who needed it more. However, Bellia had no strength to give. Still drained from her battle with Jacobb, Bellia could barely stand. And though deep down she knew it, Bellia still tried before falling back to the ground. Hat-kaptah ran to her. He dipped his cloth in the water and wiped the dust from her face.

"You just returned to us. Please, be still."

Dizzy and drained, Bellia did so. She let the sea air fill her lungs and motioned to Hat-kaptah to tell of what he knew. Hat-kaptah spoke softly of the past few weeks.

> "You and Gaia were thrown into the carriage with me. I heard them say that we were headed to Soxor. We are prized to their master as the illusive three. At least, the two of you are. "

Hat-kaptah's expression changed slightly. It became sullen, rather than mournful, with the reasons that followed.

> "I…I have been pleasure to the mistress of this ship. Torture. She revels in it. Oddly, I have become numb, for too frequent are her visits."

Bellia examined her holdings. She saw no bounds or chains in the room. There was water and the lantern lit by the stones. It was odd to have such things in a cell, Bellia thought. Still, they were captives with no exit. And had they the strength to flee, whereto would they go?

"And the big one?" Bellia asked.

"He waits outside," replied Hat-kaptah.

"How many aboard?"

"I know not. Slaves and soldiers fill the next room. Who knows how many fill the whole of the vessel."

answered Hat-kaptah.

From outside, Bellia heard footsteps coming towards the door. She scurried to grab one of the stones, placing it in her tattered cloak. She heard the thick wooden post, which sealed them in, hit the ground. The door sprang open and a curvaceous silhouette blocked the light.

"What have we here!" she exclaimed.

Bellia slightly moved her hand and Sciona came forth. She sprang towards her, staring her down, face to face.

"Reach for your rock," Sciona pleaded.

Bellia hesitated. She looked deep into Sciona's eyes and held the stare. Their eyes stayed locked, until finally, Bellia blinked. Sciona returned to her feet with a smirk on her face.

"Of course." she cried.

"You have what I allow you to have. And everyday I have returned, hoping for your young friend to indulge me. Maybe now, you will show some heart. We have a long voyage ahead."

Suddenly, the guards rushed in and seized Hat-kaptah. It was all too familiar to him. Bellia reached out to protect him, but to no avail. There was nothing she could do.

"Be patient," said Sciona, as she looked down upon Bellia.

"We shall return. Take him to my quarters." Sciona

exclaimed.

They dragged Hat-kaptah away. It had been several days since he had any strength to fight back. Bellia then went to Gaia. Bellia hoped she would soon wake up. She gazed upon her intently and took notice of her pale skin. She placed her hand on her shoulder and watched her sleep. Her torso moved up and down at an even pace. Her skin was warm to the touch.

"So here we are," said Bellia.

Bellia cradled Gaia in her arms as her mind went back to a time past. She talked to Gaia's slumbering ear of times more ordered. When there were fewer doubts present. She saw the Woodlands of the South, and the clearing where a cabin sat isolated. In memory, the grass seemed greener and the sun had shone brighter. They paused there and talked briefly about how to proceed.

"Are you sure that this is the house?" Bellia had asked.

"Of course, the scrolls are clear. Besides, the fact that there is a home here, in the middle of nowhere, seems beyond pure chance." Gaia replied.

"You have a point," replied Bellia.

"Of course, I have a point." Gaia added.

"*Of course! Of course! Of course!* Please! Pick

another phrase.," demanded Bellia.

"If it pleases...*Of course!*" stated Gaia with a quip.

"Walked right into that one. Grow up, Gaia." Bellia replied.

They both chuckled and finished the conversation with only their eyes, and then pulled up the hoods of their robes. In a stately manner, they walked taller towards the house. They did not make a sound as they made a slow march to the door. Gaia was a step ahead. When they finally reached the door, she let out four booms upon the oak. There was complete silence. Gaia turned and looked back at Bellia. The door opened slowly. As it opened, the two strangers entered without waiting for an invitation. They saw the sorrowed faces of its occupants who sat motionless. Through the shadow of Gaia's hood, Karwynn looked directly into her eyes. She spoke clearly to the expected strangers. Her tone held no fear, only grief for her time with Alee now reached a close.

"Everything is in order. She is ready."

Karwynn's voice wobbled. In a corner of the room, Alee sat with her packed belongings. Karwynn went to the young girl whose head was held so low.

"Look at me."

Karwynn asked, but Alee could not find the strength of

heart.

"Look...at me!"

Loudly, her voice rushed out toward Alee. Karwynn had her attention, but with each word that followed, her tone did more to ease Alee. She took Alee by the hand.

Bellia continued to hold Gaia and remembered how Gaia glanced at her when Karwynn spoke to Alee. Bellia thought that Gaia, who still lay motionless in the cell, would have smiled at the retold story. Despite no reaction, Bellia continued. She whispered to Gaia and rocked her in her arms.

"Remember what she said, Gaia?" Asked Bellia, rhetorically.

"Like Karwynn to Alee, I wish I could say to you now words with equal comfort."

Bellia paused.

"Because I know…that you can hear me."

For some time, Karywnn had mulled over exactly what she would say at that moment. But, when the time finally arrived, those words lost all potency and meaning. Karwynn sighed for her daughter whom she loved above all, even her own selfish desire to keep her. Gaia signaled to Karwynn that time drew near and took a step closer to Alee. Karywnn wiped her eyes. She had no strength to speak through the sorrow of crying. She needed to be strong for Alee.

> "You have always known, my love," said Karwynn, "Here, in the Southlands, was a small piece of the world you desired to see. Do not be afraid when dreams come true. Change is a part of life and comes divinely, no matter what choices we make."

Karwynn paused. She looked back at the two heavily cloaked figures. She nodded and they grabbed Alee's belongings.

> "There is nothing I can say to make this moment less real than so. Nor is there anything I can say to justify my hand in giving you over. You would not understand it now. I only hope my teachings and love for you will bring you to a place where you see there is more than us in the world. And keeping you here and keeping you safe, would be so selfish; when I know you can become so much more."

Alee sobbed intensely. She could not speak. She heard some reason in her words but, as Karywnn had said, she did not understand. Full of pain, Alee could not move. Alee blamed her own mouth for speaking the moment upon her. With regret, she pleaded to make amends. She closed her eyes, not knowing that they would never see Karwynn again upon opening. Karwynn tipped a burning candle, left the home she shared with Alee and disappeared into the Woodlands of the South. Gaia saw the extreme and grabbed Alee by the wrist.

Pulled from her meditation, Alee saw the inside of her home catch ablaze. There was no Karwynn in sight. She struggled to go back inside, to gather her precious belongings that were not packed. Things she left behind with the hope that she would see them again. In a hysterical frenzy outside her home, Gaia struggled to hold her back without hurting her.

In somno pete pacem

With a gentle touch on her shoulder, Gaia's words put her at ease. Alee did not awaken until she was a far distance from the burnt rubble of her former home. Alee's life and memory had turned to ash. Trust came from Karwynn's leaving her to the strangers. When she awoke, she remained unharmed. The thought of fleeing entered her mind on occasion, but there was nothing for her to go back to.

Bellia's memories were all that remained of a better time. In the cramped space, she thought about Alee, and then laughed. She looked down at Gaia and thought aloud about the manners in which she found a humorous calamity.

She stared at Gaia while thinking of Alee. Bellia spoke.

"What did we think, sister? That we would teach Alee all the skills we knew, deliver her to the doorstep of Changel and ***that*** be the end of it. For all we planned, who would have thought Aleeia would have been the capricious element to all of it?"

Bellia clenched her fist and hit the wall behind her.

"Our arrogance led us here," Bellia stated, "Destiny." Bellia scoffed.

"A destination without a clear singular path. And even then, there exist numerous courses to an alternate end entirely."

Bellia thought about the end as it was for her and Gaia. Defeated and beaten despite their best efforts, Bellia laid her head on the hard, moist floor. She desired a long sleep again to take her mind off such things. Though, just as she folded her arms and rested her head upon them, the door flung open. Hat-kaptah was thrown to the ground with all his wounds reopened. To Hat-kaptah, the two or so hours felt like days. He returned to the hold, hating himself. He questioned how his own body could betray his own pain and contempt. Bellia asked the obvious question, to which Hat-kaptah replied,

"I am still alive."

Bellia let out a low sigh.

"I am glad to hear it.," she stated.

Hat-kaptah's brow became frazzled, though still marked by a bitter expression.

"I would hope so, for who else is to blame," Hat-kaptah stated.

Bellia made ready her speech about the unpredictable nature of intertwined destinies. It had been told to her by her teachers; and was paramount to why she felt she could call someone as contrary to her as Gaia a sister. But before she could give it so that Hat-kaptah felt the same reassurance, Hat-kaptah interjected.

"***Not*** letting me go with Alee was a mistake. One that took me from her better graces to this pit."

He turned to Bellia with a stare that could cut through steel. His voice softened before his mouth filled with the questions to come.

"Where is she, Bellia? Where is Alee?"

All Bellia could do was shake her head. She wished she had the answers. Instead, she issued a promise.

"When my strength has returned and the ship has set

to port, we will find her. All of us, together."

Meanwhile, an ocean apart, the Ouache vessel sailed on calmer seas. To shore the vessel, the Isle of Avalon was only three days away. Alee found herself below deck in a suite meant for one of great rank. The mirror alone was accented with jade stone about the corners. She peered at herself, though it was not an act of vanity. Alee tried desperately to look into herself, to find her true worth. Only her tattered reflection looked back at her. Her flustered skin, unkempt hair, flaking lips and bloodshot eyes revealed the lowly coward of whom she did not want to believe herself to be.

The door to her chamber opened. For the first time since the Prima of the Ouache Tunnels, she looked upon the face that terrified her to such end. Alee still regarded him as Changel, but it was Alonard who entered with a tray of salt with dried fruit and meat. Alonard approached her in a cavalier manner; with the same cause as a master tossing scraps to his feeble livestock. Livestock that you would not have die for the potential that it could one day assume given regard.

Alee kept her distance, although the small room left no space for fleeing. Alonard gave her distance. He placed the tray on her bed and turned back to the door. In the corner beside the vanity, Alee thought over Changel for a moment. Without the shock of his presence to cloud her rationale, Alee quickly pondered his actions thus far. In all their time together, she realized he had not harmed her and that he only attacked Mhasika in defense.

"What will you do with me, Changel?" Alee asked. Alonard laughed. Alee did not know what to make of his reaction. Regardless of his past actions, Alee pondered his intentions for her with caution and fear. Alonard's laugh dwindled to a chuckle before his reply.

> "Your ignorance honors me greatly. Simply put, I am Alonard, second to his greatness."
>
> "A general?"
>
> "A son."

Alee was taken aback. She saw him change and felt no reason to trust anything he said. The cabin seemed smaller. Alonard moved around the bed, he forced Alee out of the corner. She sat on the bed near the wall and asked another question to occupy him.

> "I saw you change. How is that possible if you are not Changel?" Alee asked.
>
> "The simplest answers should not elude you. I learned the art from him. It took years, yet I am still limited in comparison."

Alee was surprised at the fullness of the answer. She

wondered again why he gave so much. More so, she wondered what to ask of an enemy that would stand so openly before her. Her lips curled in a sly manner. For the first time since he entered the room, Alee made eye contact with Alonard, rather than looking pass him or to the floor. Alee walked toward Alonard. He noticed the change in her body language. She seemed slightly less intimidated, a bit less afraid. Alee began walking behind Alonard. He tracked her out of the corner of his eyes until she lingered behind him completely. Although Alonard did not turn he felt her behind him. She called out to him. He heard her soft voice.

"Why have you taken me?”

"Taken you?"

Alonard turned abruptly. Alee fell back a few steps. Alonard seemed to hover taller above her. Alee reverted. She lost all the false courage she had mustered. Alonard's eyes softened along with his voice.

"Consider yourself rescued, ***Alee***!"

Alee felt a nameless sting within her. Hearing her name come forth from Alonard for the first time since his revelation jolted her. It took her a second to compose herself and refocus on their discourse.

"What do you mean by *rescued*?" she asked.

"It is obvious you are a child of Avalon. I have not yet put all the pieces of your story together, but I do know you feel burdened by the weight of destiny. Have you ever thought that I have come...that going to Avalon...are the means to help lighten this load you seem determined to carry alone?"

Alee paused. She thought to herself and of the temptation that had already begun. Alee knew that as Hat-kaptah, Alonard heard her speak many times about her duty to end Changel's crusade. Yet now, he stood before her offering some manner of assistance. Alee swayed back to the bed. The meat there looked appealing. The diversion of eating offered her time to think. She reached for the meat and chewed. The silence gave Alonard the wherewithal to speak.

"My father can teach you things you never thought possible. And through him, we can all follow the greatness of God. There is a world conceived only in dreams. Peace, harmony, and justice... We know what these things are and what they mean. But how can any one of us map out the road to achieve these ideals? They are elusive, beyond taming for mortals who remain so earthbound and corruptible. Unless you covet nothing, good intentions will always waver. He is pure! As if moved by the Hand itself, my father simply is."

Alee was deaf to the empty rhetoric divulged by Alonard.

She heard only the passion in his voice, but was numb to the recycled banter that obviously seemed impressed upon him by Changel.

"Are sons and daughters merely the extension of their parents' agenda?" Alee thought aloud.

"What?"

"Nothing," she replied.

"...nothing… "

VERSE IV

Return to Avalon - The storms subsided. From opposite sides, both vessels converged on the island. A thick misty blanket kept the shore hidden. The mist surrounded the isle like a ring and dance about like breaths of the sea. With no wind, the mist moved slowly, before rapidly tumbling back upon itself. Oddly, it never dispersed or changed its hazy consistency.

On the Eastern Bank of Avalon sandy golden shores met the crystal blue ocean. Sciona and Jacobb approached from the southeast without ever needing to see the air in front of them. They returned to the port they left all those months ago. The dock hands anchored the ship and unloaded the cargo. In addition to the captives on the ship, they returned with goods that included spices, textiles, and literature.

"Lower the sails," someone cried.

A ramp lowered, connecting the ship to its home at port. An envoy awaited Alonard and company, for the news of their ship's return spread as soon as the ship was in sight. Below deck, the mountainous behemoth, Xamare-Jacobb opened the door to the prisoner's cabin. Inside, there were three who had not seen the sky since the sunny days of Dorginarti. Hat-kaptah scurried into the corner, while Bellia stood tall. She stepped in front of Gaia. Gaia remained motionless for the whole of the journey. Bellia's worst fear was that she would never awaken. However, the slow and steady rhythm of her breathing gave Bellia hope.

Jacobb turned to Bellia. He threw three shackles at her feet, each one connected to a single leather strap. Bellia looked down upon them, then back at Jacobb. Without thought, she kicked the shackles away. Jacobb saw the insolence. He closed his shoulders inward, lowered his back and head, and then barely squeezed himself through the portal. Jacobb completely filled the room. Bellia felt no fear for herself but Jacobb looked at Gaia intensely. Repentant, Bellia looked at her and then to the shackles. She turned to Hat-kaptah.

"Here, Hat-kaptah," she grabbed the shackles, "Put these on."

Jacobb grunted. He turned his back to Bellia and exited the hold in the same cramped manner in which he entered. In the next instant, four soldiers entered the hold with a dolly for Gaia.

One soldier grabbed the tether, two stood behind the prisoners at knifepoint, and finally, the last soldier loaded Gaia onto the dolly. The end of a blade led the captives to the surface of the ship. When they emerged, they were met with a tremendous uproar. The crowds clamored and applauded for the return of those who would be either soldiers or slaves. Next, came forth Jacobb followed by a quiet awe that swiftly gave way to loud applause. On Avalon, his strength was legendary and few ever looked upon him in such close proximity. Sciona brought up the rear. She did not revel in the applause. She walked alongside the prisoners with solemn eyes fixed upon Hat-kaptah. Finally, the crowd roared louder in anticipation. The clapping became thunderous as the envoy awaited the emergence of one more. They chanted his name and shook the dock with their frenzy. Several minutes passed, before the whispers stirred.

"Where is Prince?" said one.

"Where is Perfection?" said another.

Sciona was well on her way to Changel's fortress before the crowd dispersed at the dock. She entered the forest near the docks as the sunset cast its amber sheen across the sky. When dusk arrived, the mist seemed lit by the sunny horizon. The same flourishing mist now held a silvery sheen. Finally, the sun set and moonlight filled the night sky.

The Ouache vessel approached the majestic Isle of Avalon from the northwest. The rocky shores and mountainous cliffs of the Western Bank a direct contrast to the East. Two split ridges formed a narrow pass, which came right to the precipice of Alonard's stronghold. Despite the ship's lack of crew, the small vessel stood as good a chance as any of navigating the stony seam.

It pleased Alonard to see the winds low. He knew if they could safely past beyond the mist the remainder of the journey would be easily left to the skill of his experience. For the past few days, Alee roamed free of her quarters. With the ocean all around her, the sea kept her as contained as need be. Alonard tightened the main sail as best he could and took his place at the helm. Alee emerged from the stow of the ship. She looked at Alonard but could barely make him out through the fog. By her own accord, Alee stationed herself at the bow of the ship as they entered the sea ravine.

Alee looked out into the airy blanket. She looked down and yet again reflected on the many choices made thus far. Alee returned her eyes to the sky precisely at the mist cut apart. A tall rocky spear pierced outward from the sea. Startled by the sight, oddly, she cried no warnings. As the megalith grew closer, the ship pulled hard to starboard. Stones slightly grazed the hull. If anyone had the unfortunate pleasure of looking into the face of Alee, they would have seen her disappointment. With every port and starboard dodge of the protruding stones, Alee crept closer to her enemy. Undeniably, she was overcome with a sense of dread. She had long ceased wondering how she would defeat her enemy. Instead, Alee's mind dwelled on death, her own. She no longer doubted her end was soon to come. Alee only feared the manner and the circumstance of her death. *How am I to die*, she thought. *In some horrific way by Changel's hand? I would rather be taken now.* The mist cleared and the heavy boulders were now behind the vessel. Alee looked out into sea.

> "One plunge and I no longer have to wonder. I'd have nothing left to fear," she whispered.

Alee stepped out a little. She leaned over the bow and held on to a rope fastened to the mast. Alee closed her eyes. She felt the rope between her fingers and palm. She loosened her grip. The rope fell back to where only her fingers kept the rope secure. The ship's speed placed a moderate breeze against her face. Upon the rope, five fingers gave way to four. She stood, tiptoed on the brink and prepared to let go of all her sorrows completely. Three. Two. In the final moment, when Alee felt control and choice returning, a warm hand touched her on the shoulder.

"The sea is gorgeous this time of night. Is it not?"

Alee turned to Alonard. Her face full of tears. She fell to her knees. Her mind inundated with her own misgivings. However, Alee was sure of one thing. Every decision she had made on her own had been worse than the one before. Leaving Dorginarti, despite her certainty in the translations, proved to be a mistake in her eyes. Rescuing, who she thought was Hat-kaptah, seemed too easy. Alee knew it, but she did not listen to herself. And the cost of another poor choice was still unknown to Alee. Alonard kneeled beside Alee. It confused him to see her in such a way.

"I thought your grief had passed. What is wrong, Alee?"

His concern puzzled Alee. Alonard's interest in her state was unexpected. Her mouth was dry. Even so, she had no words.

"You have heard me say these things before, weep no more. Avalon will soon be home to you, a place where you shall be free from doubt and sorrow. It is a paradise that gives beauty and purpose to everyone, even those who are lost in the heresy of the mortal realm. The outcome thus far seems unfortunate to you. But Avalon, Changel, and I, may be your chance at rebirth."

Alee looked out again, back towards the bow where a light shone brightly at the top of the rock face. There stood the vessel's destination, Alonard's home and sanctuary. Alee let out a low sigh. She whispered to herself.

"I have yet to learn what it means to be me. I do not

know how to be *Aleeia*, daughter of this Isle."

Alonard heard her whispers. He smiled.

"Aleeia, if there were any place else so meant for you to learn the way, then by God, it is this place."

Alonard stood tall and extended his hand to Alee. As the ship slowed into the shallow waters of the base cliff, he helped her up from the deck. The ship endured a modest jolt before it came to a complete stop. Alee looked up to the beacon, which seemed to prevail from hundreds of feet above her. Upon further glance, Alee saw no tunnels or stairs to climb.

"Why did we come this way?"

"You speak to me now as if you are no longer afraid," replied Alonard with a grin.

"My curiosity outweighs my fear. I have always been the curious one," she added.

"I see. Well, the quickest way to travel between two points..."

Alonard left the idiom without its conclusion. He felt the holster at his hip to ensure his newly acquired axe was secure by his side. He looked at Alee, then to the top of the mountain's edge. Alee folded her arms with as much integrity as she had shown in weeks.

"Fine," smirked Alonard, "Stay here if you wish, but

this ship will be beneath the sea in less than an hour at best."

It was not lost on Alee that only a few moments ago she wished to be ushered to rest by the sea. She quickly went from dreading every choice she had made to being left without one. Since she entered the camp of the Egyptian forces, it seemed to Alee that her foes held an overriding control of her actions.

Alee surveyed the cliff wall. A half mounted plan formed in her head. Despite Alonard's cordial nature thus far, Alee had no idea why she was brought to the Isle. She only knew she was unharmed. She briefly hoped a similar fate befell her companions before she took four or five steps back from the bow. She looked at Alonard with a slight grin, then took a running start towards the wall. After three long strides, Alee leapt into the air. Alonard tracked her until she seemed to melt into the moon. When Alee landed, she clasped her hands tightly on the jagged rock. The jump cut the distance to the top of the mountain by a third. Alee looked at the speck that was Alonard. She quickly turned her head back to the sky and attempted to flee.

Below, on the weather beaten deck of the Ouache vessel, Alonard was somewhat impressed by the spectacle he witnessed. Her escape was the furthest thing on Alonard's mind, regardless of Alee's sizable head start.

Without so much as a pivot step, Alonard loaded power in a low squat. And like cinders from a volcano, he shot up the mountainside, just above Alee's mark. By the time he landed, Alee remained several feet above him well into her climb. The race was on. With sure footing, Alee hurried to the mountaintop. She had a rhythm hastened by the chase. She felt a swooshing wind climb parallel to the mountainside. It echoed in her head, *reach and pull, step and push*. She never bothered to look back. Alee assumed she was far ahead of Alonard.

Alee was soon to reach the lip of the cliff. The sound of the crashing waters rushed up behind her. Alee turned for one last glance of Alonard before her mad dash away. When her eyes panned downward, however, she only saw the Ouache vessel consumed by the waters. A gulping thump came from both her and the waters that swallowed the sinking ship.

"Need a hand?"

The voice came from above her, slightly in front of her. She cleared all surprise from her face. Alee did not want to seem thwarted by his unexplained appearance. Alee grabbed the hand he extended to her. Alonard pulled her up with ease and smiled.

"How did you beat me?"

Alonard feigned a laugh before bragging somewhat. He led

her towards the light of his home that lay past a small orchard of forest trees. He paused and then answered her.

"Same as you." he stated, "I jumped. Twice."

Never giving Alee's hand back over, Alonard guided her. They began walking into the trees. Silence accompanied them. Alee felt something strange. There was this sensation that made her blood run, but made her body relax. It also brought a clarity that she had not had in a while. Although she did not know this land, Alee was connected to it. It too infused her with something powerful.

Though Alee wanted to ask Alonard about the weird energy, trust was still an unclear issue. Alee knew she was somehow being saved for something. And, at the very least, she would be presented to Changel before any harm would follow. So many unanswered questions fed the beast of deceit. Foremost was Asal-Iman. In the Prima, before she fell to pieces, Alee saw his body, lifeless. Alee broke the silent trek.

"Why did you kill him?" blurted Alee.

Alonard stopped completely. He let go of her hand, but did not turn to look at her.

"Kill who?" returned Alonard.

"Asal-Iman, back in the Prima," she added.

Alonard turned, looked her directly in the eye. He took a

single step in and stood face to face with Alee.

"I did not kill him," he stated surely.

Alee surveyed him carefully. However there were no reads, which suggested the contrary to his statement. Alee filled in the blanks as they appeared in her memory. Alonard heard them and understood her reasoning. His head held a bit lower, though not through shame or contrition. Alonard knew that there was little he could do to win her trust. In actuality, it was not required for the successful completion of his mission. But something within him felt Alee was due the truth. Simultaneously, he spoke and continued his hike to the stronghold.

> "Back in the tunnels, I was brought before the face of the vault by some unknown draw. I needed to enter. I needed to break through..."

Alonard's tone crescendoed. Alee listened on. She related completely to the lure of the vaults.

> "Asal-Iman, he knew me. His gift allowed him to see me truly. He never saw the shell of your friend. He could not. He assumed you knew as well."

Alee thought back and remembered the odd phrases which came from Asal-Iman. More made sense to her. Alee was concerned, still with the fate of Asal-Iman, but also how Alonard opened the vault.

"Yes, I was annoyed by him. But he always gave me

the proper respect encased with his brash sense of humor. He was wise though. And somehow, he knew more than he probably should, despite being a keeper. He told me if I wanted to open the vault, if I wanted to know myself, then I should be like you, Alee."

Alee was taken aback. Not since her training in Adindan had Alee felt humbled or pride from anything pertaining to her. Alee wondered what Asal-Iman saw in her. She wondered if he had seen the truth.

"Asal-Iman told me not to hold back, to reveal myself completely. He said you were filled with doubt. And your jabbing regret came from having to constantly and repeatedly leave behind the things you ultimately sought to keep safe. And having your doubt, having your uncertainty, you still managed to summon a power, which could will open an unwilling door. You found a strength greater than you and that was the key. For me, I became my father's son and thought of the world he would create for us all if I, as well as others, had the courage to live up to what we could be."

Alonard could get lost when speaking of Changel. He knew it and reeled himself back to Asal-Iman and the story at hand.

> "When the door opened, I felt an energy wash over me. It felt similar to how I feel upon setting foot on this Isle after time away. However, the force that poured out of the sealed vault filled the Prima. It was almost too much for me. And for Asal-Iman, one who felt the energies of the world and took them in to see, it was just too much. As I crossed the threshold of the open door, I became bare. Leaving the vault, I had to do the same in order to pass."

Alee knew what happened from there. She had a tendency to assume blame in the midst of a tragedy. The tunnels caved because of her. She pondered whether or not Mhasika could have revived him had the entry not been blocked.

> "Asal-Iman died before I reentered the Prima from the vault, long before you came," he said.

Somehow Alonard knew what to say. And as morbid as it was, she was put to ease by the knowledge of it. Before she knew it, Alonard moved aside a brush and they were yards from the beacon.

The illuminant beam came from a lighthouse that stood at the southwestern most part of the compound. A wind banner blew gingerly on the pyramid rooftop. The light had shone out to sea. It focused and intensified through three glass windows. Each lens was fashioned with a slightly steeper arc in its curvature. The beacon warded ships away from the rocks, however it could not be seen outside the ring of mist that circled the Isle. The base of the lighthouse had the guest quarters attached. An arched wall of stone connected the lighthouse to the central tower. From the central tower, two more towers were connected. With a stable on the north side, the plaza was open. There were no walls to enclose the modest castle. Atop the mountain, on the Isle of Avalon, the plaza, clearly, was not built for defense. It was open to all the people of the land.

Servants welcomed and bowed before him. Alonard headed directly for the central tower with Alee. The door flung open. Alonard led Alee upstairs to her quarters. He opened the door to the plush and luxurious trappings of the room across from his own. Out of the poorly lit hollows of the tower corridors, two guards seemed to appear from nowhere. They positioned themselves beside the portal as watchmen.

"You are safe here," Alonard said, "Get some rest and join me for dinner."

Alee said nothing. She slowly closed the door and turned into the room to see its delights. The room was warm, arranged well. The cold of stone and iron was covered by the feel of autumn in the carpet and drapes. Crimson vases sat at the two corners of the room near the entrance. The wall opposite the door was semi-circled along with the make of the tower itself. The tall window served as the bed's headboard. The sheets upon the bed were also crimson with a woven pattern of sun and stars in a yellow and orange stitching. With bathing oils beside it, a water sealed drum lay at the foot of the bed. Finally, Alee saw a few simple robes to her left. Clothes rested on the chair to a dark brown vanity. Alee sat on the edge of the bed and laid back. Her lids became heavy and her eyes closed. She tried desperately to put serious thought to her captivity. The bed's comfort overcame her. Within a few seconds, Alee was at rest, true rest. For the first time in months, she saw no darkness. Her dreams were not nightmares. Nightmares were nowhere to be found.

In the woods that stood at the feet of the citadel, Sciona and her company traveled in file with little incident. Bellia marched ahead of Hat-kaptah and Gaia. She often turned back to check on Gaia's condition. Each time she did so, Bellia was met with a fervent strike just above her shoulder blades.

The convoy hiked through the towering oaks of a quiet forest where the trees were not twisted. Each towering oak felt the presence of the other with the space to grow taller than the season before. Beneath the canopy, the terrain was plush with soft grass, accented by flowering bushes. Everything seemed to have an emerald glow below the moonlight. The stones sat along the dirt way looked like teardrops from the mountain that split the Isle in two.

In this place unknown to her, Bellia made note of the land throughout their travels. Bellia knew of Avalon only through the scrolls and teaching passed casually to her from Gaia. Its beauty and completeness inspired more awe than Bellia was prepared to deal with. Bellia felt somewhat guilty that she bathed in the radiance of the Isle without Gaia. With an uneasy felicity, a strange sensation seemed to invigorate Bellia. Bellia had felt it for a while, since setting foot upon the shores. At the time, she dismissed it. She thought only that her sea legs returned with a queasy tingle, but it was so much more. The land had power. Bellia could *feel* it.

They reached the doors to the citadel. The lofty twin doors were made of wood but strong as any tempered steel. Xamare-Jacobb stepped before the company and faced the door. Jacobb raised his hand and reared back. He pounded the door at its seam. It rang out through the citadel and went answered immediately. The double doors split open and swung outward. Bellia heard the cranks and creaks of the gears and chains that moved the doors apart. Sciona entered the menacing fortress. And although it was not her home, she gave the order to unload her things for an extended stay.

"Take the prisoners below," she commanded, "We will give them their options in the morning after his Excellency has been briefed."

The guards once again wrangled up the three captured from the Land of the Black Sand. They followed a tight corridor to a spiraling stone staircase, which connected the citadel to empty caverns beneath the Fortress.

Legend had it that shortly after Changel made his first journey into the world of man, he erected a towering piece of stone. He used his Will and moved the earth to make a monument he knew to be greater than anything he saw among men. Tempered by his own fires, he shaped the monument tirelessly. He waited for a true vision of something worthy of God. A century passed without inspiration, though clarity had befallen upon him.

Man-made monuments for the glory of men,
Built only in pride, and so grievous with sin.

Changel was disgusted with himself. He was sorrowful. Not only had he taken part in the same misdeeds, but he also went such long a time ignorant to those regrettable actions. For he had left the Isle and spent a lifetime amongst mortals. He learned of their desires and their ideals. However the purpose behind them seemed unknown, yet he himself reveled. And while he studied the nature of men, to grant them meaning someday, the monument was left to his lingering Will that was never undone.

It lingered behind and shaped the stone. As Changel learned of art and life from the mortal culture, a land afar, rock chiseled away by its influence. When Changel was finished with his research, he returned to the Isle. He saw the monument and unbeknownst, he ironically thought that God had made it for him.

Bellia and Gaia were thrown into a hollowed cup of rock together. The bars were closed then chained and locked. Hat-kaptah, however, was placed in the cell closest to the stairwell. Though still within eyesight of Bellia, who was a few yards down the cavernous pass. Bellia turned to Gaia.

> "Despite the Chasm at Abydos, I know how you hate being closed beneath the ground. You would loathe this place...as much as I loathe your cooking," Bellia stated with a grimace.

Bellia's eyes widened. She had seen Gaia's face furl as though she heard the poor and untimely joke. She rushed to her and sat beside her. Bellia grabbed her hand. For a brief moment, Bellia felt a tight gripped reply.

"It's this place…this Isle! This energy I feel, you feel it too?" She inquired of Gaia.

Bellia meditated. She stretched out her hands over Gaia. She wondered if enough of her strength had returned so that Gaia could be quickly healed. Once again, Bellia was prepared for the sacrifice of giving life energy. She stopped to think.

"If you are revived, then I become weak. I don't even know how much strength I have without testing myself. And you would have strength to do what, mount an escape for Hat-kaptah and I by yourself?"

Bellia paused. She lowered her arms then sighed.

"I will let this place work its wonders. In the meantime, I will be observant and protective."

Bellia took off her cloak. The cave was damp and cool and Bellia wanted Gaia to be as comfortable as possible. So she sat there, stained with old stale blood. Beside the cell gate, she waited quietly for daybreak.

Meanwhile Sciona made her ascension through the fortress to the upper levels. Jacobb was close behind until he realized where they were headed. Sciona sought an audience with Changel, to give her account of their journey's undertakings. Jacobb, though massive and powerful, seemed fearless to all. Fearless because there were few he knew doubtlessly to fear. Changel was one of the two, and the greater. Thus, just outside Changel's chamber, Jacobb stopped as Sciona continued. She reached out her hand to push upon the door. It opened away from her as though pulled by a taunting string. Oddly, Sciona was not startled by it. To her it only meant that the master was within his chamber. Sciona loosened the straps, which wrapped her from toe to head. She unfastened the knot that also fixed her hair in a long ponytail. The straps, which covered her, sagged. But just before the straps became revealing, she retied the knot around her neck. Thus, Sciona entered the chamber of Changel with her face uncovered and her hair flowing free.

Sciona stepped surely. She did not see Changel anywhere, but of course, she knew he was there.

"Games? Games! I love them, you know this." Sciona raised her head higher from her neck. She tipped her nose to the sky and searched the room for his unique fragrance. She looked to the tree adjacent to the hearth. She saw the owl as it fluttered quickly out the door.

"Are you up there, Master?" Sciona asked gleefully. The leaves ruffled. Sciona peered into the branches. She searched for the cause of motion. Sciona stepped closer to the trunk of the tree. She rose to her toes, with intent to climb the tree. Before she could begin, a snake slithered from around the back of the tree. It climbed upon her, down her arm, around her waist, then finally across her leg to the floor. The sensation of it pleased Sciona. She watched with a smile as the snake took form as Changel. He stepped to her wearing his white, pristine robe. They stood face to face. Sciona grew extremely excited as she watched his lips form words.

"What news?" he asked of her.

Sciona smiled for not getting what she desired. She also knew that Changel granted her that pleasure. The waiting, anticipation, then conquest was sweet to Sciona. It made her throb for the future and the actions that could occur in it. With a giggle, Sciona brought her mind to the question at hand.

> "You led us to three who have the Will. Two, the women, are strong and the boy is a novice, but none of them seem to have the power you described before our departure."
>
> "My son...?" Changel interjected.
>
> "...the boy went to great lengths to protect another, a girl named Aleeia. He went alone to ensnare her. I doubt if she alone has the power we seek. We were told she is younger than the two women we have."

Changel walked closer to the fire from the hearth. He stared into the flame.

"People say about the rivers, that you never see the same one twice. The same can be said of a burning flame, each has a life of its own."

Sciona was confused, however she was aroused by the strength in his tone. She was drawn to it.

"The two women...? Will they need to be broken?" inquired Changel.

"It seems so. They engaged in battle with us without hesitation. They fought well. Even in their defeat, they remain defiant."

Sciona paused to think for a moment. She knew her battle with Gaia and Bellia was more challenging than any she had encountered before. It humbled her to know Changel sought someone even stronger. Changel bundled up within his robe as if to gain warmth or conceal himself. He moved to his seat and rested upon it. He raised his hand indifferently, accompanied with an order.

"Make sure our guest know what we offer. They can be of great aid. And be sure to express the graveness of an unfavorable decision. Inform me at noon on the morrow," said Changel.

Well into the night, Sciona made haste with little time in which to do many things. She exited the fortress.

Jacobb rested under a tree just outside. Sciona came to him.

"Wake up, my friend. I need your unique brand of diplomacy."

Jacobb's only affirmation came in the form of a low, livid groan. Side by side, they returned to the citadel to have words with the travelers.

The table was set for a late meal for two at the central tower dining chamber. The long table was garnished with an elaborate spread of cuisine. Despite the fullness of the feast in Ouache, Alee had not seen a meal so delectable since Dorginarti. She arrived there first. Escorted by two maidens to Alonard, she sat patiently at one end of the table. Alee resisted every luxury placed in her chamber. She came to the table in the same tattered clothes in which she had arrived to satisfy her curiosity.

To her left, a bowl sat filled with furry brownish, green fruit. Alee had never seen anything like it before. She slowly reached towards it. Her left hand rose closer to the bowl. Suddenly, she heard the distant knocks of footsteps approaching. Her arm snapped back quickly to her lap.

Alonard entered the dining chamber with an air of kingliness. He wore black trousers stuffed into his boots and a long maroon vest with a high collar. The vest hung just above the knees, with a dark orange trim along its edges. A black sash wrapped the vest together by the waist. Alee saw his chiseled, bare chest and turned quickly as not to stare. Alonard wore no gauntlets or heavy metal jewelry. Having endured so many battles in his cold, hard armor, he enjoyed being free from it in times of leisure.

Alonard sat in the chair across from Alee. The long rectangular table separated them by several yards. He looked her over and raised his cup. Alee did not follow suit. Alonard noticed the old, tattered clothes she still wore. Disappointed, Alonard raised his cup higher, and then began delivering the customary words before eating.

> "Thanks be given for our safe travels. The chance to return here, to this place, where all things are possible, a template for the world."

Alee was unmoved by his words. Alonard slowly gathered food to his plate. Alee glared at the odd fuzzy fruit she saw before. Alonard caught her distraction.

"Are you not hungry? Will you not eat?"

Alee said nothing and turned away.

By the center of the table, the spread of food was symmetrical. Therefore the food to Alee's left was across the table to Alonard's right. From his bowl, he grabbed one of the fuzzy fruits. He held it just below his lips and rotated it atop his fingertips. For a moment, Alee's brow raised.

"These tasty treats come from a land far east of

yours. Gooseberries, they are called. An odd name, I have always thought. For these are rather large for berries," said Alonard.

Alonard took his other hand and split the fruit in two. The sweet juices flowed freely from it. As exotic as it was, Alee's mouth watered at the sight of the moist green and black seeds within the fruit. Beneath the table, her hands fiddled. Before Alee could resolve any restraint she snatched the fuzzy fruit and tore it open. She cupped a half in her palm then ate into it. It was sweeter than she expected, though not overwhelmingly so. It tasted just shy of fullness. It compelled her to take another quick bite so that the bite before could complete its work upon her taste buds. Alonard smiled.

"Take a fresh bowl of Gooseberries to her room," commanded Alonard to an attendant.

In that instant, Alee stopped. An abrupt gulp and swallow followed. In the brief moments before Alonard spoke, Alee gorged enough to satisfy her hunger. She felt as though she had betrayed herself with a simple bite, but before she could put more thought to it Alonard spoke.

"And what have you accomplished, my honored guest? If my presence prevents you from the peace and joy of such a simple thing as dining, then I shall leave."

Alonard folded his sash and stood from his chair. He looked up as if to the sky, then straight into the eyes of Alee.

"Tomorrow, I travel to the East of this Isle. I will be gone for six days. I go only to see that my father is well and make myself known.

Before I go I will pose a question, the option laid before all those rescued from the hellish chaos off these shores. Will you stand with those who would make the world the place it should be? Those who know that true paradise and oblivion are only separated by a razor's edge? Or would you go back to the shallow life of the mundane, were death awaits with the certainty that you scoffed at an opportunity to make the world as it was intended?"

His eyes softened before he continued. It brought a truth and sincerity to the words that followed.

"I will not reveal you to him. You have six days to make your decision. Until then, you are lord here. My home in these towers is yours."

The candles in the hall seemed to flicker more violently with every word. Alonard turned away and left Alee alone. She contemplated what such an option meant for her and her destiny, as it were.

"Home?" she whispered.

Alee saw the flames from the wick of the candle. In it was her home in the Southland that was consumed by such a flame. Alee heard again her Karwynn and remembered that her last act was an unselfish one. And in a twisted way, Karwynn's act made her choice seem not so clear.

Alee and the Tower: Day 1 - Alee slept as soundly as possible in a bed that was so foreign to her. She rose with the sun. The sound of rummaging brought her up and out of bed. Out her window was the white horse fraught with supplies for Alonard's journey to the Eastern Bank. There was no procession or brigade at the time of his departure. Alonard walked alone to his horse in an unadorned brown cloak. He topped his horse and looked to Alee's window. Alee quickly dodged to the side of the window seat. And thus, she did not see his smirk or how he gingerly shook his head before he called his horse into a stride.

As pathetic as it was, the reality of the situation arose within her. It was a sad truth for her. Even after knowing that Alonard posed as Hat-kaptah, she had been around him for sometime. Oddly, there was regret, and loneliness at his leaving. Of all the people Alee thought she would need at anytime in her life, Alonard was not one. She looked around the empty room. She still wore the tattered clothes she traveled and slept in. She then looked at the robes and garbs hung by the vanity. With Alonard gone, there was less lost in pride by wearing them. So she chose the simplest style, a tan leather tunic along with woven trousers hung beside a gray hooded cloak, which happened to resemble Kushite fashion to a degree. Alee put them on and felt the safety of Adindan, as if she was in the rings behind the great wall. Though comfortable, the ensemble became the first of many that Alee tried on. She put on corsets, shawls, leggings and jewelry, all to pass the time. And surely she did; for with every outfit she sampled, Alee leered at the sight of herself in the mirror for a considerable amount of time.

Alee enjoyed the time wasted. It was a welcomed distraction. With each combination of attire, Alee thought often about the look of someone else in it. She saw clothing in which she knew Awana and Lyla would look stunning, Gaia and Bellia would find practical, and Aalarae and Atratah as princesses would never formally wear. However, her taste favored one set in particular.

Alee pranced in a peach colored dress for hours. Though its hue could more accurately be described as pink with a subtle blend of orange. She pulled her hair back. With a string of pearls, Alee fixed her hair in a topknot so she could tie the slender neck straps that held the dress upon her. Alee noticed her arms while they were raised. The bulge of her triceps was a surprise that caused Alee to look at how she filled the dress. The elegant dress was a formfitting piece, which showed off her fit and toned physique.

Alee examined the dress even more. About her neck, the straps left Alee with a bare sensuous neckline that melted into her shoulders. The neck straps also supported her bosom. It gave her cleavage a more than moderate exhibition. The cut of the dress fell shy of her sternum. The dainty gown was mostly silk except for the wave and spiral patterned cotton lace, which ran diagonally across the fabric. The lace began high just off the outward bottom of her breast. It flowed across her midriff, around her waist, then past the small of her back and finally ended just across the front of her thigh. From where the lace ended, the solid colored silk resumed. And unassumingly, the silk poured to the floor to complete the regal and pristine quality of the gown.

Alee twisted and turned in the mirror. Alee's mind failed to temper the words, which suddenly burst from her mouth.

"***He*** would die if he saw me in this," blurted Alee. Her eyes then turned to the table stand by the door. There a bowl sat atop it. Alee walked to the bowl and saw a bunch of fuzzy gooseberries inside. Her morning of oblivious vanity left her eager for sustenance. She grabbed the bowl. It was still fairly cool by the brisk night air. She moved slowly to the chair in front of the vanity. Still in the dress, which she admired so much, she gorged on the gooseberries. Between every bite of the fuzzy green fruit, Alee looked to the door and wondered how long she could hold out. The chamber was both a self-inflicted prison as well as her sanctuary for the time being. Out of half a dozen berries, Alee ate four with every intention of finishing the rest. When the next bite was soon to reach her lips, Alee heard a pound upon the door. She naturally wondered who lied beyond it. Soon after, another knock followed along with a low bass voice.

"Do you require anything, M'lady?"

Alee was taken aback. She used her forearm to wipe her mouth of juice and seed and then walked slowly to the door. Still in the elegant gown, she opened the door to a middle-aged guardsman. He had a grim look about him accented by his dark hair and empty white pupils. He wore a simple gray robe, which held no majesty in the making of it. Despite his hollow stare, there was no mistake of where his eyes were fixed. Alee looked down at her own noticeable bust. She quickly retreated and closed the door half way as to not be completely obvious.

"What do you want?" Alee blurted as casually as one could while startled.

The guardsman looked down the hall at nothing distinct. He turned away and appeared without concern. The tone he used matched his stern demeanor as he replied,

"I am your guide and servant while the master is away."

Alee hoped a name would follow. To her it would mean, that at some point there was a mother who had named the son that stared so maliciously. However, nothing came forth. They both stood there separated by the door and an awkward silence. Alee briefly recalled the few words he did utter. *Servant,* she thought.

Alee looked back to the room and immediately spotted a true enough errand for the stalking figure. She darted back into the room with enough speed to return to the door before he could make any advancement. She felt a brief moment of shame. A glaring eye was the only testimony to the guardsman's nature. In addition, Alee admitted to herself, if he was but a little more fair to her eye, then she would probably be flattered by his ogling. She relented from the door and succumbed to what she felt was her innate better nature. Alee allowed him in and offered a seat.

"I am not permitted," he replied.

She looked into the bowl with the scraps of fruit. She felt the soft fabric on her body and wondered aloud,

"Why am I here?" she asked of the guardsman, "...not the Isle, I ask. I know that well enough. Why the lush palace, the dresses, the food? Why am I ***not*** a prisoner?"

The guardsman remained outside the room as if held by the seal of the door, responded. The low growling voice was still startling to Alee and what he said was even more unexpected.

"The master left you with a choice. And the nature of choice is that it comes freely. It cannot be coerced," the guardsman stated.

"The master...dare I say his name..." he added in an introspective tone before he continued, "Alonard knows you have experienced the best of the world you come from. You also know of its vices and flaws. He feels you should weigh those against Avalon and all that you see here. For if you bare witness to this place, yet love your place on earth, then you will choose to spread its tranquil pleasures to the place you call home."

Staggered by the consistency she had heard from the

guardsman, Alee gave in for a moment to the thought that there could be truth in their harmonious message. It was as if Alonard spoke, convinced, and pleaded for what he called the opportunity to do great good beyond a single short lifetime. Then and there her mind became more open. Her apprehensions fell to the floor. She offered the guardsman her bowl.

> "Please, dispose of these scraps. And if possible, could a fresh bowl be brought back to my chambers?" Alee paused.

She looked up with a smirk.

> "Upon your return, I will be ready for a tour of the grounds."

Alee changed into something she could bear to get a bit dirty. Within the hour, the guardsman returned to her door and began his tour. Every possible avenue of the grounds was explored from the exercise arena, library, stables, to the bathhouse. Alee especially enjoyed the library.

In design, there was nothing exceptional about the space. However, its architecture aided the lighting of the room. Two tall oval windows sat opposite one another. They captured perfectly the sun's bearings of east and west. As for noon, there was blue tint glass directly in the center of the ceiling to give the room a thematic glow during the midday that lent itself to the clairvoyant sensation that the world laid just beyond the flip of a page.

The books flowed off the shelves. There were stacks and bunches of texts and scrolls scattered around the library. Alee stayed there for hours on end. Even the guardsman, who stood waiting readily by the door, grew fatigued from his stagnant stance. She read several books, mostly poetry, which described the immaculate Land of Avalon. She later discovered the romantic and stylized lyrics that she found were the historic accounts of a land which plain prose did little to describe.

Alee only ventured to read the languages that were known to her. There were an innumerable many which the people who traveled to and fro, bringing back tongue after tongue, wrote.

> "A scholar's curiosity would ensnare that poor soul for several lifetimes. No fear then for Bellia in such a place."

Alee's quip fell only on the spines of the books before her. However, she knew Gaia would have found the humor in it. She also knew Gaia would gorge on all the knowledge from minds unknown. The day came and went. The sun traveled to its secret place, where it moderates the gift of warmth. There was no such crypt for Alee. She fell asleep; and Alee could be found in the same place. The place she had been while the sun shined and gave so freely, in a book.

The Wanting Pool: Day 2 - Morning came. Alee awoke drowning in a pool of her own making with her mouth stuck to the pages of a cookbook. Oddly, she found it amusing the night before. Her awareness slowly returned. As soon as she knew where she was and what she had done, Alee frantically wiped the book. She paid no attention to her own unkempt hair, red eyes, and foul breath, but with every stroke of her hand the page became more unsalvageable. Alee let out a childish whiny pant.

"I had every intention of making the *Exotic Fowl with the Sweet and Spicy Gooseberry Rub* tonight. I mean..."

Once again, she realized the time. She stretched out her arms. An uncontrollable yawn followed her motion. The yawn had a deep rumble and a sound not unlike the moo of a cow. It was loud enough to wake up the guardsman.

"Good morning, Sir," greeted Alee.

"What was that noise?" he inquired.

The guardsman continued before Alee could answer.

"It sounded like dying cattle."

Alee's face fell. Her expression became more flustered and

a bit of embarrassment followed.

"What noise?" she avoided his question.

Alee extended her hand and offered to help the man to his feet. He wiped the dust from his robe, but he politely rose to his feet on his own.

Alee gave him leave to go freshen up when, in fact, she needed it for herself.

> "Meet me beside the stables," ordered Alee, "As pleasing as your tour was yesterday, we never left the grounds. I look forward to all you have to show me."

Within the hour they convened at the stables on the north side of the grounds. The guardsman stood beside three horses. There waited his horse of a brown hue and two more saddle-less black stallions for Alee to choose between. Alee, clad comfortably, approached. She wore a suede tunic and leather trousers that were flexible enough for any type of hike to come. In style, the nameless guardsman dressed in the same attire as that of yesterday. However, it was a different gray robe. Alee determined so, simply because it did not hold the dirt from his previous night's slumber on the floor.

"Good morning," stated the guardsman with

impassive courtesy.

Alee replied with excitement. She had her first day of fun and peace in what seemed like a lifetime to her. Things and people, the likes of: *destiny*, *Alonard*, *Gaia*, *Bellia* and *death* were pushed to the back of her mind. Yesterday was more about the *child*, Alee. The girl who was a curious youth that dreamt of seeing the world, yet secretly held comfort by the safety of a book. A day ago, she was that girl. She traveled the world with her imagination to touch and taste.

Alee turned her attention to the horses and followed the guardsman's dry reply. Both horses had a shimmering black coat. The horses stirred as Alee approached them, though not in agitation. They jumped and stood about on their hind legs as if to garner some attention or favor from Alee. Their friendly competition was recognized by Alee as well. She smiled from ear to ear and paced back and forth to better examine them. Suddenly, she stopped with a practical question for the guardsman.

"What are their names?" she inquired.

"Names?" the guardsman replied.

"Yes, what do you call them?"

"They are the master's horses. He has named them

and I know not what."

"What a shame," replied Alee.

She turned to the horse on her left. Alee could tell she was more suited for battle. She bore a small scar across her neck and her overall bulk and tone was considerably larger in comparison.

"You have seen the blood stained fields, haven't you?"

Alee asked rhetorically as she rubbed the horse's brow. Alee made a playful, yet soothing clicking noise out the side of her mouth. The horse reacted like a child being tickled. Alee brushed her hair with the fork of her fingers, then moved to her right. There stood the second horse who vied for Alee's pleasure. Alee set eyes upon him. With hooves of pearl about a small frame, Alee saw this horse was meant for the spectacle of ceremony. Now knowing what she knew, Alee was left with a simple decision. Alee turned again to her left and spoke to the mighty beast.

"I do not know the name given to you by Alonard, but I will call you Bekemete. The name is one of a warrior so great that he brought peace to an entire nation. However, he found none for himself."

The horse moved away from Alee. She no longer made for Alee's attention. Bekemete retreated to the stable to partake in the rest Alee meant for the warrior to have. In such a short time, the two formed a bond. Alee mounted the other horse, the male, whom she was content in not naming.

"Come on, pampered prince. I'll be sure to toughen you up."

Alee spoke as she rubbed the horse's shoulders. The guardsman began a slow gallop atop his steed. Alee followed and together they quickly left the grounds of Alonard's compound.

They trotted onward from the high hills of the mountain where the Lighthouse Towers were perched. In passing, Alee saw the wonders of a land so readily referred to as paradise. The green of the trees and blue of the sky was just as sharp to her as those in the Southlands. The animals scurried as they approached. It seemed to Alee they were no more at peace, free from the fearful need to survive, than the animals of home. However, despite her attempts, Alee only proved Avalon had the best of the natural world and more.

The temperature was perfectly warm, with an occasional breeze that cooled the skin before any sweat could amass. The trail they rode was unworn. The grass was thick and tall while wilder growing bushes and shrubs lined the path. In all of her skepticism, Alee could at least admit a few things to herself. She was heartened to see a world untouched by the scar of unbalance. There was enough settlement and civilization to support the cultures of the Isle without sacrificing the natural world completely. Much like the Southland, Alee saw that the people of the Towers, who were scattered across the Western Bank respected how man and nature could live symbiotically.

Alee enjoyed the sightseeing. She saw the mills, crop rows, and the garden in the distance when she passed them. She paid no mind to their destination until finally they came upon it. The guardsman dismounted near the bank of a sparkling pool of water. Alee was close behind. They left their horses grazing several yards from the bank.

"Why did we stop here?" Alee asked.

Alee walked causally to the bank. The guardsman followed while at the same time keeping his distance from the lake. He watched Alee. He saw her full womanly shape in her form fitting attire and remembered darker times.

> "The master bade me take you here. This place has no formal name but all who have truly experienced it call it the Wanting Pool."

Alee's natural curiosity was in conflict. She needed to hear more but wanted to see the waters. The clear waters reflected like a glossy mirror upon its surface. The guardsman watched while Alee came upon the waters and saw her own visage staring back at her. It was awe-inspiring. To Alee, it looked as though a copy of herself looked at her from a life in the waters. She reached out to the person in the pool. Caught between inhales, the guardsman in that moment was breathless. Her finger felt the slightest wetness from the surface of the watery mirror and suddenly was stiffened. Alee tried to move but was paralyzed by forces unknown to her. The guardsman came closer. He saw her hair flowing in the wind as well as her neckline made bare by the breeze. Despite knowing better, he spoke of the pool as he walked closer to it.

> "In the distant past, not too long after Changel the Worthy completed his wanderings in the world of men, he decided to gather to the Isle the strongest of his offspring. All of his seeds possessed a greatness more formidable than that of the race of man. However, that did not guarantee a place in his plan or by his side. Through council, Changel decided to wade through his children's weaknesses by challenging them. And so his soldiers came. They were drawn to the Isle from across the sea and endured the physical trials of a journey from the Eastern Bank to the Western Bank where a final test of spirit and self awaited. It was a simple pool of water and the prized mission of the quest, "*Bring water from the lake.*"

Alee heard the guardsman. She tried to turn her head

towards him, but could not. She could not even seem to wrench her eyes away from herself. Alee's mind moved while she stayed frozen.

> "One by one, the men and women who deemed themselves worthy came to the pool. They reached into it but in doing so, truly they reached into themselves."

The guardsman stammered a bit. He remembered how the story he told was told to him, after the fact. While still reminiscing, he continued his oration.

> "A blessing or a curse, like most things is relative. The unweighted truth is Changel changed the waters to give service to the things that came unto it. When touched, the waters made real the desires of him or her engaged by the mirror. They saw all they wanted. However more times than naught, it was all they feared they wanted. It was a blessing for some to know.
>
> Changel would lie in wait and see the visions in the pool. He looked into the hearts of his soldiers as they themselves saw what they truly wanted for. The images were vivid and plain. Some saw themselves buried in a sea of lustful flesh or standing over the remains of a decimated army as a lord. Such as those, Changel purified the earth of

them. Desires that did not manifest were deemed more dire than the ones which did. Changel took the lives he had given them before their foul desires boiled over from some hidden place within."

Alee sunk into the waters in a vision of her own. The guardsman looked at the waters to see the images that manifested. He stepped closer to get a clearer view but was sure to keep his distance from the steady pool. Before the inner revelations of Alee spilled out, the guardsman remembered his own confessions.

"I stood where you stand, Alee, when my name was dear to me, when I was a murderer, when I took what I wanted, and wanted all but everything. Alonard found me; and before I touched the waters, he humbled me. My pride was purged and I found joy in simplicity, a purpose in a life of service."

Alee trembled. The girl in the water stared back with a smile. She looked happy. She was seated at a table with all the people she cared for. Alee was at the center of the table with a husband to her right, her neck adorned with jewels of matrimony. The guardsman smiled at the pleasant modesty of the life Alee desired, but the catch began, where determination fought against temptation.

"I was also worthy," said the guardsman, "I was in a place where greed had no life and I was the person

> I never thought I would be. But in that euphoria of meekness, the waters let go. The pool released me from stillness, but I did not move. I stayed there for days without food or water, only consuming the fullness of my deepest desire."

The guardsman looked on. Alee laughed and smiled. She was at peace. She shook the hands of her dinner guests as her husband held her tightly from behind. He gently pecked her neck. The vision continued in that joyous occasion because though Alee was free to return to the Isle, her arm was still stretched to the waters. She did not break free.

Hours passed quickly. And just as a day ago, Alee was enraptured by her own delights. With every moment gone by, the illusion became more real and the visions more detailed. The girl beneath the water grew more in the heart and mind of Alee while the girl ashore came closer to an existence as an empty shell. Alee was in danger of forfeiting the wellness that depended on the mind and body being one. Through it all, the guardsman kept his vigil. He was forbidden to pull her away and only instructed to take her to the lake and let destiny alone weave.

The guardsman knew the difficulty of saying no to a world without conflict. The trees were darkened by the shadows in the dusk. The waters grew colder and more disturbed by the winds. He looked upon Alee in all her beauty. The wet moisture of the lake fog made her hands softer. Her hair broke the binds of a brown ribbon with the help of the breeze. The guardsman took a step back.

"There is no avarice in seeing that a beautiful thing

is beautiful," he said to himself reassuringly.

Meanwhile, in a non-substantial dream, Alee experienced days that went by quickly. They were untroubled; which alone attributed to their speediness. Alee awoke next to her companion, a strong man whom had favored Alee for such a long time so unconditionally. She quietly turned to gently kiss his brow as he still slept soundly. She had meditations scheduled with Buhen later that morning. In the meantime, she stood at the foot of the bed in her nightlace and waited to serve her lover. Alee waited for her love to wake.

The guardsman looked into the waters and started to sweat. The thought of Alee performing her duties as wife gave the guardsman shortness of breath. His duty was to bear witness to her visions and report them to his master. But as Alee's partner stirred, he found it harder to carry out his own duties. He knew what was to come and doubted whether or not he could withstand the temptation.

Waking eyes fluttered, Alee's husband groaned. He quickly attained focus in the early morn. Alee teased the right strap of her blouse just as his eyes were upon her. The guardsman was tantalized; he paused and still gazed into the clear watery image. He looked upon her real flesh that still lay on the bank. The inner struggle was severe. Upon his mind and spirit, the doubt within him threatened to destroy the years of steadiness and serenity acquired through meditation. The help and faith bestowed unto him by Alonard would be betrayed. The images became more sensuous and the guardsman was left without grounds. He quickly rushed Alee and positioned himself behind her, but made sure to stay away from the waters of the pool. Alee crawled from the foot of the bed, atop her husband. She made sure that her chest just slightly grazed his body from bottom to top.

The guardsman placed his hands on her shoulders. Had Alee been aware of her real senses, she then would have felt the cold, rough flesh that now clasped her. The images were progressively more inflamed with Alee's passion. The guardsman read the lips of Alee's lover. He whispered to her,

> "Speak my name the way you do, which lets me know your love beyond any doubt."

Alee loosened her blouse and spoke as so to please. The guardsman could take no more. With his hands still upon her, he lowered himself a bit and tightened his grip. Despite his hands being so worn and rough, her skin was soft to the touch. The guardsman took a deep breath and suddenly pulled Alee away from the waters.

He jerked her with great intensity. They both hit the ground though the guardsman cushioned more of Alee than the earth. A bit dazed at first, everything was blurred in her mind like a dream. It seemed like no time had passed. Before she touched the waters and lost the anchor of her senses, the sun had shone brightly, now the waters were unsettled and sparkled in the moonlight.

"Wha...Where am I?

The guardsman was frantic, or at least he appeared to be in Alee's eyes. His head swayed from left to right. He spun around as if looking for something.

"Alee, leave." he blurted, "Return to the Towers."

Alee looked around as well. She tried to determine the cause of his hysteria. The guardsman's ploy worked. He saved himself from a long, uncomfortable explanation, but more so he kept his eye away from Alee.

"Go! Now!" he yelled.

Alee got to her feet and ran to her horse. She looked backed to the guardsman. Before she could voice her concerns, he spoke out.

"Go, Alee, please. I'll be right behind you."

She pulled the reins and galloped off into the forest. Alee only looked back once, before she turned around and returned to the pool. When she arrived back, there she saw the unsettled waters of the lake. Images of her and the guardsman together in the water glimmered on the surface as she tried to remember how the waters worked. Standing alone on the bank, she saw images that made no sense to her. In the images, she became closer and closer to the guardsman. Alee saw the back of her hand caressed the guardsman's cheek. As their lips drew nearer, the images faded. The waters became as black as the night. Only the light of the moon revealed the waters to Alee amidst the darkness. She found herself standing at the silvery bank alone.

The Elder in the Garden: Day 3 - Alee slept soundly throughout the night. The past day left her drained, both in mind and body. She lay in her bed with a faded memory of her watery fantasy, but arose with questions as well as unexplainable grief. She could not help but feel as though she had lost something. Alee had seen what could be. She saw love. And stepping into happiness in a form so pure, for but a moment was worthy of her lamentation.

The floor was cold when she placed her feet upon it. It could not compare to the warmth she felt a day ago. She thanked the guardsman for the wonders of the pool. She also prayed that he was content, wherever he may be. Her thoughts turned,

"He has been gone for two days. Two odd days. What will this day bring?" she pondered.

Alee grabbed her thick leather corset, trousers, and boots. She dressed quickly and ran towards the stables. A brisk soothing wind met her face upon leaving the tower. There were a few clouds in the otherwise clear sky. Alee arrived at the stable and, again, Bekemete was a sight to behold. The horse leapt and shuffled before Alee quickly put her at ease.

"I would be honored if you would return me to the lake," Alee stated.

Alee grabbed a dark crimson saddle from the top of the wooden enclosure. Without call, Bekemete came closer and Alee placed the saddle on her. Alee gingerly patted the back of her neck while tightening the saddle more securely.

"Ready when you are," said Alee.

Alee set out with her newest companion back to the pool. She felt odd fullness of joy that was in many ways surreal. On that day, the trail went by unnoticed. Some would say the beauty of the Isle was magnified as compared to the day before, however, Alee was preoccupied. She was genuinely concerned for the guardsman who had been her guide. Alee regretted fleeing so quickly the day before. Despite his insistence, Alee saw no danger, but that had made her even more anxious. She admitted to a larger truth as well, her memories from the pool were faint; but within them was the possibility of something Alee never knew she wanted and with someone she never thought she would need.

"Bekemete, why are you stopping?" Alee asked upon their sudden halt. "Yihh!" she exclaimed then nudged the side of Bekemete who galloped faster off the trail.

Quickly Alee lost sight of all that was familiar to her.

"Stop, Bekemete! Stop!" she yelled.

At that moment, Bekemete took a sudden jump, which threw Alee from her saddle. She hit the ground hard while Bekemete continued on without breaking stride.

"I...I guess Bekemete found her pawn."

Alee rubbed her sore hip then slowly rose to her feet. Noon was not yet upon the land, but the sun had long since erased the morning dew. Alee was in the thick of the forest and with the sun now so high, it would be hours before she knew which course would certainly lead her back to the Towers.

"Now what?" Alee asked aloud, "Bellia would lose her lunch from laughing if she knew I had been tricked by a horse."

"It would only be funny if you were not hurt."

someone said.

Alee heard a shaky voice of mild tone, which seemed to come from all around her.

"Who is there?" she shouted.

The sounds bounced off the tree trunks and echoed through the ruffling leaves. Alee spun around looking for the source of the commentary.

"Show yourself," she demanded.

"I would, but these thorn bushes are so sharp and prickly."

Alee looked to her right towards a thick wall of flowers, vines, and weeds. She could not see through it. Its vast length seemed to be matched by its undeterminable depth. While calling out to the stranger, Alee walked towards the hedge. The causal banter the stranger returned allowed Alee to isolate his location, relative to the wall.

"Can you help me get out of here?" asked the man within the bushes.

"Out?" replied Alee inquisitively.

"I entered the garden and now I want to go onward."

Alee was all together confused by the stranger's explanation thus far. However, she did not stop to further inquire. She went to work in heeding the cries from the man.

"Ok, I am coming!" shouted Alee.

She carefully reached out to the thorn bushes and tried to

push or snap the vines and branches apart. Alee was careful and meticulous as she handled the shrubs. Despite her caution, any exertion by Alee to break through the healthy green resulted in a deep cut or gash.

"Ahh!" she cried.

"Be careful, the bushes are very prickly," the man responded.

Alee let out a low sigh and retreated to lick her wounded fingers.

"I'm going to jump the wall.," she said.

"I would not do so if I were you," replied the man.

"And why not?" asked Alee.

"You might land in the briars, of course."

Alee rolled her eyes and proceeded to step backwards to get a good running start. The floral wall was at least ten cubits tall by Alee's estimation.

"No problem," she uttered to herself.

She began a sure stride and weaved very little amongst the bush before she jumped high into the air. She cleared the tall hedge with ease. While airborne, Alee looked below and took a glimpse of the elderly man stuck in the twines. Alee turned her attention to the ground, which quickly approached. The thorned briars and hedges twisted and meandered into a huge maze of flowers, branches, leaves, and trees. Alee was seconds away from barreling feet first into her own trap of bushes, bushes that were also *very prickly*.

"This is going to leave a mark." She glumly uttered to herself.

The crunch of her body upon the briars muffled what would have been a huge thud had she solely hit the ground. Alee moved hastily in order to free herself from the thorns.

"If my memory serves, the old man is on the other side of this wall," she murmured as she picked thorns out of her flesh. “No jumping this time."

Alee held her arms out front with her hands clamped together and focused. She clenched her hands tighter. At the same time, the wall of greens closed in upon itself a bit. Slowly, Alee separated her hands and the brush split apart simultaneously. When Alee was done, there was a hole in the tall hedge large enough for two or three people to enter at once.

Alee stepped through the gap. She saw the elderly man entangled in the briars but did not take his presence lightly. Alee approached the stranger with caution.

"How long have you been stuck there?"

"Are you going to leave it like that?"

Alee looked behind her to the gaping hole she had left in the hedges. She turned back to the elder with her eyebrow raised.

"It was not like that before," he added.

Alee scoffed a bit, but she knew he had a point. She had learned to respect nature as it was from Gaia. And although moving the shrubs had caused no damage, Alee acknowledged that it was no longer in its natural state. The plants and vines recoiled and seconds later the hole was gone.

"Mother Nature thanks you," the old man said.

Alee giggled a bit. The old man amused her. His choice of banter was simply odd to Alee. For him to sit there and find the time to comment on the landscape was not without some comedic merit. Alee asked a question through her smile.

"How did you get stuck like this?" she wondered.

"I tried to reach those high flowers up there. That is what I eat, you know. Good sap," he said.

"Eat?" Alee scowled before she continued, "How long have you been here?"

The old man wiggled his fingers in the direction of his forehead. He tried to scratch his head inquisitively, however the thorns and vines held back his hands. Alee let out a quiet chuckle.

"Uhmm, longer than a week but shorter than a

month."

"In the bushes?"

"No, the garden maze."

"And the bushes?"

"Since breakfast. Or at least what was supposed to be breakfast. Those flowers are so high. Very good sap though."

Alee did not want to appear rude in anyway by laughing at the old man. She covered her laugher with a cough and the grumble of her throat being cleared.

"Ok, be still. I am going to get you out. Hopefully, with the fewest pricks possible," she said.

"Yeah, these bushes sure are prickly," he replied.

Alee tried to pull the vines and branches away from the old man, but he was too entwined in them. They were healthy and strong and would not rip or tear. Alee looked around for something to cut the vines, but saw nothing, not even a jagged stone in the perfectly tended garden.

"Can you not just free me with your *magic*?" asked the elder.

Alee gave the elder a glance filled with displeasure. Something he said triggered her already rising level of frustration. She pulled away from the vines and thorns and set her hands on her hips.

"***Magic***?" Alee replied.

"Sure, I saw you make that hole in the bush without more than a thought."

Alee paused. Her rebuttal needed to be calm and non-confrontational so that it would be well received.

"Good Sir, there is no such thing as *magic*. And I can see how you could be misled, but please consider this, the natural world is as it is. Men have explored its wonders and secrets since the dawn of time. However, only the Originator of it all knows it all. The universe was made by His strength and His knowledge and He has bestowed unto me some of His knowledge and Will. No, I cannot turn the earth or fix the stars or raise the dead but I have some grace to do small wonders likened to Him."

The old man sighed before speaking.

"Does that mean no magic? I was so looking forward to seeing more."

Alee rolled her eyes. She did not know whether to attribute his behavior to senility, his personality, or a combination of the two, so she showed her respect as always and kept her mouth tempered.

"Very well," she said as she steadied her breathing

and prepared herself.

A method to free him came to her that would take little effort to perform. Alee tightly grasped some of the looser vines, which bound the old man. The thorns about them pierced the flesh of her hand and her thick blood poured slowly. The wind whistled and Alee began.

Her mouth moved rapidly yet no words came forth. The bushes trembled. Alee squeezed tighter. Her blood came more readily. The blood flowed along the vines. Her hands showed boils and the lines of time within them deepened. Age spread. While wrinkles and frailty stretched itself from upon her hands, time also made its marks against the vines. The earthy strands turned a paler green before crusting over into brown. All around the old man the ropes of nature, which had been as stout as an iron chain, became as soft as the muddy banks of the Great River.

The old man moved. The pus that had been tree and vine tore. Alee grew weaker, not from the exploits of her Will, but rather by her rapid growth in age. She called out to him.

"Do not move. Do not break the vines."

The old man was startled by her outburst and the raspy low voice that came from the mouth of Alee. The vines withered persistently until finally they fell to the old man's feet as dust and ash. He stepped away free and raised his eyes to

Alee. He saw a full grey head of hair upon her head, which quickly blackened as Alee fell to her knees.

"Step away." said Alee "I would hate to have to do that again."

The old man looked back to the bushes and witnessed the leaves and buds reviving just as quickly as Alee.

"Wondrous!" said the elder.

Alee paused.

"I would think in this place a person would see no shortness of...*magic*?"

The old man chuckled.

"Indeed, in this place there is no shortness."

Alee smiled from knowing that he now understood.

It was well past midday. The old man dusted himself off and walked the garden labyrinth as Alee followed. They pressed the ground for nearly an hour before Alee finally grew impatient.

"Sir, I stay to ensure your safety, but I must ask, do you know where you are going?"

"To the exit," he replied.

"And do you know the way?" asked Alee.

"No, I cannot say that I do."

Alee stopped. She sighed and thought about leaving him to

return to the lake but she too was lost.

"You are as cryptic as a man I once knew. It annoyed me to great ends," she stated.

"And this man, is he dead?" replied the old man.

Alee scoffed. Asking such a blunt and intrusive question took her aback. She strode ahead of him so she could look him in the eye. Suddenly, everything became still. The winds ceased. It seemed all the birds and beast were nowhere to be found.

"What are you not telling me, old man? What do you seek?" asked Alee.

"Answers. I seek answers. And you are welcome to join me," he replied.

"No riddles!" she yelled, "Who are you?"

"Very well. And I will keep my story short. My name is Daivd. More than anything I love my wife and daughter. When I left them, I was a man of thirty-two. I left them and to this day, I regret *that* day."

Daivd walked past Alee. His stride was principled. Alee followed, still to ensure his safety but also to feed her curiosity. He spoke very few words, yet from them, her heart went out with empathy. Alee paused as not to pry but Daivd continued.

"Ours was a love beyond all and my daughter the

gift of that love. A hunter I was, a simple hunter. She never asked anything more of me. How I loved her so."

His pace quickened, and with every crossroad in the maze, he moved without hesitation. Alee kept pace behind him, however, her ear was much closer.

"I thought I needed more. I wanted more for them, a future for my daughter. And so that day came a ship, larger than life, a fortress upon the waters. The men who came forth from this vessel had riches I never knew existed."

At the next turn, he stopped. He lowered his head and was then unsettled by his memory.

"I told my beloved but she did not believe me. She laughed. It was the last time I saw her laugh. I went back to the harbor in the dark of night and I boarded to plunder. I went there to steal, to steal a better life I thought. I mean, surely, I saw robes made of gold, cups made of gems. Everything seemed fine. Everything was...good. There were riches in my hands."

And saying the words, Daivd looked at his old and wrinkled hands, which he held up before him.

"I crept back to the deck and looked over the stern. I saw no earth. No earth, only sea. I put no stock in the heavens. But if there is such a thing, those who live there found game in me. The sky opened up just as I jumped into the sea to swim home and I awoke on this Isle."

Daivd turned to Alee and smiled. He made a left turn and continued.

"Gracious, me! I promised a short account," he said. "And my prison has been this Isle. No passage from anyone to be free of it, no way to escape. And yet this cursed Isle cradles me. She will not let me go. The days here are short it seems. I stopped counting them after my eightieth year. Surely, my wife and daughter are dead. For years, I have felt the sorrow of one ill-conceived choice. I would have ended my life ages ago, but I am certain I have mentioned I put no stock in the heavens. This wretched life is all I have now. I cannot throw it away with the false hope that they wait for me in some magical realm beyond what is."

Alee held her tongue. She knew it was not her place to say the things she wanted to say or teach the lessons that were taught to her. She held to her own beliefs, which were so unshakable and held to the idea that people are what they were meant to be, while still being what they choose to be.

"Why speak of death so plainly then, Sir? Is there no

hope left in you?" asked Alee.

Daivd gave nothing of himself. He walked on deeper into the maze but Alee cut him off once again. All of it made no sense to her. She blocked his way, and stayed face to face with him despite his every attempt to pass her by.

"Why are you wandering these garden halls aimlessly? Maybe I can help? Let me help."

Daivd's face turned. His tone, once wavered by age, became firm with frustration. He leaned his shoulder towards Alee forcefully and brushed her aside.

"Have you not been listening?" he exclaimed. "Aimlessly?" he grumbled, "I love them. I would give anything to see them again. In the last thirty of my years, I have only known hope when I happened to hear a small group of men speaking. They seemed to know every inch of this place. As causally as you or I would speak of the weather, I overheard them talking about visiting a place past the garden where the dead live again."

Alee placed her hand on his shoulder.

"The world can be full of illusions--" she began.

"Stop right there!" interrupted Daivd, "You offered help to me. Will you honor that?"

Alee nodded and they continued to tread along the winding path of the wild garden. She thought about Daivd's obsession and wondered if the things he told her could be true. The line between the living and the dead is sacrosanct, yet Alee had learned to be open to all possibilities in this place.

They journeyed long past the setting of the sun, yet Daivd walked on with an inhuman determination. Alee, however, grew fatigued. Her hips were still sore from both of her falls earlier that day.

> "We have been here all day. How close are we to the end? We must be fairly close if you have been in here for as long as you say."

Alee removed her boots and massaged her feet. The old man looked at her and then turned his eyes to the ongoing corridors of green and earth. He let out a low and melancholic sigh.

> "I will find the true way out. If it takes me eighty years on this Isle, I will," he stated.

Alee paused for a moment. She quickly rose to her feet and poured the loose dirt out of her boots before putting them back on. She looked directly and deeply into the eyes of Daivd but he lowered his eyes away from her.

> "I noticed before the price you paid, the toll for freeing me of those branches," said Daivd.

He took a small step away from Alee. The moonlight seemed to define more of the grief and sorrow that lay upon his face.

"It's funny. These amazing things are here in life but it seems they exist with exceptions which would appear to be all too entertaining to those who have placed them here."

Alee stayed quiet again. She held her tongue. Gaia had imparted the wisdom behind the intricacies of life such as those. But once again, it seemed to Alee that a lecture about humility and temptation was not appropriate in the situation. So she remained quiet and let him continue.

"This garden is no different. It is vast and long by nature and it grows wild, but I have not traveled it for nearly a month solely because of its size and twistedness."

While Daivd spoke of the garden, the breeze seemed stronger. It made the brush and leaves of every plant and tree in the garden speak louder. They ruffled and creaked as Alee listened on.

"No matter how tired, fatigued, or wary we become, we must not sleep. For when we do, we will find ourselves at the entrance to the garden upon waking," he said.

Alee was amazed by what she had heard.

"I am sure lost travelers who wandered into the maze

were pleased by this upon waking," Alee said.

"Yes, but the traveler who needs to find its end? What about those such as myself, who want to venture into Resurrection Valley?"

They continued on towards what Daivd called Resurrection Valley. The longer the journey became, the more Alee saw things through the eyes of Daivd. Deeper into the night, Alee fought off her own urge to stop. Stopping would mean being wrangled by sleep. They stopped every so often to consume from the very garden they struggled to escape. They ate of the many fruits from the wall of the green labyrinth. Daivd knew what was safe to eat.

Alee and Daivd helped one another and made it further than he had ever gotten before. Up until now, Daivd avoided all the dead ends by virtue of his experience and memory. Each turn was now unknown territory and Daivd admitted it to Alee. She took point and led the way from there. Her knowledge of the stars led them in the same general direction. However, they both still ran into a few dead ends.

"I am…tired," said Daivd, yawning.

Alee followed with a yawn of her own. Her eyes fluttered. Daivd fell to a crouch, then to one knee. Alee ran to him to help him up. She had been amazed by the old man's strength and resilience.

The dawn peered from beneath the horizon and the night became shadows in the garden. Daivd and Alee were sore from head to toe. It was the pain of a body begging for rest and replenishment. Alee ignored it. Daivd however was on his feet but resting on the stance of Alee. His head fell back. Alee patted his face repeatedly. She slapped him to a place just before slumber and dreams. She placed her hand on his chest and gave him some of her strength. Although she knew she did not have much of her essence to spare. She longed for the death of sleep, to be reborn, replenished, so that the day could resurrect her awakening.

The dawn increasingly beat down on them. The sun climbed higher. They scrounged around the bends of the garden only to meet dead end patches that were impenetrable. Despite Alee's generous donation, Daivd's body seemed to consume the energy quickly. And considering Daivd and the height of the hedges, Alee could not leap the walls of the garden to free them.

"Maybe one or two jumps are all I need," Alee said to herself.

Alee turned away from Daivd and set her base. She leapt into the sky, as high as she could at the moment, though not as high as before. She tried to peer through the higher trees to where she thought the exit lay. In the split seconds before she charged back to the earth, Alee tried to commit as much of the maze's layout to mind. She landed, crouched to a knee.

"One more!" she said.

She jumped again and barely cleared the hedge. It did little for her. She only saw enough to confirm what she witnessed before. It was a small victory, though it came as most did for Alee, with a price. When she arose from the crouch of her second jump, Alee turned to find herself alone.

"Daivd? Daivd!" she yelled.

She sprinted around a few corners before Alee was forced to admit what happened.

"He fell asleep." she sighed.

She sat for a moment. The path to the outlet was fresh in her mind, though not vivid. She thought about letting go and letting her own desire to sleep take her. To rest and go back to the beginning with Daivd would help them both, provided she could remember the way after a hazy slumber. Alee quickly rose to her feet and continued to navigate to the exit.

> "There is no guarantee I will awaken around the same time as Daivd." Alee stated to herself. "He could reenter before I even wake up. I would be left chasing him not knowing if slumber caused him to

continue on from in front or behind me."

And so, she went forward. Her words spoken aloud were more to convince her rather than any honest reasoning. She wanted to know if any of her loved ones could be summoned from the Valley.

The day full new, the sun continued to ascend. Alee raced through the chambers of the garden maze. She converted her scouted path into a sequence of numbers. *Lefts* and *rights* became *ones* and *twos*. Alee, now with her count, developed a rhythmic stride. Her pace hastened. Her thoughts strayed away from Daivd towards the promise of what the Valley could give her. Her mother, Nympthia, could answer all her questions. Questions about who she was and what was meant for her could be put to rest or back in motion.

Alee neared the edge of the garden. She ran and pressed the earth with only a few turns left to follow. And with her final turn, she saw the wreath-twisted archway of the exit gates. The fire-red roses and purple dragon lilies lined the vines of the arch. They bobbed with the horizon as her head moved from stride to stride.

"Almost there," exclaimed a weary and exhausted Alee.

The exit now lay only a couple of long strides out of reach. Alee lifted her left foot to move forward. Suddenly, she stumbled upon a loose mossy green stone. Her head and upper torso came piling to the earth. Alee hit the ground with the same speed she ran with. There she lay motionless in a slight daze from her impact, merely a few yards from the exit.

Upon the ground, without sleep or rest for some time, Alee's eyes grew heavy. Her dizziness made the ground feel as though it swirled beneath her body, yet it was soft and comfortable. Alee was disoriented. Coupled with her weakness, she found it hard to get up.

"I…can't..." she mumbled.

Alee yawned. She gathered what little strength she had and reached out to the earth. She grabbed grass and dirt then pulled it towards her as she felt her consciousness slip towards rest. She wallowed and inched closer to the gate. Her eyes fluttered rapidly. Her head pounded from her haze and fatigue. She rolled over twice then stopped, facing skyward. Her arms were stretched out. The bright sun above closed her already weighted eyelids. She tilted her head to the side without so much as a thought. Her breathing slowed. Thoughts subsided. Eyes remained shut. Finally, sleep had overtaken Alee.

Resurrection Valley: Day 4 - Hours passed. The sun was

now positioned for the late evening. Alee felt the cool refreshment of the late day breeze upon her cheek, then her eyes fluttered. She shook off the dull cloud that followed slumber. She looked towards the sky, no longer blinded by the sun. She saw the pure white clouds, which floated on high. Alee rose to her feet. Her eyes came into the darkened shade that stretched across her face. Alee smiled. She looked above her head and saw the dragonlilied archway just above where her elbow had stretched out during her hours of napping.

"I...I made it!" exclaimed Alee.

She scoffed at both her misfortune and the luck that quickly followed. Alee dusted herself off. She removed the loose leaves and twigs from her hair as she walked beneath the archway.

Now free of the garden, the terrain changed drastically. Brown stone pillared around her. The fragrant perfumes of the flowers in bloom gave way to the smell of beasts, which roamed the valley. The ground declined and the rocks grew taller and taller above her. The shadows thickened and Alee crept deeper into what seemed to be beneath the earth itself.

"At least the road is set," scoffed Alee.

Unlike the garden maze, there were no twists or turns on the rock-valley road she traveled. Alee steps were slow and soft. The cavernous valley was just as foreign to Alee as the plush garden, yet there was increased tension amongst the dusty walls of stone and rock. The valley evoked a sinister mood.

Alee strode onward and descended deeper into the valley. The canyon walls cradled Alee. Traveling further into the darkness, she saw very few signs of life. Scattered shrubs and aimless lizards created a more stark setting. Alee doubted what she had heard about Resurrection Valley. The canyon narrowed and the walls melded above her. There was no more sun light from above. Alee continued down a cold, dank cave. The faint light at her back reflected against the minerals in the rocks.

"This is beautiful," she murmured.

Throughout the whole of the cave a light, blue and purple from the ore of the rock and crystals, shone. The lights bounced all around the hollowed ground. With every reflected beam, the hues brightened and fused. It gave the cave a majestic and serene white light. The further inward Alee traveled, the more intense the light became. The light was full, yet did not blind her. It covered her body with a soothing warmth.

"Truly beautiful. I wish Daivd was here to see it," added Alee.

Suddenly, a shadow manifested before Alee. It was as

though the light bent and was given density. Alee looked on and saw form in both the shadows and light. Soon a face appeared from the light. A face familiar to her that she had unwittingly summoned. A startled Alee jolted back.

"Daivd!"

He wore the same garments, which adorned him when last they saw one another. Daivd took a step towards Alee with a smile upon his face.

"Its good to see you again, Alee. How have you been? It's been so long," said Daivd.

Alee scratched her wrist and raised her brow.

"What do you mean? I saw you less than a day ago," replied Alee. "Remember, I was looking for a way out of the garden. I left you alone for a second. You feel asleep."

Daivd turned away from Alee. He touched the glowing crystal walls and turned back with a look of enlightenment upon his face.

"I remember…everything," Daivd said starkly. "I wanted to be here, in this place, to be with the people whom you just called me away from."

Alee in her heart of hearts knew of what Daivd spoke. However, she refused to admit anything concerning death. Her fear of it and relationship with it, gave death too much power in her life.

"Who now has fallen during my tenure?" Alee asked herself. "This can't be real."

Daivd finished examining the cave. He brought his hand back to himself. He turned around from the wall and walked up to Alee. She saw his expressionless face, but still felt a sense of restlessness in Daivd. He spoke, though his words were few.

"May I go now?" he asked.

Alee did not understand the question. Held within it was too much of a subordinate tone. She did not know how to respond. Her face said as much.

"You called me here, Alee. I can go when you give me leave or forfeit your stay in this valley."

Daivd's face fell and emoted something more than what he said. Alee pondered Daivd's request. She had every intention of letting him leave. However, she thought about what she said to bring him here and the words that could do the contrary.

Daivd's words grew more intense. Desperation loomed behind the words he spoke. He let out a booming shout.

"I want to return to my family! Can I go to them? Will you let me go?"

Alee became startled. His sudden burst in dynamic caused

her reply to fly out, short and unhindered.

"Yes!" she blurted.

The same light, which swathed the both of them in the cave, radiated from the eyes of Daivd. To Alee it seemed as though the light of a strong spirit within could no longer be contained. Daivd gave thanks. His mouth opened and closed forming the words for Alee but the beacon of light from his tongue blinded her. She turned to shield her eyes and rubbed them clear. When she turned back, Daivd was gone.

"Peace and no more travels." whispered Alee.

She now understood. In that place, there was no need for incantations or elaborate prayers. Alee needed only to speak the name of the departed and ask for them to appear. She pondered for a moment before she made use of her new knowledge. On the one hand, there was the matter of the fate of her friends, but Alee feared to speak a name and have one appear. On the other, there was her mother, Nympthia. Her design, her will, and presence could be made clear. However, Alee feared judgment from Nympthia for all her actions thus far.

Thus, with little thought Alee spoke a name. A form appeared. Just as before with Daivd, the shadows broke the light and made clear the depth of a face and body.

"Hello, Alee." said the phantasm.

"Hi..." Alee said in undertone, “...I...I...don't know

why I called you here."

She came forward, closer to Alee.

"It is your guilt. Trust me. Remember that I was learnéd in the workings of the mind. Also, trust that I died doing my duty and guilt is a weight no balanced heart can carry."

Her words comforted Alee and gave her strength. Despite there being no wind in the cave, the silk flowed and swayed on the beautiful feminine form that came from the light.

"Thank you, Dorah. I am sorry."

Dorah smiled. A contrite Alee gave the healer, Dorah, who had healed once more, her leave. Alee tried to peer through the light of Dorah's luminously vivid eyes. She wanted to see Dorah fade as her soul went to wherever souls rest. It was like trying to track a bird flying before the clear, bright sun. The shadows, which defined Dorah's ethereal vessel, retreated back into the light, in the opposite of the way she appeared.

While her heart was full, Alee did not hesitate. Her guilty heart made her fear for her friends and matrons for Alee blamed herself for leaving and parting as she had. But now, with her guilt reconciled, so was the fear. Alee accepted it and called forth another name.

"Bellia!" she shouted.

Moments passed. She waited, longer than she had needed to

before.

"Bellia?" Alee whispered the second time.

She spoke her name for good measure. Nothing happened. No one came. She now knew that Bellia still lived. She tested another name.

"Hat-kaptah!" she called.

The light of the caves made no moves. It did not fluctuate, nor did it bend. She was relieved. Alee let out a light sigh in the form of a name.

"Gaia," she uttered.

In that very instant, the light dimmed. It was but a quick flicker. A shadow drew together before dissipating like a puff of black smoke. Alee waited. She saw nothing but was indeed concerned by the motion in the cave.

"Gaia? Gaia!" Alee shouted.

Nothing happened. No one came.

There was one more champion to call before Alee could stand to be in the presence of her mother. Beads of moisture prickled Alee's skin. The light gave off heat as well and the cave grew hotter. Coupled with the tension she felt, her hair fell damp and wavy across her face. Alee removed her thicker outer tunic and stripped to her lighter linen vest.

Alee spoke yet another name. Before the last syllable passed her lips, the shadows took shape once again. A strong, feminine figure emerged. Covered in black from head to toe, an image of strength and courage came closer to Alee. Her hair was short and frizzed. Her black linen garb looked to be a single cloth that hung across the shoulder and was fixed by another thin strand at the waist. The simple dark toga, as loose as it was, could not conceal her toned and sculpted body. In Meroe and Bellia, Alee had thought no other women could so finely weave the beauty of womanhood with the strength of a warrior. Alee looked on. She saw why those women so proudly claimed to be the daughters of Pixsus.

Pixsus, a reborn spirit turned flesh, reached out her hand to Alee. She placed her hand upon the side of Alee's cheek. They looked into each other's eyes as the heat of the caves became more intense. It was as though the caves of the valley could not hold the stronger spirits that came. Alee became dizzier as the heat grew more severe. Exhausted by it, she fell to a knee. Sweat dripped from her face. Her mouth was dry. She had trouble speaking. Her swollen tongue flopped around inside her mouth as she tried.

"Help…" gasped Alee.

Pixsus looked upon her. From her perspective, there was no heat. The air was as calm as a cool autumn day. Alee's full lips peeled and cracked. Her eyes became bloodshot. Pixsus looked at her, puzzled.

"Is there a problem, child?" Pixsus asked.

Alee gasped. The air was so thick she choked on it. The energy from the spirit of Pixsus engulfed her. Alee pondered for a moment. She considered that had she called the name of another, her mother, then she would surely be dead. Pixsus kneeled beside her.

"Who are you?" asked Pixsus.

Alee tried hard to form a simple word. Her lips shook, but eventually a single word hit the heated air.

"Go!" Alee murmured.

The black tunic seemed to flutter into nothing, like a ribbon flying away, disappearing in the breeze. With Pixsus now gone, the air quickly returned to normal. As the weighty hot air toppled out of her lungs, Alee hacked violently. Her mocha-brown skin had darkened slightly. With the strength she had left, Alee ran free of the caves. The open air refreshed her, though her mouth was still a bit dry. Alee reached behind the shadowy side of a stone near the threshold of the cave entrance. Her two middle fingers moistened from the damp moss. She placed them on her tongue, sucking away the sparse wetness. She reached behind the stone again and rubbed the mixture of mud, water, and fungus across her lips. In actuality, Alee had no important words for Pixsus. She wanted only an opportunity to honor her. For any question of Alee's, which could be answered by Pixsus, could also be answered by Nympthia.

Thus, Alee cleared her throat and strode back into the light of the cave. She went deeper into the tunnel. The light there washed over her. It seemed a million times more potent than before.

Alee stood in the center of the cave. She prepared her mind and body for her last encounter in the valley. She pulled her unkempt hair away from her face, wiped her brow, steadied her feet, and raised her hands above her head. The back of her hands met, leaving her palms faced out. She was ready. Alee called out.

Dei lux animum summam sum! Nympthia!

The words, which preceded the name of her mother let loose the power of her Will. To fight back the air and strength soon to come from the spirit of Nympthia, Alee encased herself in a pocket of existence by the light of a spirit even greater. As expected, the shadows closed and a great glow shone throughout the whole of the cave. The spirit brought light so intense that Alee could only look to the ground. The light came with energy so fierce that its radiant heat fought the Will of Alee. She struggled to keep the heat at bay and attempted to stretch out her arms and move her palms as far apart as possible. Alee held still the pocket at great strain.

Outside the sphere that protected Alee stood Nympthia. Alee could only hear her past the light like the sun. The heat in the cave carried greater intensity than before. Waves of heat filled the cave. And although Alee fought them back from a place far more habitable, she suffered with her Will sustained in such a way.

Alee made haste, but before she could speak her heart and mind, she was made to listen. Alee tried to look through the light. She wanted to see her mother. She wanted to see her face, but the light was far too bright. Alee fell to her knees, as both hands tried to stretch away the power of a spirit pure and strong. Alee's eyes were at her feet. This time, sweat and tears fell to the ground.

I am proud and humbled by you, Daughter-Aleeia. I have always expected great things from you. But I never thought you would come so far, so fast even now, to stand before you. For you to have the strength to bring me here is a wondrous feat.

Everyday of my life, I have seen you in my dreams. I have seen you grow. But now you want

> *answers. You want to know where it begins, where it ends; where it ends, and where it begins, the evil you must face, the journey you have undertaken, a means to defeat your enemy, and love in a life all your own.*

Alee heard the words that every son or daughter wanted from a parent. She could not hold back the emotions she felt. Her arms quickly became sore. Her strength drained. The once black stones of the cave changed. They were now red and began to melt and move. A sobbing Alee listened on.

> *I know time is short. Your heart is weighted and stressed, but listen carefully to what I am about to say and understand. You cannot fail! In more than one way, you cannot fail. The choice to continue is yours. It always has been. If Changel is successful, the world will still go on. Good will endure. It is an opposite*

and cannot die.

But if you stop him. If you decide to do what only you are capable of accomplishing, then the world will fly closer to what it was meant to be. God gave us choice. Trust in that, my daughter! I love you. Farewell.

"Mommy..." Alee whimpered, "...goodbye...go in peace."

Alee heard a clap like thunder and saw a flash of light. She lay bent with both hands and knees on the ground. The smell of cooling molten rock filled her nostrils. Alee coughed. Despite her fatigue, she had to escape the fumes from gases and minerals unknown to her. She rose to her feet. Alee stumbled to the edge of the cave wall and scorched her shoulder. She cried out in pain, but still moved forward.

From all that had made her body weary, Alee's heart was full. She climbed back up the valley trail to the archway of the garden exit. The afternoon breeze grew cooler as the sun sank behind the horizon. Alee became limp and fell upon the soft plush grass of the garden. While crying and smiling at the same time, Alee passed into a much needed slumber, which ended a very long day.

The Counsel of Caim: Day 5 - At the verge of the garden entrance, the cool morning dew blanketed everything that lay still from the night before. Alee's skin glistened with the grass that was both moist and refreshed by the day anew. Very soon however, the damp, weighty beads fell and flew away. The lightened grass rose up and so did Alee.

Alee yawned and wiped her eyes. They were still red from all the crying done the night before. Her journey thus far had hardened her. She had a greater sense of her own emotions as well as more control of them, but that control was broken yesterday. Alee was humbled by her mother, who was a light too great to look upon. However, more befittingly, Alee looked to the ground, to the darkness, where all rays of the spectrum are absorbed, communed, accepted, and kept. Nothing is jettisoned, but seen as the color *called* black.

"Impressive! To know what black *is!*"

Alee was startled. The voice she heard came out of nowhere and spoke words, which commented on the thoughts in her mind. Alee's head swayed and swiveled around. She saw no one. She stopped and listened for a moment, but heard no more so she headed northwest, back in the direction of her temporary towered home.

"Most people in *this* age have no grasp of such things."

Alee turned again to where she thought the sound had originated. No one was there. Except a few bustling shrubs and an owl, there was nothing in that direction.

Alee stared at the owl for a moment. The owl seemed to glare back. Alee slowly crept closer to the bird. Uncharacteristically for any type of beast, it did not flee. It stayed perched upon a tree branch that stretched out a few feet beyond Alee's reach. The owl was larger than any Alee had seen before. Its plumage was dark brown and the tips of each lower feather had a sharp red and black accent. Alee also noticed how sleek the owl was compared to the others she had seen in the Woodlands of the South. Its wings extended with a length more akin to that of an eagle. The bird was truly an amazement. It almost caused Alee to completely forget her reason for looking in that direction.

"Show yourself," Alee exclaimed.

"No need to shout."

Shocked, Alee's face fell. Her eyes widened. Of all the things she had seen, she was not prepared to see an animal that could speak. For Alee, only the stories of old were saturated with serpents, lambs, and other more fantastic beast that moved and spoke with men. *Do my eyes and ears deceive me?* Alee asked herself. The owl fluttered to a lower branch. Alee thought intensely about how the owl could speak and how it seemed to know her thoughts as she thought them.

> "The thoughts of human beings are too predictable to start with. You all have simple needs," said the owl.

Alee walked closer. Naturally, she thought maybe her ordeal in the valley, which had weakened her, also caused her to imagine the things she saw and heard.

"What? Who are you?" she asked.

The owl moved his wings in a flurry and twisted its head back and forth. The motions had no meaning with regards to the question Alee presented. Seemingly, they were only the actions of a beast. However, the eyes of the owl widened, before it spoke in reply.

> "A better question would be, *Did your mother give you the key to defeating your enemy when you spoke in the caves?*"

Alee once again was taken aback but stopped wondering about *how* it knew *what* it knew. Instead, she was curious to know the extent of what it knew about her. Naturally, Alee held a few secrets. Secrets kept about who she was, what she had done, and the destiny laid down to her. So she grew more defensive in discourse.

"You hold me at a disadvantage. You seem to know a great deal about me, but I have naught that same courtesy," she stated.

"You are right. Perceptive." replied the owl with a tone of admiration, "In fact, I am what just *occurred.*"

Alee became more confused.

"What just happened?" she whispered to herself.

"Your mother told you nothing. Well, she gave you words to encourage your troubled mind and even more for your dithering call to action. I asked the question to lead us here, where now you know to a greater extent of what I know and a bit more about *who* I am."

Alee wanted to scratch her head and thump her brow. The owl spoke in riddles. However, it was right. It did reveal a bit more about what it knew. Alee stood still. The owl hopped to another branch, this one even closer at eye level to Alee. She could stretch her hand out and touch it if it pleased her.

"Come now, Aleeia. I am sure Gaia instructed you better than what you show."

Alee thought a moment. She considered all possible reasons for the things the owl said. It said just enough to keep her curious, and that curiosity did indeed grow. However, suddenly, her thoughts cleared and only action remained.

"Where are you going?" the owl asked sincerely. Naturally, Alee's mind went to the question, but quickly her thoughts became random. She saw the trees before her and the sky above. Once again she thought nothing and was left with her actions alone. Now facing Alee's back, the owl left its perch on the branch and flew skyward. In just a few seconds, it settled on a stone a few strides in the path of Alee.

Alee quelled her interest yet again. She still burned to know the owl's purpose and as a result her thoughts ran deep again. Until she glanced at the moss below the stone. It guided her westward and she moved with no aim. The Tower of Alonard was no longer her focal point. She simply wandered and the owl ruffled and rumpled its plumage. The language of its fowl form was clear. The owl was frustrated. Alee was slowly besting him.

The owl called out to Alee. It bade her stop and insisted she wanted to know what it had to say. For the first time, Alee listened in the moment. She heard the owl’s call and instantly filed it away in her mind. When the owl was finished, Alee heard the wind and the leaves with no thought to the sounds that came before them.

Relatively silent now, Alee and the owl continued to

square off as adversaries. No one spoke a word while the music of the forest played on for Alee. In between each sweet note of nature's melody, Alee pondered briefly, *why does the owl persist?*

The owl could not hear or see much of Alee anymore. It only heard what she heard, only saw what she saw.

"I am knowing. Call me Caim," stated Caim.

His voice softened. His beak opened and closed quickly, it was akin to Caim smiling.

> "Alee, you are truly one who is touched by God. No one before has shown such wit or strength against me. Yours is quite strong."

Alee was intrigued, but only listened. She had restrained her thoughts to simply wanting knowledge for its own sake. She never grasped for anything in particular. She allowed Caim to continue to speak.

> "I was at the right arm of God. Now, I am here to guide you. To help you fulfill your destiny."
>
> "Well, you definitely seem to know a lot about it," replied Alee.
>
> "Yes, yes! But let's move past that." scoffed Caim, "Tell me, what do you think you have to do?" asked Caim.

Knowing that Caim already knew so much, she did not hold

back. Alee also decided this ominous bird could do little to alter anything by speaking freely.

"It has fallen to me to *order* Changel. A misguided watcher, who is both treacherous and wise."

"Misguided *and* wise?" Caim asked with inflection.

"Scrolls tell the story of how he stole the mantle. He knows a great deal. His knowledge is a threat. He is wise indeed, but uses his wisdom to run amuck in the world of men," said Alee.

"And you would stop this?"

"I must."

Caim finally leapt to her shoulder and together they traveled back northwestwards to the Towers. Alee had not yet taken three full steps on the grassy graveled trail before Caim spoke again. Now he sat on her right and spoke directly to her ear.

"How will you stop him?"

Alee did not hesitate. Her reply came forth so quick and freely as though it were rehearsed a thousand times.

"I have been trained to defeat Changel. Our gifts from the Creator are only separated by the Will, which drives it. I will prevail."

"So brute force is your ploy?" returned Caim with a weighty inflection.

"No, the pure majesty of it takes cunning and

discipline to wield successfully. Besides, what else do I possess above any other that will grant me success?" Alee asked.

Caim cackled loudly. He lowered back down and whispered into Alee's ear. Alee entered a familiar clearing. The lake she had visited a few days ago was not far. Although she no longer had any desire to return there, she followed the trail back towards the Tower.

"Remember what just happened. You certainly have more resources available to you besides your parlor tricks," said Caim.

Alee did not know whether his words were meant as compliment or ridicule. She let out a barely audible scoff.

"Parlor tricks?" she asked.

"I simply mean this, Alee. It took true cunning to best me back there. It took real intelligence to translate the scrolls, to break that code. And for some reason, people follow you. You should consider using that to stop Changel."

Alee was flattered. She saw the point behind Caim's words. However, to Alee, it still seemed a little too farfetched.

"So do you really thing I can talk down Changel? Persuade him to abandon his madness?"

Caim left her shoulder and flew ahead to a branch a few

paces away. They were once again eye to eye.

> "I just gave you praise and your thoughts turn narrow," Caim retorted, "Of course God would be pleased if simple words could stop the bloodshed to come. However, it may take more than that alone."

He paused briefly.

> "Whether you know this or not, Changel's most beloved, his first among many, Alonard, is open to your will. As we speak, he returns from his father's council and will do so with a fiery hatred for Changel. And his passion as it is has never before filled his being in such a way as it soon will."

Now, Alee completely followed what Caim insinuated to be a plan of action for her. She did not question the validity of the information he imparted. Caim was right about her thoughts and history so she believed what he said.

Even still, Alee was doubtful. She did not know how to put a plan like that into action or if using Alonard was a viable option for stopping Changel. Caim made sense, though. Peaceful words seemed to be more in line with the God she knew as opposed to a battle to the death.

Alee saw the Tower perched atop the ridge through the trees. The massive stronghold shimmered with the sun as part of the horizon. Alee had nothing more to say to Caim. She wondered about the timing as well as the messenger. *Why now? And why not foreseen or suggested by Nympthia?*

"Were those questions for you or meant for God's ears?" asked Caim.

"Its seems both. I ponder what I ponder and you have God's omniscience to respond on His behalf," replied Alee.

She stopped and then quickly ran into her next thought.

"Can your all-knowingness bring me anything more than doubt?" she asked.

Caim knew of what Alee spoke, Gaia and Bellia. Alee had grown increasingly wary of Caim and just as weary of their banter. For the conversation to continue on she required it to be of some immediate benefit. At least she knew they were not dead. They did not come to her in the Valley, but knowing was not enough.

"There is nothing I can tell you about your two companions."

A scowl of disbelief was written all over Alee's face. Her eyes inflamed and her tone grew more severe. To know so much about so many things, yet nothing regarding Gaia and Bellia seemed inconceivable.

"Think whatever you will, Alee," stated Caim. "I know only what God allows me to know. Consider that knowing anything about your friends could affect you adversely no matter what their fate may be."

In an instant, Alee realized that Caim offered nothing but confusion. Her head was jumbled with all he had said. Fatigued, Alee rubbed her hand across her brow and cheek. The past few days had been trying. She needed rest. She looked past Caim to the Tower and thought only of the food and refreshments that awaited in the luxurious manor. She walked through the brush on the beaten trail back to her defaulted home. Caim did not follow her and at no time did Alee turn back to see if he had. She did not care. She only wanted to rest her body and mind.

A warm bath and soft bed awaited Alee. And, though it was the midday, Alee indulged in it. She walked by every attendant and servant with a simple nod as she made her way to her room. Her sullen clothes hit the floor as quickly as possible. The warm bath waters that steamed at the foot of her bed were tempting, but Alee was impatient. She took a warm wet cloth and wiped away the grit and grime from her face and body. She was clean enough to enjoy her slumber without the putrid itch of a dirty body. Her sore and weary body hit the cushioned bed and again Alee felt unbridled peace.

Prey of Flesh: Day 6 - Hoofs played the earth like hands on drums. Alonard rode at a frantic pace. From Changel's citadel on the Eastern Bank back towards the West, he strode on yet he veered southward. The horse galloped with a consistent downbeat. Four thuds pulsated through the forest as Alonard made his way to the mountain peak. And while he rode onward, his mind went back hours in time.

In the courtyard, two imposing men walked. The enormous citadel, although made from mountains, was green all over. In the center of the hold, the courtyard held a straight polished stone path from the north end to the south. The walls surrounding the courtyard were adorned with life as thick and fragrant vines scaled higher to reach the sun's warmth. The plush grass and full trees called Red Maple lined the walkway. The branches were twisted but the foliage was not yet primed to have its autumn fall. The sun shone upon the courtyard inside the steep and narrow walls for brief moments around noon. Despite the wall being so high and the swirling binds, which funneled off them, these living things flourished. It seemed the cold shadows were more to the liking of the Red Maple and plush green grass. The blue and white stained glass windows embedded in the walls staggered with respect to the Red Maple. Changel entered the courtyard with his First Among Many. Dark silhouettes filled the stained glass windows. Hidden eyes from on high looked upon two figures, admired and exalted.

The awe behind the windows poured into the courtyard as the two men walked tall and cleared the archway. Alonard knew his place. He remained half a step behind Changel. It was a slow leisurely walk from the north end to the south. Alonard had his arms folded inside his long brown robe. His black boots knocked upon the stones of the walkway beneath his feet. His hair was tied back with his pale blue eyes fixed on Changel who also wore a robe. It was ivory white, and otherwise pristine, except for the aberrantly assorted black spots that covered the garment. The dark blemishes were thick, as though woven into the fabric. His right sleeve was black to the shoulder. It was a profuse concentration of color that dispersed into permanent, yet artistic specks. Changel knew how the artistry of those marks accrued, and soon so would Alonard.

> "...so we decided to split up. Knowing the other would soon come to save the slave whom we had captive. I went after one of them alone and--" said Alonard.

"And you think to insult me?" Changel added.

His voice was calm but instilled great fear in Alonard, who knew to choose his next words carefully. With a conscious effort not to stammer, Alonard spoke. Still, his voice trembled.

"I am sorry, Father. I do not understand my misdeeds, but I assure you I mean you no disrespect."

Alonard looked to Changel. They stopped at one of the Red Maple trees along the path. Changel pulled gently at a bud, and then suddenly snapped it away.

"Do not patronize me with details already known to me. You are here to explain, what seems to be your failure. Sciona and Jacobb returned with their cargo days ago. And you, my son?"

Alonard was distraught. His father's tone dug out his insides. The words that accompanied stung like salt. He took heart of Alee and remembered his promise to her, to not give her up. However, Alonard never anticipated he would be in such disfavor with his father. He discovered from Alee so much related to Changel's past and his plans to come. He still had no choice but to regain favor.

"Father, I must--"

Alonard tried to speak but was quickly interrupted.

"You must set yourself right and become the son you were on your way to becoming."

"Father, please...I…"

"No apologies, son. I take my share of blame for your faults. Because of me you know duty, loyalty, and love for men. But my message must have gotten lost."

Changel raised the black sleeve of his cloak. It was a symbol to him of the last time he had worn it. He enjoyed the smell of the stale blood.

"The cause of your weakness is gone. I removed it. He is no more."

Changel spoke quiet words, not as a reflection of his disappointment, but rather, to impart the severity of what he had done. It instilled a monstrous sense of foreboding in Alonard.

"He?"

In a single word, Alonard asked the question that would soon lead to his own unraveling. Giving over Alee was no longer at the forefront of his thoughts. Changel had done something but in his usual manner, remained cryptic. Alonard turned. He grew more impatient while his curiosity continued to pique. His face showed the emotion.

Changel, once again walked slowly along the path. Alonard followed.

"You look at me as though I owe you something." Changel said, "Indeed, I do owe you, son. I owe you the best life, the chance to be and not just mildly, but to the utmost. I owe you the chance to reach your full potential without the things that hold us back. I took that thing away. You can now be whole and grow unhindered."

Alonard reached out and grabbed Changel aggressively. Dozens upon dozens of onlookers gave a simultaneous howl at the sight of it. Changel stopped. He looked at the hand that clasped him by his elbow. He raised his eyes to Alonard who then let go.

"What is the world coming to when sons raise their hands in such a way?" demanded Changel.

He casually glanced downward. Between the openings of Alonard's robe, Changel caught a glimpse of an axe that rang in his memory. Changel completely turned from Alonard.

"Father, just say it," pleaded Alonard.

Changel grinned to thicken the spurn.

"Say it!" yelled Alonard.

"You were weak for him. Weak for Kain! That is why his life is no more. Or at least, what I left it as atop the mountain."

Alonard turned and set free his robe. It fell to Changel's feet. In full armor, Alonard made his way back to the north exit of the courtyard. Fire burned within him. He made haste to the mountain peak of the isolated isle. He did not look back, though he felt the stabbing glare of Changel cleaving into his spine. Changel let out a low sigh.

"Why must our children disappoint us so?"

Only a few steps from the courtyard archway stood Alonard. He had never behaved in such a way in the face of Changel. But he had never felt the rage he felt towards Changel who showed him disfavor for the first time in his life. A part of him wanted to go back and fall at his knees to ask both Changel and the God they served for forgiveness. But his hate was too strong. And his concern for one so loyal and true kept him moving towards the mountain.

Before his next step to the exit, two hands graceful yet still scarred and coarse, seemed to appear from nowhere. One hand swathed from beneath Alonard's arm, across his chest. The fingertips of that hand rubbed the metal chest defined in the armor, making circular motions upon it. Her other hand wrapped around with the arm rested against his waist. The hands began high on the pelvis and made a slow motion downward. Alonard could feel the warmth of the hands through the metal he wore.

"I have missed you," said Sciona.

Alonard clutched her by the wrist, removed both hands, and pushed her away from him. He was not in the mood to deal with Sciona.

"Stop," he stated simply, "I do no not have time for

you."

Sciona walked around in front of him. Her hips dipped and swayed in a language that did more than imply her sensual desires. She turned to him and stood directly in his path.

"You just got here," she moaned.

Alonard did not reply. He continued to walk back towards the stable, to ride on to the mountain. His patience wore thinner by the minute. Changel's words would not leave him and the thoughts of a dear friend potentially being dead were unsettling.

"I will go with you," said Sciona.

"No!"

Alonard turned quickly. The back of his right hand met her cheek that was wrapped in her leather garb. An off-balanced Sciona hit the ground with a thud that echoed in the hall. She touched her cheek and then placed her hand out in front of her eyes. She saw the blood from her mouth, moist on her hand. Alonard continued and walked onward.

"I smell her on you. On you." she cried.

Alonard clenched his fist and turned back. He came upon her quickly and grabbed her by the throat with his left hand. His right hand raised to a fist beside his grimacing face. He let loose a fierce and merciless strike right between her eyes. His eyes swelled, his nostrils enflamed and he delivered another punishing strike where his knuckles closed her mouth.

"Shut up!" he yelled.

Alonard then let her go. Sciona was still conscious, but fell to the ground and did not move. She lay there with a red ring around her neck. And there Sciona remained, gagging on her own blood while Alonard walked on.

Alonard reached the foot of the mountain. The palette of a crimson dusk filled the sky. He dismounted and looked to the top of the mountain. He removed his bronze chest plate and the iron chain mail beneath. He stood there with his chest and back bare. His skin pulsed as if the muscle beneath his shoulder blade was growing cancerously. The flesh on either side of his spine ripped itself apart. A large, oozing black mass stretched out from the back of Alonard and a pair of full black wings pointed skyward. Wind whirled as the wings made motions up and down. The wings dried more with every stroke, leaving a flurry of loose gigantic feathers, which fell slowly to the ground. The dust stirred and the black wings flapped faster and faster until finally the wind pushed with the strength of a hurricane. Alonard leapt to the sky and flew into the sun. For just a moment, he was light and free. His well-formed body shone in the sky, which was now painted in the many colors of the spectrum. He flew higher than the mountain peaks and danced on clouds like Heaven's messenger. But free flight was not Alonard's aim on that day. He came back to the earth on top of the mountain. From on high, he saw an inauspicious boulder. However, when he finally touched down he saw that it was so much more.

"Kain," he sighed.

"You arrived. It took you long enough," said a voice. Alonard looked to the base of the petrified statue that was Vale-Kain. There sat Caim.

"Kain died well, Alonard," added Caim.

"What do you know of it?" sneered Alonard.
Caim fluttered to the top of Kain's head.

> "I saw the entire display. Your father, as you consider him, showed no mercy."

Alonard lowered himself to Kain and looked him over. His sweat and tears were stone as well. Alonard placed his hands near his chest and abdomen where there were strange lumps and markings.

"What happened here?" asked Alonard.

> "If you are asking me what prompted Changel's wrath, I have my theories. Changel ran his arm through him as though it was nothing, and he did it with a smile. Though just before Kain could find

rest, Changel froze him in a prison of stone."

Alonard looked up.

"Frozen before death?" he uttered.

"He is still alive. But his state of living is only a formality. He is nothing," said Caim.

"He is everything!" cried Alonard.

Caim cackled. He fluttered his wings to show his amusement.

"Now, I see," said the owl.

"You see nothing. If I know one thing in this world, it is that true virtue is a finite thing. It cannot be created, even though evil can be destroyed. For all that Changel has taught me of these things; it is devastating to discover he has extinguished a light such as Kain for no reason."

"No reason!" scoffed Caim.

Alonard stood up and looked directly into the beady eyes of the owl. Alonard knew that Caim was not of earth and that his knowledge was vast. Changel trusted his counsel as that of the Lord's sweet song, long unheard. Thus, in that moment, Alonard looked to Caim just as Changel had done on so many occasions.

"It was both a show of power and a test of your reaction," said Caim, "In simple words, your father fears your strength and power. You are stronger than you know. Thus, you were challenged. A thing you loved to great heights was taken. And did you confront he who took it? No! You stayed in your *place* and misplaced your frustration on the woman."

Caim cackled again.

"It was all to Changel's delight," he added.

Alonard lowered his head and looked into the stony grey eyes of the statute Kain.

"But why fear me and to such an end?" he asked.

"That is a question for Changel himself. In the meantime, Alee remains the key. Finish your business here quickly. You should know Sciona followed you out but travels straight to the Tower to meet Alee."

"Fear not for Alee," Alonard uttered.

He turned to the setting star. The shadows of the dusk grew larger beneath the mountain. The amber sheen became fainter as the dark night was soon to befall.

"Was this the view last afforded to you, Kain? Or did you look into the eyes of a great man gone mad?"

Alonard returned to Vale-Kain. He shed no tears. He examined the form of Kain and knew what he had to do next. It was a moment Alonard needed for him and Kain alone.

"Take your leave, Caim. I must put things to rest," he commanded of Caim.

"Any words for your father?" asked Caim.

Alonard was silent. No words came to mind. In unison, he waved his hands and wings. Caim knew to fly on. Alonard was consumed. He had nothing to spare on thoughts of what Caim said of Changel.

"I pray for you, brother. You are one whose loyalty, honor, and virtue assures you a place at God's side."

Alonard gathered himself. The words he spoke in eulogy were difficult to find. Yet, he continued.

"And knowing you'll see him, speak testimony on behalf of me, so I may have pardon for my sins past and sins to come."

The black wings of Alonard crashed back into his shoulders in the same moment the stone that was Vale-Kain softened and peeled. The rocky flesh became grey sludge, which covered the pale skin of Kain. Alonard saw the fissure carved in Kain's chest. He lowered to pick up the barely living Kain. Suddenly, the earth ripped apart and tore the mountain in two. Alonard looked at Kain, who moaned both faintly and ghastly.

"Let go. Please, my brother. So much more awaits

you," said Alonard.

"FFfff...ORrr...gh…ive."

Allowed to utter his final penance, Vale-Kain, son of Vale-Ode, passed on. Kain's body was then cast into the abyss. Alonard closed the crater and left an entire mountain as an unmarked tomb.

"What was made of Earth returns to decay and the immortal part of man flies agelessly from the shell."

Early Return: Day 7 - Nightfall came. Alonard galloped intensely to the Lighthouse Tower. His mind was filled with misery. His best companion was no more. His father was the cause and for a reason that was unfathomable to Alonard. And Alee was now the target of Sciona.

He traveled towards Alee. He did not doubt her ability to protect herself, rather he credited Sciona with a persistence that could only end by her death. And from what he knew of Alee, she was not capable of a battle to that end.

At first, Alonard rode with the certainty that Caim's warnings were true. However, at some point along the journey, Alonard questioned the paradox of that trust. He trusted in Caim solely due to the loyal counsel given unto Changel. Changel revered Caim as an old one and believed his words to be greatly divine. But now, as Caim's words came to Alonard, they spoke out against the one who taught him to revere Caim's counsel. Ultimately, Alonard believed in the evidence. Changel confessed to killing Kain. Caim's reasons were as plausible as any.

Alonard approached the Tower toward the westward path where the passage inclined more steeply. There the briars tore through his clothes while the muddy hillside slowed him immensely. As to why it was a road less traveled was obvious. The horse was knee deep in the thick, moist earth. Alonard dismounted and sank a bit himself. He reached into the mud and pulled at his horse's ankles, trying to free the horse. But with every tug, they both sank deeper. Alonard let out a low sigh. Despite the time gained using the straighter path, Alonard was now losing precious seconds. He unfastened his travel gear along with the saddle.

"In nature, it is the fit who survive," he stated coldly. Alonard took his things and moved on alone. The mud was thick; however Alonard possessed the strength to wade through the grime. He traveled easily enough. He refocused quickly on the task at hand and never looked back.

"The key!" he uttered, repeating the words of Caim. In a matter of moments, Alonard reached the hilltop. He saw the Lighthouse Towers and followed the emanating glow up the mucky slope. Yards away from the manor, he began a full out sprint to Alee. There were no servants, guards, or citizens in the vicinity. Alonard ran unhindered up the spiral stairs. He reached the door and pushed against it. The lockless door would not open. He knocked violently but there was no response, no sound. Instinctively, Alonard reared back and kicked down the door.

"Aleeia!" he called.

Alonard's face fell. His expression was a testament to what his eyes took in. The room was in total disarray. There were clothes everywhere as well as rotting gooseberries on the floor. He stepped inside to see a motionless Alee, her bare and perfect form so still in the bathing drum near the foot of her bed. He kneeled beside the drum.

"Aleeia," he sighed. "...whatever was our destiny is sadly no more."

He reached out to her and ran his hands along her brow then through her hair. Suddenly, Alee's eyes fluttered. She stirred a bit before she focused on Alonard.

"Ahhh! Get Out!" she cried.

Alee erupted quickly and stood up from the waters of the drum, thigh over thigh. She covered herself with her arms and hands.

"Alee, you are--" began Alonard.

"Out!" cried Alee.

Alonard motioned for her to settle down. Seeing that

Alonard made no motion to leave, Alee quickly reached for her gown upon the bed. She wrapped the gown across her bust, and then reached for a cloth. With it, she tilted her head to the side and dug the herbal paste out of her ears.

"What is the meaning of this? I barricaded my door for some peace but still you enter while I bathe."

Alonard understood and quickly tried to explain himself.

"Alee, no. No, the door would not...I saw the room...and the sound from the...you were...sleeping," Alonard stammered horribly.

Alee waved her hand with the force of her Will and sent Alonard flying through the doorway. He found himself in the hallway with pieces of the doorframe all around. Alee rushed to the nearside of the room by the door where Alonard could not see her. She untied the gown and put it on properly. Alee also reached for her trousers and a pair of gauntlets, while Alonard rubbed the back of his head in the hallway.

"Alee, I have to talk to you. Please, may I come in?"

"Your request comes a tad bit late. Does it not?" Alee inquired with sarcastic anger.

Alee stood with her back against the wall. And although now clothed, she still did not care for Alonard to see her. She finished fastening her gauntlets before she ripped away the lower part of her gown below the knees. Still infuriated,

Alee called out.

"Thank you for reminding me that Changel, and the like, take what they want. I've certainly been reminded of why I am here."

Alee paused. Just before Alonard answered, Alee said more.

"For a moment, I believed you were more. More than your father's son."

Alee eyed the window. She began a hard sprint toward it and came into Alonard's line of sight.

"Alee, wait! It is not..."

Alee jumped out of the window, intent to travel East through the forest to Changel. Alonard gathered himself quickly and ran to the window seal.

"It is not what you think. It is not safe," he said.

Alonard looked out but there was no sign of Alee. He went back down the stairs and gathered nearly two dozen guards for a search party. He had to find her.

Meanwhile, a figure concealed spied Alee's jump from the window to the tower's roof and then her climb to the ground. Alee ran towards the stalking form hidden in the forest. Unknowingly, she ran right past the dark and ominous person who stayed perched quietly in the bush. She quickly made distance between her and the Tower. However, the figure followed at a cushioned distance so that

Alee remained unaware. With the moonlight above and the lighthouse at her back, Alee ran until she could not run anymore. She halted suddenly in a clearing to catch her breath and despite there being no wind in the air, Alee heard an inauspicious rustle of branch and the crack of a twig. Alee knew she was not alone.

Though a thick cover of clouds hovered through the sky, the moon shined bright. It was a moon so full that it seemed closer to her on the Isle than anywhere else Alee had seen it. She felt the wind pick up. Her eyes and ears were still at work, trying to target the stalker about. Suddenly, the sky opened up. The sound of raindrops by the thousand filled her ears. The pouring rain in the dark cluttered forest blurred her already limited vision. Alee knew that she was now at the mercy of whoever stalked her.

She turned around slowly and scanned the area for any trace of someone there. Without hesitation, she ran out of the clearing back into the woods, trying to bring out the stalker. *If you want me, you will have to keep up with me,* she thought. Alee ran swiftly with the certainty that if someone wanted to continue a pursuit then they would have to forego all stealth. Alee continued on. Her wet clothes clung to her body. Her hair stuck to her face. She ran smoothly and relaxed, though with a speed that could not be matched by the average man. She approached the bank of a river, which was of considerable length across. While still in stride, Alee set her left foot a few feet shy of the bank and went straight into a huge leap across the river. She began ascending into her jump. Before she could reach her apex, she was tackled into the waters of the flowing rivers.

The blow shook Alee and knocked the wind out of her. Instinctively, she inhaled just as she hit the water. Water flowed down her throat and through her nostrils to her lungs. Alee surfaced, coughing violently as the force of the river pushed her further down stream. Bobbing above and below the waterline, Alee continued to cough and take in water. She struggled and eventually made it across to the riverbank. Convulsing and coughing, she crawled atop the mud to drier land.

She flipped to her back to catch her breath and to regain her composure. The cool night air felt soothing despite the rain that beat against her face. Alee's eyes fluttered. She focused. A figure above her blocked the silvery orb amongst the stars.

> "Your death would mean little, if you knew not who ushered you unto it."

The words came from the dark figure above her, concealed in a black hooded robe. Alee rose quickly to her feet. Still a bit dizzy from the waters, she steadied herself. However, a moment later she convulsed again and vomited the cold, murky waters from the river. Yet again, Alee regained herself and spoke boldly to the figure in reply.

"So," blurted Alee. "You have found me. You wish me dead. But as you said what will it mean if death comes from a phantom."

Alee raised her arm, held out her fist and called out.

"Show yourself so this may begin. And by that as well, it will soon end."

The hooded phantom raised its arms. The sleeves of the cloak receded to reveal strong yet feminine hands. They touched the brim of the hood and slowly pulled the hood back.

"What?" gasped Alee. "This can not be."

A fair skinned beauty with braided brown hair appeared before Alee. Alee remembered her. And now, as she stood before the rushing waters, which make all rivers ever-changing, she understood.

"I brought that evil to you," said Alee. "If I could, I would forfeit my life to make amends. But I have more to do and in all that I have before me, know that it is for a better world. For now, all I can say is that I am sorry. Please forgive me."

Mhasika's face was as cold as a blizzard hailstone. She had shed all the tears that could be shed for her father. Every teardrop poured out the love and compassion she had for him. Now, weeks later, Mhasika stood before Alee with only her hate and contempt left inside her.

"I do not need a lecture about you or your destiny. We were the keepers of it and our society was made to hold its secrets, but had I known our society would fall for the sake of you, then I would have said to hell with it all."

Mhasika began her slow walk towards Alee. Alee stood ready. She could not read the face of Mhasika but prepared for a potential attack. Mhasika removed her robe just as the rain subsided. Alee stepped back slowly as Mhasika advanced. She favored one last attempt at pleading with Mhasika. Alee was knee deep in the waters of the vigorous river. She spoke once more.

"Your father would not want this, Mhasika. Please do not do this." implored Aleeia.

"And you know, right?" said Mhasika, "You looked into his eyes, saw him smile, and heard his voice when he told you these things?"

"Mhasika, I--"

"Shut up." Mhasika blurted. "What I am about to do, I know it is wrong. Then again, my father always ***said,*** *'No ills can come about when you follow you heart.'* So you see..."

Suddenly, Mhasika's head jolted back. She let out a loud

gasp. Mhasika felt the rough damp leather tightened at her throat.

"The suspense was delightful." said Sciona.

She had crept behind Mhasika so quietly at the perfect angle to remain out of Aleeia's line of sight. There they all stood. Sciona held Mhasika by the hair with her left hand. And with her right, she tightened her straps around Mhasika's neck, using her forearm against her back as leverage. Aleeia did not move. She waited.

"But there was too much dialogue. I became so warm and tingly when you said that stuff about following your heart. But you ruined it. Yes, you did!"

Sciona pulled her head back and tightened her neck hold yet again. Mhasika scratched at her own neck to get beneath the straps. It was a hard jerk that caused Aleeia to flinch toward Mhasika.

"You should have tried to kill her then. More action, less dialogue," said Sciona.

"Who are you? What do you want?" Aleeia asked.

"Like our friend here, I want to kill you. My reasons are no more or less viable as our little lady's here. Alonard favors you above me and that is not acceptable. No one can please me like him and since you have come along it has been lonely down below," replied Sciona.

Aleeia looked for a better angle and took slow steps to her right. She needed to determine whether or not Sciona held Mhasika at knifepoint. However, in the dark of night she found it hard to see anything.

"Please, let her go. I have no concern for Alonard or the troubles that come from his company," said Aleeia.

"Spoken so eloquently, but she wants to kill you too. Ah well, I just hope you put up more of a fight than your two friends and the slave boy," replied Sciona.

While Aleeia's eyes widened, Sciona pulled Mhasika by the head and throat and slammed her into the muddy bank. She then drew her daggers from the stay at her sides and went straight for Aleeia. Aleeia retreated into the waters. A little more than waist deep in the river, she kept her eyes on Sciona. She looked at Sciona and guessed that speed and agility, rather than strength and power were her tendencies in a fight. Thus, she lured her into the water so that its flow and rush would slow her down.

"Coward," Sciona slandered.

"What did you say before about dialogue?"

Even in the moonlight with the fading trickle of rainfall, Aleeia saw Sciona's face turn red. Sciona made an inside thrust with the dagger in her right hand. Aleeia easily sidestepped. Then, with her right arm extended, Sciona swiped the dagger back around to her right. Aleeia ducked to avoid it. It was a weak combination thought Aleeia.

> "There is no way you could have defeated Gaia or Bellia alone. You had help, didn't you?" taunted Aleeia.

Sciona let out a muffled grunt held back by the clench of her teeth. Mhasika stirred. Aleeia looked to her out the corner of her eye. Inside herself, she rejoiced to see Mhasika was well enough. Aleeia quickly returned all of her attention to Sciona whose loose straps waved distractingly. But Aleeia remained poised and prepared for the next offensive. Sciona, however, was more cunning in warfare than Aleeia gave her credit. She paused and stared at Aleeia. The sound of rustling splashes quelled. Aleeia looked back at Sciona and saw an ominous smirk upon her face. It grew into a full foreboding smile. Out the side of her eye, Sciona glanced at a dazed and wobbly Mhasika. Aleeia realized that she had made her advantage in the water, her weakness when it came to protecting Mhasika. Sciona ran against the vicious river towards Mhasika. Aleeia, deeper in the water and further from the bank, shouted.

"Mhasika! Ready yourself!"

Mhasika was a bit dazed. Her hand felt the huge bump on the back of her head and the moisture of the blood that stained her hair from it. She did not hear Aleeia. Mhasika rubbed her neck and struggled to catch her breath. Her head rang from meeting the muddy gravel with such force.

"Mhasika!" Aleeia called again.

Sciona closed in. Aleeia, despite her exceptional strength and speed, could not make up the distance. Sciona cleared the water. As soon as her foot hit the mushy threshold of earth and water, she took two hard strides to a vulnerable Mhasika. As Sciona directed both daggers in the direction of Mhasika, Aleeia emerged from the water like a phoenix from the flame. She leapt high in the air with enough force to take most of the river with her. The sky, it seemed, filled with hundreds of small twinkling crystals that shimmered around her. Sciona was so close to Mhasika she could see the likeness of her blood amongst her sweat. However, she smirked and began twisting her torso to head back to Aleeia.

"Got you," uttered Sciona.

Faster than a serpent strike, Sciona swung her arms back and released her daggers. She hurled them towards Aleeia who had left herself open while coming to the aid of Mhasika. Sciona finished her attack and burrowed her shoulder into Mhasika's abdomen. Mhasika immediately stumbled back and fell to the ground with the wind knocked out of her.

Aleeia saw the daggers flying toward her. They were perfectly on course with her trajectory and there was no way for her to dodge them while still in midair. But Alee had no intentions of attempting any evasive maneuvers. Still surrounded by the sparkling beads of water that emerged from her awe-inspiring leap out of the waters, Aleeia spread her arms wide and opened her hands. Her palms faced Sciona. Alee quickly clasped her hands together.

The crystal beads of water launched outward and flew opposite the course of the daggers. A rapid tapping rang out as the water struck the daggers. It was the sound of metal on metal; for the clear water became as hard as diamonds. Thousands upon thousands of rigid droplets rained down and threw the daggers harmlessly to back to earth. Yet thousands more spread out towards Sciona. Aleeia's counter attack had a range so wide Sciona could not escape it. Within seconds, Sciona was blanketed with nothing to shield her as the barrage fell upon her. The projectiles were too small to deeply pierce her flesh. But they moved quickly enough, and in such large numbers to cause Sciona concern.

Sciona set her feet. Arms raised above her shoulders, she folded them across her face in order to protect her eyes. When the first petrified bead hit, it felt like a splinter in the shoulder. A sensation likened to a hornet's sting followed. Soon the water crystals met her body one after the other. A few bounced to the ground, leaving welts and bruises. Others dug into her, settling just beneath her skin. Between the straps Sciona wore as clothes, numerous scratches cascaded across her body. Her body was bombarded as though small pebbles stoned it fiercely, until she felt worn.

The last bead hit. Sciona wobbled, her body tender from the assault. She lowered her arms slowly, away from her face to the sight of Aleeia. A stride's length away, Aleeia aggressively made up the distance with a hard right that connected with Sciona where the neck met the jaw. Sciona hit the ground harder than Mhasika. She was unconscious, out cold.

"Mhasika, are you okay?" asked Alee.

Alee ran to Mhasika. A few stray water crystals had hit her legs, but there were no major injuries to her.

"Come on. She is strong, there is no telling how long she will be out," said Alee.

Alee looked Mhasika in the eye. She lowered a bit to lift her to her feet. Alee ran into the woods, towards the Eastern Bank, with Mhasika propped across her shoulders.

"We can settle your quarrel later if you wish," Alee

said.

Mhasika gave no reply.

Time in Captivity - A week went by in the Eastern Bank. Time staggered along in the hold of Changel where the prisoners rested from an arduous routine. Left alone beneath the surface, Bellia laid asleep beside a still unconscious Gaia. Hat-kaptah mustered what little peace he could in order to rest for another day of work and servitude.

For the seven days since their presence was imposed on the Isle, the three captives, who formerly resided in Nubia, were ruled by their rigorous routine. Several hours before daybreak, the crack of a whip and the rumble of a deep call to rise awakened two of the three prisoners. Jacobb, accompanied by two soldiers of lower stature, issued the strict orders.

"Up! Work time!" Jacobb said.

With Gaia still in an unfavorable condition, Bellia could do nothing but comply. She instructed Hat-kaptah to do the same. The dew from above coupled with the moisture in the caves made the cell blocks unbearably humid. The heat was intense in the cramped space. And there, Gaia was left throughout the day.

Bellia still wore the tattered leather she had worn

during her battles on the black sand, minus her thick vest and all her metal cuff bracelets. Hat-kaptah walked mostly bare with nothing but a loose, shredded rag bound around his waist to cover him. His scars and bruises were in plain view all across his body. When Jacobb waved his arm towards Hat-kaptah, the two guards rushed him. They entered his cell and hurried him to his feet. Jacobb himself took sure strides to the hold where Bellia tended to Gaia. He let out a low grunt. All Bellia could do was sigh. She rose to her feet and walked out leaving Gaia alone.

In the time since their arrival, Gaia's condition had been difficult to assess. Although she had not awakened, her body told the story in other ways. Aboard the ship and upon their first days in the dungeon, Gaia laid motionless. Her breathing was so slow and steady, she appeared to be dead. However, Bellia with eyes so keen could just barely see her chest make subtle movements. Bellia continued to care for Gaia. From the scraps of food they were given, she placed small servings of honey and food paste under Gaia's tongue. It was just enough nourishment. Bellia funneled her returned strength back to Gaia, though not too much at once. If she flooded her with more raw energy than Gaia could handle, it would kill her. About midweek, her brow crumpled as if she struggled and battled in a dream. Though Gaia's eyes stayed closed and the improvement small,

Bellia still gave thanks and continued to pray for her friend.

"Be safe, get well. I will return my friend, my sister." Bellia said to Gaia before being shoved out of the cell.

It was a slow march up to the surface. They walked in file, Hat-kaptah between the two guards and Jacobb trailing at the heels of Bellia. The sun had yet to rise. Hat-kaptah was familiar with work at such hour. He had been ripped from a life of servitude in order to be placed in another. The stables awaited. In the shadows of daybreak, the first job of the day was less than pleasant. They were made to feed and water the livestock as well as clean the mounting piles of excrement.

Alone in the stables, but their solitude was merely an illusion. The perimeter of the stable teemed with guards and the Children of Changel who trained nearby. Bellia committed every detail of their routine from the layout of the land and the time of day to the stature and changing of the guards to memory. The war-master's mind churned day and night. And as soon as Gaia was able, Bellia needed to have their escape plans and contingencies ready.

"Put your shovel away, Matron," said Hat-kaptah. "Do not sully your hands."

"Hat-kaptah," Bellia sighed. "It was not necessary

the first day and it is still not today. We are in this together. You...me...and Gaia."

Bellia's words were reassuring. Throughout the week, Bellia was the only example to Hat-kaptah that hope still remained. For Hat-kaptah, it was hope he might live and in that life renewed see Alee again. And so, they continued to work til the sun rested upon the horizon trees.

Their warden returned. Jacobb served as their slave driver for the past few days, a duty which was chiefly of Sciona's until her sudden departure from the Citadel. Hat-kaptah feared the behemoth but preferred his presence to that of Sciona. She had made him a commodity of her own personal interest. Her interests were written in almost every scar upon him since Abydos.

"Hat-kaptah! Snap out of it!" shouted Bellia.

The memory of it all froze him. Jacobb called for the two prisoners to leave but Hat-kaptah did not move.

"Come, Hat-kaptah. We are called to our next task," Bellia urged.

The stable was open at both ends. Hat-kaptah trailed behind Bellia who walked towards Jacobb at the northern end. Bellia slowed her pace a little. When Hat-kaptah caught up to her, she placed her arm around him. Hat-kaptah pulled away. He was not weak and did not want Bellia to think him as such. He also saw half of Alee in Bellia and could not bear to be near any semblance of her.

"Alas, another prison. My heart remains bound by her," Hat-kaptah said as he walked ahead.

Bellia saw her surrogate family waver. After a sudden pause, she realized that it had long been so. For the past week, Bellia had been waiting. It was atypical of her to be so reactive, to not be the initiator. But everything still rested on Aleeia and she could play no role without Gaia whom she waited on to recover; whom she needed.

Bellia hated the upcoming chore, yet still found it useful. Jacobb led them to the training grounds. There, the children of Changel numbered well. They continued to gather from across the entire Isle and all of the world. It was the second of four sessions that would commence throughout the day. As it was, the grounds could not support all four units at once. Bellia and Hat-kaptah approached the dining tents in order to serve meals to the first group. After an early morning session engaged in the practice of war, all the uneasy warriors clamored to be fed.

The weeks of simulated warfare quelled the study of art and culture in paradise. Everyone on Avalon was devoted to the cause of Changel, except for three. Gaia, Bellia, and Hat-kaptah were expected to decide where their loyalties lay. Unbeknownst to Bellia, almost half of the warriors on the Isle had also come unwillingly to Avalon in similar servitude. But upon bearing witness to the peace and truth in the world as laid out by Changel, a decision was usually made quickly.

Bellia served drinks and bread to start the meal. She had come to know them from what she overheard of their conversations. There was Taeryus who hailed from lands further north of the Nubian plains. He sat, by chance, at the head of the table. Seating in the Isle had no particular meaning except when in the presence of Changel. Bellia placed a tray of bread at the center of the table. She then went from person to person and offered wine.

"Here, lady!" Taeryus called.

Bellia made her way to him. He was one of the few warriors to train in full armor. He wore a chest plate made of bronze engraved deeply with an emblem. On the left was a lion raised upon it hind legs and on the right was a bear on all fours facing the lion. Between the lion and the bear were the sun above and the moon below. Bellia saw the same design mirrored on his helmet, which rested atop the table, fashioned as the head of a mighty bear. Taeryus saw the scowl upon Bellia's face.

> "My lady, how long have you been here?" asked Taeryus. "How long will you be stubborn? It took me but a single day of living in this place to know

that it was special. You may speak."

Bellia ignored Taeryus and continued to serve the meal. Her face cleared and became expressionless once again. Taeryus clasped Bellia by her wrist. He was angered by her unresponsiveness and took it as a complete display of disrespect.

"Listen woman!" shouted Taeryus. "You can either clean, cook, and serve in disgrace as a slave or as an honored fellow of this Isle. Either way you will know your place!"

Bellia feigned discomfort in her demeanor, but did not cry out. Taeryus twisted her arm and forced her face to the table. She held back. Bellia remained calm while Hat-kaptah continued to serve. They both knew that now was not the time to reveal anything. Until Bellia's plan was set and Gaia was able, they would have to endure.

The other attendants at the table did not skip a drink or miss a bite. The actions of Taeryus lacked their concern. On the Isle, Sciona remained one of a handful of women that battled and were granted a reluctant respect for their prowess. Taeryus released Bellia and arose from his seat.

"Excuse me all. I am off to attend the second session as well. Jacobb will be center circle and I am suddenly in the mood to be challenged."

Taeryus left the dining tents and made his way to the

training grounds. Bellia hurried to complete her current tasks. She placed the food and wine on the tables for all the famished warriors. She moved with urgency while appearing poised and unfettered.

"Is there anything else that I can do, my lords?"

Bellia asked.

She paused half a second for a response. When she heard no reply, she darted out of the tent. She followed Taeryus to the training grounds and caught the last part of his warm-up. Taeryus looked ready for the giant Jacobb who stood in the middle of a huge circle made up of onlooking warriors. Bellia was anxious to see Taeryus fight. But more so, she wanted an opportunity to ascertain the tendencies of Jacobb's style. Bellia looked around and saw the soldiers assigned to her. They did not hinder her from viewing the spectacle. They only observed her to ensure she made no plans for escape. And so, the contest began.

Taeryus was of a greater stature than most men, yet still he was dwarfed in comparison to Xamare-Jacobb. He removed his chest plate and the two combatants stood before one another to compete hand to hand. As soon as the two men were in the enclosed circle, they sanctioned the battle to start. The two stood still for a while. Finally, Taeryus took side steps to circle Jacobb so that he could attack from a more favorable angle. Most fighters would counter step, but Jacobb remained completely still. His head faced forward, stiffly while his eyes followed Taeryus. Taeryus eventually shifted out of Jacobb's visual periphery.

"Do not fall for it!" Bellia said to herself as she looked on.

Taeryus felt taunted by Jacobb. He believed all fighters were due respect no matter how inferior they are considered by the other. However, Taeryus was an accomplished solider, a general in his old life off the Isle.

Taeryus stood still for another second. He then let out a long aggressive yell, but did not attack. With his right foot, he kicked a small amount of dust and sand at Jacobb's ankle. Jacobb timed the yell and turned around with a forceful back fist, but Taeryus was not there. Jacobb was open. Taeryus took his left foot and plowed it just below the surface of the sand. This time he kicked a clump of sand straight into Jacobb's eye. Jacobb reacted as he moved both hands to his eyes. Taeryus quickly and quietly moved behind him. He let out an aggressive kick to his right side. Jacobb turned with an overhead strike to the ground where Taeryus once stood. Taeryus then struck Jacobb's left side just below the rib cage. Jacobb tried to counter but without all his senses, he looked like a man swatting at a swarm of wasps, just hoping to hit one. And like a wasp, Taeryus' best blows were little more than stinging annoyances.

"So with no weapons, when will this fight be at an end?" Bellia wondered.

Taeryus' strategy did nothing to grant him the advantage. He continued his agile barrage at Jacobb's ribs and stomach. He moved in and out so Jacobb could not hone in on his whereabouts. However, time was running out. With every moment that passed, sweat and tears made Jacobb more to form, clearing his eyes to return his sight. In an instant, the tide turned. The spectators that lined the ring were pushing from behind Taeryus. Jacobb had him cornered. Taeryus had no choice but to go straight at him. He led with a right cross to the jaw that did nothing to slow the giant. Jacobb closed in. Taeryus tried an inside front kick where his boot connected with Jacobb's kneecap. It did as much damage as if he struck a stack of stones. Finally, Jacobb was upon him. He lunged out and grabbed Taeryus by the face with his mammoth hands. Taeryus grabbed him by the wrist while Jacobb lifted him off the ground. The pressure against his face and skull rose and fell at the whim of the brute. Taeryus tried desperately to break free. He tried to chop downward against the forearms of Jacobb but to no avail. Bellia looked on until she could stand no more. She began her advance into the circle. Just as she committed herself, she felt worn hands grab her wrist and shoulder.

"Stop, Bellia," said Hat-kaptah.

Bellia turned and looked the young man directly in his eyes.

"Are you kidding? He is about to kill him!"

Hat-kaptah let out a low sigh. He held her arms tighter and spoke his mind.

> "How is this death different than the ones that occurred a day ago? Or two days ago? Less than a moment ago that man demeaned and dishonored you," he said.
>
> "We cannot pick and choose. I am here now and there is something I can do. Now let me go," shouted Bellia.

Her yell was faint amongst the crowd who called for blood. Hat-kaptah did not let go.

> "It is pride, Bellia. See that! See that it is. You want Jacobb. You want him for yourself as well as for Gaia. Let him go, the time will come. Let him go."

The physical tension between them lessened. Bellia stopped pulling away at the very instant Hat-kaptah let her go. Taeryus called in agony as his head folded over his neck. He was dropped to the ground like the carcass of freshly scored game. The ring dispersed and all the attendees went back to their training stations. As for Bellia and Hat-kaptah, they continued to set tables and serve food. They worked until the midday past. No other warrior lost their life in the circle that day. Some had injuries, but no one fought with the brutal ferocity akin to that of Xamare-Jacobb in the bout with the late Taeryus. Bellia stayed composed, but could not forget about Jacobb. He became the face of the enemy to her. However, Bellia focused on getting back to Gaia. She pocketed miscellaneous items from the food brought for the soldiers. Hat-kaptah looked at her. The setting sun brought a glow that brightened the west side of the tent. Bellia seemed dark in comparison, as though she were trapped in a shadow.

"The work day is done. Will you not go to the Tabernacle? You have yet to do so," said Hat-kaptah.

Bellia's brow crumpled. She dropped the plates and trays she carried away to clean.

"Do you forget yourself, Hat-kaptah? This is not our land and that is not my temple," replied Bellia.

Hat-kaptah kneeled before Bellia. It seemed a bit extreme to Bellia for the young man, but she quickly learned not to underestimate his mind.

"It was taught to me days ago in Abydos that the house of faith becomes the temple wherever it may be. Pray not to the paintings or the statues. Read not their scriptures and sing not their psalms. But let go and believe what you say you believe."

Bellia's eyes widened. Gaia's words and teachings were retold with a pure clarity as though spoken by Gaia in her very first lesson. The memory was poignant but Bellia failed to see the current relevance.

"Plainly!" commanded Bellia.

"Gaia needs you. But as much as the food and the aid and the hopes to recover, Gaia needs your faith. Gaia needs your trust. She needs them both as part of your prayers to God. Let go."

Bellia had nothing more to say. She exited the dining tent. Outside, two guards waited to escort her. When Hat-kaptah left the tent, he made his way to the Tabernacle alone and Bellia returned to Gaia and the cell caves. The guards left the caverns as soon as Bellia was again locked away. She ran to Gaia. Bellia glanced at her lying there positioned on her side. She looked down to her pockets where she had hid meat and bread. She ripped away a small piece of each and chewed it into a smooth paste. She then spit the paste onto her palm. She looked up at Gaia's mouth and gently pulled down her bottom lip. Bellia paused to wipe her cheek. Had it not been for the spec of dirt on Gaia's cheek, Bellia would have never seen Gaia's marble-brown eyes staring back at her. Gaia had finally awakened.

Armada - The moonlight through the stained glass windows was brighter than the torches on the wall. Hat-kaptah, in the center of the Tabernacle, bowed before the altar. The best fat of cattle and ripest fruit from the land was placed upon it. Hat-kaptah had no offering but knew the nature of offerings and tithes. He painfully pulled away seven locks of his long, bushy hair from the crown of his head. It was all he could give.

In the throne room, three generals, soldiers of elite, status stood shoulder to shoulder eagerly before their master. But there were only three where there should have been seven. Xamare-Jacobb was center to Lucien III on his right and Aspalta to his left. Missing from their ranks was Tal-Taeryus, Mage-Sciona, Vale-Kain and Alonard. It was to be Changel's final address before he unleashed *his* mercy on the world. The generals by land and admirals by sea had only two days to convey the wishes of Changel to the hundreds of soldiers and crewmen on the thousands of ships. When the sun set, Changel took form as his younger self. Fire lit his eyes. He wore the same blotted white robe he wore for Kain and Alonard. It was now very symbolic to him. Changel rose from his seat. At that very moment, his subjects kneeled to the ground. He gazed at all his manifestations upon the walls and began.

"Who but One can not achieve greatness alone? Greatness as a good, not greatness as a stature. Coveting stature is selfishness but good makes seeds for many. Those *many* wait beyond the mist, on the shores of a broken land. That land is the world of men made by God, now changed by men. It is further from what it was by those who dwell therein. Changed, I say. Changed. And yea, I know of change.

Change is time observed, a comparison made discretely from moments bound continuously. In one moment, the land flourished by mortal hands which knew no sin. It was laid upon me to keep it so.

But Faith...Ah, Faith! It works two ways.

Men explored the world as well as themselves. They found such pleasures along the way and those pleasures made them happy. As a father spoiling a son, I let them be. I let them pursue their happiness without moderation, without restraint. A new moment came and with it, some change.

To right their wrongs as best I could, I revealed a shade of myself. I let them know through me there is a path to God. So I became their dreams and fears. I became their *gods.* And for a moment in each incarnation, change came for the better. Yet in every instance, there came along a people that skewed my words. They claimed they knew my mind and wrote falsely by their own politics and interests. Some have even claimed to know Him truly. But how could they hear what I have not heard in ages? They who have fallen and corroded to wicked, beastly men that find pleasure in flesh and deceit.

Alas, I look at you, my generals, and say again greatness cannot be achieved alone. Alone I let them slip and alone I tried to pull them back. But, it was too great even for me. Ha! Too great had there even been three.

Now I come to my children, humbled, and I ask for help to right both wrongs, mine and man's alike. So it is said *the sins of the father are passed to the sons*. If it is indeed so, then may redemption be passed back and my providence be restored.

Offer swift mercy to the lands to which you return. Remember those lands as well can be as majestic as this Isle. Take your seats at the heads of every city-state and be my vessels. And when the liars, thieves, hoarders, and murderers are no more, then the people who remain will cry out with joy. My leadership will usher in a new age from there.

I trust you three to make all ready for our deployment in two days. Prepare in all ways. I go now to the Tabernacle so God remains with us. Dismissed."

Changel exited his throne room through his own personal passage, which lay behind the eastward wall. He entered the corridor way that was lit only by the glow of his eyes. A narrow spiral stairway took him directly to various locations on that side of the citadel. Changel stopped two flights down and opened the door. He entered and emerged from the curtain hung behind the altar. He walked with his head lowered and proceeded to step down from where the altar sat atop a pedestal. Changel looked down. He looked with pride upon a boy, clearly downtrodden, who was bowed and bent before his Creator. Hat-kaptah opened his eyes upon hearing the footsteps of Changel.

"Pardon me, young one, I do not wish to interrupt," stated Changel.

Hat-kaptah said nothing. He did not know the identity of the man beside him, but was cautious of everyone on the Isle.

"This was the first altar I built. I gave it to the

community. There is a power in its simple design," said Changel.

Hat-kaptah looked around. He saw only stone walls, a few tapestries, and the altar made of granite. Hat-kaptah agreed that it was simple. In Abydos, great care and detail was given to the construction of shrines and tombs. Hat-kaptah stayed lost in thought until he realized what the stranger said and what that could mean.

"Yes, ages ago. This place called for a tributary to be built," said Changel.

Changel smiled and placed his hand on Hat-kaptah's head.

"Go now. Take your leave. You are done here, for your prayers are certainly small compared to what I must say to God."

Hat-kaptah hurried to the doors now knowing full well the company he kept. As he passed the threshold of the Tabernacle, no longer on sacred ground, he saw a watch-bird owl that flew on to the altar.

"I thought you were more perceptive," said Caim.

"What riddles do you speak now, old friend?" asked Changel.

"Nothing," Caim replied.

He fluttered from the altar and flew closer to Changel. Changel rose to his feet. Caim flew to his shoulder.

"While you are here you could at least make yourself

useful?" said Changel. "What of my son and Sciona?"

"He pursues two women past the river headed in this direction," replied Caim, "The two women injured Sciona. She is still alive."

Changel paused.

"Who are these two women?" asked Changel.

"I think you know, Master. Look no further than the axe," said Caim.

Changel's mind went back to long ago and the axe that came through the fire. He saw Pixsus charge with the axe in hand. He remembered just a while ago to when he broke the news of Kain to his son. Changel remembered again the axe upon Alonard's hip.

"Ask yourself the questions, Master," said Caim. "Why did Alonard not return with Sciona, Jacobb, and the other prisoners? Why did Sciona follow him back to the Western Bank with such scorn? And most of all, where and how did he get that axe?"

Changel walked to the stone altar. There was a goblet of oil on the left and a candle on the right. Changel reached into the oil with his two middlemost fingers then slightly touched the top of his brow. He then reached to the remaining container of oil and poured it on the fats and fruits that were set upon the altar as offerings. The candle was tipped, and a blaze erupted from atop the altar. Changel turned towards the exit.

> "You now advise me my son is a complete traitor? That he has harbored a descendant of Pixsus since his days in Abydos? Is this what you tell me, beloved Caim?" demanded Changel.

Caim fluttered his wings as a sign of severity and sincerity. Still upon Changel's shoulder, he leaned over a bit towards his ear.

"Not Pixsus," stated Caim, “Nympthia's!"

Changel stopped. Caim jumped to the ornaments that protruded from the door. He sat upon the snake ornament now at eye level with Changel.

"The pacifist!" exclaimed Changel.

> "In your eyes, Changel. But think for once with your pride and arrogance aside. You betrayed her and killed her sister. Nympthia sees you as the enemy to all that is righteous. I am not saying you were wrong in assuming your mantle, but *Nympthia the Pacifist* is the illusion she put forth. Nympthia the Patient or Nympthia the Vigilant is more to form."

Changel made a low, nearly inaudible groan. What Caim said made sense, but he argued in favor of Nympthia as a means to redeem the news of his son, his First Among

Many.

"Send word to Jacobb. Have him take a hundred of his best soldiers. I want my son and those women by mid-day tomorrow."

"And what of the three retrieved from Abydos?" asked Caim.

"They all die tomorrow."

With an ominous cackle, Caim flew off to deliver the news to Jacobb who then set out immediately.

Upon exiting the Tabernacle, Hat-kaptah again felt the loose presence of the guardsmen assigned to him. He walked back towards the cell caverns. With every step he took, the five soldiers that surrounded him drew nearer. Finally, he reached the stairwell of the caverns, his wrists and shoulders bound and held by the guards. They led him downward to his hold. Hat-kaptah entered the row where he was thrown into his cell. He hit the ground and laid there still until the guards left. When they departed he spoke.

"Bellia! I think I saw--"

"Hat-kaptah!"

Bellia tried to interrupt him but he was so overcome with

his news. He continued.

"...back at the altar, I may have been--"

"Hat-kaptah…"

Hat-kaptah heard his name from a voice he had not heard in several days. The sound of it stopped him in his tracks. He heard frailty in the faint voice that called. His heart filled. He called out.

"Gaia! Gaia, is that you?" asked Hat-kaptah.

"She is still very weak but she is awake," replied Bellia. "She is awake!"

To Wroth - Off the beaten path, a fair distance from the river, Aleeia and Mhasika rested in the bush under the cover of darkness. They took pause from a hasty escape as they tried to place distance between them and Sciona. Still hindered by the strays of Alee's projectile barrage, the hobbled Mhasika slowed their pace. After hours in flight, Aleeia finally thought they could spare a moment to catch their breath and tend to her injuries.

"Let me see," Aleeia ordered.

Mhasika and Aleeia sat on a fallen tree whose thick trunk served as a suitable bench. Mhasika sat beside her and raised her leg on top of Aleeia's lap. A deep gash within her thigh caused most of her discomfort. Aleeia placed her hand above the wound.

"This should not hurt," said Alee.

The crystal daggers embedded in her fleshed reverted back to the soothing waters of the river. Aleeia continued to work her Will to heal Mhasika. It took very little of her strength to mend and seal the wound. It left a small scar, but Mhasika did not feel a thing.

"There," said Alee, "how does that feel?"

Mhasika stood up. She took a few cautious steps then ran and jumped in place. Alee smiled, but their recent history came quickly back to mind for both of them.

"Now what?" asked Mhasika.

Aleeia was surprised. She posed the same question on the tip of her tongue. There was a mixture of contrition and gratitude in Mhasika's voice. Aleeia stood.

> "Mhasika, I still grieve for your father. He was a great and wise man. I know he taught you so much. I thank him and you for the knowledge and quarters you spared me."

Mhasika looked at the moon. She heard Aleeia, but also heard the voice of her father within the words Aleeia spoke.

> "You know, I sat on that ship, stowed away in the cramped space of the cargo hold, hidden behind crates with no room to stand. Suddenly, the ship crashed and took on water. For a moment, I thought

to myself that it would be so easy not to struggle. To just let the waters take me so I could be with my father again. I lived for him and to have him taken when he was did not seem right."

Mhasika paused. Aleeia knew to just listen. She also knew the lost of a loved one, four times over. Mhasika's story was all too familiar to her.

"As I let the waters overcome me, I thought about my father and all his principles. He did not raise a weak daughter. So in that moment, I clung to the next emotion of my heart, aside from the debilitating grief that seemed to overrun within me."

Aleeia heard her impassioned memories retold. However, she was also mindful of the pace they kept before. She knew the time they had to rest drew to a close, but wanted to hear what Mhasika had to say. She did not have the heart to stop her.

"There was *blame*. And that blame quickly turned to hatred and vengeance towards you. But it is not my way or my father's. But without it, what way do I have? I ask you, Aleeia."

Mhasika's eyes widened. They sparkled in the moonlight. They were full of uncertainty as they looked upon her. Aleeia touched Mhasika on the shoulder. She looked into her moonlit eyes.

"I am not as wise as those who have tried to teach me wisdom. I cannot offer any guidance that is purely suited to what you have asked or the confusion you feel. But I will say this, you are a good person and your father's daughter. Follow your heart with all the wisdom your father has imparted to you and you will not go wrong. You will be fulfilled."

"What about you?" asked Mhasika.

Aleeia smiled, but her face fell quickly.

"I would be lying if I said I did not need you. I have a great task before me and I do not know if I am ready. But at the same time, I will ask no one else to risk their life for me, my mother, and my mission."

Time was up. Aleeia heard the thump of runners not too far away. Her acute hearing also picked up the strange ruffle of stirring treetops when there was only a weak wind about the air.

"They are closing in on me. Go south and be safe my friend, my sister." said Aleeia.

Before Mhasika could say a word, Aleeia embraced her and ran eastward in the forest.

Aleeia ran with the grace and speed of a gazelle. Her

senses were as tuned as a hunter-wolf. She felt the world around her and knew there was someone close behind her and more than a dozen others who followed as well. She smelled their sweat and knew Alonard was one of them. Visibility was low. Aleeia turned suddenly to stand her ground. She saw her pursuer.

"Mhasika!" she cried.

"I have no place else to go. Besides, if you need me and I can be of help, then I am here." replied Mhasika.

Aleeia had no time to argue the safer road for Mhasika. She heard the pursuers scatter and sensed the scent of their musk all around them. They closed in slowly from their position as Alonard walked out of the shadows of the forest.

Aleeia wasted no time or words. She charged Alonard fiercely with her right arm cocked. She made up the space quickly and landed a right to his jaw before he knew what hit him. Two quick rib-shots followed and Aleeia ended her combo with a crouching sweep that brought her enemy to the ground.

"Get out of here." Aleeia cried to Mhasika.

Upon Alonard's collapse, the forest quivered around them. Thirteen soldiers emerged from the cover of the brush and began their charge against Aleeia.

"Wait!" called Alonard as he held his jaw.

Mhasika and Aleeia were surrounded. The sharp end of thirteen lances kept them motionless. Aleeia made no sudden moves for the sake of Mhasika. The stalemate was for but a moment but felt like hours.

"Aleeia, listen," pleaded Alonard.

"You ask for my ear. You have it but only because of the thirteen spears upon us," replied Alee.

"Will you listen if they are lowered? Will you be still?" he asked.

"Yes." replied Aleeia.

The soldiers of the Tower, personal guards to Alonard, stood down. In the same instance, Aleeia grabbed Mhasika by the hips and flung her southward into the Forest. It was the strangest thing to the eyes of the soldiers. Aleeia knew Mhasika would land a bit bruised but better off overall. However, while the soldiers were still dumbfounded and lances low, Aleeia rushed a guard to her right. She broke the blade from the end of the staff and twisted it away from him. She twirled it around and about and with each move she struck the head or knees of her enemies. She moved so quickly that in the next instant all thirteen were toppled.

"Alee!" Alonard shouted.

She charged again. Alonard drew his weapon. It was the axe

of Pixsus. Alonard blocked high with both arms as Aleeia struck downward with her staff.

"Stop! Listen!" cried Alonard.

Her pace quickened. She remembered how she dishonored herself back in the Prima. She disappointed everyone by not standing up to him then. She remembered how she froze. She remembered his lies and especially his extended time disguised as her beloved friend. Alonard remained defensive and the clap of iron against wood rang out like thunder. Alonard was tested. He found it harder and harder not to counter, for it was instinctive for him to do so.

The soldiers reoriented themselves but Aleeia was well aware. Beneath four of the soldiers, the earth opened like a trap door. The cavity refilled quickly and left them buried to the neck. Aleeia continued fighting without pause. Alonard could not help but look past her to see her focused Will at work. Three more soldiers let out battles cries and rushed Aleeia. They continued to wail louder as they charged. The closer they were to her, the more intensely they called out. Soon, their breath was expunged. The three quickly became lightheaded and fainted. They fell at her feet. They could not stop calling for the Will of Aleeia.

Of the six men left of Alonard's company, there was only one who did not pause. The others were halted by caution and fear, having seen their comrades quickly fall.

The lone soldier reared back his spear and launched it at Aleeia. Aware, yet still in combat with Alonard, Aleeia twirled her staff to strike Alonard's shoulder. She anticipated a block and when Alonard did so, he left himself open to a hard sidekick, which knocked him yards backwards. Aleeia was now face to face with the spear. She fully extended her arm as her hand became the point of impact. The spear seemed to sink deeper and deeper into the palm of her hand. As swiftly as the spear hit her, it seemed to almost fully disappear into her arm. As the base of the spear burrowed into her, her mouth opened wide and the spear shot out of her with all the speed it hit the palm of her hand. The lance flew back out and struck the ground right in front of the feet of the soldier that threw it. With that feat, they all scattered and fled as Aleeia turned to Alonard, pressed deep into the trunk of a nearby tree.

Aleeia walked towards him. She picked up the axe Alonard dropped following her devastating kick. The dew formed as the twilight hours came to an end. There was no sun, moon, or stars, however, light still shone from both horizons. Alonard sat there impaled through the hip by a strong jagged root.

"I will finish with your father, but I will start with

you." stated Aleeia.

"Wait!" Alonard cried again faintly.

Despite his exceptional strength and power, he was injured. If Aleeia attacked, Alonard knew he would not be able to dodge it. He pleaded more as she drew nearer but she refused to hear him. Aleeia raised her axe and Alonard was left with no choice.

"Alee!"

Aleeia stopped. She almost dropped her axe. The softer voice hit her like a blow but what Aleeia saw was an even greater shock. Alonard had changed. A soft young face stared back at Aleeia with long braided hair and deep brown eyes. Aleeia was motionless at the sight of the young woman whose form Alonard had taken.

"Alee, I saw this face," said Alonard, "I saw your mother."

Alonard broke the root that pierced his flesh and tried to get up, but Aleeia placed her boot on his shoulder and put him back down.

"How?" asked Aleeia.

"My door. The door that was meant for me back in the Prima. Your translations were right, I was meant to be there," stated Alonard.

Aleeia knew Alonard only as a liar and that his ability to change and manipulate was his primary tool to deceive, but for some odd reason, unbeknownst even to Aleeia, she listened and allowed Nympthia-Alonard to continue.

"I saw the past. I saw everything from the very beginning. Pixsus, Changel, and Nympthia made for this world, together like a family."

Nympthia-Alonard's face turned to where her brown eyes no longer connected with Aleeia's. It was a sign of shame. Aleeia wavered. Her anger became harder to sustain yet she still remained skeptical.

"I saw my father as well. I saw his betrayal and how he turned his back on Pixsus and Nympthia for nothing more than greed. It did not exist before that moment. I guess he created it. I saw him harass Nympthia and kill Pixsus. I saw the sacrifice your mother made for you."

Aleeia clutched her axe. She swung it around and it burrowed into the tree just beside Nympthia-Alonard's neck.

"What do you mean *sacrifice for me*?" asked Aleeia, "And do not think your form makes you safe."

"Your exploits earlier were amazing. But I know how they drain you. It is the nature of our Will. Energy on this plane is finite," said Nympthia-Alonard, "Your mother used an extraordinary amount of power to bring you here. Her Awakening came far before Pixsus's and she plotted with patience so you could save us all. She was never the same afterwards."

Aleeia heard the story of her mother and had no choice but to believe Alonard, for there was no other explanation for what she heard and even what she saw.

"What do you want?" she asked.

"To help," he replied.

"That is the second time I have heard that in the last few moments. And from you, it seems too convenient," said Aleeia.

"I had questions. I could not wrap my mind around what I saw. That is why I left you at the Tower to see my father alone. But when I came to him, I saw first hand the brutality and malevolence that was shown to Nympthia. Changel killed someone dear to me. And I suppose greed was the root again."

Aleeia extended her hand to him. When Nympthia-Alonard reached his feet, he reverted back to Alonard. He held his wound. Aleeia issued a brief apology to him.

"What about your friend? That was a little drastic, don't you think?" asked Alonard.

Suddenly a voice came from the bush. Both Aleeia and Alonard turned to the south. With daybreak upon them, there was no longer the cover of the night to hide and conceal them. Sciona stepped out into the clearing, she held Mhasika by the end of her dagger.

"Traitor." called Sciona.

She tightened her hold over Mhasika with her left arm around her neck, the dagger at her cheek.

"Let her go." cried Alonard.

"Oh, you were not here. We already did this," scoffed Sciona.

"You are outnumbered, Sciona," added Alonard.

Aleeia heard the forest move again. And where before there were about a dozen, there were now about one hundred soldiers around them. Jacobb stepped out into the sunlight with his company to retrieve Alonard and Aleeia as commanded.

"What did you say about being outnumbered?" mocked Sciona.

Alonard leaned slightly towards Aleeia and whispered.

"It's your move. I am ready." He stated.

"No, patience," said Aleeia.

Aleeia threw down her axe. Jacobb let out a barbarous groan and all his cohorts rushed the bounty of three. Mhasika, Alonard, and Aleeia were placed in iron chains and shackles. The morning dew had dried and the convoy marched eastward to the Citadel. The Armada was set to depart in a little more than a single day. The eve of tomorrow had arrived.

VERSE V

Eve - The procession made its way to the Eastern Bank. The landscape along the journey was a marvel to behold. Everything from the tall trees to the mountains in the backdrop was a beauty that seemed to color the clear blue of the sky. The air was fresh. It was filled with the aroma of the flora and foliage, both known and exotic. A focused Aleeia looked around and took in all that was there. She saw the history of the land. Her imagination peered through space and time to see those who dwelled on the Isle near the very beginning. In her vision they were all together: Pixsus, Changel, and Nympthia. They enjoyed the wonders of Avalon as well as the pure joys of their service to God. Aleeia gave an untimely smile.

Alonard saw her. His brow wrinkled in confusion. Aleeia's expression reflected the parallel between Mhasika, Alonard, and Aleeia to the ancient inhabitants of the Isle.

> "There are at least five legions here. Not to mention, two of Avalon's finest warriors." whispered Alonard.
>
> "How many soldiers make one of your legions? It looks like way more than five legions around us." replied Aleeia.

Alonard was taken aback by her oblivious reply for her tone

was inappropriately light. Aleeia then looked to Mhasika.

"Are you okay, Mhasika? Sorry about throwing you into the forest like that."

"I know why you did it, but it hurt just the same," replied Mhasika.

"Your feelings or the landing?" teased Aleeia in inquiry.

"The latter," stated Mhasika with a smile.

Alonard was beyond confused but wasted no time trying to determine Aleeia's state of mind. He glanced at Sciona at the front of the procession. Just as he looked in her direction, she turned and met his eyes. She slowed her stride until she walked side by side with her former lover. For the longest time, Alonard was the object of her twisted and lust-ridden interests. The whispering subsided when Sciona neared.

"Look at what you have become," said Sciona. "You were once everything; a man to be feared, respect and desired. Now, you band with these drudges. You plead to follow that dog."

Sciona pointed directly at Aleeia. Aleeia heard everything, but smiled gingerly to Mhasika. Sciona took Aleeia's behavior as one gone mad.

"Look at her! A crazed dog only fit to be put down,"

Sciona scoffed.

Alonard then had his own inauspicious smile. All the portentous grins and snickers quickly frazzled Sciona. Alonard spoke through his smirk.

"Yet you are not fit to even lick her heels."

Sciona reared back and came across his cheek with the back of her fist. It was a forceful strike. Alonard took a half step to his left and then corrected his balance. Aleeia heard his retort. Inside her heart, she felt his loyalty. In her mind, she stayed weary of possible betrayal for a second time.

The Citadel rose behind the trees in the horizon. They inched closer to the doorstep of their enemy as captives. Aleeia took in the terrain, the soldiers, the time of day, and the weather. For no factor could be ignored on a day of such importance. She looked to the rear of the procession. Jacobb trailed the line of allies and enemies with the axe of Pixsus in hand, propped across his shoulder. The shadows signaled a few hours before the midday. Aleeia looked to Mhasika with a sisterly concern written on her face. The hour of discord drew near as they came upon the Citadel of Changel. By way of his trembling grumble, Jacobb called to the sentinels. The gate opened. Both Aleeia and Mhasika stood at the base of the fortress. In awe, Aleeia gazed at the huge structure of smooth, black stone. The outward facing walls shone like glass and gave off a distorted reflection from its glossy surface. Aleeia grimaced. The slightly angled walls reflected her as taller. In the dark warped mirror she looked like someone else. Rapidly, her emotions turned. Uneasiness set in.

At the same time in the hollowed space of Earth beneath the fortress, the three detainees were allowed to rest. No servitude was placed on them; for the tasks of the day were too plentiful and vital to be left to mere slaves. On the surface, the morning was riddled with the comings and goings of soldiers in force. So great was it that there had been a slight tremble that rocked the prisoners awake from slumber.

The evening before was filled with smiles as well as tears. Gaia's upturn kept everyone awake throughout most of the night. Bellia and Hat-kaptah told the story of their life in captivity since Gaia's fall in battle back in Abydos. A new day began and Bellia was full of joy and optimism. She never denied herself the reality of how much she needed Gaia. Gaia was the grounded strength that complimented her brash aggressive nature. With Gaia back, it was time to put the final touches to a plan of escape. Bellia's eyes fluttered open. She was the first to awaken.

"Hat-kaptah? Are you awake?" asked Bellia.

Bellia called to Hat-kaptah at the end of the Hall. She heard the sounds of the young man stirring, which came from his cell. She then turned to Gaia with a smile. Gaia was bundled in as many warm clothes as could be found. They were sure to make her as comfortable as possible. Bellia kneeled beside her and rocked gently.

"Face the day." she said.

Bellia stopped. She did not hear anything from Hat-kaptah's cell. She walked to the iron bars and called out to him.

> "Hat-kaptah, wake up. You have seen and experienced much. We need your eyes and ears to plan this escape," Bellia called through the empty cavern.

She turned back to Gaia who looked anew and peaceful. There was a glow about her that Bellia had not seen from her in months. Despite lacking the light of day, her skin was as colorful as it had been in weeks. Bellia always admired her beauty, nearly to the point of jealousy. She gave her a nudge.

"Wake up, princess," she said mockingly.

Gaia's cheek drifted to her shoulders.

"Gaia?"

She shook her again, this time a bit more aggressively. Gaia remained as she was, unmoved, still lying peaceably.

"Gaia? Gaia?"

Bellia was afraid. She had tended many wounds on the battlefield, seen comrades fall in seconds by the sword, however, Bellia had always feared the subtle death. She did not know what to do. She needed Gaia to answer her question. Was this *real*?

"Gaia. Please!"

Bellia did not plead *to* Gaia, but *for* her. She needed strength and courage to answer what she feared she knew. Finally, Bellia ran her eyes across her clothes and saw no motion. She put her hand before her mouth and felt no air. She placed her ear upon her chest and heard no heartbeat.

"Gaia! No! No! No!" she cried repeatedly.

She placed her hands on Gaia's chest and forehead. Bellia offered her own essence, her own life-force in an attempt to bring her back. It was too late.

Think of the soul as a glorious ship, truly homeward bound, and the spirit as the winds that give power and direction to the journey ashore.

Gaia had sailed away in the midnight hour. Her winds were strong by her faith, her loyalty and her love. Her direction was true by her deeds and her charity.

A sorrowful Bellia continued. She tried to revive Gaia but could not and nearly gave all of herself in the process. Bellia grew faint. All the energy she expelled was wasted on a shell. She was now drained. Though she still possessed the strength to cry and mourn the loss of her friend and sister. She draped herself across Gaia's body and sobbed and wailed. The tears ran across her neck and down her spine. Hat-kaptah heard the cries and recognized the pain in them. Instinctively, he knew his friend and mentor was gone.

Bellia became unbalanced by grief. It was a rapid transition that escalated within her. There was nothing more to restrain her as sadness became anger. She was replenished by it. Her body quaked and trembled. She folded Gaia's arms and repositioned her for her final resting place. Bellia placed both hands on the ground. The earth sprang up beneath the body of her friend. Gaia lay on an unmarked mount of squared stone. Bellia then turned to the bars and rammed her shoulder against the iron cell. In a single forceful charge, the cell door gave way. Bellia shook the entire cavern. She walked to Hat-kaptah's cell and reared back again. A loud bang rang out as she slammed against the bars. As though a giant tuning fork was struck, the cave resounded with tremors that became progressively violent.

Bellia could have opened Hat-kaptah's cell using the more elegant side of her Will. However, metal pressed against flesh left bruises, and for Bellia, any external pain felt better than what she suffered in her heart. Hat-kaptah saw Bellia. She had the look of a wild beast, though he understood full well. Her eyes seemed empty to Hat-kaptah. They no longer possessed their former warmth or impassioned vivacity. With eyes like stone, she tore through the stiff iron holds. The bars bent; until finally, they ripped away like autumn leaves from a wind-struck tree. Hat-kaptah stood aside as the door came crashing down. Bellia entered the cell and trudged to the back wall. She began striking the rock wall with all her might. Boom after boom filled the cave. Her knuckles scarred and reddened as they sank into the rock. A fearful Hat-kaptah ran to where Gaia lay. He could still hear Bellia's quaking blows as he looked upon Gaia, who had been so beautiful to him.

Hat-kaptah saw the matriarch who had guided him into maturity. He was the weak child who had met them back in Abydos. Now, through time and unfathomable experiences, he was a young man -- smarter, stronger, and more upright. He now knew that he too had a purpose and that a *destiny* was not reserved for only the progeny of the powerful. Hat-kaptah had been separated from his own mother and father when he was young. To him, they died on that day of parting. His life of servitude had also seen its share of pain and death. He brushed the stray locks from

Gaia's brow and smiled. It was time for his final goodbye.

"Thank you…mother, sister, friend," he said.

He had nothing more to say, for most of what he felt could not be conveyed. He kissed her brow and turned away. When he reached the door, he noticed that the banging had stopped. He rushed back to Bellia in his cell. He found her curled against the wall, sitting on the cold, hard gravel floor. Her arms folded across her knees. Her head rested against her thighs. Faint, muffled moans of woe drifted out from her. Toppled and stricken by loss, her hands bled but no longer trembled. Hat-kaptah walked towards her and loomed above. Bellia raised her moist, red-eyes to Hat-kaptah. He extended his hand to her.

"Come on," he said assuredly. "It is time to go."

Hat-kaptah feared the commotion caused by Bellia's shock and grief. Surely someone would soon come. Without an injured companion in their company, there was no reason for them to delay their escape any longer. However, Bellia, still weak with the pain of loss remained recoiled. She ignored Hat-kaptah's outreached hand. In that moment, Hat-kaptah heard the hollowed, echoing knocks of steps descend the cavern stairs. He closed his eyes to visualize the sounds he heard. The rhythm and rest between the beat of each step suggested that two guards approached. The change in tone announced their speed and distance. Within a few moments, they would be in the cellblock.

Hat-kaptah quickly became concerned. Back in Abydos, Hat-kaptah had received his fair share of training alongside Aleeia. He knew a few tricks as well as the basic means of how to defend himself. Against the likes of a mainland warrior, he would be able to hold his own. However, in his time on the Isle, Hat-kaptah had seen the children of Avalon train relentlessly. He doubted his ability to survive for even a second if he had to engage in battle with one of the Avalonian warriors alone.

Time was running short. He looked around for something he could use as a weapon but only saw stones. He kneeled and grabbed a rock the size of his fist.

"This is it," he said to himself.

He turned back to the entryway. The two soldiers were there before him. The leftmost solider stood about six feet tall with a cold pale complexion and a short blade in hand. Although the other held no weapons, he looked more menacing to Hat-kaptah. With a scar down the side of his face, he was tattooed and pierced with metal through his brow, lip, and the bridge of his nose. They saw Hat-kaptah beside the fallen cell door that was broken and bent. With Bellia huddled and shaken, they assumed Hat-kaptah bashed the cell and had the strength to be formidable against them. They spaced apart and took flanking positions. Hat-kaptah tightened his clasp on the stone in his right hand and waited for the first move.

In their tongues, they both called out in words unknown to Hat-kaptah. Two against one, they charged him. The swordsman of the two was closer and quick. He was a more urgent threat, thus Hat-kaptah turned more directly to him with the other assailant coming yet accounted for out the corner of his eye. A slash came downward against Hat-kaptah, who had his stone firmly in hand. He met the attacking blade's angle with an upward thrust of his own stone to defend. As the rock met the blade, sparks and cinders flew out as flames from the clash. The blade quarried into the stone and the flash made from rock and metal blinded the two assailants. Hat-kaptah hurled the stone at the swordsman. With precision, the hard stone struck him where his throat met his collarbone. The swordsman fell immediately.

"Bellia!" Hat-kaptah called.

The soldiers gathered themselves rather quickly. Their vision cleared from the blinding flash. They set their sights on Hat-kaptah. They both took a sure stride towards him, but only one. Without warning, the toppled cell door flew upon them and crushed them against the cell door opposite Hat-kaptah's cell. Propped between the two metal frames, the soldiers were not killed, but severely injured. Bellia emerged from the hold for the last time and turned to Hat-kaptah.

"Let's go."

She reached for the short blade dropped by one of the incapacitated soliders. Hat-kaptah retrieved a piece of iron bar broken from the cell that was slightly longer than his forearm. Bellia dashed up the stairs with Hat-kaptah closed behind. The commotion from the surface intensified. The afternoon sunlight filled the stairwell and beamed brightly as they approached top ground. The warm beams of the solar gem hit Bellia. Her eyes adjusted quickly, she looked out over the courtyard along with Hat-kaptah.

"Look!" Shouted Hat-kaptah with excitement. He pointed towards the opposite side of the yard near the gate.

Bellia smacked his hand away and ordered him quiet, but it was too late. The busy guards, the Children of Avalon, noticed the armed and unattended slaves. However, Bellia saw what Hat-kaptah had seen, Aleeia bound and being led towards the very prisons from which they had just escaped.

The bells rang in alarm. Any soldiers who carried no cargo immediately rushed to the courtyard as well as those un-amused by their tedious labor. Bellia stood battle ready in a well-balanced stance. She pulled Hat-kaptah behind her with her free hand as the warriors charged.

At the same time across the yard, the soldiers surrounding Aleeia stood curious about the commotion. Aleeia saw they were distracted, Sciona and Jacobb included, and took action.

"Now." she called to Mhasika.

Mhasika ripped apart her shackles and Aleeia's restraints fell from her wrist like grains of sand. Mhasika whirled the chains connected to her wrist as a weapon and set her sights on Sciona. The hard chains from her right arm wrapped around Sciona's neck while the left was flung around her waist. Then, using her extraordinary strength, Mhasika pulled the chains. Sciona hurled towards her. As she approached, Mhasika brought her fists together below her hip. She swung them upward across her body and struck a devastating blow to Sciona's jaw that left her dazed.

In the same encounter, Alonard took on the other soldiers. In a single second, he made his body withered and thin, almost skeletal to where no muscle or fat lay upon him. The chains slipped off his wrist and ankles easily. Then, in the next moment, Alonard's frame was full again. With a stronger, muscular body, he attacked the soldiers. Many of whom were too timid to effectively attack someone whom they esteemed. They knew he had almost limitless power.

Amongst all the conflict, Aleeia stood a few paces

from Xamare-Jacobb. They stared each other down and prepared to face-off. Aleeia wiped her hands on her tunic and pulled her hair back away from her face. She tied it in a nice secure bun. When she was done, Aleeia cleared her throat.

"My axe, give it back." Aleeia paused, then smiled.

"Now."

Jacobb let out an earthshaking yell. His muscles flexed. He reared back with the axe that once lay dormant upon his shoulder. As the axe came down, Aleeia stepped in with her back foot across her front. She caught the axe by the hilt with her right hand and lunged her front foot behind his ankle. With the open palm of her left arm, Aleeia pushed with all her strength and Will. Simultaneously, she pulled her front foot from behind his ankle. Jacobb was left unbalanced. The sheer might of her counter-attack hurled him backwards. He flew yards in the opposite direction with enough force to crash through the gate. Aleeia twirled the axe from the upper hilt to the lower handle and smiled.

"Thanks." she said.

Aleeia looked back towards the center courtyard. She could not see clearly the cause of all the forceful attention, but thanked God for the diversion. Alonard and Mhasika looked to Aleeia and followed her lead.

"Alonard, where is Changel?"

"This way!" he replied as he pointed diagonally across the yard.

"Alonard, you come with me. Mhasika, find my friends and with their help sink as many ships on the docks and near the shore as you possibly can."

Mhasika nodded but did not know where to start. Aleeia readied herself for what she hoped would be her first and final confrontation with Changel, the Betrayer. Just as she had set her feet to stride, she heard her name and peered through a seam in the crowd.

"Hat-kaptah!" she cried.

The connection and calls between Aleeia and Hat-kaptah drew more attention and more warriors. Axe in hand, Aleeia cut a swathe through dozens of troops in the yard. Alonard and Mhasika followed closed behind. Sciona came to Jacobb. They rumbled back into the Citadel from the rubble of the shattered gate. Aleeia, Alonard, and Mhasika fought through the ranks of soldiers until they stood beside Bellia and Hat-kaptah.

The Five Agents of Nympthia stood side by side: Aleeia, Bellia, Mhasika, Hat-kaptah and Alonard. There were new faces for everyone amongst them except for Aleeia. But Aleeia saw that someone was missing.

Suddenly, the bells rang again. The soldiers surrounded the Five and looked to the tower. Looking out through the window was not Changel but Lucien III with Aspalta who then emerged from the base of that tower to the courtyard.

"Working soldiers, continue with the preparations. This day will not be delayed by five miscreants," stated Lucien, "Consider my words as the orders of Changel himself."

Lucien leapt from the window and landed in the yard with a thunderous boom. It shook everyone but him. The count of warriors surrounding them dwindled from about sixty to twelve. The soldiers who still out flanked them held them by the edge of their spears. In addition, Sciona waited behind the north side of the ring, Jacobb the south, Aspalta on the east, and Lucien on the west.

During the pause, the Five stood at attention. They were ready to fight and ready to defend. Aleeia looked to Bellia. Her eyes widened. Without words, Bellia shook her head. Aleeia knew full well its meaning with regards to Gaia. Aleeia had no time to be somber or mournful. However, there was room for anger and it began to swell greatly within her. Alonard saw Aleeia and the force that stood against them.

"General Lucien, stand down now," he commanded.

"You give no orders here! Not anymore, you

traitor!" replied Lucien.

"It is not an order. Consider it a suggestion, ladened with wisdom. You are outmatched!"

Lucien laughed. His was a story of strife and triumph. The six foot tall man with icy pale skin was a no one as a young boy on the mainland. Discarded and left to die, he was much like Hat-kaptah. He lived a humble life of servitude in the Icy Northern Realms. He was a nomad who had found his cause when Changel discovered him nearly half dead. Lucien learned of the strength that lay in all Children of Avalon. And for one who came from Changel so distantly, he still wielded a remarkable amount of power. He began his new life as a liberator who took on warlords and tyrants who praised themselves as gods. Until finally, he became one himself on behalf of Changel.

"Outmatched!" replied Lucien "I have waited for this! I know not how exactly I am kin to my Master, but I have always believed that I was *more* than you. Worthier!"

Aleeia glanced to Hat-kaptah out of the corner of her eye. She looked him over and saw the scars and wounds that Hat-kaptah-Alonard had feigned. He was visibly angered and confused by Aleeia being with Alonard but knew enough to know that now was not the time. He trusted Aleeia no matter how much he did not trust Alonard. All the looks and signals were exchanged in seconds. Tension mounted.

> "Alonard, why do you lead this rabble?" asked Aspalta, "Your father has given so much to us. Just look at this land. Avalon is a pillar of peace. Your father only wishes for the world to follow."

Aspalta was the diplomat of the General Corp. She always looked to negotiate and barter as an alternative to brute force. Though she was formidable in battle, as all the generals were, the beautiful, pristine warrior assembled most of the allies and acquired most of the goods and labor from the mainland. Her Will was weakest amongst the General Corp, but she had an uncanny ability to predict the minds of her opponents, which aided her both in diplomacy and combat.

"I do not lead," said Alonard. "She does."

Alonard pointed to Aleeia with pride and loyalty. Sciona had heard enough. She'd grown weary of the standoff. She drew her daggers and broke rank. In an ill-advised act that displayed no restraint, Sciona pushed through the ring of soldiers that surrounded the Five and closed in directly towards Aleeia. As the daggers came towards Aleeia she turned her back to Sciona and called forth a thrust of gusting wind, which pushed six of the soldiers behind her to the ground. A clank resounded as Bellia deflected Sciona's attack with her short blade. Alonard raised his arms. His torso elongated and another set of arms sprouted from his ribcage. He ran between two soldiers and knocked them aside, both of them struck with a double back fist. Then he strode towards Lucien. Mhasika faced down Jacobb, Aspalta, and the remaining four soldiers alone. Aleeia tended to Hat-kaptah.

"Hat-kaptah, listen. There is little time. Find cover. This struggle is too great for you. Go." insisted Aleeia.

But Hat-kaptah did not move. In fact, he reared back with his iron bar towards the six soldiers Aleeia had pushed to the ground. Aleeia grabbed the bar and pulled him back.

"No, Hat-kaptah. I will not lose you," stated Aleeia. She pulled his bar and twirled him around. She pulled him close to her. Their lips met. Aleeia gave him a full, impassioned kiss, though it did not symbolize just her love for him. Hat-kaptah's eyes grew heavy. Quickly, his limbs grew limp. Aleeia continued to kiss him until he laid flat across the gravel of the courtyard. Aleeia then pulled back. She delicately waved her arms as though she played an instrument that was not there. The sand and gravel fashioned an orb around his still body, with enough air inside to last more than a day. Finally, the airtight ball that housed Hat-kaptah was buried below the surface. Aleeia rose to her feet.

"I will return, my friend." said Aleeia.

She looked at all the commotion and the match-ups between friend and foe. Alonard now took on Lucien and Aspalta. Bellia, with more motivation than anyone, fought furiously against Jacobb and Sciona. Mhasika was alone against the ten soldiers still well enough to fight. Aleeia knew this conflict could not be drawn out all day.

The sun was just above the trees and walls set in the horizon. The forming clouds looked unfriendly. Aleeia needed Alonard as well as all her strength to stand a chance against Changel, but her friends were in trouble and Gaia was no longer around to offer her wisdom. She took deep breaths and said a very quiet prayer.

Mhasika still wielded her chains. Two soldiers attacked from directly in front of her. Mhasika jumped in the air, flipped behind them and clasped them by the throat with her chains. She then pulled as her feet left the ground to kick the two warriors in the lower part of their backs, just below the tailbone. They did not rise again.

The other eight soldiers with spears drawn towards her charged her from all angles at once. Mhasika whirled the chain in her right arm completely around and knocked the spears off target. Some of the spears mistakenly impaled the soldiers at their side. Three assailants fell with fatal wounds immediately, while two more were punctured through their thigh and calf.

Mhasika pulled the slack of the chains in both hands around her fists until they were tight and thick around her knuckles. She charged the last three soldiers. The remaining forces came at her simultaneously from a triangular flanking position, still armed with their spears. The first man, nearest to her on the right, lunged for Mhasika's heart. She knocked the blade with the back of her right fist covered by the chain. With the spear away from his body, an opening was left for Mhasika. She took advantage of it and kicked the soldier in the groin. As he fell, she turned to her left but still hopped to the side and dodged the thrust of another spear. With the lance extended, Mhasika struck through the bladed staff and then hit the soldier with a hard jab followed by a low ankle sweep, which brought the man to the ground.

Finally, there was one more face to face with Mhasika. She waited with her left and right forearm parallel to the ground. Her left arm above her face. Her right arm below her torso. The solider closed in. He lunged his weapon directly at her chest. Just as the blade was about to near her flesh, both her arms moved forcefully towards the other in the opposite direction. She broke through the spear like a twig. The soldier quickly dropped the splintered lance and came at Mhasika with a right cross that was too wide.

She grabbed his wrist with her right hand while she delivered a crushing blow to his sternum with the other. She then slipped her left hand behind his neck and brought his head to her knee. She ended with an uppercut that lifted the soldier flat off the ground. Mhasika had quickly and skillfully dispatched her lot and now looked for an ally to help.

Bellia's struggle began long before the conflict itself. The moment Gaia died and she moved to save Hat-kaptah through force, Bellia knew her grief would be realized through vengeance, not sorrow. At the same time Mhasika and Alonard began their bouts, so did Bellia. Because of the demons before her, she had lost a friend, dear and true. Bellia was quiet and still. Sciona circled behind her while Jacobb stayed to her front.

"So here we are again," said Sciona. "Where is your friend so we can have a full reunion?"

The attempt to rile Bellia did not work. She was completely focused on the task at hand. This time she had knowledge of the enemy. She knew the strength of Jacobb and the agility of Sciona. She also knew their minds, Sciona who reveled in pain and Jacobb who was slow in wit.

"Oh, no reply," said Sciona. "How I hate to be

ignored."

She showed a sinister smirk.

"No, foursome. Pity!"

Quickly Sciona hurled one of her daggers at Bellia. As the dagger approached, Bellia turned and used her blade to knock it away with little worry or effort. Jacobb used the opening and pounced quickly upon Bellia. He wrapped his arms completely around her and held her with a sturdy bear hug. Bellia grimaced but stayed calm. She tilted her head forward and reared back. She struck him with a blunt butt to his nose with the back of her head. Jacobb grumbled. He raised her higher so she could not strike again.

"Hold her still," said Sciona. "This will be fun."

Sciona picked up the blade deflected by Bellia, and with both daggers drawn she walked towards her. Jacobb squeezed tighter. Bellia did not grimace this time. Suddenly her short crop of hair grew longer. It crept more to the length that Aleeia's was, or that Gaia's had been. As her hair grew, the strands encircled Jacobb's throat and rang tighter and tighter. As Sciona approached, Jacobb loosened his grip, for Bellia's hair continued its slow creep. The hair behaved more like tentacles and entered through Jacobb's ears and nostrils. He cried out for the first time, due purely to pain. Sciona heard his cry and hurried her stride. She loomed closer and reared back. As Bellia's hair exited through

Jacobb's tear ducts, Sciona thrust both her daggers. Jacobb could take no more. He continued to call out as Bellia's hair repelled back to its short crop. The thick hair that ran all beneath his skin and through his skull caused him to let go. Bellia hit the ground and ducked just before Sciona stabbed Jacobb through the abdomen with both knives.

"Aagggghh!" shouted Jacobb.

By little more than reflex, Jacobb lashed out with a devastatingly fierce straight punch that connected directly with Sciona's head. He struck her right through her nose. She flew several feet backwards and hit the ground, bloodied and broken. Bellia quickly grabbed the daggers and twisted them as she removed them from Jacobb's stomach. She then took the blades and rammed them into his feet. Another agonizing roar came forth. Jacobb raised his huge hands and brought them towards Bellia. She dodged the blow. Jacobb's hands sank into the gravel. She hardened the gravel around his wrist and the brute stayed bent over and pinned to the ground. Unlike before, he had no leverage to break free.

Stray hair still fell from Jacobb's eyes, nose and ears. It made every move excruciatingly painful. Bellia approached him. She squatted low and placed her shoulder beneath his chin with her hands upon his shoulders. Bellia let out a loud, horrific battle cry. She straightened her legs and jumped towards the sky with all her might. As her shoulder rose higher, Jacobb's chin and neck rose up and back. With Jacobb's arms still fixed to the ground, Bellia heard a crack just as her feet left the ground. When she came back to the ground, the entire monstrous weight of Jacobb rested upon her. She walked from beneath him and his body fell to the ground. Then Bellia walked beside Sciona who lay there blinded by the gushing blood from her broken nose and cracked skull. Sciona struggled to breathe as Bellia finally spoke.

> "Know this," said Bellia solemnly, "the both of you ***do*** have souls. To say you do not is to give you free reign and a life without consequence. But you do have a soul. And by your soul, you will spend an eternity paying for what you have done. Ashes to ashes, dust to dust."

Bellia rose to her feet as Sciona let out her last few merciless hacks. Bellia gave her own silent prayer for forgiveness.

Meanwhile, Aleeia and Alonard had engaged Lucien and Aspalta to a stand still. With Bellia and Mhasika finished fighting, they now outnumbered their opponents two to one. Lucien and Aspalta fell back. They looked at the bodies of the fallen soldiers, as well as Sciona and Jacobb and decided a strategic retreat would be best. Before they left, Aspalta spoke boldly to Aleeia.

"You cannot win," said Aspalta.

But Aleeia and her friends were strong and sure. Thus, her words fell on deaf ears.

"I will not forget this day," Lucien said to Alonard.

"No one will," replied Alonard.

The Tower Bell rang loudly again and the remaining generals went to the docks. Over one thousand ships were soon to sail and the forces that were not enlisted to leave would soon return to the Citadel. Aleeia was running out of time.

"Let them go," said Aleeia, "Bellia, Mhasika! Go to the docks. Do whatever you can to stop those ships. Alonard, let's go!"

As Aleeia turned to depart, Bellia grabbed her by the wrist. Her expression was easy to read. It was full of frustration and defiance, as well as doubt. The cloudy sky opened and became black and foreboding as did Bellia.

"Aleeia, what are you doing?" said Bellia, "Gaia is dead! She lay in that cavern. You act as though nothing is wrong. And you would order me around and let those dogs go free."

Aleeia pulled her arm away.

"What would you have me do?" replied Aleeia. "Our enemy is up there, the cause of all this pain. We do not have time to deal with those two as their reinforcements are soon to come. They have stalled us even now."

Aleeia let out a low sigh. Thunder broke. Rain trickled as dusk approached.

"I love you, my friend. Please, there will be time. And if Alonard and I are not successful, I will see Gaia soon."

Bellia's face softened. She now saw Aleeia was not the same girl she had known, for the Aleeia before her did well to weigh her duty and her grief. Bellia embraced her with a hug.

"Come now! Mhasika, is it? We have a job to do. Try not to slow me down, kid," said Bellia despite her mournful state.

"Uhm? Are you joking, *granny*?" replied Mhasika.

Bellia smiled.

Appointed Shepherd – In the temporary quiet of the courtyard, the group exchanged their final goodbyes. Muddled with their subtle best wishes versus the prospect of never reuniting, Bellia and Mhasika left for the docks of the Eastern Bank. There was but a brief moment's distance between Mhasika and Bellia and the outnumbered duo of Aspalta and Lucien. They hurried to catch up. Alonard and

Aleeia traded quiet looks. Alonard turned to the north portion of the courtyard. Aleeia followed his eyes and set them on the gates of the main hall. The gate was made of tall oak and steel hinges. Sitting between slender pine trees, the door was vast, yet unadorned. No image or iconography symbolized where or to whom the gate would lead. Alonard stepped ahead. The doors opened to a chamber with rooms and passages to the center and spiraled staircases to either side. Together, Alonard and Aleeia climbed the stairs to the upper levels of the Citadel. Unhindered, Aleeia stopped.

"Where is everyone?" she asked.

"Aleeia, you have to understand," said Alonard, "In all of time, or at least the lifetime of my father, there has only been one person, for any reason, foolish or brave enough to face him. In this chamber of this land, amongst his children, there is nothing for him to fear."

Aleeia was still skeptical. The commotion in the courtyard, the ringing of the bell, as well as the betrayal of Alonard was known to Changel. Those reasons should have been cause enough to raise the defense.

Meanwhile, beneath the surface of the courtyard, a young man began to wake up from a sleep induced by a kiss. Hat-kaptah had not seen Aleeia for quite sometime. She knew him as he was but he had been through so much, both mentally and physically. His increased strength of body also mirrored the strength of his spirit. Aleeia had used her Will to quell him, but not enough. Hat-kaptah was now buried alive in a pocket of thick air, surrounded by earth. For a moment, he did not know up from down, but slowly he regained his bearings. The forces of the earth pointed the way. He began his upward dig through dirt, root, and rock. He held his breath as he burrowed to the surface. His right hand was first to feel the air and moist beads of the raindrops. Covered in mud, he heaved himself free of the hollowed subterranean chamber. After a mild cough to catch his breath, he slowly rose to his feet and surveyed the empty courtyard.

His eyes panned the area. Not far from where he stood, he saw the lifeless bodies of his former captors. Jacobb laid faced down in thick mud mixed with the remnants of his blood that oozed from all his open wounds. To his right, he saw Sciona lying there way past life, yet still shaken. With faint motion, she twitched from the blow to which she had succumbed. Hat-kaptah had no words for them. His concern was still Aleeia.

The tracks and markers in the mud told more of the story. Four people departed out the eastern gate, two by two, towards the waters of the shoreline. Their size and shape told Hat-kaptah the first pair was made up of a man and a woman. The smaller tracks of the other pair were both female, which lay atop the first set.

"The other two generals were followed by two of my comrades," Hat-kaptah thought aloud.

His eye was perceptive. He had learned to be observant and ever studious from Gaia's teachings in Abydos. He noticed another pair. There was another male and female who did not rush to the main chamber entry, for the footprints were not spaced or deep enough. Hat-kaptah saw the steps as sure and determined yet possessing caution. He looked back to the eastern gate.

"Bellia and that other girl followed the retreating Generals...that way," he said.

Without the hesitation of another thought, Hat-kaptah grabbed a nearby lance and raced into the chamber entry.

Mhasika and Bellia came to the port of the Eastern Bank. With no visible sign of Aspalta and Lucien amid the hundreds of ships in staggered formation from shore into sea, Mhasika and Bellia were ready to begin what seemed like a task without end.

"Ready, kid?" asked Bellia.

"You do know the moment the first ship sinks, the warriors will come like ants from a mound," said

Mhasika. "Or maybe like wasps from a hive."

"I get it," replied Bellia. "Bugs! And we will have to fight a lot of bad guys."

Bellia turned to one of several stakes embedded in the sand by which the ships were anchored. She unsecured the rope and upheaved the stake. Mhasika followed her lead and did the same.

The rain fell violently. With the aid of the mist, they were now hidden in the blanketing night. Bellia walked fiercely to the edge of the shore then waded into the ocean until waist deep.

Despite her witty and blithe exchanges with Mhasika, Bellia still reeled in the pain of losing Gaia. She doubted whether or not she would ever see a day completely without mourning. That point in time where a person's anguish turns into a fond appreciation of memory was unfathomable to her. Her grief was devastating, but it kept her from remaining static. The salty waters of the sea covered her from below while the weeping sky accosted her from above. Finally, Bellia took a deep breath and submerged beneath the subtle waves of the coast. She swam deep into the watery abyss by the dim blue moonlight that came from the surface. Her feet peddled her onward. Her left hand grazed the hull of the ship, and so, by touch, she guided herself directly below it. Still in the other hand was the stake. Bellia drew back and unleashed a blow with more force than the waters and the wood could withstand. When she removed the stake, the water engulfed the hold of the ship. Water gushed inward and flooded the cargo store causing an unexpected suction from the flow into the hole. However, Bellia was strong enough to pull away and move on to the next ship. In that same single breath, Bellia inflicted similar damage on three more ships before she had to resurface. Mhasika saw the ships begin to dwindle and capsize into the sea. When Bellia resurfaced, then Mhasika too knew how to capsize the ships. Mhasika clutched her own stake and ran into the water to assist the cause.

The women continued. They delivered crippling wallops to about a dozen vessels. But they did very little in their mission to stop or weaken the armada. When the first ship was nearly submerged, a horn resounded. The sound gave the signal to castoff. The ships set course to the four corners of the world and everywhere in between where mortal men and women dwell.

From the tons of sinking lumber, dozens upon dozens of warriors emerged from the waters. The ships classed as *Negotiators* held, at a minimum, sixty crewmen. Larger ships classed as *Peace Makers* held at least one-hundred and fifty crewmembers. Out of the fourteen ships dismantled by Mhasika and Bellia, only a few were the larger.

"Here come the hornets," said Bellia, who stood beside Mhasika.

"Wasps! I said *wasps*," replied Mhasika.

"Whatever," Bellia exclaimed. "Some type of swarming, stinging insect is coming for us."

Bellia watched as hundreds of ships sailed off into the moonlight, while out of the ocean came at least a thousand displaced soldiers. With regret, Bellia felt a sense of failure.

"Had Gaia been here she would have been able to use her Will to do more," she said to herself.

Mhasika looked to Bellia for their plan of action. Her eyes held worry. Yet, in the brief time they were together Mhasika somewhat instinctively recognized Bellia as a force in war. The soldiers called out and took an organized phalanx at the edge of the beach. In three triangular units shaped like giant arrowheads, the phalanx closed in on the women.

"What do we do?" Mhasika plainly asked.

Bellia did not turn to Mhasika. Her eyes stayed fixed on the troops.

"Either we fight them here and now, or Aleeia must fight them later. We did not stop the Armada, but we can stop them," Bellia boldly stated.

Back in the Citadel, Aleeia and Alonard approached Changel's main chamber. The door was as grand as any that Aleeia had seen before. It was as though the entry was the gate to a castle rather than a door that led to a single room. Aleeia took deep breaths and made herself as calm as possible for the moment to come. Her final march to the door ensued. Suddenly, Alonard grabbed Aleeia by the arm and pulled her back.

"What are you doing?" he whispered.

"I am about to end this," Aleeia replied.

"And your plan?" he added.

Alee paused.

"To face him," said Aleeia.

"No," Alonard was flustered. He whispered, "That would be suicide. No, I have a better idea."

The massive chamber doors opened. Lucien and Aspalta entered. Both were in full battle gear, slightly sullied by dirt. Aspalta walked in with an elegant stride, more womanly than warrior with very little movement from her arms. Changel stood beside the fire mantle beneath a tall oak that grew in his chamber. The roots of the tree seemed to rise and sink out of the marble floor like eels in water.

The stained glass windows, which lined the westward side of the hall, were backlit by the moonlight. Coupled with the roaring fire, the room was bright.

Changel stared vacantly into the fire as though somehow disconnected from the world. For the master of the isle, it was the beginning of a new era. Hundreds of vessels had set out on that day to forge into existence a world of justice, compassion, and devotion. Changel stayed beneath the branch and leaf of his massive oak. Before two of his most trusted generals came any closer, Changel spoke. They stopped when he posed a question to them.

"Why are you not aboard the flagships?" he asked.

Lucien took a step forward. Aspalta glanced at him and stepped away, placing a good bit of space between them. Lucien lowered his head and answered.

> "Jacobb and Sciona are newly returned from where we travel," he said. "I thought it best that they go with the first tour."

Changel turned away from the fire although the blue of the stained glass kept his face of full glow. His steps knocked and echoed against the marble floor.

> "You thought," stated Changel. "I do trust your expertise, but for a decision that huge, I would ask you consult with me first."

Changel spoke as would a noble statesman to his general.

He paced a bit before he noticed Aspalta. She seemed stiff and favored her right side.

"Any more news, Aspalta?" Changel asked.

"As you know, a disturbance in the courtyard involving some prisoners ensued." Lucien answered.

Changel moved closer to Lucien, yet still under the cover of the tree leaves. His face turned. His voice deepened. He then walked slowly to Aspalta.

"On this blessed day, it pains me that Aspalta can not speak for herself. To have worked so hard to be one of my elites."

Changel turned his back to them and once again faced the flames in the fireplace.

Suddenly, Aspalta moved in on Changel with her arm raised awkwardly. She did not cry out. However, as she moved from having the smooth, high ceiling above her to the leaves and branches of the powerful oak tree, her body changed. The guise of Aleeia-Aspalta faded the moment she crossed into the shadow of the oak tree. Her oddly raised hand revealed the Axe of Pixsus held high with the intent to cut down her sworn enemy. For Aleeia, her destiny had finally arrived.

The Evil That Follows - In the Woodlands of the nearest

land, Aleeia, the princess nymph of Avalon awoke. Created with the powers of the magical isle, she was born. And in her creation, her birth, was the hope and faith in a God that could live inside of every being no matter who or where they were. It was the belief that the commonality of that intrinsic spirit could bring everyone together.

At that moment, the young life of Aleeia was the summation of her mysterious journey through space and time to the present. As a young girl, indeed a nymph in carefree play, she had wished to be and see more of the world than the Southland could afford. Aleeia wanted knowledge, more than the books and lectures of her own small realm back home. Adventure, far off places, and meaning were her desires before she even knew them to be her destiny.

She did not hesitate at the idea of a quick and shiftless assassination as a means to an end. To end it, for the sake of no more lives being lost was reason enough for Aleeia. She held the same axe that faced him down ages ago. In silence, she dashed ever closer with her final play to strike down The Betrayer, The Lost One.

The axe was but an arms length from the skull of Changel. The impact was less than a moment away and with it the end of it all. Changel turned with his hand as hard razor-talons and the snout of a feral dog. He knocked the axe away with his long left claw and grabbed Aleeia by the neck with the other. Alonard saw Aleeia deterred and called out to her. He stepped closer beneath the tree and lost his semblance as well, no longer Alonard-Lucien. Changel raised his hand and the roots of the tree entangled Alonard from ankle to waist. Changel let out a horrific sound. It was the laugh of a growling, snarling beast. Changel returned his face to his own and was as he had been the day he was appointed shepherd of men, when he was once a part of a great Triumvirate.

> "In this place, your Will is nothing. Beneath this tree the truth is revealed," said Changel, "Do you think I am foolish enough to have no sanctuary amongst sons and daughters with power and ambition?"

Changel squeezed both his hands. His grip upon Aleeia and the wreathing roots around Alonard tightened with the clutch of his fists. Aleeia hacked and looked at Alonard out the corner of her eye. He was wrapped in roots that surrounded and buried into his flesh. Her eyes became veined and bloodshot. She dug into her own neck to loosen his grip but to no avail.

> "You learned a trick or two. He taught you to change your look but not how to alter your voice."

Changel paused and looked with judgment back towards Alonard.

"My son, I forgive you," said Changel, "her strength and beauty is clear, even to me. I see it all over her, this lost child of Avalon. I am glad you found her for me."

Changel raised Aleeia higher and squeezed harder, now with both fists. Both Alonard and Aleeia grimaced and cried out. Though Aleeia had no breath to have any power behind her voice.

"That axe, first seen with Pixsus who intended to murder me. More than a millennia goes by then I see it in my tree orchid with my son. And finally with this girl, who tried to murder me as well. The cycle of time affords me no surprise."

Alonard saw the life being pressed out of Aleeia. Despite his own agony he called out to her and pleaded to Changel.

"Father! Please!" said Alonard.

"Right," Changel replied, "And mercy will be granted as swift death. Farewell."

Aleeia's hands fell by her waistside. Her head throbbed as her heart pumped blood frantically. The end for her drew near. Without warning, a lance cut the air with speed and precision to meet its target. Changel was struck in the ribcage, just below his heart. He loosened his grip on both Alonard and Aleeia. As soon as she fell to the ground,

Alonard went to her and grabbed her by the wrist. Aleeia gasped for air. Alonard pulled her up and then towards the stained glass windows. And as they burst through the shining glass rainbow from the lofty Citadel chamber, Aleeia looked back. She saw Hat-kaptah at the door. Changel removed the lance and picked up the axe. Hat-kaptah now stood alone against Changel.

"No!" shouted Aleeia.

Alonard and Aleeia fell from the sky and the high tower where Hat-kaptah was left to face death. Alonard grabbed Aleeia and secured her underneath her arms. Free from the restraint of Changel's chamber, the black wings of Alonard manifested. They spread far and full and caught the wind.

"We have to go back," demanded Aleeia.

"And do what?" replied Alonard.

A loud screech resounded through the air. The noise caught Alonard from not too far behind. He turned to see a grand winged beast with an axe clasped in its talons behind them. An eagle of epic size and ferocity gained in pursuit. Aleeia turned to witness what loomed closer. In seeing Changel, she feared Hat-kaptah's fate. Her rage went untempered and reflected in the winds. With the rains came thunder and lightning that dyed the dark heavens a purple hue with every strike.

"Alonard, take me to the valley," said Aleeia.

"Quickly! He is gaining. I will make my stand there."

Alonard gave no objection as he lowered his altitude to gain more speed. They flew past the mountain that split the island where Kain met his demise. They crossed the river where Mhasika and Aleeia had stood against Sciona. They neared the pool and maze where Aleeia met and lost a pair of strangers in a very short time. They flew through the jagged rocks that peaked just before the land dipped far below sea level. Alonard dropped off Aleeia and immediately flew back skyward.

"I will hold him off. Whatever you are planning, make yourself ready." Alonard said bravely.

"Alonard, wait." shouted Aleeia.

Aleeia watched him fly upward until he was covered by the clouds and stinging rain. He flew towards his father and what would be their final encounter. His skin darkened to the color of his wings before it peeled away to reveal the stiff feathers of a falcon. And so two birds of prey took passes against one another. The sky was filled with the sound of thunder and the squawk of hostile birds at war. Swooping attacks ensued. Changel dropped the axe not too far from the feet of Aleeia. The eagle and the falcon rolled together in the sky. Their claws threatened to remove meat from bone. The birds fell from the lightning filled sky into the maze. When the father and son reached their feet, they were once again in the form of men.

With a hard thud, they landed roughly in the center of the green labyrinth with its high thorn-laden walls. Changel stood quickly and made himself ready for the battle to come. Alonard, however, took his time and ripped away as much mud and muck as possible from his body.

"It seems that my efforts to make you a strong and worthy heir to carry out the will of God came too late. Killing Kain came too late," said Changel.

The words riled Alonard but he knew whom he faced. He stayed his rage as well as his desire to protect Aleeia, for whom he cared greatly. To match his strength and speed in whatever form Changel was to take was one thing, but to match his knowledge of war and combat which had been acquired throughout the centuries was a disadvantage Alonard doubted he could overcome. Changel had done it all and seen it all, and for that reason Alonard was slow to move. He had already begun to second guess himself.

Changel sprang out with his right fist cocked behind his head. He unleashed a blow of unbelievable force that struck Alonard against the jaw. Changel followed through fully with the punch and sent Alonard hurling through the sky. He flew through three walls of extremely sharp branches and vines. When Alonard landed, the fight was already near its end. There were lacerations all across his body. He was slow to get up.

"Too fast," Alonard said grimly to himself.

The earth quaked beneath Alonard and *bad* quickly changed to *worse* for him. Changel grew to three times the size of a normal man. He stepped over the hedges towards Alonard just as he rose to his feet. Alonard was amazed at what he saw. He had never known the gift of change could be used in such a way. The only thing Alonard could think to do was become, in form, as Xamare-Jacobb who was a little less than twice the size of a normal man. Alonard-Jacobb charged the giant, Changel. He let out a punch aimed at his chin, but Changel leaned back. Alonard's fist hit nothing but air. The miss left him open. As Alonard leaned over, Changel brought his knee into his gut. The wind released from the lungs of Alonard blew fiercely against the flowering green. Changel then raised both hands as one fist and lowered them into his spine. Alonard hit the ground with enough force to shake the earth far and wide.

Alonard returned to his natural form, but Changel was not done. He raised his boot until it was higher than the trees. He began stomping him in the back, just below the neck. With every stomp, Alonard grunted faintly and his face pressed deeper into the mud. The grunting stopped. However, Changel did not stop. He continued to unleash unrelenting punishment to he who was his son.

Finally, Changel returned to normal size. He lifted Alonard up from the grime by the hair. Alonard's eyes were closed, he did not move. The right arm of Changel became that same black talon. He recoiled and struck without hesitation. His arm pierced through the lower right side of Alonard's abdomen. Changel let him go. The moment Alonard hit the ground, he immediately turned into stone. Changel displayed no courtesy in how he left Alonard. Unlike Kain, he did not pause to position him for a respectful memorial.

"And son, if you are alive when I return, then wish now you were not." Changel said.

Aleeia heard an ominous, yet not too distant howl. With her axe, she took her position and waited in the caves of Resurrection Valley for her long coming and inevitable engagement with Changel. The sound of the howling wolf drew closer. Aleeia heard the staggered patting steps of the four-legged beast approach. When the wolf entered, she pounced from her hiding space. From the ceiling of the cave, she brought her axe downward and cut through the wolf. It let out a horrendous whimper and fell dead.

"It was not him." said Aleeia.

She held out her axe and backed into the dark cave. Aleeia

stood still for several minutes against a wall. She saw nothing come in and nothing go out. Her mind began to lose focus. Her thoughts turned to Hat-kaptah in the chamber.

"I will come back for you. You are okay," babbled Aleeia quietly.

She then heard a creak from outside the cavern.

"Alonard! Alonard, is that you?" Aleeia asked.

No answer came from the stormy air outside the cramped hollowed cave. Thunder rumbled and the lightning struck. Aleeia became impatient. The moonlight afforded her little light inside the cave. Aleeia crept slowly towards the opening. One step after the other bought her closer to the moonlight. Her heart began to beat faster. She looked to and fro as the rain fell with greater intensity. She reached the edge of the entry and looked out. She saw nothing, but heard and felt the rain. More thunder crashed. Aleeia took a breath and turned. The sight of a bruised and beaten Alonard startled her.

"You are okay," cried Aleeia.

"I have seen better days," Alonard said. "Quickly, we have to leave. I only slowed him down."

"Right." replied Aleeia. "You *are* your son's father."

Without warning, Aleeia swung her axe. Alonard took a hop step backwards to avoid the attack. The ploy had played one time too many. Aleeia was not fooled. Changel reverted to his natural form. He sighed, but said nothing else. His face turned. His grimace was a signal to Aleeia. She prepared for his unrelenting onslaught.

Aleeia's senses were at their peak. Even the electric sky seemed to become rhythmic and predictable to her. She stood with a strong base in a solid defensive stance. The crash of thunder echoed in the cave and the flash of lightning vanquished the dimness. Changel advanced as the beastly sky roared again. The battle that began in the pristine trappings of a chamber made by Changel resumed in the hollowed dwellings of a cavern fashioned by time. Changel's speed was only amplified by the low visibility allotted by the cave’s darkness. He closed in quickly and threw a stiff right fist that threatened to take Aleeia's head. She barely eluded it, but ducked and struck him in the gut with the hilt of the axe. The blow had no clout. Changel continued. He threw a left-right combination. Every move that followed came closer to meeting its target.

An unending flurry of assailments, parries, and counters shook the cave. With every attack, both combatants grew wiser. Changel threw a high right hook that Aleeia ducked once more. He then followed with a straight jab from which Aleeia leaned backwards and away. Changel held his ground and came back with the exact same combination. Once again, Aleeia ducked. However, when the jab came towards her it did not cease until his fist met its target. Aleeia was hit square in the nose. Dazed and confused, she glanced at Changel's arms that stretched lower than his knees. *He made his limbs longer,* she realized. Despite the blood that dripped from her nose, Aleeia reset. This time she took the offensive.

She drew back her axe and came across with a swipe towards Changel's neck. He took an inward pivot and with his left hand grabbed the upper hilt near the blade. With his free right hand he struck through the handle and then landed a swift back fist to Aleeia's jaw. She was left holding a wooden stump. She threw the stick to the side just as Changel tossed away the remnants of the well-preserved relic.

The rain poured endlessly from the cloudy sky and trickled into the murky break. The earth and rain pooled into thick clumps of muck. Sounds of the mud were now an ally to Aleeia for they helped her follow his movements, and surely, she needed some type of turn in the battle. She had yet to land an effective strike while his assaults were already beginning to take their toll. The sounds Changel made as he tried to navigate through the dark towards Aleeia were loud and clear.

Changel laughed with a taunting fashion that clearly suggested his mind. His body became as full as the cave would allow. Aleeia now stood before a huge mass of aggression that afforded her no path of evasion or escape. She was cornered. Changel charged with his forearms crossed. With a horrendous amount of force, he crashed into Aleeia and drove her backwards into the rigid walls of the cavern. He pinned her deep into the firm rock. The impact alone made her head throb and spin. Still grafted to the cave, Changel took open shots at Aleeia's gut. He reared back four times and unleashed a barrage of uncontested punches to her body. Folded in the chasm, Aleeia slumped over as much as her positioning would allow. Changel snatched Aleeia by the wrist and pulled her to the ground. Blood mixed with the moistened earth. She hacked and coughed away all the unsettled fluids that had gathered in her belly. Changel took easy and confident steps towards her. He then kicked her stomach just below her ribs. It was the first time Aleeia had experienced pains so sharp and severe.

> "Is this it? Is this all?" asked Changel, "The agents of evil grow weaker as time moves on. As it has always been, God is with me."

The disillusioned words of Changel lit a fire within Aleeia. She struggled and soon found her way back to her feet. Changel, still of a grand size, allowed her all the time she needed to stand again. He waited for her next move.

Aleeia's hands stayed to her side, though her fingers

moved with slow grace. The mud moved at the feet of Changel like restless serpents in a fruitless garden. They seemed to become more rigid and firm as they ascended Changel. The slithers of once earth encircled Changel by the torso and the throat. He let out an uneasy groan then exhaled. The ropes of rock quickly reverted back to wet grime and fell to meet the rest of the ordinary sludge.

Aleeia did not waste time in the failed maneuver. She quickly turned back to the rock and reached into the chasm wall. Her hand sank into the rock as though it were as fluid as the sea. She pulled out a strong yet unrefined stem of ore with her right hand. Her left hand became red hot. Aleeia ran her palm across the ore and all the coarse and bumpy malforms melted away. Aleeia held in her hands a smooth, full blade. A sword fashioned from the earth. Aleeia held it in a low position, pointed outward towards Changel. Her other hand favored her stomach and ribs.

Changel was blunt and less gracious in how he acquired his weapon. A jagged spike hung low from the crown of the cave. He pulled it free and returned to his normal, more agile size. Aleeia took deep breaths though with each draw she felt the soreness of a wounded body. She tried to use her energy to heal her own injuries, but had little stamina to spare. She clasped the blade with both hands and waited.

When the next echo of thunder resounded, she attacked. She continued with a grimace and proceeded through her pain. Aleeia swiped at his neck, then towards his hip, followed by a turn and thrust to his chest. Each move was well received by Changel. He blocked them all with little strain, but Aleeia did not relent. Her sword came downward and was met by Changel's club. She followed with a kick to his midsection that forced him back several steps. She rushed in towards him and leapt from an adjacent stone to deliver a harsh kick to his cheek. Changel took two staggered steps to his left. Aleeia kept coming. She held the blade in her left hand and slashed back towards his shoulder. Changel dodged the strike. The sword of Aleeia hit the cavern's stone and unleashed a flurry of sparks. And still, Aleeia proceeded to strike.

Changel dropped the club. The flesh of his skin peeled and gave way to his feathered talons yet again. His razor sharp appendages glimmered from the faint light recycled by the cave walls. Each fingernail was a blade unto itself. Aleeia closed in on him and slashed across at him from her hip. Changel ducked and swung wide with his right talon. Aleeia came back around with her sword to stop his counter. However, Aleeia was then left open and Changel cut into her thigh with his free hand. Fighting Changel with both his hands as the deadliest of weapons was like battling a dual-bladed swordsman. Aleeia had to be twice as fast to counter the quickness of Changel. Once again, she found herself on the defensive.

The clank of their weapons continued. Aleeia backpedaled and took step after step away from Changel. He slashed at her head. She dodged to her left with her hands still at high guard. Aleeia saw an opening. Changel's arm was fully extended and his left shoulder was directly beneath the downward strike of her sword. The cold metal of her weapon moved closer to Changel. Aleeia was a moment away from a blow that would turn the tides. Despite her soreness and bruises, she was calm. The battle was soon to reach its end. Destiny was soon to become a moment in the present made footnote of the past. The moment of impact came, though not as Aleeia had foreseen it. Changel made a quick turn clockwise. He knocked her sword away with the very same hand that missed her earlier. Aleeia was knocked off balanced with a slight turn away from Changel. He reared back. Eyes fixed on her abdomen, he attacked. His talons gouged deep into her side. Four wounds made with bird-like claws penetrated her flesh. Aleeia let out a loud scream. The scream could not match the pain she felt. But to her own great misfortune, her pain was just the beginning of the torture planned by Changel.

Aleeia fell to one knee. She would have collapsed completely had the fingers of Changel not been so firmly embedded in her side.

"I will ask again. *Is this it*?" mocked Changel, "Is evil a true adversary or just the manifestation of our inner fears and weakness?"

Aleeia did not move. Her breathing intensified. Her pain was twofold, from both her physical afflictions and her failure. She could barely move to stand. The slightest tremble spilled more blood from her wounds. A still defiant Aleeia threw a back fist towards her enemy. Changel did not dodge the slow, weak strike. He laughed then wrenched his hand. Aleeia cried out again.

"I hear your cries and you will know my mercy." said Changel.

Suddenly, a grainy grey salt bubbled from each wound. Her skin hardened slowly. The dark granite spread like the shadows at dusk. Aleeia tried to concentrate to stop Changel and counter his Will. However, she was too weak. Her agony, the memory of her friends and the weight of death kept her from focusing her waning abilities. The lurking stone crept from her side to cover her abdomen and lower thigh. Aleeia pulled away from Changel and fell to both knees. Though she was no longer impaled, she was still afflicted by the scouring rock. Her eyes became heavy. The stone was now to her chest and lower back.

"I weep for you, little girl," said Changel, "If only there was guidance. If only you had not been led astray and left alone."

Thusly, he turned to the exit and left Aleeia to the clemency of his Will.

Alone! The word resonated in her ear. It painted a picture in her mind and burrowed deep into her heart. Alee was there in the gloomy hollow with her sworn adversary. Moments away from a death that would be eulogized in failure, Alee looked back on the friends and family who had brought her thus far. She thought of them: Karwynn, Hat-kaptah, Aalarae, Buhen, Meroe, Faras, Asal-Iman, Mhasika and Bellia. Her eyes watered and the tears rolled down her cheek. And for the friend who had most recently gone but who would never be forgotten, Alee lamented with a sigh.

"Gaia," she cried.

The mud in the cave bubbled and boiled. Water and earth parted as the heat intensified in the cave. It was just as had been days before when Alee summoned Pixsus. She said Gaia's name with the mind of joining her soon. The pain inflicted by Changel caused her to forget the wonders of the cave. Warmth filled the cavern. The air became humid and thick. The walls and rocks of the chasm glowed red, and then became a bright, hot white. In the rainy night, the once darkened hollow was illuminated with Gaia's spirit.

The spirit of a being so strong hit both Changel and Alee like a tidal wave. It filled the room. In awe of the phantasm that formed before him, Changel stopped in his tracks. The land of Avalon had been fashioned with the rules and ways of someone greater and there were still mysteries unknown to him. Changel at no time in his life had the need to enter an unassuming hole and speak the names of the deceased.

"What is this?" asked Changel.

Alee struggled with the energies that surrounded her. Coupled with her injuries, the forces of her spirit were as abrasive as when Pixsus had manifested before. Alee lay on the ground that was now stiff and hardened by the heat.

Changel reached out towards the smiling face that belonged to a woman so beautiful. A face that looked downward to Alee. When Changel's hand reached her face it burned. He quickly pulled back. Gaia turned to him with an intense and unfavorable stare. Alee saw what happened to Changel while the threat of her statued-grave loomed.

"Can you save me? Can you end this?" asked Alee.

"No" replied Gaia, "But you can Aleeia. ***We*** will always be with you, in both memory and in spirit."

In that moment, Aleeia saw destiny become more than a word. She saw the events of the past shape themselves into a singular resolve rather than any type of choice to be made. To defeat Changel, Aleeia knew what she had to do. Aleeia staggered to her feet while Changel looked on, amused at the gesture. Suddenly, Aleeia called out.

"*Pixsus! Nympthia!*"

The walls and floors resounded with the cry. The light, already magnificently radiant, became more brilliant. Rocks tumbled and the ore of the cavern walls ran. The heat was so intense. Despite his curiosity, Changel looked to the cave's exit. Alee used what little Will she had to hasten the melting earth above the exit. Once again, the earth moved like magma. The molten earth fell and dripped from the entryway until the weakened arc caved. They were sealed inside.

The ethereal bodies of Pixsus and Nympthia amassed on the terrestrial plane along side Gaia's. The light as before became blinding to both Changel and Aleeia. The spirits of Aleeia's three matriarchs brought about extreme pressure in the cave. Coupled with the heat that still proliferated, the cave felt more volatile than the center of a star. Changel pounded against the stones that blocked the entryway. However, the iron ore and minerals had already tempered to hard steel below the molten surface. Alee closed her eyes to ready her mind. Upon her last call to Nympthia, Aleeia was forced to encase herself within a shell of her own energy in order to protect herself. For this, the final battle, Aleeia had something else in mind.

> "Thank you, my mothers. I am strong, smart, and free because of you. I am all that you have instilled in me. My *Will* won't let you down."

Changel heard the heartfelt discourse from Aleeia and moved on her as a means to free himself. With every step closer, the stone that preyed on the flesh of Aleeia seemed to spread more rapidly. Aleeia had but one thing left to say.

Cupiam nostro animo esse meam fortitudinem

It was a plea for her Will to be empowered. It was the converse of the shell she had made all those days ago, which was to keep Nympthia's spirit out and away. Now, as the cave quaked and flesh burned, Aleeia spoke the words that would make their spirit her strength. The air spiraled and swirled with one of the purest of heaven's creations made for mortals. The forms of Gaia, Pixsus and Nympthia dissipated into their own distinctive hues. The colors filled the cave and nipped and cut at the flesh of Changel as they passed around him. Their essences coalesced into a black wave that rushed over Aleeia. She was not afraid as the black air surrounded her. She saw it. She tasted it. She breathed it. Their strength was now her own. Their Will was hers to wield.

When the air cleared and the black wave had filled her, Aleeia stood tall. The viral granite receded from her body. Her Will was now strong enough to overpower it. The four wounds created by Changel's talons closed and mended, but did not fade. Despite the scars that left four unsightly black circles at her side, she was more than well. She stood ready for Changel who drew closer. Once again, he made his body as full as the cave would allow. They stood toe to toe and wasted no words.

Still reeling in confidence from their last encounter, Changel made a move. He cocked his left arm back and delivered a blow with twice the force that had toppled his son, Alonard. For Aleeia, the moment was now and the world seemed to idle in it for longer than the rules of time would normally allow. An attack, which moments ago, was too fast to be tracked seemed to last for ages. Changel's fist was a hair length from Aleeia's face. With all calm and speed, she spun around behind Changel. She wasted no time. She did not taunt nor pause. Her opening was there, and with a body that emanated the strength of the spirits within her, she attacked. She reared both arms back behind her head. Her two open hands recoiled like cobras. She lunged out towards Changel with her fingers pointed outward and closed together. Changel turned just as Aleeia struck her blow. Her hands and arms had the same scorching hot intensity as the spirits that melted the cave before. Rapid as two canonballs she thrusted her arms. Her hands pierced and burned through Changel completely. Her hands protruded out of his lower back. Aleeia placed her foot on his chest and kicked herself free. She pressed him away. He flew violently through the air. Changel hit the wall with a crash that seemed to shake not only the cave, but the whole of the Isle. He then hit the ground and proceeded to bleed profusely. Aleeia walked closer. Desperate, Changel flailed another right fist with little force behind it. Aleeia caught his wrist and twisted backwards. Her right arm rose with a sense of the past, love, and faith that shared a place inside her. She unleashed a blow that spoke from the pain of all who gave her strength. Her fist met the wretched flesh of his visage. It burned through his tissue to break through the bones of his skull.

Changel the Misguided, the Betrayer, fell dead. And from the parts of Nympthia, which spoke from within her, Aleeia felt tremendous regret that he never found a truer path. She felt pride and hope from Gaia. And from Pixsus, Aleeia let out a low sigh, for the day had finally come when all was resolved and justice had prevailed. Aleeia said a silent prayer on her own behalf for Changel. It was a courtesy, a right owed to all of God's creatures.

She was done with the strength that was not her own, the power loaned to her by the Will of others. Suddenly, a ghostly dark green wave of air released itself from Aleeia. It split into yellow and blue as the bodies of Gaia and Pixsus manifested again. Their images became whole again along with their spirits. The cave brightened, but this time Aleeia was not shaken by their presence.

"Where is Nympthia?" Aleeia asked of Gaia and Pixsus. "I wanted to say goodbye."

Gaia smiled and turned to Pixsus who replied with a clear answer.

"You will not have to say goodbye. We will return home, to peaceful death where our spirits can walk with God."

"And my mother?" asked Aleeia.

"I have this message she wanted me to give you," Pixsus recited to Aleeia. As she spoke her own lips moved as though she knew the words already,

You lived inside me. In that, a bond was made between daughter and mother where we lived as one with the mother living solely to nurture. I felt this as any mother, but I felt

your strength even then. It filled me and allowed me to go on. You nurtured me. And now I wish to stay as part of you. What strength I have is yours for all time, and forever we will truly be together."

Aleeia was both flattered and saddened by her mother's choice. Which Heaven to reside in had not been a choice for many who had walked on God's earth. Alee smiled. She nodded courtesies to Gaia and Pixsus. And though she would miss Gaia, she did not mourn. Alee was a part of them and knew the joys that they would return to. So without further selfish delay, Alee spoke.

"Thank you, my friends. Rest in peace, Gaia and Pixsus. And when my days are done, I hope that I have walked a path that will allow us to see each other again."

Her family faded and returned to the place beyond space and time. Alee took one last look at the body laid a few steps from her feet. She turned and walked to where the entry way caved. Alee nonchalantly reached out to the pile of boulders that stacked to cover the exit. She touched it. The moment she did so her form blurred out of phase. Alee took instantaneous steps in and out of the terrestrial plane.

For moments at a time, extremely brief instances, she traveled into another space and time. Thus, as she reached for the stone, she never touched it. She simply walked through the entry's blockade. Alee smiled and knew from whom her new understanding and strength of Will came.

> "You sent me here to do what I have done. It took so much of you, more Will than you had available to stay with me. But here you are...with me."

Alee left Changel buried. Once she emerged through the rocks, she saw the sunny dawn and smelled the fresh air. She gathered herself and made ready for all she had left to do. Another smile set upon her face. It was one akin to those she had as a young adolescent in the Woodlands of the South. She set aside her accomplishment and remembered those who had fought and those who may still be in need. She closed her eyes. In the blink of an eye, she vanished.

Resolute Revelation - On the ground, a young man lay alone near the edge of the garden maze. He was Alonard of the Western Bank, who before a little more than a week ago, continued to make the protection of his father the sole purpose of his life. Ironically, he laid still at the entry to the grand garden due to his father. He was pushed aside, evicted by the green labyrinth the moment he lost consciousness. Since Changel was no more, his Will could not be sustained.

Alonard was free of his stone prison with more good news to come.

Blood still flowed from the crevice made in Alonard. Barely able to move, he covered the gap with both his hands in an effort to stop the bleeding. His vision blurred. His legs became numb. A stark chill emanated across his body. He felt less and less of anything as time went on.

Suddenly, Alonard heard the sound of unsettling leaves. A strange and powerful gust of wind stirred from the air. Alonard listened for footsteps but heard none. Yet, for some reason, he still sensed someone was there. Alonard could not speak. He wanted to call out to ask who was there. Only a low inaudible moan came where words were intended.

"Be still. You are going to be alright."

Alonard heard the voice of Alee and rejoiced. He took her words as comforting rhetoric for he simply did not wish to spend his last moments of life alone. Alonard felt he was beyond any aid Alee could possibly give to him.

Alee kneeled down to him. She gently moved his hands away from his hollowed gash. She placed her own hands there and breathed with purpose. In and out, he inhaled and exhaled her energies. She spoke to his tissue and flesh and pleaded that they take the strength she offered.

Alonard's body was invigorated. His wounds mended. His flesh moved and reshaped like eager vines reaching to the sun.

Ego vestrae salubritati meum ardorem consocio

Alee smiled. Alonard then returned his own after he set eyes upon her. She had been dragged through the mud in the fight of her life. She was bloodied and bruised. Alonard had never been so happy. He saw only the beauty in the woman before him. He rose slowly to his feet, still suffering from moderate pains while his body worked to repair itself. The jumpstart given to him by Alee was great enough to pull him back from the edge of death. But the wounds he endured, courtesy of his father, would take time to be completely undone.

Alonard extended her a hug. She was caught a little off guard by it for she had never seen him express his feelings in any manner outside of words or warfare. Alee felt comfort in his arms despite that fact that Alonard leaned against her to remain upright as well. She looked into his eyes and saw the changes that made Alonard a man of good. He placed his hand on her cheek and pulled her near. In the form of a kiss they gave thanks to one another. Just as her eyes closed and her heart started pounding, she pulled away with the thought of her friends.

"Hang on," said Alee through a blushing snicker. In an instant, she refocused. Her happiness for the life and wellness of Alonard was stayed. Alee had not forgotten about Hat-kaptah. Her body soon followed her mind. An instantaneous charge happened in the air. Both Alee and Alonard became phased and then material in a flash. They were now back in the chamber room of Changel's Citadel.

Alonard fell to the ground. The journey, though brief beyond imagination, caused an unsettling lag in him. His body was still too weak to be put through much more of an ordeal.

"Rest," Aleeia said to Alonard.
She looked around the chamber for signs of a struggle, trying to use her tracking skills to put the pieces of the altercation together. Nothing she saw gave her an indication of what happened since their escape. No body. No blood. Hat-kaptah was nowhere in sight.

"Hat-kaptah, where are you?" sighed Alee. "Where are you?"
Alee's face fell. Not knowing where her friend was or even if he was alive was troubling. With the sorrow of her uncertainty, she loudly called his name.

"Hrrrrmm!"
Alee heard the muffled reply that came from the top of the

huge tree in the chamber. Aleeia walked closer to the trunk and looked upward through the branches. Alee gasped. She saw a cocoon made of vines and roots and the dark bronze feet and hands that protruded.

"Hat-kaptah, is that you up there?" asked Alee.

"*Hmmmm! Mhhhm!*" he replied.

Alee cried. Her tears were so laden with happiness and joy that she paused. She became lost in her emotion and remained aloof until she heard his muffled bellows again. Aleeia walked to the trunk of the tree and extended her hand, twiddling her fingertips against the bark. The tree rustled as though hit by a strong breeze. Alee reached out with her other hand and began the same massage to the tree. The wooden coils that encircled Hat-kaptah lowered and loosened. Alee smiled increasingly.

"Coochie Coo, little gal!" She exclaimed to the tree. She tickled Hat-kaptah's ensnaring vines to the ground where he was free of the roots that had bound him. He sprang up and gave her a huge, endearing hug. Alee returned his embrace while smiling from ear to ear. Alonard regained his composure and made his way to her side. Alee stood squarely between the two. She quickly became flustered and felt the tension that passed through her, from one to the other.

She was rescued from her predicament as she heard

ordered footsteps draw near. Alee remained calm. Though weakened from the revival of Alonard and her shiftings through space-time, she stood ready and with more than enough power to deter any threat. The soldiers entered with two women bound.

"Master, these two women overpowered eight legions near the beach. They fought nearly until exhaustion and tried to escape into the woods. We ran them down. What is to become of them?" asked the captain of Changel's guard.

The captain looked upon Changel. He glanced at the tattered yet alluring woman as well as the slave who shrank away as Changel spoke.

"Eight legions?" repeated Changel.

Alee glanced at the prisoners and gave Changel a slight eye.

"Yes, my lord," replied the captain, "they sank twenty ships."

Alee saw smiles on the faces of Mhasika and Bellia when the captain gave the final tally.

"How many ships have confirmed departure?"

"The first wave of three hundred twenty has left. Two more waves of three hundred thirty-seven will depart upon your order, Sir."

Alee heard the news and saw her partial failure. She was too late. She lowered her head. More had to be done.

"Excellent! Leave the prisoners to me. They could be an asset if broken properly," ordered Alonard, again in the guise of Changel.

"Yes, Sir."

"Bring all maps and reports on the location and status of the ships that have already departed," Changel added.

"As you command."

The captain turned to his subordinates and ordered the prisoners release. The guards unhinged their chains and both Mhasika and Bellia rubbed the discomfort in their wrists away. They looked upon Changel-Alonard with a smile. The soldiers left and Alonard reverted to form. The three women hugged one another. They embraced and swapped pleasantries while Alonard and Hat-kaptah exchanged glances, their show of respect. Instinctively, everyone looked to Aleeia for comfort, leadership, and encouragement. She stood center of a semi-circle of friends and allies.

"For years, I have been the recipient of wisdom and words meant to help me become all that I was meant to be. On this day, Changel is no more. However, no one can say that life has unfolded as it was supposed to."

Alee looked to Alonard.

> "In a perfect world, a son does not have to choose between right and the will of his father. For in that world, they are one and the same."

Alee turned to Hat-kaptah and Bellia.

> "In a perfect world, a mentor does not meet a violent death through the selfish folly of their pupil."

Bellia began to speak to ease her guilt, but Alee raised her hand and turned to Mhasika.

> "And in a perfect world, good people are not ripped away from all that they know by destructive strangers; no matter how *just* those strangers claim their intentions to be."

Alee turned to window and the cloudy open of the sky.

> "Before we can rest and study war no more, there is still work to be done. For though Changel is gone, his misguideds are now scattered across the earth. It is our responsibility track them down and bring them here. It is our charge to ensure the peace and safety of all people who walk this earth. So they might have the means to live as God intended."

Alee's words were stirring. The daughter of Nympthia, so called the princess nymph, spoke with the strength of her convictions. In one fell swoop, she released them from the weight of Changel and granted them peace. At the same time, she empowered them to act against the residuals of Changel's centuries of misguided ambitions.

A new day had dawned. And for all the days that preceded and followed the sun seemed to shine with a bit more clarity and luster. On that day, one could look upon the sun's undiminished glow and take it in without harm. Warmer was the air as the sky sparkled blue from the sun-kissed mist of the Isle. Avalon was still. War had no voice. There was only the sound of the soothing roar of the waves crashing from coast to coast. They washed over the Isle and drowned a joyous, yet sinister cackle. It was Caim who laughed as he pecked against the entryway of the cave in Resurrection Valley.

EPILOGUE- The weeks since Egypt made war with Nubia were marked with bloodshed, enough to stain the Nile for years to come. However, the Kingdom of Kush remained secure behind the Wall despite the endless barrage that was unleashed by the orders of Pharaoh Isohhim. Atratah attempted peaceful negotiations. In an act of diplomacy, Atratah went as far as offering Isohhim a position as an advisor. Above all, Atratah cared for the lives of her people, even those who followed under the misguided orders of an impostor. Her messages were returned as all others before, with the severed heads of the emissaries that delivered them. Nubia was running out of time and Atratah was running out of options.

The Last Emissary - The battle took its toll on all those who played a role in Nubia. Of those affected, Aalarae seemed the most regal and unshaken of any leader. Ashur lamented perpetually for his Princess at the wall. He received word of her daily but the report came with a delay of about a day-and-a-half.

Meroe remained concerned for the safety of her women and men. The Egyptians had grown bolder mounting several sneak attacks at night. The Wall was climbed and breached. With Meroe's leadership, the Egyptian phalanxes were beaten back. In the battles, Faras remained distant. He fought autonomously. Since the departure of Alee, his will to fight and his will to live seemed to lessen severely.

Buhen's legend continued to reflower. He had become Meroe's second in command. And now with the fifth body of an emissary brought to his feet, Buhen prepared a plan to enter the city of Abydos himself. He would be the last emissary.

Focus of the Warrior - Faras left Buhen's meeting in the same trance that had gripped him since Alee left. The plan was not too complicated, though extremely bold. Buhen was to go as an emissary and get close enough to assassinate the Pharaoh, while Faras and Meroe were to personally escort Atratah covertly into the Temple of Amon-Ra and return her bloodline to its rightful throne. However, Meroe could not endure Faras's state of mind anymore. His attitude was detrimental to his duty and could not be allowed to pass any longer. Meroe ran him down as they exited the meeting.

"Patron! Wait!" she called.

Faras stopped and turned slowly.

"Yes, General?" he replied.

"Please, call me Meroe," she said.

"How can I be of service, General?" he asked.

Meroe placed her hand on his shoulder. As she spoke to

him, she touched his neck and cheek with the back of her hand. She looked deeply into his eyes to convey her sincerity.

"You have been distant. And for those of us who were here when your melancholy began, we know why. Do not let this be your undoing. If you were not as skilled as you were and we were not at war, I would give you leave to right yourself," said Meroe.

Faras's eyes shifted. Meroe moved closer. She held his face with both of her hands to focus his eyes on her.

"General..." Faras tried to explain, but Meroe continued to speak.

"Faras, know there is more to lose if you continue this way..."

Meroe paused.

"And more to gain if you let the past go," she added.

Meroe kissed him with her full, supple lips. Her kiss was warm. It came so unexpectedly that Faras could not offer any objections. He did not pull away, but closed his eyes until the kiss was complete.

Meroe led Faras to her chamber and that night, they laid together. Faras enjoyed the sensual exchange of passion between them. For Faras, his mind became clearer and his spirit was invigorated. Alee was not forgotten, but rather through his relations with Meroe, Faras saw the futility in dwelling in the past. After that night, he understood that life was meant to be lived. Meroe, on the other hand, simply wanted her Patron of Guard to return. She knew the risk involved in such a ploy, but also knew that Faras was already broken. For her, the choice was an easy one and the night of enjoyment with the handsome, virile captain just happened to be an additional perk.

Clausulam Carmen - Everyone rose from slumber hours before the sun. In Meroe's chamber, Faras awoke to an empty bed. He dressed quickly and hurried to the final debriefing. When he arrived, Buhen, Princess Atratah, and Meroe waited. They went over the plan once more before they left. The gates to the Wall of Nubia opened. Out walked Buhen, Atratah, Faras, Meroe and half-a-dozen soldiers. All except the soldiers were dressed in diplomatic robes. Buhen walked behind three soldiers and Atratah walked behind Buhen with Faras and Meroe to her sides. The remaining three soldiers marched at the rear. They entered the Egyptian camp and carried their diplomatic flag. As planned, the three black robed ambassadors and the principle emissary, Buhen, were allowed to enter the camp. However, the soldiers were ordered to turn back to the Wall or forfeit their lives. The rest were escorted to the Temple in Abydos and walked before the Pharaoh Isohhim.

"Greetings and welcome to the great kingdom of Egypt and its capital city," said Pharaoh Isohhim.

He spoke with sadistic sarcasm. Behind ever pleasant words was the intent to kill them after he lost amusement in the foreplay. Buhen was unarmed, as were all the peaceful contingents that came before. The Egyptians had become complacent. They saw Atratah's desperate attempts to negotiate as sending lambs to the slaughter. Once Buhen was searched and the soldiers relented, the others in robes were not examined, though Meroe and Faras had short blades strapped to their inner thighs, four in all.

"Would any of you care for refreshments? Some wine perhaps?" asked Pharaoh Isohhim.

"No, Great Pharaoh," replied Buhen.

"So, straight to the affairs of rule, I see," stated Isohhim. "What terms of peace does that banished whore offer? It is laughable she barters with what she does not have."

The ten sentinels in the chamber moved closer and surrounded the four Nubians.

"I came to discuss surrender," said Buhen.

Isohhim smile.

"Ah, finally! Kush speaks wisely," he said.

"Yes, Pharaoh," replied Buhen. "*Your* surrender!"

In that instant, at the center of their ranks, Princess Atratah let down her hooded robe.

"Kill them!" yelled Isohhim.

Meroe and Faras pulled away their robes and released the short blades form their harnesses. Meroe grabbed both her blades. Faras secured one and kicked the other towards Buhen. Isohhim sat atop his altar-throne and witnessed the fray. The ten sentinel-warriors closed in around them. The protection of the queen became the simple part of the plan. Buhen, Meroe and Faras intended to protect her until everyone who opposed her re-ascension was dead.

It was like a dance. Meroe leaped over Faras's back to the other side of their enemy's front. It was an effective maneuver that split them in half and removed the advantage of their position. Meroe stared down three sentinels. The remaining seven were left to Faras and Buhen.

Meroe and Faras moved with speed and power. Buhen fought with superiority and certainty of movement that did not waste energy. He threw his blade at the nearest sentinel and impaled him through his torso. Another converged upon him with a fierce yell and a wide downward stroke. Buhen took a calm sidestep to his left and countered with a strike through the sentinel's eye-socket with his pointer and index fingers. He grabbed his attacker's wrist and bludgeoned his head with the reserved side of his own blade. He then pried the short curved blade from the sentinel's hand as two more made their way towards him. Buhen reached into his pocket and pulled out a small silver coin. He flicked it at the soldier to his right, and then warded off the other with a lateral swipe to his left. The coin hit the sentinels squarely in the face. With the soldier dazed for that split second, Buhen thrust his sword through the sentinel's neck. The remaining soldier saw Buhen's back. He came down upon him with his blade. Buhen dislodged his sword and turned clockwise while bringing his weapon upward. As the soldier’s sword came down, Buhen's blade continued to rise. A fatal blow was made that cut the sentinel from his inner thigh, through his abdomen and torso to his shoulder.

At the same time, Meroe and Faras fought the other six sentinels. Their battle was far more spirited. Meroe lunged and struck a blow that pierced through an assailant’s hip but her back was turned. Faras called.

"Meroe, watch out."

Meroe was calm and aware. She ducked a lateral swipe at her head and turned with her blade to sever the legs of the attacking solider.

"Mind your own men." she said.

Faras and Meroe continued to fight and talk.

"I can't help it. You have my concern."

The sound of swords clanking ensued.

"I do not need your concern. I need your focus," she

grunted.

Another two soldiers fell from the skill of Meroe and Faras.

"Was that what last night was about? You needing me to focus?" asked Faras.

He parried a few wild attacks but, like Meroe, remained completely calm and in control.

"Couldn't you have just told me?" Faras added.

"I tried! Repeatedly! Besides, where is the fun in that?" she responded.

Faras smiled as he put the finishing touches on the solider he occupied. Meroe toppled her assailants as well. Faras held no hard feelings. Her direct and unemotional approach reminded him of his old cavalier mentality. The boldness of her actions reminded him of Alee as well.

The room was cleared of soldiers but Isohhim remained seated at the altar-throne. He did not move. He did not cry out for he knew his time had come. Buhen gave Atratah his blade. Bravely, she stood unmoved in the center of the room while the battle proceeded. She remained still and stared at Isohhim without a single blink. When she received the sword from Buhen, she ascended the stairs that stretched out before her throne. Meroe, Faras, and Buhen walked closely behind. When Princess Atratah reached the throne she offered her blade to Isohhim.

"The gods favor the Pharaoh," he uttered solemnly.

Isohhim took the blade. Atratah turned her back to him. He then raised the sword, angled it downward and drove the blade through his own throat, chest, and out through his lower back. Faras removed the body and placed it respectfully on the ground. He covered Isohhim with one of the robes. Atratah sat atop the blood splattered altar-throne as Pharaoh of Egypt. The kingdom recognized her rule immediately. The people rejoiced in her ascension. They were relieved to be free from the tyranny of Isohhim. And so, Pharaoh Atratah spoke.

> "Let this be my first decree. I will have a formal marriage to the Prince of Nubia-Kush, Ashur, and together our kingdoms will become stronger, just as we are strengthened and stronger from the union of our love. A new nation-state is born!"

And so it was for all the people of the Nile and in the Land of the Black Sands to the Barren Sea.

THE END

POSTFACE

Sophomore year of college, I had a friend that I would e-mail. She was an old friend that I had known since grade school, and we both subconsciously endeavored to keep in touch. We would e-mail regularly, sometimes with nothing in particular to say. They were just letters to let her know that I *cared* and we were still *cool.* From time to time, I would send poems rather than a comment or inquiry because I did not want her to feel obligated to respond. She was a busy college student afterall. After a long hiatus, in which I neglected to write, in conjunction with a day's lesson involving the Iliad and the Aeneid, she wrote to me and asked *Where's my poem?* And I responded something to the effect of *Oh, man! I guess I owe you an epic poem.*

History, Religion, the Epic, and the Black Diaspora

At no point did I undertake the writing of this novel with any deep-seated agenda. As the "author" with my audience of one it was natural to have a protagonist of African descent. What followed was simply an attempted exercise at responsible and compelling writing since it was now up to me to write something that was entertaining to read, enjoyable to write, and had a depth comparable to my poems of the past.

My friend and I both took an "Intro to Engineering" class in high school where one of the class projects was to report on different civilizations' mathematics and engineering discoveries and innovations throughout history. The only caveat of the assignment was that Greek, Roman, and traditional European cultures were *somewhat* off limits. *Somewhat* because the study of these cultures and accomplishments were the norm since elementary school, and the teacher forewarned any groups which chose those civilizations would have to produce a top notch report, as the availability of more information made researching them easier. Teams were formed in the haphazard manner which occurs in high school, and as the Mayans, Aztecs, Chinese, Egyptians, and Persians all were quickly spoken for, we were left with Nubia Kush. *Who?* I thought. And later the question became, *And how are they different from the Egyptians*? Needless to say, as we all scavenged for engineering facts pertaining to the Nubians, we all reluctantly learned other stuff too. Facts about Nubian monarchs, both kings and queens, as well as theological and ideological hierarchies were a fortunate and interesting byproduct. While I do not claim that this novel is 100% accurate to Nubian history and myth, I will acknowledge that it was the perfect mutual seeding grounds for an epic that the two of us could enjoy.

However, the epic poses a problem for any diasporic group, especially those groups who have suffered from a "cultural genocide". In the spirit of treading lightly with no intent to dismiss the actual physically violent history of African-Americans or both the violent and psychologically devastating residuals of what occurred for other groups, the concept of cultural genocide must be briefly explained as it relates to commonly known concepts of genocide and enslavement.

For African-Americans, the disconnect from what is African history and culture was quick and forcefully blunt. Other groups experienced cultural shifts where time and willing assimilation were the main factors. People spoke, dressed, ate, entertained, and learned differently over generations and generations of what can be considered subtle change. Willing assimilation is somewhat of a paradox because in most cases people assimilate in order to avoid oppression or to be granted some perceived benefit afforded to the majority. For early colonial blacks there was no decision to speak differently to fit in with the neighbors or to eat differently to fall in line with the regional cuisine. Blacks were made to forego their customs, forsake their language, and as a result their history. Not to belabor the point, or to make this introduction purely about the disconnects and residuals of slavery, it should suffice to say that it may be easier for a Scottish American to trace his lineage back to William Wallace than an African American to track his lineage back to Shaka Zulu.

The spatial and cultural disconnect also relates to time. Epic stories and legends are created like a fine wine and while the heroes and heroines of the American Emancipation Era are beyond epic, they are not far enough removed to ferment and become fantastic. Fantasy is key. If I were to write about a Harriet Tubman-like character with amazing super-powers and the ability to talk to the stars, it simply would take more to suspend a reader's disbelief. John Henry and Paul Bunyan fit into this folk hero category, where exotic people are set in a familiar places and not so distant times as opposed to Frodo, Odysseus, and Dante who are more normal, yet still exotic and who are set in an exotic place because of the far former, so-called, "ancient" period in time. Lack of grandeur answers the question as to why not another story of a John Henry set in 1810s America.

Men, Writing, and Pathos: The Heroin Cop Out

The character of Alee was made to mirror the female

audience of one, to allow her to feel engaged with the hopes that the character was relatable. However, Alee, Gaia, Bellia, and all the other characters were met timidly. As a man, I had no intention of belittling or dismissing the complexities that come with being a woman. I could only try to emphasis the similarities afforded to both genders. Needless to say we have the same emotions, but differences in the manner in which we choose to express them. Traditionally, women are free to explore the full range of emotions with a full spectrum of expression. While men, on the other hand, have a full range as well but cannot, or will not, show them with the same depth and transparency. Men must remain masculine by adhering to the self-imposed archaic cultural stipulations which define masculinity. Conversely, an asexual, humble woman can assume masculine traits with relative ease without the unfortunate side effect of being called a vamp, tramp, or bitch.

Perfectly embodied by characters like *Buffy Summers*, this archetype is not new. In actuality this character is the norm and something of a Godsend to a generation of men and women who seek to push the boundaries of stereotypes involving sex, emotions, and physical capabilities that are contrary to traditional gender roles. The women who were smart, patient, strong, moral, and compassionate took on character traits of who I ultimately wanted to be. Even Sciona has a philosophy of certainty and confidence to be admired, although she draws from the "primal" in a manner that is often associated with man or beast. On the other hand, the men were who I am: brutish, arrogant, crass, aloof, and lacking clarity. And while all characters in order to be whole have both sides of the equation, a general line can be drawn just as described.

The novel does not seek to demean nor idolize women as creatures without flaw. There are instances in the story when a male character finally opens up but is met with an unexpected coldness from his female counter part. Essentially man's fear is that his emotions will either be seen as weakness or quickly exploited thus deeming it, in effect, a weakness. The "push Jenny off the seesaw instead of telling her you like her" paradigm.

There is this basic and probably flawed idea that children learn from both parents. Boys learn the most from fathers and girls learn the most from mothers. Having an example and being able to see yourself, a younger version of your like-gendered caretaker, means that your imagination does not have far to go in order to conceive certain possibilities. There are only a handful of father-son duos in this story as there are only a few men, even where fathers are figurative. However, the men are riddled with defects either from a father's absence, his example, or his negligent tutelage. The women appear to be more sound, nurturing, and stronger as they have seen the examples of brave, fierce, and capable women through one or more *matrons*.

Lastly, the word *matron* was troubling. As defined by Merriam-Webster, it means:

- a married woman usually marked by dignified maturity or social distinction;
- a woman who supervises women or children;
- a leader of a women's organization;
- a female animal kept for breeding;

Throughout the story I referred to the highest military rank of Nubia as either matron or patron. *Patron* is defined several ways but stands out defined as:

- a person chosen, named, or honored as a special guardian;
- protector or supporter or the chief male officer in some fraternal lodges having both men and women members;

In order to show literal symmetry between men and women holding the same rank, *matron* means the exact same thing in this story as *patron*. I simply thought it would be weird and a bit absurd to call Meroe, Patron of the Guard.

Life Goes On: Stories of *the One* vs. the Reality of an Ensemble

The legends and myths surrounding larger than life "Christ-like" figures are a staple in fiction, especially the fantasy epic. Stories with chosen ones allow a reader the ability to more easily invest emotionally in the success or failure of a character. Otherwise, the relationship to the character would be based purely on the ability of the writer to convey the importance of a comparatively lesser task, such as finding a date or getting a job, and in these scenarios the character's personality, subplots and humor hold the story in place at a greater strain.

Larger-than-life goals require larger-than-life characters in order for them to be brought to fruition. However, the real world dictates more often than not that huge world-changing accomplishments take more than the deeds of one person. And should one person, even if that person be at the forefront, fail or be removed from a movement to affect great change, life still goes on, and others take up the cause.

I once had a discussion with a friend who was a fan

of a particular fantasy. And of my friend, I asked a few skeptical, critical questions of the story. "Why is this character so special? Why is he or she the chosen one?" Could the story at all survive or hold water if the main character, who is chosen, were to die?" and then to which she slowly replied "no". So as a reader (and watcher) of fantasy, the notion that a character is the chosen one is thwarted quickly by the notion that he is at any long-term risk. Even fake deaths and resurrections are to be expected when the audience is fed the notion that *only* one person is able to solve a problem. Therefore this same person is the primary, by far, to hold your concern.

It may not seem as though people are all connected, but no one is more or less important than the next. That is not to say that certain people do not possess an abundance of power and influence; it is only to say that everyone is in possession of some power and influence by way of their decisions and actions. Even when the door is closed on one person, it is not realistic to assume the door is closed on everyone. So in the absence of an ascendant Christ there is a commencement, still a task at hand. And we ask of James, Mary and Peter, what now? What next?

Fantasy: a "Means" of Allegory not an "Ends" of

Imagine an architect commissioned to build a tower with the mandate that this structure sparked an emotional reaction unlike anything ever felt before to anyone who would look upon it. Now imagine that the architect was given the ability to defy the rules of physics in any way he or she wanted. Would you expect the architect to use this amazing ability only to cut corners for a structure that is grand but can be seen on any Chicago street or use every bit of this ability to create something that fulfills the mandate and is amazing, unlike anything ever before seen?

I have long felt this way about fantasy and magic in stories. To defend against those who innately see science fiction or fantasy as childish, I try to explain the genres in the following way. *Sci-fi* is the allegory of a possibility in the future: A "*what if*". *What if mankind continues to war? What if technology continues to advance at this rate?* While *fantasy* is a metaphorical look at the present set in a fanciful past. *What if elves did not allow dwarves to drink from the Great River?* (How do you feel about that, Mr. "1940s Mississippi diner owner"?) Ultimately, they are a writer's attempt to disconnect you from your reality only to reconnect you to it later through the characters of the story. Fantasy and sci-fi are not spectacle. A dragon that actually is just a dragon, a fairy that is only a fairy, or a wizard that does not act, think, or feel who uses "magic" to miraculously escape from dangers, is the architect ignoring his or her mandate and who simply just builds that big mundane tower in Chicago.

Often when I read sci-fci or fantasy with magic or spectacle used, I will ask myself, was that necessary? Did this have to be set in "a galaxy far far away"? Does that ***ring*** represent something more in terms of the grand scheme? And what I have found is that when the material is good *yes*, when the material is trite, lazy and uses fantasy as a means to write out of holes and dead ends, *no*. Granted, in the tough publishing world of fiction, people need a gimmick to be seen and sold, but when the stars align, that gimmick enhances the story's thematic premise as much as it does the bottom line.

When all is said and done, the writer's tone does not matter if the material does not spark some type of mood in the reader. For my friend, as well as others who have taken the time in this journey with me, I am proud that some merit was found in it.

www.ingramcontent.com/pod-product-compliance
Lightning Source LLC
La Vergne TN
LVHW020645110826
845149LV00012B/1920

* 9 7 9 8 9 9 5 8 0 8 6 0 2 *